What people are sayin

The Chernobyl Privileges

This atmospheric novel introduces a powerful new voice in British fiction. I was gripped by Lockwood's tale which brings together the personal and political, the spectre of Chernobyl and the continuing controversy of Britain's nuclear deterrent. A haunting message for our uncertain times.
Andrew Crumey, Booker-longlisted author of *Mr Mee*

The Chernobyl Privileges is a compelling, well-wrought and sharply intelligent book. In haunting and thought-provoking ways, it draws the reader into a complex understanding of what connects the Chernobyl disaster in 1986 to the UK today and the future of Europe.
Nicholas Royle, author of *An English Guide to Birdwatching*

An exceptional piece of writing… What extraordinary detail and characterisation; I was gripped by so much of it.
Jemima Hunt, *The Writers' Practice*

A great read. And a fabulous idea to combine old and new, Chernobyl and Trident. What an interesting and gripping story.
Adam Strange, Sphere Publishing (Little, Brown)

A tight thriller for the modern age that entertains as easily as it provokes.
Thomas Hocknell, author of *The Life Assistance Agency*

This is a well-researched and thoughtful book on a contemporary theme – the use of nuclear power. The central character, Anthony, is a scientist working at the submarine base in Gare Loch, Scotland when a nuclear incident occurs. He is caught up in the dilemma of how to deal with a possible cover up. However, there's a terrible extra dimension to Anthony's predicament which is gradually revealed through flashbacks. The author skilfully racks up the tension of this nightmare scenario before bringing it to a resolution.

Liz MacRae Shaw, author of *No Safe Anchorage*

The Chernobyl
Privileges

The Chernobyl Privileges

Alex Lockwood

Winchester, UK
Washington, USA

First published by Roundfire Books, 2019
Roundfire Books is an imprint of John Hunt Publishing Ltd., No. 3 East St., Alresford,
Hampshire SO24 9EE, UK
office1@jhpbooks.net
www.johnhuntpublishing.com
www.roundfire-books.com

For distributor details and how to order please visit the 'Ordering' section on our website.

Text copyright: Alex Lockwood 2018

ISBN: 978 1 78535 872 2
978 1 78535 873 9 (ebook)
Library of Congress Control Number: 2017963700

A CIP catalogue record for this book is available from the British Library.

Design: Stuart Davies

Printed and bound by CPI Group (UK) Ltd, Croydon, CR0 4YY, UK

We operate a distinctive and ethical publishing philosophy in
all areas of our business, from our global network of authors to
production and worldwide distribution.

Other books by this author
The Pig in Thin Air
ISBN 978-1-59056-535-3

For Simon,
and for HK

Acknowledgments

Much of the research for this book draws upon the detailed and essential work of Svetlana Alexievich, the Nobel Prize-winning Belarusian investigative journalist and non-fiction prose writer who collected so many stories of victims and survivors of the Chernobyl disaster in her book *Chernobyl Prayer: A Chronicle of the Future*. It is a book all humanity should read. I also drew upon Grigorii Medvedev's *The Truth about Chernobyl*, Adi Roche's *Children of Chernobyl*, Anna Reid's *Borderland: A Journey Through the History of Ukraine*, and particularly Adriana Petryna's *Life Exposed: Biological Citizens after Chernobyl*. There are many other works that helped me create the world of this book as it is set both in Ukraine and at HM Naval Base Clyde in Faslane, Scotland, and I thank all of these authors for their scholarship, passion and commitment, while of course noting that in this work of fiction any errors or diversions from the factual accounts of history are my own.

I wish also to thank a great number of readers and friends, in particular, Viccy Adams, Liz Bostock, Jill Clough, Lisa Davison, Glenn Gaetz, A. Marie Houser, Richard Kerridge, Hannah Kirkham, Stephanie Knox, Emma Lawrenson, Martin Rowe, John Tollitt, Mick Walker, and Becky Williams. Thanks as always to Simon Gill, Elliot Jones and Liam Walker for their support, and to Andrew Crumey, Tom Hocknell and Nicholas Royle.

24th August

Brother,

It is your sister wishing you Happy Independence Day, and by the time this letter reaches you, your birthday. They celebrate here with all the usual drinking and fighting. And you? I'm only teasing. The old people complain that we're always joking. I do not think that's true. I wish it was. I need to laugh.

I'm sick. It is nonstop. But I celebrate our independence, as you may still do. Even so, we're not so independent, are we? At least, you remain part of my story.

My husband doesn't want me to write to you. Yet here I am, writing to you. What do I risk for this? Tonight I've cooked his dinner and now he's sleeping on the sofa. Not like father used to—not like that. My husband is a good man. This is what all wives say, isn't it? Perhaps to admit our husbands are no good is to take the blame for our choices. I know two girls from the hospital who whisper in my ear their husbands aren't satisfying them, but what can they do? We meet for coffee at the sweet place on Taras Shevchenko Boulevard near the hospital—what is its name? Large slabs of poppy seed cake, our eyes too big for our stomachs. The cream makes me feel sick. *Don't drink the milk!* The politicians came on television and said not to believe the foreigners, the milk was fine. But it never tasted the same, did it?

I don't fear my husband. I cooked tonight a stew, and he appreciated it. He's a good man, regardless of what you might think when I tell you he pleaded with me to stop writing to you. But can you blame him? I've told him all I have to tell. He sees what I could not, what father never did, what perhaps our mama knew but would not admit. That you were the wolf, brother. How does it feel to hear this?

1

Some think my Drago is possessive and controlling. If he found out I was writing to you, would he strike me? Would he let his anger brew like the *buha* in the shed? Would he burn a thousand holes into my skin? He wouldn't have married me if that was his temperament. He says I am a *survivor*. He married me knowing the scars on my body and the withering of my breasts. Perhaps a sister should not share this information with her brother, but my breasts will never produce milk. They hang over my ribs like the empty sacks we used to take into the forest. My husband makes love to me despite this, perhaps because of this. There is pity in his love—can love not be this mix of pity and passion?—and when he kisses my breasts in the heat of our lovemaking he is blowing to make them full. Even if love makes for a shorter life, and the doctors' medicines a longer one, I will take his love over their prescriptions. It is not the length of life that matters. We walk together along the Dnieper to the city, he encourages me to meet the other girls, to keep my ties to the Privileges, and I cry with the nausea of knowing that at least I have survived long enough for love.

And you, brother? Does your wife make you feel like this? Do you fight alongside her for what is important? Does she tell you to write to me? Or *not* to write to me? (It would not matter; what matters is that she stands beside you.) This is what I have with my husband. It's why I'm able to write to you, even with my husband saying I should not. Can you argue with him, can you tell him why he's wrong?

But he is wrong. Your life has been full of the privileges that come with being a man. I'm not writing to take those away from you—as if a woman could do that—but there are tales you should hear that are not the ones we heard as children, about wolves and foxes. These other stories are the ones that matter now: about our bodies, our lives. You are a man and married; you understand a woman's body. And

I am not a sister anymore but a frail thing shivering in a harsh wind. You were caught by this wind too, but your sails faced the opposite direction and you were blown away.

I'm no poet. Forgive me.

I have been happy these last few years. But there's misery too. I'm too young for this body, for what happened. We were children. What else could we do? But we're not children now.

Wisdom scares me. Does it scare you? Are you ready to hear what I have to say? I don't want to, my husband doesn't want me to, but if I don't tell you I won't know how to live. I am no poet but I can write a letter. I must. You see, without knowing what is happening to me, you will never know what has happened to you.

Monday

He's on his knees, leaning forward with both hands wrist-deep in the earth when an electric shock, or something like it, flows up from the hole along his arms and across his back. He shakes it off, looking like a sopping dog crawled out from the loch, trying to subdue the sensation before it overwhelms him. It settles at the nape of his neck, and he shivers at its candescence. He blinks, looks into the hole he's dug. Once he's sure he's not cut across an electrical wire, he laughs. *Still alive.* Perhaps his aluminium augur struck a mineral vein? The feeling lingers regardless, unpredicted, enthralling. He looks again into the puncture of earth, dug to collect ten centimetre monitoring samples. There's nothing there. No buried phalanx of wires running from the base to carry away transmissions of upmost national importance. No crystalline strike of quartz or gold. He grips soil and it smudges through his fingers; he lurches back on his haunches and wipes his hands on his trousers and then smacks off the dirt. Whatever it was, its afterimage loiters around the back of his head, tingling like lips after blowing a tune on trace paper. He stares, but feels the pressure to get on. He has one more sample to take so he grasps the top of the auger and untwists it from the ground and then brushes away the loose soil. The new channel slowly fills with trickles of dirt rolling down the sides. He halts the sabotage by pushing in a probe. It slips into the loose earth and the soil compacts. When he feels the probe is full, he squeezes the sides inwards and pulls the tube out. He holds it up to the dim morning light. Black mulch. Nothing strange captured, no fizzing electrical fuse, no bug of strange heritage and stranger power having used its antennae on him like a Taser. From an equipment case he takes a strip of label with his loopy handwriting in red pen, peels the label onto the tube, and secures the sample in the case with the others.

He pushes himself up. From here, outside the perimeter of fencing, the naval base looks like a stack of grey boxes and black spikes and enormous soup dishes spread out across both sides of Gare Loch. Even from this far away there is the sweet mechanical hum and play of machinery, a constant wash of generators and air-conditioning, the infrequent wail of metal turning. His new home, as much as their little cottage. The sky is gunmetal grey. When is it not, here? He registers the occasional movement from Navy personnel, engineers working on the outer skin of what he's already come to think of as a huge dormant beast. His job is to check on the health of the creature, to ensure the beast's excretions do not foul its lair; or — with this extension of the testing parameters he's implemented — beyond. Radiation respects no boundary, is his argument. Atoms stop at no arbitrary gate.

The lab is empty when he gets back, although there's a fresh pot of coffee still warm on the central bench. He puts on his whites. He's taking out the vials of earth he's just collected when Mariam strides in.

'Anthony. You're here.'

'Aye, I am so.' His Scots accent is terrible but it sometimes makes her smile. Attempts at self-deprecation have, at least partially, smoothed over what was a bumpy arrival. They're the same grade, he and Mariam, and she still hasn't accepted the need for his appointment. So a few planned errors, some lapses in standards — nothing serious — and attempts at humour... He hasn't won her over, but they've reached a concord, of sorts.

'There's a meeting,' says Mariam.

The energy that has sat itself at the base of his neck pulsates, and the hairs on his arms stand on end. If everything is working well there are no sudden meetings.

'Everyone's needed.' She reappraises her words. 'Everyone from *this* lab.'

They leave and cross the road, Mariam a step in front. She

knows where she's going. He's not often visited control; only twice, for the security interviews. No reason to; he's not Navy. He'd thought it a necessary distinction for accepting the job. Now he's been here for two months, what does it matter anyway?

The central administrative building of HMNB Clyde is ordered and practical, as he knew it would be. As they walk through the corridors fake wooden flooring becomes crimson carpet and oak panelling. The walls are lined with pictures in baroque frames of ships and the commanders of ships. There are wooden plates with lists of names in gold lettering. Mooring points of the service's lineage, days of fleet superiority. He's been told many times the Navy considers itself the primary defense; the line of last resort entrusted with the nuclear deterrent. A launch of the Trident missiles would be coordinated from along this very corridor, where Radio Four never stops playing as indication that all is right with Britannia. When the broadcast stops, so he's been told, the commanders know what to do.

They reach a large reception. A woman behind a desk regards them. There are four soldiers in muted uniforms; their presence and the presence of their weapons are not lost on him. He's thankful he's wearing his whites.

'Doctor Burnett and Doctor Fahey,' Mariam announces. The receptionist checks their faces against her screen and waves them in.

Commodore Thompson, who Anthony knows from the pictures on the base's website, is standing behind a huge desk in front of a window overlooking Gare Loch. The room is decorated with more iconography of submariner history. Anthony scans the desk: phone, small laptop, a large writing pad, a framed picture turned away from him, which he assumes is the Commodore's family. The water beyond the window is a deep unyielding slate.

There are three others, all men. David, Doctor Edgecombe, is the director of scientific services and Anthony's boss. The two others are in their fifties, four chevrons on each of their shoulders.

'Come and join us,' says the Commodore, waving them towards seats. In the centre of the coffee table is a pristine spray of purple flowers. Anthony hears another arrival. It's their colleague Elspeth. She sits next to Anthony.

'Doctor Jurnickel,' David introduces her to the men. 'Elspeth.'

Commodore Thompson is in his late fifties, with reddish skin but otherwise impeccably turned out. He's not quite what Anthony was expecting. Anthony listens as the Commodore finishes off a conversation with one of the other officers. He doesn't speak cleanly or commandingly. There's a dullness to his voice, maybe a tiredness that's the only way to deal with the enormity of relaying instructions to blow up the world. Finally the Commodore sits on the sofa and lays his hat on the table.

'I'm assured of your prudence,' begins the Commodore, turning to each of them. It's not a question—assurances on their behalf have already been given. 'There's a situation with *Tartarus*.' The Commodore catches his breath, looks around, almost unsteady. This alarms Anthony more than the words. But then the words come too. 'A reactor situation.' The words are a thumbprint against Anthony's eardrums. 'We thought we'd dealt with this after *Vanguard*...'

'The test reactor?' asks Elspeth.

The Commodore turns to her, and the uniformed men follow suit.

'Not the test this time,' the Commodore clarifies. 'But the same cause?' He looks to one of the uniforms for confirmation, but whose nod is unconvincing.

'We spent all that money,' says Elspeth. 'On the cladding.'

'Indeed.'

The Commodore's not fazed—that emergency was reported in Parliament, after a bit of kicking and screaming from the press to hand over the FOIs, Anthony remembers from the research he did for his interview.

'Is it contained?' asks Mariam.

'How long was the exposure?' adds Elspeth.

The Commodore's eyes widen. Anthony keeps quiet, but it's not for the officers' benefit he says nothing.

'All good questions,' says the Commodore, while his stiff back says otherwise. '*Tartarus* has been evacuated. As has her restocking team. We brought her back—'

'So she was at sea,' Elspeth says. The Commodore glares at her. 'We are scientists,' she carries on. 'We *are* paid to question.'

'She was coming into base,' explains the officer sitting to the right of the Commodore. A sturdy man, the aiguillettes of his post trailing over his left breast. 'On regulation action.' Anthony scrutinises the man's face. The commander of *Tartarus*? Was he on the ship? In that uniform?

'So we have a widespread problem in the ship and the water,' the Commodore continues, blowing his nose into a handkerchief. 'Is that right, David?'

'One of the engineers flushed the system,' David explains. Anthony watches a line of sweat inch down David's forehead. 'It wasn't procedural. But it probably helped. With ionised water. Into the loch.'

'Bloody wreckers,' says the other uniform. It's strange to hear slang used by an officer. Anthony sees it's a deflection from something they aren't saying, and suddenly understands the Commodore's tension.

'So we need readings. Immediately. Before our next action,' says the Commodore. 'From this team. I'm sorry for the inconvenience. But...'

The Commodore stands and Anthony feels the future suddenly stick, then start again into a new rhythm.

Anthony and Elspeth walk along the pontoon at the southern edge of the harbour, the point nearest the submarine's route to sea. They're dressed in waterproof waders and boots over radiation protection suits. The suit covers his whole body with

Alex Lockwood

the gloves on. They wear goggles and masks that are too tight around his face.

The far end of the pontoon is a long walk in these suits and the equipment is not light. They squeak as they walk. The planking is wide enough for trucks to get down and his footing need not be too careful, but the water lures him with its blankness. *What it would be to just step out?* He shakes the thought away.

At the end he catches his breath. This farthest point is less than a hundred feet from land, but to reach it the pontoon runs parallel with the shore for over half a mile and so it's taken them half an hour to get to its farthest reach, and they both need a rest. He looks back. There are six small Navy frigates moored in braces along the pontoon, just before the turn that juts out into the sea. To his left, maybe a mile away, the great engineering hangar looms over the water, solid grey apart from its entrance, which is all shadows, and inside where *Tartarus* now rests. From here the base looks surprisingly abstract and ordered, considering how up close, when he was given his induction tour, he saw its disorderliness: the nest of thick red hoses and enormous canary-yellow crane parts and custard-yellow security cabins and red Portaloos for the contractors, and huge black brick warehouses with steel roller doors with television-shaped portholes, around which zip dozens of blue and white oxygen and water trucks that refill the subs when they're in port. The white vans that seem to ignore with impunity the 20-mph speed limit, carrying the fifty-six thousand kilos of oats and blankets and apples that go down into the water with the crew when they disappear for their three months at sea, when nobody except two or three people, the Commodore and the Rear Admiral and the Prime Minister, know the exact location of each submarine. And everywhere huge trolleys full of broken pipes and recycled cardboard and shit and piss from the tanks taken off the subs when they come back in. He's never met any of the actual crew, but he's been told it takes at least a fortnight for the smell of the recycled air to be

9

scrubbed from their skin.

'Why flush the water if you thought there might be leakage?' Elspeth asks. Her words are like crumpled paper through her mask but their suddenness shocks him. 'How much would it disperse?'

'Something must have—' he begins, but stops. He doesn't know what *must have*.

Elspeth is the physics modelling expert and unused to detection. He's worn the suits before. As the senior biomonitor it's his task to explore environmental dosages, cell cycle status, typologies of damage and repair. It's his responsibility to identify carcinogenic conditions in soil, leaf and bug, vertebrates, humans. All in the job description. He's pleased to be out taking samples related to something evident and real. He's aware that there's a military way of seeing things seeping into him.

'But if there's a crack?' Elspeth's accent is full of cadences, a sweet intonation at the end of the breath. She'd told him it was Orcadian, which he thought magnificently alien, until she explained that it meant from the Orkneys.

He stares at the equipment he's carrying. Even now he knows the radiation is around them. In them.

'They weren't talking about the cladding.' Her voice is sharp in his ear; she's taken off her mask. 'Anyone with half a brain could see that.'

He doesn't want to entertain her thoughts, which he's thought too. Instead he imagines who they were: the men who plugged the leak. As they reach the end of the pontoon, Anthony puts the equipment down and bends on one knee and sets up the sampling. Elspeth turns on the dosimeter and begins to scan.

'If it's in the water it won't have spread to the air—' He stops. Is that true? He's not a marine expert. He knows Elspeth isn't either, so no point asking.

'Oh God,' she says. He looks up, alarmed. But she's not reading the meter. '*Wreckers*. If it *is* the reactor, then what we're doing here...'

'They would've evacuated the base,' he says, opening the sample kit.

'It took them two years to let anyone know about the last leak.'

'That wasn't so serious,' he replies, taking the vials out of their packets.

'Ninety-nine,' she says. 'Ninety-nine failures at the last Evening Star.'

'Some of those contraventions were paperwork.'

'They need more scientists on board.'

'You want to go down in a sub?' he asks her. 'Be in charge?'

She laughs. 'Playing with their toys? No. You, Anthony? You must want...'

'Want what?' he asks, as light as he can. Elspeth chooses not to answer.

He kneels, indicating they should get on.

He fills eleven vials of water at two-metre intervals down to twenty-two metres, using the extending rod to push and release. He pulls them up and hands them to Elspeth. She wipes them dry and places them in the rack. As the rod deepens into the loch he feels a pull. Each time his arm is heaved away a little more. *There. Again.* The electricity as he dug into the hole, tingling his neck. *Tartarus* was at sea when the accident happened. Yet he felt the disruption. *That's what it was!* He thinks of telling Elspeth, but it's too far-fetched.

Would Aggie believe him? Yes. Because of its mystery— or because she was desperate to reward anything he shared? Something else gnaws at him. A memory. He sees it. Hears it. The surprise pushes him forward. He wobbles and grips the rod but the rod is no good, it's resting in the water.

'Steady,' says Elspeth, catching his shoulder. 'I thought you said you didn't want to go down in a ship?'

At the lab they dry off and remove the waterproofs and put them into decontamination buckets. Mariam and David are back from *Tartarus*.

'Suits in the bins too,' says Mariam. 'Quickly, then we'll get them sent off.'

Anthony takes off the underlayer of the protective suit, scrunches it up into the laundry trolley and takes off his gloves last. He stares at the pile of clothing. It should have been discussed who went on *Tartarus*. As the senior scientist, David would take the more dangerous job. But Mariam? Anthony throws his gloves in the trolley and goes over to David, who's plugging a dosimeter into his laptop to download the data.

'We should've discussed who went with you,' he says quietly.

David ignores him and calls Mariam and Elspeth over, looks at them all.

'We need a new set of guidelines put into place immediately,' he says.

'Our procedures aren't—' Mariam begins, but Anthony interrupts.

'We need to strengthen them again.'

Mariam glares at him.

'Look,' says David. 'The Commodore is—this is by far the worst that's—although it's…it's, look…when this gets out, and it will, it's going to be…a shit storm.'

Anthony's never heard David swear.

'There's nothing wrong with *our* safety procedures,' says Mariam.

But that, Anthony thinks, is because he's introduced new processes, widened the scope of the testing routines, made links with experts to develop the knowledge tables. He's tested more soil and flora, the trees and leaves outside of the base as well as inside. That wasn't easy to get past the Navy comptrollers, but it was all done efficiently, with a successful PR push to the local media so the story didn't become a conspiracy. This is what irks her. It passes judgment on a status quo she'd forged. But which ambitious scientist would follow the handbook? When it's Parliament scrutinising your handiwork? There weren't any major gaps in the procedures, he conceded that. But that didn't mean Navy staff were compliant. Or that nuclear energy didn't have a life of its own, beyond the base's fences.

'You're right,' says David. He looks at Mariam. 'You both are.'

Elspeth laughs bitterly. David glares at her and she swings away.

'Now is definitely not the time for in-fighting. We need a review of everything. Especially how we test in water. The water evacuation. Shit'—and David double-takes—'That is, if they hadn't evacuated the water...'

'They had to,' says Mariam.

David passes out a portion of the existing procedures to each of them for review. Anthony's given the marine testing. It's a rebuke to Mariam; they both know it. David glosses over the injury with a suggestion that 'fresh eyes' will do the whole process some good. And now's the perfect time to introduce the schema for looking into the fish and water insects, any water mammals.

There's far less known about how to test within the marine environment than he's expecting. Lots for on the boats. But in the ocean? Fish? Who has done fish? The Japanese, after Fukushima? He's been out of the conference circle for a long time, although he still reads the proceedings when he can. And here they have access to *every* journal. He sits at his bench drinking cold coffee and sets to work.

It's six o'clock when he looks at his watch. The others have the same bowed posture, leaning into their work as if the pressure of gravity might squeeze extra results from the labour. There's been no interaction since the morning. No debrief on the water samples, which were handed over to David. Anthony's made good progress in the procedures for marine testing, on what he's

13

been able to read up. What's meant to happen now? He wanders over to David's perch.

'It's gone six,' Anthony says.

'Has it?' David grimaces. 'Oh bloody hell. Christie is going to drag me by the balls through the roses. We've got her sister over for dinner.'

'Get off now,' Anthony says. 'You'll make good time.'

There's a look on David's face that says there's a separate set of commands that Anthony's not privy to. He can't help but glance at Mariam. She doesn't look up from her work. Six o'clock is not on her radar, either. His gut swims knowing he's not included. He gulps it down.

'I didn't know your wife was a gardener?'

'Hmm?'

'The rosebushes.'

'Oh. Look, you get off. Have you completed a review?'

'I've emailed everything I've done so far. But there are gaps.'

'Well, get off home. And you two, Elspeth, Mariam.'

Anthony looks at Mariam, pleased that she's being ejected.

'We're happy to stay.'

'Look,' says David. He blinks a number of times. 'It's not a four person job. I can take the results over to the C when I'm done.'

David makes his body big and the three of them find themselves outside with their coats and the subjects of orders that only David has received.

It's dark except for the bright spots of the base lights. He meanders over to his car. He watches Mariam and Elspeth get in theirs and drive off. He thinks of going back in. But he doesn't have that rapport with David, yet.

He gets in the car and in the stillness accepts the new burden: what he cannot *officially* share, not even with a spouse. Aggie called him out on it straightaway once he'd taken the job. *Perfect excuse,* she'd said. *You like your secrets.* Marriage was meant to make it easier. He still believes it was an oversight—that he'd not thought it through when applying for the job. He never imagined there would be something secret enough, dangerous enough, to keep from her. *Whatever,* Aggie countered.

All the same, he hopes that tonight he will know what to say.

Anthony gives it—he counts—seventeen turns of the key before he phones for the recovery van. After going through the script with the call handler and confirming a mechanic is on the way, he phones Aggie.

'Ant?' Aggie answers. 'Is it the motor?'

They've been having trouble with the Hyundai. The starter and sparks. It's this West Coast damp, or the car rebelling against the rubbish he strews on the back seat. The soil he tramps through its footwells.

'Fucking engine,' says Anthony. 'I've phoned Green Flag. They won't be long, but I've got to get them security checked onto the base, or push the car out into the road. I've no idea how long that will take. Sorry.'

'I'm making soup,' she says.

Not, *don't say sorry.*

'Okay.'

'You can heat it when you're back.'

Not, *I'll wait for you.*

'If the garage is still open I'll see what bread they've got.'

She's fuming, he thinks. She is aghast at his failure to do this simple thing: to come home. So they can talk. After a while she says, 'Not the white.'

It's too late for soup when he's back with new plugs, another hundred and fifty quid down, too much time thinking about what's become stuck between them. The delay and the cost has curdled in his stomach. This wasn't how the week was meant to begin. They were going to have the evening together. Is their week already ruined for the next six days?

Aggie is in the kitchen, the only properly warm room in the cottage, leaning against the Aga. They kiss lightly as a greeting, and he gets a mouthful of her black hair as it falls over her shoulder. He hands her a loaf.

'It was all they had.'

'It's fine. Thanks. Soup?'

He shakes his head, takes the bottle of Oban from the dresser and a tumbler and sits at the kitchen table.

Aggie doesn't say anything, then offers to make toast. He shakes his head again. She makes herself a slice while he gets out his phone and pretends to check Facebook. The toaster pops, Aggie rattles for a knife, spreads the margarine. He wills her to put on the radio to fill the silence. She offers him a bite. He flicks his head. She lingers for a moment in the doorway and disappears into the corridor. It's half past ten.

They thought they'd have more time away from the city, engaged in village life, the Trossachs less than half an hour away, walks, Munros, air. But this new life has been lonelier than expected. The cottage is too damp to linger in. Neither wants to be there alone, waiting for the other. His job has been a saviour at least—not exactly all-consuming but Anthony's gone at it with a graft and zeal that even he's surprised by. This show of commitment makes Aggie happy. Happier. She's taken up a project management role with a social enterprise in Glasgow working with people in poverty, but that's only part-time, so she's gone back to teaching mindfulness too; her classes are usually in the evenings, outside his work hours, so they keep missing each other. Only Mondays and Saturdays do they both find themselves, like startled shrews, at home together, this place that they have not yet made their own, unpacked boxes lining the hallway. Mondays and Saturdays when they can eat, and talk. Apart from when the car breaks down. He flicks between apps on his phone, alerts that he's cautious not to check while at work. He suddenly feels a pang for his wife's name. Not

Aggie, her full name. *Agatha.* Its goodness. *Do you, Agatha, take...* When did he hear it last? He has a memory of them launching themselves into waves on the Atlantic coast, her swimming top torn away by the force of the surf, laughing and shivering over hot chocolates, his hands cupped around hers. An old friend of her family happening upon them in the cafe, calling her, *Agatha?,* interrupting their privacy.

Aggie comes back, munching her toast under which she hovers the plate to catch crumbs. She stands by the table, puts down the plate and then puts her arms around his neck, nuzzles the side of his head. Her breath is warm and yeasty. He feels the strange tingling from the earth under her kisses. He twists away, puts the phone face down on the table.

'Porn?' she says. 'We can go upstairs.'

'After you've eaten Marmite?'

'That gives you away. You're not British until you love Marmite.'

'I thought you could love it or hate it?'

'Not truly.' She reaches over to her plate, picks up a quarter of toast and takes another bite. She's chewing loudly in his ear. 'Are you hungry? I can get you something.'

'That really fucking irritates me. The whole Can't-Be-British thing.'

'Don't be stupid,' she says, peeling herself off him, falling onto the nearest chair. There's a long strand of her hair caught in the spread on her toast. He stares a moment longer then rubs his face with his hands.

'For work,' he says, tapping the phone. 'There's a...lot going on.'

'There's a lot going on here, too.'

Aggie notices the hair stuck in the Marmite and lifts it out with a finger. She takes a final mouthful and puts a single crust on the plate. She can never quite finish anything. She won't admit it when he points it out. It's something to do with her parents, and they can't talk about that now, either. The death of her father another excuse. Aggie washes up her plate.

'There's a letter for you,' she says over her shoulder. 'On the dresser.'

'From who?'

'It's for *you*.' He stares at her back, stretches for the Oban. 'Looks like it's...'

She doesn't finish. He continues to stare, then pours out two fingers.

Three fingers.

He climbs into bed and lays there, heartburning, unwisely philosophizing. It's chill in the bedroom and when Aggie comes in she throws on her Edinburgh half marathon T-shirt, its legend faded. She climbs in and puts a hand on his chest, her leg over his. It's palliative, unsexy. They don't say anything. He stares up into near black.

'Did you open your letter?'

He grunts. He did.

'Are you going to reply this time?'

He closes his eyes. He can't begin to think about that as well, not yet.

'But at least work is going well?'

Even in this mood, her patience astounds and belittles him. It *is* going well. Even more so because of things he cannot tell her. He doesn't want to say what else he's thinking but knows he's going to say it anyway —

'*At least*? Implying that...?'

She blows out her cheeks. 'Implying nothing.'

'It's the cottage,' he says after a while, for something to say. 'It must be haunted.'

'What do you mean?'

'It's been like this since we got here.'

'It's not the cottage.'

'Bad blood. Dead bodies in the walls, maybe. Miserable women who—'

'—only *women* are miserable?'

'—who were lured in by the charming proprietor—'

'—who wears big knitted jumpers—'

'—that's not the—'

'—and then married him.'

He pushes her off. She rolls away. Their awkwardness becomes overwhelming.

'Sounds like that fairy tale, the one with the cape,' he says.

'Bluebeard.'

'No, the one with the wolf.'

She turns on her side and faces him in the dark.

'I know the one *you* mean. That's not the one *I* mean.'

'It's not the cottage,' he admits.

'*I know it's not the bloody cottage.*'

He doesn't reply. They lie there and drift into silence until Aggie is breathing through her nose, not quite a snore but enough of a whine so he knows she's sleeping. Now she's asleep he can reach out a hand and take hers under the cover. She grips, but doesn't wake.

And you, brother? Does your wife make you feel this?

It has slipped away in the last year, their marriage, like the way a tree loses its leaves. Those first few arguments he thought were only bickering, and the fallout immaterial, as they would come together again, and grow. But the storms have stripped him bare. Worse, however, was this: when they didn't really argue, but just went over the same old ground. They used to talk. He'd felt safe with her. And then something closed around him, and from inside he cannot fathom his way out.

But there's a toe in the door. This move north, the new jobs. If there's a toe in the door, the marriage counsellor said, there's a chance. And work *is* going well (*at least*). Those failed jobs before put pressure on them. Not *only* the jobs; he's smart enough to know that. But while this one lasts they have a chance to settle and regroup. They just need some time to find their grip on each other again. He'll fall asleep holding her hand until at a moment during the night they roll away from each other, and he is able to rest.

Tuesday

Light enters through the curtains. There's no noise. He's awake, listening to nothing. A dream fades, and he registers something ill-fitting in his body. He wriggles towards Aggie, and she stirs and allows him closer. He slides an arm under her pillow and wraps himself around her and lays there for a while before the events of yesterday overcome his inertia. He gets up, and while her eyes are still closed he tiptoes over to the dresser. He opens her accessories box and pokes a finger among the thin wire necklaces and silver rings, tiny tinklings that sound, in the silence, like a car alarm. There it is: the pebble. He's not needed it for a while; he's not even sure why he wants it now; then he remembers the letter from his sister. He picks up the pebble, carries it into the bathroom. Downstairs he fuels up on two pieces of shit white toast and heads to the base, but is wishing the car to splutter to a stop before he gets there. He doesn't have to drive. It's just another habit. He could cycle. Aggie cycles to her classes. He prods his abs, as soft as marshmallow as he sits behind the wheel. He takes a right onto the A616. He half recognises someone from the village at the bus stop. They wave but he pretends he doesn't see.

There's a permanent protest on the verge by the entrance to the base that's been there well over a decade. It's outside the jurisdiction of the Ministry of Defence, covered by the same exemption as the peace camp at the Houses of Parliament in London. He has enough of a grasp of politics to know the Scottish Nationalists don't want Trident, so they encourage the camp. Turn a blind eye, at least. There's one main tent, taut and apple green, and four smaller of different shades of blue. A lot of milling around, although he's seen it swell to a hundred people, like a few weeks ago when a convoy of missiles was driven up from Bedford where they're assembled. The atmosphere was carnivalesque, and he drove slowly that morning. There were TV cameras. He and Aggie watched the news that night but there was nothing on the bulletin.

There they are: the two ever-presents. An older man in a rainbow of waterproofs wearing a beanie, anti-everything patches sewn on his jacket. There's a woman about the same age, a sweet face, brown hair and a big red jumper under a Berghaus windcheater. They're sitting in camp chairs around a low table and kettle. It's a very British protest, stewed tea and limp flags. The woman waves, and it startles him. The old man laughs. He accelerates into the base.

David is sitting where they left him last night. Mariam is standing at his shoulder. Elspeth is at the bench reading through a printout stapled at the top left-hand corner. He takes his whites from the door and walks over to David.

'I have a job for you,' says David. 'Some whales have washed up on the beach at Kilcreggan, on the other side of the loch. Half a dozen. You need to get over there immediately.'

'Whales?'

'Probably porpoises. Someone from the cafe reported it.'

'To us?'

'Well, you know about the bombs.'

Anthony had heard about it on the news a few months before. They'd spoken about it in the lab, not in an official capacity, but there'd been a *communiqué*. Nineteen pilot whales stranded after the Navy exercises at Cape Wrath, when the bombs had missed their targets and sunk into the water and been detonated after.

'Every time a whale washes up the locals think it's to do with the Navy.'

'They're probably right,' he says.

David stares at him for a moment.

'Why are they sending us and not a clean-up team?'

'Both,' says David. 'But you need to test them before the clean-

up finishes. It shouldn't take you half an hour to get there. Take
your suit. And Anthony...'

'Yes?'

'Be discreet.'

'In a radiation suit?'

'Just don't let anything slip out.'

He drives out of the base, passing the protest encampment. The
same man with his jacket and myriad patches, the woman with
the brown hair, and another woman, short, younger, sporting a
bobble hat the shape and colour of an aubergine. He doesn't slow
down. As he passes they look, but no one waves. He catches a
glance of the younger woman's face. Pretty, but also serious.

He's on the small road round the head of the loch. The
Hyundai is spluttering, and he swears, *just paid a hundred and
fifty fucking quid for those new plugs.* The sun flashes through the
scansions of the security perimeter running along on his left, and
he notices how it changes in increments the farther out from the
base he gets. Twelve-foot fencing with thick metal riveted panels
halfway up and topped with razor wire. Then twelve-foot fences
and the metal panels. Then ten feet, no panels just fencing. All
this sitting alongside the normality of small village life. A bus
stop; pavement that disappears into verge for no reason; the
occasional touring cyclists with panniers packed with gear. Then
the perimeter fence shoots off sharp left, revealing a clear view of
the loch, or what remains of it here at its head. Little more than
a small, inland pond. He looks the other way. The Trossachs,
hardly towering but magnificent all the same. A welt of green
that at this distance spreads out like a hundred kinds of moss. He
and Aggie should spend more time in the forest.

He enters Garelochhead and passes four new Scandinavian-
looking cabins going up on the waterfront. The prices around
Faslane are cheaper. Who'd live on top of nuclear weapons? The
cabins are an attempt to attract more pragmatic tourists. If the

clichés about the Scots are true, then perhaps they don't mind the nuclear proximity for a cheap price. But the clichés aren't true. Aggie is one of the most generous people he knows. They all are.

Anthony drives past the strange, museum-like collection of local buses and minibuses parked outside two large roller-door garages. A yellow double decker from at least twenty years before—too new to be beautifully shaped, too old to benefit from modern comforts—looms like a mutant canary over the smaller buses more suited to the country lanes. The image of a hundred buses parked in a town square floods his memory. He pulls over out of breath, as caught for air as the car's engine. Those ghost buses are lurching, biting on their clutches, spewing out a spume of oil and smog like a great bubbling pot, a multicoloured burn on the skin of an old, lost town.

He falls over the steering wheel and gasps loudly like an old man. Words come unbidden: *tekhnohenna katastrofa*. The floor of the car has rolled away. Awkwardly he thrusts his spare hand in his trouser pocket. He rubs his fingers over the shiny surface of the pebble, retrieved from Aggie's jewellery box. There are words coming at him like tiny shocks. Spoken, but not by any voice he can put a face to. They're sung by a chorus.

Sviaz po bolezn'iu.

He's shocked back into the present as a car drives by and honks—his rear is sticking out in the middle of the road. He looks up, sees only the local buses. Parked, silent. The memory is gone. The words too. He finds first gear and pulls into the car park of The Anchor, where he and Aggie visited when they first moved up and left after two halves of lager each, the second only to be polite.

His breathing returns to normal. He starts the car, wipes saliva from the corners of his mouth. His eyes are blurry. He drives as soon as he can. He rounds the water and begins the drive down the western shore. The view of the buses is hidden and then the base also, by trees and bushes. Every now and then he catches a glimpse of the loch through a gap in the foliage.

Tekhnohenna katastrofa.

He knows what the words mean. They don't need much translation.

Technological catastrophe.

Sviaz po bolezn'iu.

Those too. In connection with the illness.

He's not been this side of the loch before, but Kilcreggan is on the main road according to the map on his phone so he's not expecting to miss it. All he knows is that there are whales, possibly porpoises, somewhere on the beach. He can't believe Navy security is so slack to send him on his own if there's something seriously wrong. So perhaps it's not as bad as he thinks. He hopes.

He drives into the village and pulls into the parking bays opposite a row of shops by the waterfront. There's a cafe, a barber's next door, and a little trinket shop called Strawberry Fields next to that; a restaurant, The Kilcreggan Bay. Outside there's a dinky bright orange 1960s Land Rover.

The cafe is painted white with pale turquoise woodwork and some bare pine. It's comfy, smart and bright. It smells sugary. There are a handful of people, all locals or tourists from the caravan park in Rosneath. He thinks of Aggie, knee deep in mindful breathing, and the ails of the local pensioners who are her clients, coming here to fortify themselves on Earl Grey. There's a girl behind the counter in a white T-shirt and black apron, her short blond hair tucked back in a ponytail.

'Can I help? If you want, you can just take a seat.'

'I'm looking for the person who phoned in about the whales,' he explains. 'Someone called from here?'

'Aye, they're over at Portkil Bay,' she says. 'Doris phoned the base. You Navy?'

He nods briefly. He's not used to it yet, and neither is it true.

'Portkil Bay?'

'Back along,' she says. She's drying a mug with great care. 'Along Fort Road. Then there's a place you can park.'

'Poor things,' says someone, and he looks around. An older woman sitting on her own is looking at him. 'You keep killing them, don't you?'

He doesn't say anything. The woman tuts at him and goes back to her crossword. He looks to the counter for the young girl but she's disappeared into the kitchen. He leaves the cafe and stands by his car and searches for Portkil Bay on his phone. The signal is slow. He looks out over the water. The beach is little more than gravel, then disappears around a corner. In front of him there's a small jetty that runs about twenty feet out into the water advertising a ferry to Greenock. How much water is between here and there, he wonders. How much radiation would it take to register, to be dangerous?

The map on his phone loads. As the girl said: *back along*. Down to the right, around that hidden crest to his left as he stands.

There's no missing the whales. He doesn't know what a porpoise looks like in comparison up close, but they're surely smaller than these sad, lolling beasts. There are, he's able to count as he drives up, six. But what captures his attention is the small crowd at the edge of the beach and the two boys sitting on top of two of the carcasses.

He pulls into the layby where a handful of cars belonging to onlookers are already parked. He's not in his radiation suit, but there's more pressing needs. He runs down to a beach of black gravel and grey stone.

'Hey! Get off there,' he shouts, waving his arms.

They're what people in their village call radgies, boys about eleven or twelve wearing jeans and T-shirts and trainers. One has a cagoule slung loosely around his waist. One has bright red hair and freckles, the other is darker but just as pale.

'Get off!' he shouts again.

The crowd are pulled in by the altercation. He's by the boys now. He can see the slick, black skin of the whales glistening under the sun. The boys sit staring at him astride the carcasses as if they've been there long enough to claim them.

'Hey, who are you?' asks a woman.

'It's not safe, boys,' he says, and then adds, 'they might have diseases.'

The boys look at each other. They know about diseases, mumps and nits and worse. What can kill a whale can kill a boy?

'Hey, who are you?' the woman asks again. She's standing by him now, pointing a finger. Her face is blotchy. 'What do you mean diseases?'

'Boys, get off,' he repeats. 'Or you'll get your parents into deep shit.'

The redhead boy gets off, making a disgusted noise as he does, sliding his hands down the thick body of the whale and its mucus skin. The other looks at Anthony grudgingly and then sneers, gets off too.

'We were just having a ride,' says the redhead.

'Wash your hands. It just might not be safe, that's all,' he says, and curses David for sending him out here alone.

'Are you going to answer my question?' the woman asks him.

'We just need to check what's wrong,' he explains. 'To find out why they beached. If there might be anything wrong with them.' That's not enough of an excuse, certainly not by the look on her face. But what does he care? He's doing them a favour. 'There's a disease in whales around here that's possibly contagious,' he says, and immediately regrets it. What if that makes it into the *Herald*?

'What are you, one of those animal people?' the woman asks. It isn't a nice question. Her friends are with her now. 'You having your animal rights?'

He almost laughs. *What the fuck?* He turns to the whales, their great smooth black bodies like slippery onyx, barbed on the stony flat beach. If they're not victims of the *Tartarus* leak, then they're victims of something. Plastic, pollution? The desecration of their corpses by ignorant kids?

'Whale conservation,' he lies, easy enough. 'We need to know what caused them to beach. If they were sick, it could be dangerous for you to be here.'

'It's too late to save the whales,' jokes another woman, the middle of the three who've come to question him. One laughs, but another chastises her.

'Pity the beasts. Oh pity,' she says. She looks like she could be the mother of the dark-haired boy. She's staring at the whales. 'This is the Navy's fault. That sonar. It makes the whales deaf.'

All he wants is to get his equipment out of the car and test the whales. But waving a dosimeter around would be explosive. They've lived opposite a nuclear base for long enough, they can't be that ill-informed, surely? Even if they were, someone they told would describe it to someone else, who'd put two and two together, and it would get out. *Jesus.*

He hears another vehicle. He turns and sees a truck from the base. It pulls up behind his car and half a dozen guards get out. They're not immediately recognisable as Navy but wearing security uniforms. He looks more closely. They're walking like something out of B-movie horror. Underneath they're all wearing radiation suits.

He's patting his coat pockets for his wallet, fishing out ID. Soldiers are coming over and waving the crowd away. Two unroll an eight foot high canvas fence along the edge of the beach around the whales. Two more channel the women and the boys away. Some of the women have their phones out, taking pictures. He's looking at the boys who are going off behind their mothers.

'Wash your hands,' he shouts in their direction.

He only has to nod for David to grimace; it's fast becoming David's standard expression. Anthony downloads the dosimeter readings into the laptop. He wonders what will happen now to the bodies of the whales, and if the Navy is prepared for such manoeuvres that require the disposal of half a dozen contaminated leviathans. He fires up Google and confirms the identity of the species. He searches for validation of his intuition that the whales didn't go anywhere near the subs, and so their deaths would indicate that the radiation has spread far into the water. But what he finds is counter to that guess. In fact, there's so much noise pollution that the whales don't know which way is up when it comes to avoiding boat strikes. And the subs don't make much noise. They're silent compared to tankers and cargo carriers and cable layers. There's as many deaths caused by noise in the water as by plastic. He was not expecting that. But it makes sense. It's how whales navigate their world. And sound travels four times quicker in water. Most of this from the website of a charity he just pretended to be representing.

He adds to his report: *While there is no way to measure the proximity* –

'David. Do we have coordinates for the location of the sub when –'

'We've not been told. Why?'

'Proximity for the whales. To triangulate where they washed up.'

David swivels to face him. 'Were they all dead?'

'Yes. I think so.'

He writes: *It is possible that the whales were in immediate vicinity to the evacuation of the irradiated coolant water due to the increasing levels of noise pollution at depth from commercial and military marine activity.*

Which makes it sound perfectly reasonable.

David is at his shoulder, puffing out his cheeks.

'You'll finish that this afternoon?'

'What do we do about the boys?'

'We pass the report up,' says David. 'Not in our hands.'

'But they were on the whales. You've seen the dosimeter results.'

David wraps his lips and makes a sucking noise.

'This is the Navy's jurisdiction. Make your recommendations—'

'My recommendation is that those kids are going to get very sick,' and he knows he's said it too loudly, but carries on anyway, 'and then someone at the hospital is going to find out that—'

David doesn't wait for him to finish but turns around and walks away.

Khlop.

Anthony grabs the side of the bench and steadies himself. He closes his eyes but all that does is brighten the memory: a child walking but her leg not working; someone asking a question: *Ty tut sviaz po bolezn'iu?*

'Anthony.' Suddenly David is towering over him. 'You're still new. What we do here is provide the research and data for the Navy to make decisions. You make your recommendation. I will take that and make mine. Then the Navy will act. They're not monsters. They'll take those boys' safety seriously. Do you understand?'

He shoves a hand into his pocket and grabs the pebble.

Khlop. Little boy.

At the cottage he parks and sits in the quieting car. He takes a deep breath, not ready to go in. He looks around. A few driving CDs (*Tracy Chapman; Masters of Rock Remixed*) and ordinance survey maps. Receipts for petrol and a set of hair clippers he bought now there's not a barber's in fifty miles he'd trust with his hair. A chewed-up tennis ball, as if they had a dog. *Where did that come from?* Aggie must have picked it up—she was always going soft over other people's dogs. Aggie had taken the car before she got organised with her cycling; then she insisted she'd rather, as exercise. He doesn't like her coming back in the dark along that road. Why doesn't he make her take the car?

The tennis ball. Maybe she has a secret dog? A flash goes through him like a vein of gold in rock, leaving an empty stripe. He considers it. An affair? Aggie wasn't shy. She was always talking to strangers, she had a way of touching them and smiling that... But an affair? Wasn't there the guy at Oxford, her old friend from home who gave that talk in Waterstones when his book about the fishing industries was published? He knows nothing happened between them — *do I?* — but he'd still sat there in the audience not looking at the author but watching Aggie constantly tuck her hair behind her ear, sitting forward with a straight back, and not turning once to look at him, her (soon-to-be) husband. And that was when the relationship was going *smoothly*. Now sometimes the only word he can think of to describe their marriage is *terrible*... so what about now? If she was — having an affair — the guy *would* have a dog. A Border collie. This other man would have Scottish written through him like a stick of rock, he'd have a beard and thick hair, he'd speak Gaelic, his dog would be black and white, he'd wear Aran jumpers that actually suited him — what she'd meant last night by *knitted jumpers*, perhaps — and he'd be called Connor. There was no one like that in the village. But Aggie's classes — where did they take her? He scrutinises the tennis ball. Yellow and mushy, the brand all but chewed off, half-hidden under old papers and a plastic bag. How this car has fallen into such disrepair, as if the vehicle was, well, the *vehicle*, for the unsaid between them. Marriage hadn't resolved as much as he'd hoped. Then her father died. But there *was* a time when they spoke. Would they get that back? All he had to do was... Only that. Slowly, word by word, pull himself out of the morass of fear and shame and whatever other terrors ruled his unconscious like a wordless demagogue. Share his life, again.

But the tennis ball. She's given her lover a lift home. Or they've taken the dog to the beach. Anthony doesn't want to touch it, in case it's still warm and covered in dog drool. Who is he, this man, this dog? Anthony slaps his hands on his thighs. It's one of her mindfulness clients, and Aggie's given her a lift, an older woman from the village and her dog is a little shih tzu, or a terrier, or... he can't think of any more breeds. Every client at her mindfulness classes would in some way be mindless, right? They'd forget their dog's toy. But would the dog?

He can't think of this. It will ruin him. A vein there, a flash from brow to gut like a twanged string, and all night he will feel the fret. How could he talk then?

But Aggie's not home. It's Tuesday and she has a class at the spa in Carrick for rich golf widows. Maybe the chewed-up tennis ball belongs to one of them.

He warms up the leftover soup. Barley broth, salty and filling, even better twenty-four hours later. Now he's inside their home, eating the food she's cooked, the stupidity of his jealousy strikes him. How lucky he is that she's come this far with him. After eating he sits at the kitchen table and listens to the noises of the cottage. He gets out his laptop and opens up the report he'd submitted to David before leaving, on the condition of the whales and his recommendation to find and treat the boys with potassium iodide immediately, at least. Surely their families could be brought in and instructed not to break silence? Surely the news was going to get out?

The Navy will act. They're not monsters.

He cleans up the soup bowl and saucepan, looks once more at the report and closes the screen. He moves to stand but stops as if he's been punched in the solar plexus as someone's words engulf him:

Ya ne khochu buty na tsiy storoni svitu.

He sits down. It takes him a while to clarify, but in the end, he remembers.

I detest being on this side of the world.

Wednesday

They wake up together. Aggie climbed in after he'd fallen asleep reading the new biography of Richard Feynman. This morning is a lovely drag; the tennis ball is forgotten, a crazy idea after a crazy day, and they don't let go of each other way past the fifth snooze. Then everything's rushed. He burns the toast. She pelts through the shower like a greyhound chasing hares and then stands in the kitchen in her bathrobe and a white towel whipped round her head like an ice cream. But there's always occasion for tea. While the kettle boils he glances out the window at the buddleia tumbling across the view. It needs cutting back. He has an urge to tell Aggie what's happening. Sod David, sod the commanders. Aggie makes tea in today's teapot, its yellow and green stripes unevenly painted the closer he's looked. It is their Wednesday teapot. They have seven. She has seven.

'The Wednesday teapot,' he offers. 'Your mother would be proud.'

'She is proud.' They sit down, and Aggie puts the pot in the middle of the table. 'It's not an obsession. If it were I'd have a lot more.'

'There's nothing wrong with obsessions. Or routines.'

'Seven is enough.'

'And if the challenge to routine becomes the routine?'

'Then you break it. And them.'

She pulls the teapot closer, and pours herself a cup.

'And it still tastes different every day,' he says.

She knits her brow, takes a suspicious sip. Then smiles.

This is easy, he thinks.

He finishes his breakfast and washes up. In the bedroom they busy themselves dressing. Years ago they would have taken any nakedness as a chance for sex. Now it's enough they're ready without reprisal. When the Hyundai starts first time they both look at each other, share a surprised smile. He's dropping her at the train station. She's going to the Glasgow office of the social enterprise, and then the team is coming back together for tonight's big event they've been planning.

'You'll be there at six?' she asks him as she unbuckles her belt at the drop-off outside the station. They've made it with three minutes to spare.

He nods. 'Just a lot on,' but then says quickly, 'I'll be there, of course.'

They kiss and she runs up the ramp into the station. Now is when he should throw the tennis ball out of the car into the gutter, while her door is still open.

As soon as Anthony enters the lab David swivels round and motions for them—Elspeth and Mariam as well—to gather at the central bench. There are sick crew, six men and two women. Five from the engineering team of *Tartarus*, two navigational staff and one senior officer. They're in isolation at the base's clinic, extra medical staff brought in to provide care. The military used to have its own hospitals, Elspeth tells him to the side, but now if anyone gets sick or injured they're usually helicoptered to the military wings of the Western in Glasgow. David's explaining: water was flushed into the sea before they reached the loch, but there were no later emissions. The cooling rods were not damaged, so there were no further leaks from that source. But some need replacing. Engineers are working on that. There's a pause. Antony tallies the injury count with turns of the pebble in his pocket. He estimates what stage of their sickness they've reached. When he'll be asked to start testing on human samples. When will the crew get—he searches for the word—it arrives—but not as he wants it—

Pidlikuvatsyia.

'This is separate from the clean-up—' David is saying.

'Clean-up?' Elspeth crosses her arms. 'Is that how we're talking about exposure?'

Mariam leads Elspeth away by the elbow and begins asking about the new models that Elspeth has been working on for updating the procedures. It's not subtle, but Anthony doesn't care, as it means that Mariam isn't available for what will necessarily come next. And it does.

The clinic is at the far south of the operational command block. After Elspeth's explanation, it's a more sophisticated set-up than Anthony was expecting–a dozen isolation rooms as part of a large modern clinic. It's at half a level down from the ground floor, dug into the earth, and the small slits for windows let in only a dim light through translucent panes. They're met by the chief medic, a tall man with dark hair and a cheery smile, out of place, Anthony thinks, in this half-submerged scene of crisis. Of the eight crew, the medic reports, six are getting worse. One of the women is worst of all. Is the woman an engineer? He shouldn't doubt that, nor think about the gender of those in the bowels of the subs, prowling the oceans. To his shame, he does.

In the changing room, he and David wash thoroughly up to the armpit, and put on blue airtight gowns with crinkled hoods to the hairline, then tight, gauzy facemasks and clear latex gloves. He pulls the mask down from his mouth.

'Are we the first to take readings?'

'What?'

David's fiddling with the hood around his face.

'Haven't they had readings already?'

'Anthony.' There's exasperation seeping through. They stare at each other a moment, then David puts his mask back on and unstraps a mobile monitor and hands it to Anthony and leads the way into the corridor. There are four crew members in isolation on one side, and four on the other. David points to divide the hallway between them, left and right.

'It was emergency treatment first,' David mumbles through the mask, 'and *now* we get the advanced blood work.'

Anthony nods, but even so... When the Navy's got it wrong, even then? He knows the answer. An image of the two boys sitting on the whales flashes through his mind.

He and David separate and go into opposite rooms. The first submariner is a man, perhaps early twenties. No crew cut—that's only in the Hollywood version. He's asleep, thinks Anthony. Unconscious since arrival? A forced coma? Or painkillers? He's not been told anything, and there's a ball of anger gathering in his chest. It would be inconceivable they'd not taken blood already. Tested for specific radionuclides? *Fucking hell.* He looks at the man, a boy really, in the bed, and pictures what's been discharged through his system. His young body a gauze for catching ions. Perhaps this is medical procedure under military protocol, on a war footing—heal first the emergency, investigate the outcome later. Identify those who might live, limit the pain, remove bodies from the scene. But testing for the specifics, surely that? His chest tightens, his temples narrow. He knows so little of the procedures for actually treating the radiation. He sucks the frustration back into his chest, but it does not go away.

Sarkofag.

The word hits him. He runs a hand down the side of his leg but there's no way through the overalls to his trouser pocket and the pebble. He breathes in deeply.

Sarcophagus. The concrete chamber they built around the nightmare.

He looks at the man in the bed. The boy.

Don't think about yourself. Concentrate on him.

The room beats with the monitoring machines, heart rate and breaths. There's the odour of iodine in the man's sweat. Sandy haired, a healthy skin underneath, perhaps more jaw and brow than what's on show through the puffed malaise. Around the eyebrows the skin is beginning to blister. A tube runs out of the left nostril. Cannulas in the back of both hands hooked up to drips, one filled with blood, the other saline. He's seen radiation sickness before—but not for a long time. He looks around. Nothing else in the room. No clothes, no slippers reeking of feet. No uniform. No tag or name. Anthony's not a medic, doesn't know these systems, but understands sterility and understands secrecy. He puts his kit down on the chair beside the man's bed. Switches on the dosimeter for a general reading. Waves it across the man's body. He looks at the face. It's swollen, not quite beetroot but not far away. There's a deep stillness in the room despite the noisy medical apparatus. He takes readings. Fifty millirems per hour. Even now, forty-eight hours later. A lifetime's safe cumulative total was only a thousand. He'd absorbed all of that in two days.

Anthony takes out the blood kit. No names for the labels, they were instructed by the chief medic; they should write the number of the room on each tube. No names: so the families haven't been told. The Navy has seventy-two hours to inform the families. *So that's why we're here now.* To provide answers for when the Commodore has to pick up the phone. Anthony takes the blood. The arm is strong but not particularly hard-worked. This boy was not an engineer. He puts away the vials and scribbles on the room number. He does the next two crew in the same way, two breaths in, one long out, the churning in his chest spreading through his body. Once, he and David exit into the corridor at the same time, give each other a short glance. Anthony enters the final room and shuts the door.

She's puffy all over, the sheet can't hide that. Her arms are swollen, as if caught in bands and the blood has nowhere to go. She's lost her hair. No uniform. No tags. He walks over, dosimeter out. *For her hair to have fallen out, now, after two days...* He makes the calculation. Higher than six Grays.

She was the one sent to evacuate the water.

There are tufts of hair on her scalp. White and red patches. Blistering. Nothing burnt. No burns because there was no heat. No explosion. Her eyes are sunk into their cavities. Her nose is swollen like a drunk's. There are tubes running out of both nostrils.

There is a more vigorous smell in the room. Of a woman's body. He can smell the difference, whatever it is, the oestrus in sweat from apocrine glands swelling to her body's monthly rhythms. And perfume. There it is, in fact. Someone's brought a bottle and left it on the side table. Pastel orange, matte glass, the shape of a woman's torso, half empty, against all regulations.

He trembles with the syringe and barely fits the needle. Steadies himself with a hand on the rail of the bed. Draws blood. Can't help but picture what is writhing through her central nervous system. What it will bring forth. The apathy, the lethargy, seizures, ataxia, prostration. If she wakes up, what awaits her? Weeks and months of gastrointestinal syndrome: anorexia, nausea, vomiting, fever, severe systemic infections. And in the inner cavities of her skeleton, the gestation of hematopoietic bone marrow syndrome: the failure of her peripheral lymphocyte and granulocytes, a count below what's needed for survival, an increase in leukocytes fluctuating over months, lifetimes, many lives beyond her own as she is buried in the ground, or if her wish be it, at sea. Living on, eaten by fish, for half a billion years.

He fills the vials, disposes of the needle and closes his equipment case. He stares at her face. A memory writes itself over her image, over the sheet that covers her. *My child is ill: fevers, rashes, allergies, thyroid problems, leukopenia. Can you not help us? She's lost the ability to walk. Her leg functioned okay before. But now, this. You see how she drags? Is that normal? Is that her? It's as if something is not letting that leg walk. Hear the other children. What they say! Something has taken her, it holds her. She used to be quick, a runner. A gymnast. She performed for the mayor at the May Day Parade. For the Party. Now her leg hurts. She falls over. She's dragging it all through her life. Can you not help us? Please, can you?*

The mood in the lab is shadowed by what he and David have seen. David gathers in the samples and puts them through the microRNA scanner. Anthony is aiding, when asked, but struggles to remove the lid from a petri dish that sticks. David is preoccupied with the task—this RNA serum test is a new one, barely out of the lab itself. Anthony unsticks the lid, places it down for David, then wanders off to pour himself a coffee. Five minutes later David unexpectedly gathers them for a briefing. Anthony asks if the blood tests have shown specific radionuclide exposure. David doesn't answer. Can't or won't. They're not medical staff, they're not included in those who need to know. His task is complete, or rather, wholly incomplete. He knows only his part, and no other. The anger flushes his insides like barium.

'So what do we do now?' Elspeth asks.

'We carry on doing what we're told to.'

'What about the boys?' Anthony asks. Elspeth and Mariam both look confused. 'When I got to the whales, there were two boys sitting on the carcasses.'

'I've asked the Commodore for advice on that,' says David.

'Shouldn't we be *giving* the advice?'

David rubs his face, looks away.

'I've got to agree,' says Mariam, to Anthony's surprise. 'They're children. Civilians. It's not as if we can just sweep *that* under the carpet.'

'No one is sweeping *anything* under the carpet,' says David hotly. 'I worded that wrong. I've passed on your report, Anthony, to the Commodore. We're waiting for his decision. There's not much else we can do. But don't think it's not being considered. The readings were not off the charts. Less than a Gray. Yes, we need to act—'

'Bloody right we do,' says Elspeth.

'—but there's not a single one of you—of us—who didn't understand that this job operates under military authority. Is there?'

David's temples are red, his eyes bloodshot. In a flash, Anthony catches a glimpse of who he'll be if he stays for a year, a decade. Who, yesterday, he *wanted* to be. David's is a role of international standing. And this place is Anthony's last chance. Maybe his marriage's. He's had too many career dead ends. He swallows down the bile that's been building since taking the blood, thinks of Aggie.

'What about the marine environment testing?' David asks. 'Anthony? You'll be done by tonight?'

Anthony nods, then stops.

'Aggie's got her community meeting this eve, if—'

'Oh, the poverty alleviation thingy?' asks Elspeth. 'I think we'd said we'd—'

'Don't worry. I'll make excuses.'

David rubs his face. 'God, we've got parents evening tonight.'

'On a Wednesday?' asks Elspeth. 'Have I forgotten?'

'It's the upper form,' says David. 'Your Janna, she's only—?'

'Phew,' says Elspeth, smiling.

Anthony's last to disperse. He's thinking of his interview, four months ago. The psychological tests as well as the Full Level Disclosure: all past jobs, past relations, the whole history. The grilling over his childhood. He'd expected it—and been passed fit. *Not* a threat to national security. A surprise; even he'd thought it was less than fifty-fifty. Perhaps they didn't have any other candidates. But what he's recalling now are the final questions the Navy's human resources manager put to him.

'No,' he'd answered. 'I've never felt that. I was only a boy. A child.'

'But then how did you survive?'

He'd shrugged, said the only words that had ever made sense to him.

'We didn't die. But we don't know how we survived.'

By half past five he's rushing to get the new procedures complete, but there are too many holes in the knowledge of marine testing since Fukushima, and there's no way he's going to get everything he wants done to make Aggie's event on time. He walks over to David who's pulling a sheet of paper out of the printer.

'If you need me to stay…'

David isn't listening. He takes the pages he's printed and walks over to Mariam. They talk quickly, then Mariam stands. David turns around.

'Anthony, get off. And you, Elspeth. That's all for today.'

Elspeth looks up from her computer.

'I've nearly finished.'

'Tomorrow,' says David. 'Please.'

It's this final entreaty that tells Anthony exactly how bad the blood results are. David and Mariam both leave the lab. Elspeth is talking, but he's not listening. He's looking at David's laptop, which David hasn't flipped down. He watches from the corner of his eye as Elspeth carries on grumbling, shuts down her laptop and starts gathering her gear. He does the same but slowly, willing her to move. He's got two more minutes at most. When she's ready to leave she makes motions to wait for him, but Anthony sits down and opens his laptop again, says, 'Shit' and 'I've just thought of something. I'll make excuses for you tonight, seriously, it's going to be dull,' and Elspeth looks at him one last time and leaves.

As soon as she's through the door he runs over to David's laptop. The screen lock hasn't come on yet. The test results from all eight crew members are arranged as tabs in the open spreadsheet. He flicks through to her room number. He scans the different columns. Massive drop in white cell count, internal bleeding due to a lack of platelets, acute anemia due to a near absence of red blood cells. The radiodermatitis was obvious to the eye, but the numbers back it up. Six Grays minimum. At the lower end, she'll survive. But at the upper end, she won't. And even if she does… He scans for the serum microRNA, and it's the same story. Significant increase in residual hematopoietic stem cells for one measure, and significant reduction in four, just like the Harvard paper found in the humanised mice.

Anthony clicks to the tab that David left opened, shuts the laptop, then lifts the screen again and leaves it open, and walks back to his bench. He should wait. What he's just done—he should wait, and prise it out of David, so they can talk about it, so that David tells him exactly what he's just read on screen, so he won't have to pretend he doesn't know. But he'll be late for Aggie's event. And David might not tell him. Not until the Commodore decides on what action to take, at least.

It's nothing to do with him. He has no authority.

But he's read the figures. He can't unread them.

He loses track of time. When he looks again at his watch, it's past six o'clock. What he's just—but he needs to get going. He prays the Hyundai starts.

The community centre is a single-storey brick block building set in an acre of lawn gone to seed, a rash of yellowing turf and scratchy mud. It stands on the edge of the village. Its low roof makes him think of American motels he's seen in films. One 'wing' is all glass walls, a kind of conservatory. Early 1990s, cheaply made, a home for activities such as the one they're coming to, or rather which Aggie is already at and he is a late arrival. The building makes him prickly. He goes through the doors into the sanitary-smelling reception, just like administrative buildings in the towns the Party built for plant workers. Those were more substantial, but there was something in their distance from the urban living spaces, the expansive grounds around them a symbol of privilege, that always brought back a memory of his father. Would he have gone to any of those buildings with his father? He doesn't want to remember. So how does he remember, then? Maybe he's mistaken; another memory wired wrong.

He enters a corridor of grey linoleum and bright strip lights and flowery art prints. At the end are large doors, and coming through those doors is Aggie. She sees him, waves him along.

He hurries and then he's with her. He realises how much he's missed her today. He's not thought of her since the morning, their easiness before getting out of bed, and he's glad to see her. He reaches for her hand as she moves off.

'You okay, Ant? Has something happened?'

'Yes, fine. No. Just… Sorry I'm late. Good luck, that's all.'

He gives her hand a squeeze and they both let go.

Inside the main hall are a crowd of people. Some are sitting in rows of chairs facing the front. More are standing at the back in pairs or families alongside a foldout table with three large, translucent plastic cisterns of squash and water, and two silver urns with taps at the bottom, bright red lights switched on. There are jars of coffee and old ice cream tubs full of tea bags, litres of green-top milk and a big brown bowl filled with silver spoons. People are helping themselves to the tea and coffee and plates of biscuits, custard creams and bourbons and those useless Rich Tea things.

'Take a seat,' says Aggie.

She walks off. He watches her talk with a man and woman standing by the table at the back. Not audience, he thinks, fellow organisers from the social enterprise. He stares at the man, young with a wispy beard, straight out of a *Monty Python* film. He loved *Monty Python* all through university. It was the craziest thing he'd ever seen. It made Britain more liveable and loveable; even though the chaos reminded him of life before. The guy Aggie is talking to looks like one of the People's Front of Judea. *'Faeck off!'* he whispers, making himself laugh. A wave of relief travels from his stomach to his head. *There is no way Aggie is having an affair with this guy.* Anthony studies the woman, a few years older than Aggie, with bouffant hair, an old sweater with the sleeves pushed up. The three of them are talking earnestly. Anthony moves in beside a man and woman helping themselves to tea. The man wears a loose, crumpled sports suit although his belly is generous evidence he's never been jogging. The woman is in jeans and a shell top. The man takes three biscuits and puts them in his pocket. Anthony pours himself a coffee and sips at it. It's terrible, instant, shit. He thinks about a biscuit and takes a bourbon.

'Anthony.'

Aggie's there with the other two.

'Grace, and Scott,' Aggie introduces them but he cannot think of a thing he wants to say. After a moment's awkwardness, the three move off to the front of the hall, and he's left with his shit coffee and a hall of locals in poverty. He identifies an empty stretch of seats towards the front. He sits at the end of the row, an easy exit around the back if he needs it. He watches Grace and Scott manoeuvre a table. Another group come into the hall, in sportswear and casual clothing, who spot the table at the back and make a beeline for it.

Aggie isn't having an affair with Scott, he thinks. Scott does not wear Aran jumpers. Does not have a Border collie. Suddenly the biscuit tastes better, even the… no, the coffee is still shit.

This is what Aggie has involved herself with since they moved up: working part-time for a social enterprise focused on reducing poverty in Scotland. They'd moved up to be near her mother after her father's death. It was also a way for them to get out of London, and away from behaviours that were doing them harm. *His* behaviours. His different jobs. Always falling out with the bosses, always needing to move on. They both looked for work, but it was when he got the job at the base that Aggie could *make a home of change* (as one of her podcast life-coaches put it). Looking around the hall he feels… It doesn't matter, because the problem is that it's not directed at the people: it's at *her*. For devoting her time to these people. Dressed in fake sportswear, drinking shit coffee from crap plastic cups and stuffing biscuits in their pockets for later.

He can hear the disembodied life-coach chiding him in cool tones: *Judgment says more about you than them.* It's true. He knows his failings in a place like this, his mean judgments; but it's too much to battle them, not with the knowledge he holds. There's nothing that he doesn't understand of this life—but he doesn't want to think about that. And yet the only other thing he can think about is the woman in the clinic bed. Her scrappy, bald, blistering head, the tabulated pages, the plotted microRNA of her blood work bearing no secrets, what he has compromised by looking at the results on David's laptop.

He's slouching. He sits up.

Aggie and Grace and Scott have introduced themselves and are getting things going with an activity, a mini-play of sorts to get them all warmed up. There's a lot of shuffling in the seats at the idea of taking part.

'It's okay,' shouts Scott, 'you're the audience!'

It's about being in poverty—although those aren't the words they use. You can't just tell people they're poor. They're looking instead at people's *resources*. There's a big list of them written on a whiteboard on the stage. Financial. Emotional. Mental. Spiritual. Physical. Support Systems. Knowledge of Hidden Rules. Relationships. Role Models. The list is centre justified, and on the left is a column that says 'More' and on the right a column that says 'Less.'

'Poverty's not all about money,' Aggie told him a few weeks before. They were sitting on the sofa in the lounge. It was morning. Her head was buried in his armpit. He was dozing, not yet awake, while they listened to one of her American wellbeing podcasts. Aggie would occasionally lift herself to scribble down some notes for shaping into teachings in her mindfulness classes. The West Coast and LA came to Dumfries and Galloway through Aggie's well-meaning wellbeing, into the minds if not the hearts of the women of Dunfermline. And where to then? What was the half-life of that kind of knowledge? Of snippets from monologues downloaded in a cottage that was not yet a home, was too damp for lying around in for long?

Aggie was reading at the same time, switching attention

between the podcast and the page. He didn't know what book. Her fingers were curled around a cup of tea in one hand and holding the book with the other. Every time she wanted to turn a page she put the cup down, balancing it against his leg. He stared at the crown of Aggie's head for a while, thinking she might look up. He used to know that he could learn from her as a model for kindness. He watched the way her head rose with her breath, the silver hairs latticing her roots, glimmering in the lamp light. Grey hairs. He noticed a few of his own when getting into the shower, not on his head but on his chest. Not grey though, in fact. As white as the wings of a gannet. Age had caught them both, sneakily, and dabbed its frosty touch on their bodies.

'What are you reading?' he'd asked.

She raised her chin but not her eyes. He tracked them as they finished a sentence. She lifted the book, turned it to show him.

'*The Rules of Poverty*?'

'Aye,' she'd said, returning the book to its reading position, looking up at the clock on the wall. 'You going to be late?'

'Any good?'

'It's for a community event in a couple of weeks. Looking at poverty in the home.'

'Hence the book.'

'Hence the book. Planning meeting, today.'

He nudged her upwards so he could stand. He *was* going to be late. He went into the kitchen, put his plate and cup in the sink, the knife sliding off into the bowl with a clink. He ran the hot water, pulled up his sleeves. Then Aggie was beside him.

'What's the book telling you?' he asked.

'You don't like to be late,' she said. 'Did you know Scotland has the largest disparity between rich and poor in Western Europe? There are some parts of Glasgow where the life expectancy for young men is the same or worse than in parts of Africa. It's called "The Glasgow Effect".'

'Not "The Africa Effect"?'

He waited for her to swallow her irritation.

'And around here?' he asked, rinsing the plate and cup. 'The life expectancy around here is beyond the national average, right?'

'Everyone moves here to get away from the city. Like us,' she added.

'Like us,' he echoed her.

He tried to imagine himself as a different man living that life of poverty, but a tiredness flowed up from the bottom of his feet like a dark brown liquid, and he was rooted to the slate tiles as himself, Anthony, and not someone else. He picked up the tea towel and began drying.

'You would have four years left to live,' Aggie said.

'It's not my birthday for another few weeks.'

'Thirty-nine. A life expectancy of thirty-nine.'

What are you reading? A simple question. To be interested in her, his wife. He wanted to know what she was learning. What subjects, what knowledge and the form in which it was absorbed. It was important to him. Knowledge was not a fixed thing, but a process. A life leading oneself out of the shadowy cave. He'd read enough quantum physics to know nothing was fixed. And the mind too, within the physical world, worked that same way. Knowledge was mutable. Memories, too, were changed as present thoughts. Except in trauma. Then memories stayed as they were during the event. Sufferers could smell the same sulphurs, see the same wallpapers, feel the same scratch of metal on their face, hear the same wailing. Then knowledge was not verb, but noun. As solid as tablets of stone.

His path deviated from quantum physics a long way back, if one took time as linear. *His* physics, the operation of atomic structures in the practical world, didn't have much time for time, except in half-lives, or in the present moment of the catastrophically destructive. What memory was, in that context, was a trivial question. As trivial as *What are you reading?*

The crumpling sound of his plastic cup brings Anthony back to the hall. He looks down. Lukewarm coffee has spilt over his thumb and fingers onto the floor. He uncrumples the cup and puts it down. The mini-play is over. Had Aggie acted? At the whiteboard, Scott is asking the audience to tell him where to put his tick to illustrate what Knowledge of Hidden Rules, Relationships and Role Models the characters in the play had had: 'more' or 'less.'

There are shouts from the assembled.

'Nothing.' 'Nada.' That gets a laugh. 'Fuck all,' says one man, and a few people giggle but then his wife tells him to stop embarrassing her.

The characters in the play that they've watched (everyone apart from him) have 'less' in all categories except relationships and emotions. And now Grace is talking about how having 'less' is multifaceted—she checks, and thinks of another word, decides upon 'mixed up'—and that the worst form of having 'less' is not financial, not even emotional. The having 'less' that people never get out of, she says, is having no relationships. Everything else you can climb out of, you can learn, or acquire. 'Get,' she corrects herself. As long as you have people to love and rely on; to look after you.

The people around him are on board with this. Most of them have other people. In other people, they're rich. A good place to begin when tackling poverty.

The doors to the main hall open and in walks a man. Early forties. Dark hair. *Big fucking knitted jumper.* Anthony leans forward looking for dog hair on the man's trousers. But Anthony's too far away, and the man's legs are hidden behind the backs and heads of the people in the front rows. The man walks over to Aggie and Grace and greets both of them with a hand on their arms.

'Sorry I'm late,' he says, pushing a hand through his *wavy fucking hair.*

Aggie is smiling and introducing him to the crowd. It's Greg—

of course—from the main office in Glasgow. The social enterprise that Aggie works for. She's had to go once or twice a week for meetings, stayed over with her mum. *Stayed over with her mum.* Anthony can't quite fathom the painfulness of the adrenaline that's surging in him, it's so painful he's disassociated from his own body. All that's left is his headiness, that locked-up turret. *So, this is jealousy,* he thinks. *This is the streak of light through the body that is called by that name.* He is 'rich' or rather has 'more' of the emotional resource that is known as 'jealousy.' And perhaps he is soon to be having 'less' of the resource known as 'relationships' (the having less that people never get themselves out of). This is how his body reacts; leaves him a stranger outside of the event, looking in.

Greg catches up on where they've got to, and takes over. He's talking to the audience about what it is they can do to have 'more' in all the categories. He goes through them one by one. They all get it. It's clever, Anthony thinks, this presentation. The audience is on board. The only place it gets stuck is three from the bottom: Knowledge of Hidden Rules. They don't get this easily. They're all white, of course, so using race isn't going to work. They've heard of feminism but the women still aren't sure if they're being treated badly. *Class*, class is the thing here. The thing they're bound by, so this is where Greg starts.

'Even having the television on loud,' says Greg. 'That can be a hidden rule. Think about it, do you ever see the television on loud in the houses of people with class?'

He says it in a way that makes people laugh. They know whose side Greg has taken. 'Nivver,' they say. 'Ya nay hear it.'

'But when someone comes around to yours for a cuppa tea, don't you turn your tele *up*?'

More laughter, shifting in the seats. It's true. It's all true. (*Apart from me and Aggie don't have a* fucking *television,* Greg.)

But as much as they've tried to steer the evening, it comes back to money. How much they pay for their televisions, the license fee, how little money the government invests in their community, how those people down south don't care about people like them. When the moment comes, he understands he's been waiting for it.

'They'se got all this money for that Trident,' says a man in front of him, late fifties, bald. 'What, billions? And they got nae nothin' for the nurses, the NHS. Those doctors' striking, they'se like us. They'se be having less resources, and that's not right, ain't it? After looking after thay likes of us.'

There's a lot of agreement. And then one of the women is looking at him.

'Aye, you work there, no?' she says to him.

'He does,' says another woman. 'He's Aggie's hubby, ain't it, Aggie?'

Aggie doesn't know what to say. She's smiling helplessly. He can't tell whether that's because of the mood in the room or that the woman has just given away Aggie's secret to Greg. Does Greg know about him? Her *hubby*?

'You don't care about us,' says a woman. 'Do you?'

She's asking him. Greg's looking at him too. Smiling, encouraging him to contribute. The alarm of adulteration like a crisp, clipped nerve. He looks at the many pairs of staring eyes. Why wouldn't he tell them what's happened at the base? The leak, the eight crew in the clinic. That would shut them up. Send them home to watch their fucking teles and turn the sound up so they couldn't hear what he has to say.

'It's not that simple,' he says. 'You read one thing in the paper. It's another to work there. It's more complicated than the money. Isn't that what they're trying to tell you?'

He waves a hand at Greg. The crowd look at Anthony as if he's just told them they're thick. He looks at Aggie. She glances away.

'It's all those public school educated officers,' says a woman.

'Oi, my son works there,' says a man in the row in front, who looks around at Anthony and winks.

'The thing is,' says Greg, 'our friend is right. It's about the stories we are told about money. Those people who talk about money, like for Trident,' and Greg gives him a quick glance, 'the stories you hear on the news, well, it's not just about money, is it? It's about this *register* we've been talking about. When *they* tell stories, they use beginnings, middles, and ends. On the news. In the papers. That's their *formal register*. But it's not how you were taught. You begin your story with the most important element—the big point. Think about the story of Christmas. Those who use a formal register begin with "A long time ago, there was a man and woman—"'

'Mary and Joseph,' says a woman in the audience.

Greg nods patiently. 'Yes. But if *you* tell the story—'

'Eeeh, look at this new baby,' says the woman. The audience erupts into laughter.

'That's it,' says Greg. 'You begin with the point of it, and fill in with—not gossip. But you get what I'm saying? When you speak a different language, and one of those languages is privileged and one isn't, you see where the resources flow, right? To the people using the formal register. Right?'

They all nod, agree.

'So getting out of having less to having more,' and Greg's sweeping an arm at the whiteboard, 'you have to stop thinking about money, think about these other resources, and about the register—formal or casual—that the person you're talking to understands. That's why they look at you like they do when you get a prescription at the doctors, or claim your benefits. They're not talking your language. Right?'

'And they look down at us,' someone says.

Greg nods again, like a *fucking nodding dog*.

'That's right. And that's what we're here to look at. So no one gets looked down on.' Greg looks at Anthony. 'Even people who work for the Navy.'

They all laugh, and turn to look at him. His face is incandescent, and the tight line of copper has wound its way round his stomach, until there's no space inside him. He stands and ignores the eyes, goes to the back and pours another coffee as the room settles and Greg begins talking again. *There's no way*, he spills the coffee over the lip of the cup and his shaking hand, *absolutely no way that man is not fucking my wife.*

They drive home in silence, apart from the spluttering of the engine. All he has to do is say to her *that went well, well done*, and their life together will be okay. A toe in the door will become a foot, an ankle, a leg. As it is, his toe is somewhere on the step of Apollo 11, out of the door on the moon landing, and their cottage door, the door to their marriage, is sinking into this Scottish soil. Submerged Of Dunbartonshire.

In bed a tape plays in his head. *Just say it. Just speak to her.* There's no reason to be jealous. He knows there is a place inside where he's not jealous at all. But he has no trust of that place. He wants to tell her what's happened, about the woman crew member, her readings. What he's seen. That those other words are coming back, after all this time. But there's the feeling like wading through thick liquescence, and all he can hear are words muffled by the liquid: *tekhnohenna katastrofa, ducha, khlop.* And *sarkofag*, a casing: something he's inside and she is not.

He listens to the cottage. The mice in the night. The dead bodies tapping at the walls. Only fairy tales. He closes his eyes. There are words straightaway. *Ducha, ducha.* He opens his eyes, but they're tired and he closes them again. He's wearing his new pyjama bottoms, Tartan of course, and in the left pocket is the pebble. He thinks of the stories they both know. Beginning, middle, end. Bluebeard. Red Riding Hood—all stories he learnt only as a man, not as a boy. They're not the tales of his childhood. What were *they*? He thinks, but it's hard to remember. He doesn't want those stories anyway. Doesn't want to know what he saw on David's laptop. Doesn't want any of it. But they are known to him. He to them.

'I know you're not jealous,' she says quietly. 'Not really.'

After his sulk all the way home, still she is this kind to him. Can't he just tell her? Can't he just say, *you're right, I'm not,* and hold her? If she were having an affair with *Greg,* she wouldn't be this kind, would she?

'I'm not interested in doing something stupid,' Aggie says softly.

Ducha, ducha, ducha.

'That's not the same as not being interested in someone.'

'Look at me.'

Her patience is running out. He can feel the bed drop away under him. *Tell her now.* About the memories coming back. That'll stop her telling him about Greg. But she'd need to know why. What's triggered them. And then he'd have to tell her about the base, his sister's letter, the woman in the bed.

The woman in the bed is going to die.

But they won't let her. If she dies, that's it. That's the end of Trident. There's no way they would... But he doesn't know how this will end. He can tell her though, can't he? At least about the words, the memories flooding back, as he did before they got married. Then it was because he allowed himself to feel vulnerable. Now?

He turns and puts his arm through hers. Perhaps it *is* jealousy. He's kissing her neck, silently. He dislikes himself even as he moves into her. He's holding her down. She's not moving, but neither does she throw him off. He shifts her around so he's behind her and he closes his eyes and sees the loch, flat, implacable, keeping its secrets. He puts a hand on her shoulder and holds her around the belly. She begins to breathe more rapidly. The bed creaks and if someone was listening someone might think they were making love. He puts his hands to her face and lifts her chin.

'I don't even know what I'm doing,' he whispers.

'Just keep doing it,' she says back.

26th April–14th May 1986, Radynka

He's standing at the edge of the fir trees watching smoke rise on the far side of the hill. There must be a great event for so many fire trucks. He's never seen such a convoy, not even on Victory Day. He wants to go and see the fire. But this is as far as he's allowed: the line where the forest ends and the fields of buckwheat and potatoes begin. The fields are part of the *kolkhoz*. One day he'd asked why he is not allowed to go into the fields if they belong to him. His father had laughed, did not explain but repeated the rule, then added that individuals don't own anything in a collective, and certainly not young boys. His mama said it was because of the machinery. If he could go into the field he'd be able to climb the hill and see where the fire trucks are going. The smoke is not black, but blue. It smells like the stove once the fire has gone out. It burns his nose. Great swirling things in the sky fly over their house. Not planes; these things have blades on top which lift them up. *Vertolit*, his mama told him. *Ver-tol-it*. They carry great bags that swing to the side; they look how his mama looks when she comes home from the market, walking in zigzags up the *rynok pahorb*. There are more than he can count. When they're directly overhead they block out all other sounds, and a wind covers him and the fir trees bend and he feels very small. If only he could figure out a way to cross the field and not get found out. But he has Sveta with him. He's dragged her to the edge and that was hard enough. She couldn't climb the hill. She's too young. She's not interested in the fire trucks or the smoke. He wishes she was still unable to walk. She follows him around all the time now; mama makes him take Sveta to forage in the forest or get milk from the barn whenever he goes. He doesn't like getting milk, because Strokat is always there, with his leather vest and breath of sour plums ('*zduril*,' he's heard his father say). Strokat always milks the cows, and asks him questions to which

54

he doesn't know the answer.

There's snow all around, from his feet to the top of the hill. The forest floor is littered with needles poking through the crystals. Sveta is tugging at his arm. His sister has a small face, her blond hair braided into plaits.

Shcho tse.

'What are they?' she asks.

'*Vertolit*,' he says.

'What's that?'

'You don't understand.'

'Do we have enough stumps?'

He shakes her hand off his sleeve. He imagines taking a sled up the hill and sliding all the way down into the field.

'Why don't we go back?'

'Don't you want to see where the smoke is coming from?'

She shakes her head.

'Why don't you want to know?'

She's tugging at his arm. 'I want to go home.'

He moans and picks up his bag of mushrooms and the bag of sorrel and orache and nettles and slings them over his shoulder. He looks one last time at the smoke above the hill, poking out like a dark, rippled tongue. He hears another truck come past on the road from Radcha, where his grandparents live. Maybe if they go to church tomorrow he might see the trucks. He hates church, but it will be worth it. Maybe it's the church that's burning, he thinks brightly, but then is afraid in case God is listening.

He leads his sister along the path through the firs and beech and aspen. The path that sometimes has wolf tracks. He never tells his mama. His father knows. It was his father who showed him how to tell the difference between a wolf and a fox. *Vovky.* Wolves know how to survive in the forest. When he was sent to pick stumps that first time, his father put a hand on his shoulder and gave him the small knife and said, '*Anatolii Nikolaevich, buty yak vovk.*' Be like the wolf.

He tells Sveta to hurry up if she wants to go home. The trees thin out and stop at the edge of land where the houses begin. The ground turns from pine needles to muddy grass, semi-frozen from the snow that fell before, although it's thawing. Muddy grass becomes gravel and stone. The houses have small porches and wooden fences, facing each other. The women try not to leave their houses but instead shout to each other across the narrow road. They're happiest, he knows, in earshot of the *samovar* or the baby in the *shparhalka*.

They're nearly home when he sees his mama. She's not standing on the porch but running towards them. Shuffling side to side like the bags hanging under the *vertolit*. Her headscarf, the blue one with the pattern of horses, is wrapped around her face covering her mouth. She looks stupid, he thinks. She's waving and pointing. She pulls the scarf away from her mouth, and begins screaming, pointing at their bags.

'*Poklasty yikh vnyz! Poklasty yikh vnyz!*'

Put them down. Put them down.

His father is working what the women call *vakhta*. It means two-week shifts. If mama sends Anatolii to bed early then he won't see his father until next Sunday, which means they won't be driving to Radcha to see his grandparents either, which means it will be three weeks before he gets to see if the church has burnt down. He's beginning to think it's not their church. They wouldn't make such a fuss over that. He pushes his knees together and leans back against the wall and sulks. It's only eleven days until Victory Day so he'll see the fire trucks then, he'll climb into their cabins and steer the big wheel. The women all talk at once.

'They've offered him three times his salary,' his mama says. Someone else says her husband is getting four. There's murmuring. 'That's because he's *underneath* the fire,' the woman adds. No one says anything to this.

'He was driving people out,' his mama says. She's pouring

water into the *samovar*. 'But now he's driving people around. Why not out anymore?'

'Around what?' one asks.

'Who?' another woman asks.

'*Nachal'nyky*,' his mama says. The women laugh and still their breasts with folded arms. It makes him queasy.

'*Durak*,' another woman says. His father calls his grandparents *duraky*.

'We're the ignorant ones,' says another woman, a voice like his feet on gravel. 'What do they tell us? Nothing in the paper. Nothing on the radio. What are we meant to do, sit here? Where is the news? Why don't they tell us anything?'

The women talk over each other. Then one woman speaks.

'I heard it, it's true. My Ivanivna heard it from Ira, whose husband is driving the *nachal'nyk*, Pitrov. He said, "Boys, do your accounts this way: better bury one thousand than one million." One million.'

The women are silent. He doesn't know what accounts are.

'He didn't have a choice,' his mama says, pouring tea from the *samovar*. It splashes onto the floor. 'You drive or you're thrown in jail. You aren't given a choice.'

Anatolii hears the car pull up outside. His father eats at the kitchen table and drinks vodka from a little glass but many times over, and sleeps on the sofa. His mama takes his father's clothes away, puts a blanket and her fur coat over his body. His father talks in his sleep. At one point his father wakes and shouts to put his clothes in a black bag and bury it. His mama leaves the house and when she comes back she has no black bag. He, Anatolii, and Sveta watch their father sleep. When Anatolii takes a step towards his father, his mama runs from the kitchen and waves him away. She is wiping her face with her scarf and muttering the same words over and over. His mama puts a bucket next to the sofa. In the night he hears his father being sick. In the morning his father is gone.

A man on the radio called Medvedev is speaking to a reporter. 'It has killed four thousand hectares of pine forest in a matter of days,' he's saying. The reporter asks if pine trees are particularly sensitive. 'Pine trees may be more sensitive to radiation than oak trees, but they're much more resistant than rodents and vertebrates in general,' says the man called Medvedev. Sveta asks their mama, what is radiation? What are vertebrates? Are there hectares in their pine forest, and what do they look like? Are they like rabbits? Their mama turns the radio off.

No one is going to school. This would be the best news, but he's not allowed into the forest either. No other children are playing in the street. He cannot go anywhere, so he stays at home. They're cleaning the house every day. Sveta is too young so she sits in the *kvartyra* and plays with her dolls. Anatolii is tired of cleaning, angry that he has to do women's work. He wants to go and pick stumps and follow wolf tracks or meet Pylyp and Aleksandr and run across the farm. The farmers are still in the fields, so why can't he go out and play? The men are sowing according to the Plan, his mama explains. The men can still work. They've been told there's no danger, but it's best to keep the children inside. Stop them causing trouble. But before long the boys are too much bother and they're let outside. He and Pylyp and Aleksandr run around the village. The rain has made puddles and they are green and yellow, they shimmer like sheets of metal in the sun. The boys stare at them, dare each other to jump in. There's no milk to drink. He wants to believe it's something to do with Strokat but Anatolii knows better. It's to do with the emergency. The cloud that his father is fighting by driving important people around the Zone. It's called the Zone now. Something blew up and burnt down at the centre, but it wasn't the church, it was not God. They only just got the church back, his mama says. He doesn't understand. Hasn't the church always been there? No, his mama explains. Religion was only reintroduced a few years ago. How can a whole church disappear and come back? She tells him about Gorbachev; about *glasnost*. Anatolii's heard this word before. His father says it's a bad thing. It makes churches come back, and makes power stations explode.

On the news, a female presenter in a buttoned-up brown suit sits in front of a map of their region. There's a dotted line around the edges. Radynka is a small black circle on a yellow background and it is inside the dotted line. The presenter calls it a 'zone of ecological calamity.' There is nothing on the news about it again. The next evening it is a different presenter.

Mama whispers his father's name over and over: *Nikolai. Nikolai.* His father is pale and can barely walk through the door before falling on the sofa. His father lies like a centrepiece to the living room. The house is silent and it makes Anatolii angry and afraid. Anatolii's uncle Kulyk arrives from Kyiv. His uncle is a big man, his mama's older brother. Kulyk has sandy hair and a big dark moustache and a wide smile, usually. He works in a furniture factory and his father is always saying that Kulyk believes he's better off in the city than they are on the *kolkhoz*. Kulyk and his mama are arguing. His father calls out. 'I feel heavy! I feel dizzy! Bring the vodka, put goat droppings in the bottle, it's meant to soak up the radiation.' His mama stands in the doorway between the kitchen and living room, a hand over her face. Kulyk whispers in her ear, she bats him away. The shutters are closed during the day. The light hurts his father's eyes, worsens the headache. His father vomits into the bucket even when there's nothing in him, not even goat shit. When his father is being sick Anatolii takes Sveta onto the porch and they play a clapping game but she is frightened and keeps crying and can't clap and he slaps her hands, turns and looks at the trees. The aspen have no leaves left, the branches are stripped. For the first time he notices there are no birds. No sparrows. The forest is completely silent. He peers into the trees. There is a light, a flame, and then it's gone. In the house he hears the shouts of his uncle and mama, the retching of his father.

Stovpotvorinnya. A car drives past and someone announces they're being evacuated. *Uchasnyky likvidatsii.* Liquidated. Ikarus buses are parked in the town square with their engines running. They're ordered out of their houses by the soldiers in white gowns and face masks. 'What is this? What are we being moved for?' he hears his mama and the other women ask. 'Are we at war?' 'Don't ask us,' the soldiers reply, sulking. Even he can see they're young, and don't know what they're doing. 'Ask them, in the white Volgas.' He turns to look at the cars, thinking he might see his father. There are men in the cars wearing uniforms and masks, but none of them are his father. The Volgas drive off smartly. He looks around. There are dozens of buses: blue, orange and grey bubbles, facing every direction. They have hand-written signs pushed up against the inside of their front windows. Some for Korosten', some Kyiv. No one knows which bus to get on. The drivers are aggrieved, urging them to hurry, hurry. They want to get out of this place. What place, his mama asks. 'The Zone,' they say. The drivers are all smoking in quick puffs. The square is covered in ash.

Some of the women refuse to go. Their husbands are working in the Zone. Clean-up workers. Drivers. They cannot just leave in the middle of the day while their men are at work. His mama is refusing to get on the bus. 'Only three days,' says a soldier in a greatcoat and fur hat. The soldier bends down, looks Anatolii in the eye. 'You'll be back in three days to dig up the potatoes, hey? Gather in the winter squash?' The soldier pulls the mask down from his mouth. His teeth are bad. Then the soldier stands up, puts out an arm to stop a woman carrying a bundle of clothing and a fluffy white cat in her arms. 'No animals,' the soldier says. 'Leave the cat here.' 'No, no. I won't go without her,' the woman says, and the soldier half-heartedly tries to get the cat from her. There are mewls and swearing. Sveta is crying. He can barely breathe, doesn't know what to do. While the soldier is wrestling with the cat they walk quickly away, his mama pulling him, he pulling Sveta. At home his mama slams the door and sits on the sofa and begins to say his father's name. *Nikolai. Nikolai.* Anatolii stands in the middle of the living room. Sveta is holding his hand.

'Your stupid sense of duty!' Kulyk shouts at his mama. 'Both of you.'

'Go back to Kyiv!'

'He was a man, now he's a skeleton. His sense of duty's killing everyone!'

'No one asked you to come.'

Kulyk looks at Anatolii. His uncle's eyes are the blue of schoolbooks.

'Let me take them at least,' his uncle says, 'for the love of God.'

Anatolii's crying. His father looks up at him from the sofa. His father's eyes are red and also cloudy. His father smells of fire, not of charcoal but of something else. His father swings his legs onto the floor.

'Nikolai,' says his mama. 'Lie down before you fall down.'

Anatolii steps over. His father takes his face in a hand and lifts his chin. His father's hand feels coarse and shaky, but Anatolii rests his chin into the palm, feels like a man as he is held by a greater man.

'Anatolii Nikolaevich, buty yak vovk.'

He's dreaming. They're walking through the forest, he and his father, tracing the path of the wolf. They reach the edge. The smoke rises above the hill, and it has that same strange bluish tinge. This time his father tells him to *go, go*. He jumps the fence and runs over the troughs of the plough-cut earth, feet sinking into the sod, trying as hard as he can to get across. His father is urging him on. Ahead of him there is a kind of shining.

He opens his eyes. He sees the back of his uncle Kulyk's head, the sandy hair. Feels the rumble of the car as it bumps over potholes. Feels the leather seat under his cheek. He sees his sister's legs curled up and smells her skin and examines the red creases over her knees. He smells the stale gummy cotton of her favourite doll, with the big black eyes like the spots that were the villages on the newscaster's map. He closes his eyes and tries to go back into the dream, to find his father. The wolf in the forest. But the wolf is gone.

You will have noticed already, but look, I'm writing in English! But not really. I've been learning at night school for more than a year, but it's a lie to let you think I've done this. Our teacher, Alina, has translated much of it. She's a friend, too, which is why I let her read the parts about my husband. She's lived in America. She wants us all to come and live there with her—she's going back soon, once her father is recovered. She doesn't say from what, but her family is not from the Zone like ours. She lives in a place called Pittsburgh; it's where her relatives emigrated in 1920 when the Whites and Petliura killed all the Jews and forced the rest out.

When we first began, someone in our evening class asked Alina: but perhaps Petliura and the Ukrainian People's Republic were not such great wrongdoers? Weren't they patriots for an independent Ukraine, and it was the Bolsheviks, even with Jews like Trotsky in charge, who were the killers? This is what was taught in schools after Independence. But Alina says this is rubbish, this is history gone mad. Our country is trying to distance itself from its past. She says that even though Independence has been a good thing, despite all the violence on our doorstep in Crimea, it cannot be at the expense of the victims of history. She tells us these things in class. That's not quite right. She tells some of us when we stay behind for help with our letters. (I'm not the only one with family who have left.) What we learn from Alina is the opposite of what we learnt in New History after Independence. But then much has happened in the last twenty years. Alina's story amazes us and we worry for her. The authorities threaten anyone who challenges New History. When I tell Jelena, she cries for me to stop, it hurts her ears. You remember Jelena? She was at mama's funeral. She took me in. I'm so grateful, and will always be, despite her worries.

Alina is half-Jewish. Her mother married an American 'gentile' she calls him, we all thought it meant 'gentleman' in English but it means non-Jew. I wonder what you are now, brother, who once had two parents from Ukraine and now has two from Great Britain? Or rather, one from Ireland! Are you two halves? You have lived twice as long outside of our country as you did inside.

My night school is wonderful. I can't believe it's taken me so long. Even with my health, late is better than never. It's better than any school I remember from the Zone, or in Korosten', where all we did was change the colour of our badges depending on whether you had a cold or not. Alina says, 'Sveta, you are bright, you learn well,' but I do not feel bright. I feel very slow, I feel as if I'm only now learning to speak. I have to lay down a lot with my headaches. Jelena says I must not get my hopes up about a job after college. I need to stay close to the hospital. But mama stayed close and what good did it do her? Alina says I should be thinking of studying more. Perhaps one day enough to go abroad. I can get my treatments there. In England, are there not brand-new hospitals and doctors from all over the world? I used to share such things with Jelena, but she says mama would not have wanted me to leave. She says Alina is planting dangerous ideas in my head, and that the West is a terrible place. But Jelena is an old woman and doesn't want to hear it. Perhaps you do not want to hear it either.

But my brother... Anthony. I've not been able to get used to this name. Who is this person? Who am I writing to? You'll always be a new brother with this name. In England, where you eat off plates of marble. Where you drive a sports car, and are friends with the Royal Family. Where you live in a city of ten million people and go to the theatre every night. This is what I dream when I think of you—and because you never write back, I have no other truths to correct my fantasies. But I've seen the magazines. One is called *Hello!* and it's full of amazing people, rich and beautiful! People are travelling all the time to Europe and America and they come back with new magazines and jeans that fit. With the war in Crimea people want to leave. It's a second great emigration like during the pogroms, or 'The Great Patriotic War.' The things we have learnt since the accident!

You know Jelena had a daughter who died? Of cancer. Who can say what the cause was. When she looks at me I know she sees her Masha. Jelena says I mustn't worry myself with woes. Woes is a new word. Alina teaches us English by teaching us literature and poetry. She's teaching us Emily Dickinson but we don't all have books, so we read Alina's book she brought from America.

'If you should get there first / Save just a little place for me / Close to the two I lost!' This poem makes me think of you. Save a place for me, your little sister. But I can't travel on planes. The doctors don't think I can go far now. Will I ever leave this country? Where would I go, if not to you, my only relative? (Except Uncle Kulyk of course. Don't tell him I said such a thing!) Does your new country have old tales, like your old home? Do you learn them, and think of yourself a child again? Tell me.

I should be more like Emily. Listen to this:

'We are hardly ever sick at home, and don't know what to do when it comes...'

Isn't that wonderful?

Thursday

He's missing a flight. He rushes around, packing his bags, leaving so much behind. Then he's in a smoking shelter outside the airport lining up to play a fruit machine, as if the only chance he has of getting his flight is to win a ticket. It's his turn, but the spinning wheels are covered with printed paper, computational results of radiation levels. He tears at the paper to get to the hidden wheels of fortune, the fruits that are contaminated, the strawberries and cherries he can no longer forage. Someone is telling him you're late, you can't fix this, you have to go.

He reaches for his phone: 3:27 a.m. Does he believe it?

Where is the light coming from? Outside, the moon.

Where is Aggie? Next to me.

What was behind the rolls of paper? A chance.

He looks at Aggie in the darkness. Thinks of why they came here, her father. When did he last put his arm around her shoulder and comfort her?

On his way to the lab he's met by David outside the entrance. David indicates Anthony must go with him. David makes small talk as they walk and asks about Aggie's event. Mentions the weather. Anthony grinds his teeth, tries to relax his jaw. Does he admit that he looked at the results? Or does David already know?

Two men are waiting at reception. Military but without appendages, nothing that can be polished. Military *police*. One of the MPs says his name and he nods and they escort him, one in front and one behind. It's procedure; it wouldn't matter who he was or what he had done. A breach, a small one, curiosity killed the cat but the cat has nine lives. But how could anyone know? Are there cameras in the lab? He won't make it past probation. He and Aggie will move to Glasgow, he will leave nuclear and work in some other area. Aggie will stay with him, won't she?

The twine of jealousy wraps around the stone in his stomach.

The MPs lead him to the Commodore's office. Not an interrogation room. The Commodore is at his desk on the laptop. Anthony looks around. Brown filing cabinets he'd not noticed the first time. A second desk pushed up against the wall. Brown slatted blinds across the windows. Standing lamps behind the desk. He waits between the two MPs. He puts his hand in his trouser pocket and manoeuvres the pebble and rubs it with his fingers. *One two three, in. One two three, out.* He places his attention on one thing at a time. The desk. The picture frame. The Commodore looks up.

'Ah, Doctor Fahey, come, sit, sit,' and he gestures for Anthony to take a chair opposite. The Commodore looks at the soldiers. 'That's all.'

The two turn and walk out, shutting the door behind them.

Anthony watches the Commodore run a tongue around his teeth, digging out some of the morning's porridge, or just a tic the Commodore has, perhaps, when thinking. He seems to Anthony much more in control of his alarm than at their first meeting, when the news broke. 'Sorry about that formality. Security is on a higher footing across the base.'

He nods. 'I understand.'

'It isn't routine to meet like this, but, well...it's not extraordinary,' says the Commodore. Anthony gets a throat full of bile. 'I'm meeting staff who are new to the base and involved in this situation.'

Anthony nods. The Commodore opens a folder.

'And we should've done this a while ago, under different circumstances. What with your background...' The Commodore flips through. Anthony guesses they're the forms from his application. The Full Disclosure. The signed copy of the OSA. The history of his arrival on the Catholic Church's rescue transports. His adoption papers. 'I wish I'd brought you in earlier. To speak to you personally—off the record. I saw your file when you were hired. Having gone through all the security checks. If I can say, it was quite sensational in a couple of ways. There were a few jokes about Soviet spies going around my senior officers— forgive us'—and the Commodore waves a hand around, but he's still not smiling—'some of us served through the Cold War. We remember those times—and they're coming back, by the way. But what's more interesting, why I would've brought you in for a chat earlier, is... You know something of these emergencies, correct?'

'Something,' says Anthony. How small the size it boils down to.

'You passed all the psychological examinations. But we don't know each other well enough...and, you see, under these new conditions—'

The Commodore continues, going through Anthony's file, then switching to the report he's submitted on the water samples. The Commodore taps the report, draws out a list of data on printout sheets with perforated edges. Anthony grimaces and rubs a tired hand up one side of his face. They're the papers from his dream. He thinks the Commodore is about to ask him things he's not able to answer.

'Can I ask...?' Anthony says abruptly. The Commodore stops, irritated. 'The *Tartarus*. It's a much higher level of radiation than should be caused by...'

Is Commodore Thompson going to humour him? There's a passage of time where he's not sure. He can see uncertainty creep back into the Commodore's expression, that tiredness with the burden of the deterrent and all the arguments around the worth of nuclear missiles in an age of ISIS and cyberwarfare, of the many faults already found with the base over the past ten years that have ended up on his doorstep. All the contraventions, the exposés in the newspapers. But then the Commodore smiles, or makes what's close enough to a smile for Anthony to know his background hasn't got him into trouble. Yet. 'It looks like an accident in the handling of a control rod during the scheduled tooling, which may have led to the leak.'

'Do SEPA know?' he asks.

'Civil codes don't apply.'

'But...' Anthony says. 'After last time, you...'

The Commodore looks strained.

'A voluntary agreement.'

There are many things he could say to that. '*Disclosure would be likely to prejudice the capability, effectiveness and...*' Wasn't that the line?

'Trust us,' says the Commodore, almost, Anthony thinks, as if he's convincing himself; after all, why would the Commodore need to convince *him*? 'We've got a good handle on things now.'

'In 2010, that leak, it was a melted ice plug?' he asks quietly. 'If it was that now, why would a wrecker flush that out? It wouldn't make sense at low levels.'

The Commodore looks at him.

'I thought *I'd* asked *you* here for a chat.'

He grimaces. 'Sorry. I'm just doing my job.'

'As am I,' says the Commodore. If he wore glasses, this is where he'd take them off and tap them on his leg. Anthony wonders for a moment if he's on a film set. 'We don't know all the outcomes. What I do know is that we don't have a full set of procedures to ascertain all the outcomes. So we've got to carry on with that work today.' The Commodore pauses. 'Rather, you have.'

Anthony can't help himself. 'The crew?'

'David says you're a good recruit. You've implemented some innovative procedures already. So. Do what you normally do.'

Our parents say that they're tired of thinking about the radiation. That is why they don't ask any longer if the food is from contaminated areas. We just eat it now.

When Anthony refocuses, the Commodore has moved and is sitting on one corner of the desk, legs crossed. An elbow on one knee. His face is set, waiting for Anthony to speak. Anthony blinks, fearing what he's missed. What should he say? That this is what he wanted? For his past to promise some privilege. A career.

'Aren't we?' says the Commodore. Anthony blinks again. 'We're on the same side now, aren't we, Doctor Fahey?'

The faces he sees are not the Commodore's, nor David's. Not even the woman in the isolation room in the clinic.

Do not forget, little lapochka, that people from the same place are called rodychka, people from the same ground. The same soil. We are rodychka.

'On the same ground,' he says.

The Commodore's eyes narrow. Anthony feels a sliver of sunlight make its way through the wooden slats over the window, and fall across his chest.

'On the same side. Yes. Of course.'

It takes a moment but the Commodore stands, says, 'Good,' and they shake hands. As they reach the door, the Commodore pulls him back.

'Those boys. Don't worry, we've made a decision, we're going to act on that. You were right to emphasise the seriousness of the issue. It's a shame we couldn't have got there earlier.'

Anthony looks the Commodore in the eye.

'A shame,' he says.

It's midmorning, the September air is chilly but the payoff is a bright blue sky. He's not ready to return to the lab. What he most wants is to be able to go to the top of one of the loading cranes by the large hangar and survey the water. He settles for getting to the highest spot he can, the roof of the refectory where the smokers congregate. On the way he buys a coffee and a seed snack pack and climbs the stairs. He has the roof to himself. Four stories up and he can look along the length of the facilities. The large hangar at the north end where *Tartarus* is in quarantine. He can look directly into the command tower—or could, if the glass wasn't silvered. South, the two large football pitches, one newly laid, one in ruins, for the naval staff to exercise. They rarely leave. He's one of the lucky ones, the three hundred and sixty civilians on the base, one for every degree of surveillance, but at least they aren't cooped up here twenty-four hours a day.

He walks around the edge, kicking together leaves that have blown up here from the oak, elm, and aspen scattered among the pines around the lake. He spots a maple leaf the colour of yam. He should take an armful, test them too. If all the trees needed to be stripped of their leaves, who would do that? Who would bury them? How would they do it without being seen?

It won't be in the leaves. Not yet.

He sits on an air-conditioning unit, a thrum through his sitting bones. He sips his coffee and stares at the Trossachs. After ten minutes he lets go of the pebble in his pocket. He tosses a load of the seeds to the pigeons who gather along the rail. He watches the birds battle for the food. They never stop, pigeons. Every half second there's movement, the crick of the head to another vantage, the blink of the orange-rim eye. The three red claw toes, many scarred or lost. He understands people's dislike of the birds, although that is not his sentiment. Intelligent survivors. Incredible earthy talents for traversing a world where they're never lost. He wonders if they've picked up any of the radionuclides from the water. He doubts it. It's only the loch and the machinery of the submarine itself, the body of *Tartarus* held in harbour, that are contaminated; and the ocean is a great dissipater. They didn't stop to think about washing the cooling tanks of Fukushima into the Pacific. The ocean can take it all. Except that it can't. Even the oceans, not any longer. Too much misplaced romanticism in the planet's ability to absorb humanity's ills. Just here, the Irish Sea, always contaminated from the runoffs. It is not pigeons who need worry though, nor, here, the hedgehogs or badgers or beavers or cats. It is the gannets, the puffins, razorbills and guillemots who feed on the mackerel and sand eel. It is the pilot whales and the harbour porpoises. The last family of local orca. *A shame.*

He knows he's been given a reprieve. Whatever his foolishness yesterday. Whatever his background. But it doesn't matter now. In fact, his suitability is *because* of his past, his work commended *because* of what he has seen and known. And it's *his* new schema that is going to dig the Commodore—and David, for that matter—out of a hole. It's his work on the marine environment that is going to be noted—that will be the buffer behind which this shit storm of a situation will be presented to Parliament when it reaches that juncture. That yes, there was a situation. (Pick a euphemism.) Yes, there are casualties. (Ditto.) Yes, the environment has taken the brunt of it. (Those poor whales.) But new procedures are in place. *'This is a risk we all take for an at-sea deterrent,'* he can already hear the Secretary of State for Defence saying to the green benches. But no. No one will dare mention *risk*.

But if it *is* to be his work that rescues the situation, he's going to need help in filling those gaps in the marine testing. He takes out his phone and dials.

'Hey, Anthony. Ant, buddy?'

'Hi, Michael. Are you busy?'

'Getting things finished so we can get up to you. It's a bloody long drive.'

'Same the other direction,' he says. 'I've got a request. Say no if you want, but it could lead to something significant.'

'The Navy trying to tap me up as a spy? Hold on. Yes, what is it? I'll be with you in, what—ten? Thanks. Sorry, Ant. Yep, go on. Did you sink a sub?'

He knows he should laugh. He forces one out.

'Your lab does marine, right? Testing?'

'Not really my area, it's James's. Bensham. Did you ever meet?'

'Don't know. Is there any way you could borrow a machine? We don't have the latest here, and we've got something urgent.'

'Urgent?'

He can hear Michael tuck his chin in.

'It's political.' Not a lie. 'We've got a deadline for review of procedures.' He pauses. He knows this will massage Michael's ego, and the weekend will be ruined by that; he's not seen Michael for a few years as it is, but the last thing—'It'll be a massive favour.' Another pause. Overdoing it? 'I've let things slip.'

Michael laughs.

'Into the shit? I can't just pick up a marine spectrometer and tuck it in the back pocket without signing off about sixteen forms, you know.'

'It'll be worth a paper at least. And a contact.'

'I've already got a contact. You. Not that we want it. The military, Ant?'

Should he have phoned? They were coming up anyway.

'I'll bring you into the base, you can have a look at what we do differently here.'

'We were going to hit Glasgow and do some galleries tomorrow, before the party.'

'Galleries?'

'Shut up.'

'I'm sure Rachel will be okay for a few hours. Aggie might be free.'

'You don't know wives well, do you, buddy?'

That one strikes the jealous thread. It's still crisp. He lets it go.

'No problem then,' he says. 'I just thought you might be curious.'

He's overdone the bluff. Michael finally answers.

'Okay, James is probably using the big machine. But I don't know, not seen him. Shirking the teaching prep. They've got us starting two weeks earlier, can you believe it? Fucking *foundation* students. In physics? Ant, hold on, the poxy post-doc is outside the window of my office again. They're all too good these days, so they demand constant attention. *I* fucking got the money for his job, he should remember.'

'Okay, I'll let you go. You'll get here...?'

'About seven, I think. Got a half day.'

'Aren't all your days half days?'

'Har, har. Is that a shit physics joke, or a shit academic joke?'

'Both. Thanks, Michael. I really appreciate it.'

'It's a spy thing, I know it. Okay, buddy, I'll see you anon.'

Buddy. Anon. Better words than *lapochka, rodychka...* Stupid, but bearable. Should he have done that? The door to the roof opens and two men and a woman stalk out for a cigarette. The pigeons explode into the air, a flock of wildness and fear.

At the lab Elspeth looks at him as if he's marked. But David swivels around from the bench, and smiles. The Commodore has done the dirty work, thinks Anthony, that's why David's happy. Mariam is giving nothing away, as if she, perhaps, is closest to understanding what's happened. But has anything happened?

David enquires after his progress. It's the most cheerful he's seen David since Monday. Anthony's confident he can get the tests completed by tomorrow. In fact, sure he can. It doesn't matter what words come now, they can't catch him out. His past is acknowledged, and they are *on the same side.* It will be his work that he'll tell Aggie about when all this hits the news. It won't only be a toe back in the doorway, but a foot on the ladder to the career he was always meant to have, and the marriage.

He works with a renewed focus, doubles down on efforts to make the base's safety procedures watertight. He picks up the soil samples he collected on Monday. Before he arrived, the base's fence was the testing boundary. But there had been too many instances in the historical record of radiation moving out beyond such limits. Through soil picked up and trodden by animals who showed no respect for restricted perimeters — the badgers, hedgehogs, and squirrels of Britain, the wolves and bears of Russia, the coyotes of wild Pennsylvania, the stray dogs of Fukushima. These were his fascination. Nonhuman life and its way of outwitting humans: the way nature undid every engineered blueprint. Even when they culled the coyotes and groundhogs at

Three Mile Island, they only went for the megafauna. That let the mice and rats run wild with their glowing little paws. He found himself cheering for the animals, those who seemed to do better once humans had been driven from radioactive sites. (Not all. There were always the deformed births, in the first few years. The unidentifiable masses of jelly where limbs and wings should be.) And the bugs, of course. The bugs could not be stopped, nor protected. There wasn't any point trying.

His soil samples have been tested, but he tests them again. He sets up the apparatus in the secure box unit, and goes around and slips his hands into the protective gloves. He draws from each vial of soil and separates earth into subsets for various tests. The gamma spectrometry, the gas flow counter for alpha and beta. He's calm. Soil composition was his area of expertise: the interrelations of soils and leaves, and their transport by animals, worms, insects. Radiation in wild places. He finds nothing, again. He'd not expect to, either.

He sits back and looks at a picture he keeps on his section of the bench, of him and Aggie and Michael and Rachel from the holiday in Los Angeles. They're somewhere in Silver Lake, eating 'Bowls of Soul' from a hippie restaurant where the dishes and drinks are all salutations. 'You are Blessed,' the waiter told him as he got his barley-based coffee replacement, post-Soul Bowl. He thinks of Aggie. He listens for her but she says nothing. Instead he hears the air-conditioning, the suck and propulsion of oxygen into their windowless, sterile lab. But there is always the knowledge of what's in the air. What cannot be cleaned up. He screws up his eyes and rubs the ball of his palms into each socket. Words come again.

Ducha.

Soul.

What is 'Bowl of Soul' in that language? He cannot recall bowl. He cannot see a bowl, let alone remember the word. It's not his language any longer. And now as words from that old life circle above him, he no longer fears their coming.

We used to believe them and do what they said. But the children were hungry. What were we to do? So we drank the milk, ate the meat. We didn't think about it.

He sits in the car for a while staring at the cottage. He's parked on the road—Michael's car is in their small driveway. It's a stylish car, an Audi. He listens to the creakings of the Hyundai as it winds itself down. Oil draining into the sump and the brass fidget of cooling engine shafts. He listens for his heartbeat but can't hear anything. The kitchen light is a rectangular beacon in the stone wall. The kitchen is always murky in the low-ceilinged vaults of their new home, dark enough to need the lamps on in daytime. It faces the narrow drive, its exterior covered in the thick roots of that buddleia he needs to take down before it pulls the cottage apart.

This lingering isn't fair on Aggie, although she's a good host. And it's only Michael. And Rachel. He should go in. But he doesn't want to. He can't shift the faces of the crewmen and women from his head. He imagines the crewmembers lined up, stood on parade. An invisible lieutenant calling them to attention. Their puffy eyes. Their pitiful salutes. He can see them vomiting down their white bedsheets, lime green glowing saliva speckled with dark red blots.

He turns the pebble over in his hand. But its magic works only to block old memories, not new ones. When did he last see Michael? Last year? No, before. *Good. Think of then, not now.* He lets the memories come, they push the faces away.

The three of them are waiting in the kitchen. Aggie's wearing the green apron with the nuclear warning sign emblazoned on it. (They came across it for sale in the artisan market at Byers Road and he regrets, even now, not buying the matching oven glove.) Rachel and Michael are sitting at the kitchen table. He kisses Aggie, who's already made their guests welcome. They've not seen each other since...

'Two years?' says Michael, standing. 'Different ends of the country...'

'That's no excuse,' says Anthony. 'Inexcusable really.'

He puts an arm around Michael's shoulders.

'I don't know,' Michael shrugs. Anthony drops his arm.

'We didn't know if you were going to join us,' says Rachel.

He goes around and kisses her on the cheek. Smells Rachel's perfume. It's not the same but it's enough to bring back the image of the servicewoman's bloated face. He closes his eyes, hides behind his hands. Fakes a yawn.

'They're working you hard,' says Michael. 'I see tonight's going to be fun.'

They're all sitting down now, apart from Aggie who's boiling the kettle.

'A lot on at work. You've not been waiting long though?'

'Didn't know they had you working overtime,' says Michael.

'It's not common.'

'You're tired too, Michael,' says Rachel, prodding Michael in the belly. She has a Home Counties face, thick lips and a perfect smile. The opposite of Aggie: Scottish, raven, pale, thin lipped. He agrees with Michael. Tonight's not going to be fun at all.

There's a cup of tea steaming in front of him. The Thursday teapot, a sleek Japanese stone urn, sits in the middle of the table. How's Michael looking? His face a little fatter, perhaps. Matured, but not aged.

'It's not regular,' Anthony says again, feeling a need, 'late working. Just—'

He stops. His story's straight. He doesn't know if Michael's told Rachel about bringing the equipment. He hopes his old friend will pick up on the cue.

'But your deadline,' says Michael. 'I reckon overtime, maybe weekend working's going to become a lot more regular. What, you've been here three months? They've been easing you in, buddy.'

'Two,' he replies quickly, but it's too late, he feels Aggie staring and trying not to at the same time.

'What deadline?' she asks finally.

There's a play in her eyes that's he's not used to. He doesn't know if she's angry or excited, pissed off that their weekends are gone or that she'll be free to spend more time chucking the tennis ball for *Greg's* collie.

He can't help smiling to himself. *Chucking the tennis ball.* An awful euphemism.

Your wife is not having an affair.

The blistering bald scalp of the woman in the bed.

When my little child is in the sun he turns white and his lips turn black. He was exposed to airborne radiation for seventeen days after the accident. Evacuated on 15th May, to family in Kobleve on the Black Sea. Returned in August. Diagnosis of symptoms: vertigo, nausea, head pains, vomiting, loss of memory, high blood pressure, insomnia, pains in the heart, auditory hallucinations, lost limbs, numbness, a chronic internal alert.

The others are looking at him. He smiles at Michael. Without saying a word they both stand and go to bring in the spectrometer. It's too expensive to leave in the car.

'You've got house insurance, right?' asks Michael, matter-of-fact.

'Why, is it going to blow us up?'

They leave it in the hallway, the profoundly odd luggage of an itinerant superhero, Electric Man and his man-bag, stacked against the unpacked boxes. Anthony gives Michael a final look, and Michael nods.

Back in the kitchen Anthony stands at the head of the table.

'Shall I open a bottle?' he asks, looking at Aggie. 'Welcome our guests.'

'Well happy bloody birthday at last,' says Michael.

They cook dinner. The two wives do most of the talking. They open another bottle. Dinner is Aggie's mushroom and lentil pie. He's bought Swedish Glacé at the supermarket in Dumbarton, and they have it with stewed apples from the orchard of one of the members of the Balernock moot. Reverend W Wilkes. The apples, not the villager. The apples round these parts sound like characters from the Wild West. The stewed fruit is acerbic but not unpleasant, not with all the cinnamon and sugar. Always too much sugar, Aggie complains, but it's how they used to stew them in the collective, and Aggie knows better than to question the revival of such memories when Anthony shares them, even if it hurts her teeth.

He pushes himself back from the table. Aggie is clearing their bowls. They've been talking, but Anthony isn't listening. He's been in the old orchards. More than half of their trees were apples. Summer, autumn and winter they'd be in the orchard. Even as children they'd help, from two or three years old. In the summer the *Paprirovka* and *Doneshta* trees, the small, hard red apples his mama would steal from their mouths—*zocmpi!*—and dry out in the stone rooms of the main house. The men would take extra baskets and collect the windfall and bruised apples for their *buha*, which they brewed in large wooden caskets and that was rumoured to make you blind overnight before returning with a gift of foresight, a wish wished for in the drinking but not remembered and so its bequest came as a surprise. In autumn— now, he thinks, the apple trees that are fruiting now—the *Antonivka*, the *Pepinka*, the *Putivka*. And then the last of the year in the snow. He would be looking for wolf tracks, trying to keep up with the men and other boys, the snow over the top of his legs, and he would disappear into the footsteps of the men who kicked the snow away in front of him. They carried their baskets on their heads and many would fall over and the other men would laugh. The *Snow Kalvil, Symyrenko's Renet*, and the *Champagne Renet*, the last of the year, and the men would eat and drink and the women would make dried fruit and marmalade, and there was always a tub of apple sauce on the table, it didn't matter what meat. He had no idea there were other condiments for the table such as mint sauce until he arrived in England. He hated the mint sauce until Linda, his adoptive mother, told him to fight the monster at the bottom of the teacup. She made the sauce herself from vinegar and jelly, and the monster was the congealed mint that settled to the bottom. For a long while it lived in his dreams, more than the apple sauce of his mama. For a while.

Laughter stirs him. He claws his way back into the room. He's not sitting down anymore, he's drying up. Aggie is washing dishes, and he has in his hands a dishcloth and a wineglass. The idea of the glass breaking under his fingers is for a moment more real than the glass he grips. He slowly wipes the glass and puts it away in the cupboard with extra diligence.

'I guess people change,' Aggie says. She clatters bowls as she washes them. 'Not guess. They do, of course. Michael, you have different priorities with Rachel now?'

Michael smiles, reaches across the table and puts his hand over Rachel's.

'Oh, Anthony was the supernova,' says Michael. 'But then, what, buddy? You sort of found your black hole, didn't you? A wormhole?' Michael pushes back in his chair. 'It was the chance of a lifetime, wasn't it?'

'There are other lifetimes,' he says, waving the tea towel around, hoping it hides the fact he hasn't got a clue what's been said. 'This lifetime.'

'But you've got a career?' asks Rachel, innocently.

'He does,' says Michael, 'but you see he was going to stay in academia with me, take up a role working on the impact on vertebrates of exposure...'

'Of what? Go on,' Rachel asks him.

Michael stops, the damage done.

'Better not, love. Ant can't want me coming in here after these years...'

'You're right, he doesn't,' says Anthony.

There's a cold silence as he and Aggie carry on with the dishes.

'I'm just sad my friend went over to the dark side, that's all,' Michael says finally. 'Sorry if it sounds like I'm knocking your life. You were a terrific researcher, Ant. Before that conference paper. The military doesn't know what it has.'

He can see on Rachel's face she's desperate to ask. *What paper?* What Anthony's finding hard to believe is that Michael's not already told her, in the years they've been together. But perhaps what was central to his life didn't register in the everyday events of others.

'I left,' Anthony says, before Rachel asks. 'For something practical. University was starting to feel...' he pauses. He picks up another glass to dry.

'Oh, it's not so bad, really,' says Michael. 'We can take off for a day or two to visit friends up north without too much bother.'

'And you should be grateful,' says Aggie, nudging Anthony in the hip, 'that he's come all this way for your birthday, you brute.'

Aggie rolls her *r*s and it's a cavalcade of comedy and love in one sound, but it's come too late for him tonight. He doesn't even know what was said, but it's done no one any good, and the dinner lies in his stomach spoiling. He and Michael sit at the table not looking at each other while Aggie brings out a new teapot, covered in the print of ivy leaves and fern fronds knitting their way round the bowl. He wonders what place it has in their kitchen cosmology. Two Thursdays? Aggie is looking at him wide-eyed and wondering.

He lies dead still, listening to Michael and Rachel settling into bed. Aggie is beside him, reading another book, not the one on poverty. He doesn't look across to see what it is. He can feel the heat of her body under the covers, so he is surprised when she rubs her feet against him—they're freezing and he pulls away, but then pushes his leg out for her and she takes the advance, plants toes and balls firmly into his flesh. The cold subsides. In three hours he knows the wine will have him awake and twitchy. But for now it's good enough to lie still, drift to sleep. He's put the pebble in the pocket of his pyjama bottoms and folded them over a chair in case he has to get up and go downstairs in the dark.

He used to tell Aggie when the memories came back. They used to talk about it. But there didn't seem an entry point now. He imagines she's forgotten about the pebble, his totem of distress. But then this morning—the Commodore. The words didn't matter now. He could do the job. Do it well. That was all that mattered. Fuck Michael. Fuck that paper. Fuck the past.

Aggie turns a page. It's a long, protracted sound, as if the book is fighting back. He glances across. In the other room Michael and Rachel are talking. Perhaps Michael's telling Rachel he can't spend the day in Glasgow with her tomorrow. Or she already knows. Even if he could smuggle a meter that large out of the Bristol physics department, there was no way of putting it in the car without Rachel seeing it. Her suitcase had to go on the back seat.

Aggie rests the book on her chest.

'You okay?'

'Fine.'

'Did he upset you?'

He stares at the ceiling. She picks the book up and sets it down again.

'He's very laid back these days.'

'Michael?'

'He was saying Bristol's somewhere they both love. Maybe it's that.'

'Maybe Rachel is pregnant. Michael always wanted kids.'

'She was drinking. Didn't you notice?'

He shrugs. She turns towards him, her feet lifted off.

'How did they get together again?'

'You were there.'

She pauses.

'Maybe I've forgotten.'

'At a fetish club. She dressed him up in a nappy.'

'Shush!' She hits him playfully with the book. Strands of her hair are loose and streak his view of her face. 'I suppose it's good,' says Aggie, digging her hands into his chest, 'you can't imagine your friends being sexually active without cracking a joke.'

'They'd better not be. I don't want to hear it through the wall.'

'Didn't you tell me once he had a crush on me?'

'Only in a nappy.'

She shakes her head, but at least she's smiling. It's good for them to have a common enemy that is not his reticence. He wants to tell her about the meeting with the Commodore, but doesn't know where to start without telling her everything, and he knows why he doesn't do that. Not because of a bit of paper he's signed, but because of the burden of what knowledge is, of how it proffers in its sharing an assessment of life and death, of what is worth having and what is brought to an end.

'And so why has Michael brought up that big machine? For your *deadline*?'

Does she hate him, he wonders, for choosing this job?

'Do you want to tell me what's happened?' she asks, with less patience.

'Only parts of it,' he whispers. 'You know I can't really.'

'But you can tell Michael?'

He shakes his head. 'No, not really.'

'Not *really*?'

He can't say. He wants to.

'What deadline then? Can you tell me that?' She drops the book. 'You chose a job that gives you an excuse not to tell me things. Not to have to tell me how your day was. That's why you took it.'

'We came here for you, remember?'

'No, we came to Scotland for me.'

'Because your father died.'

She flips away. 'And that's somehow my fault?'

He throws out a hand, lays it on her.

'Of course not. No.'

He remembers the day they moved into the cottage. All the hope of that inauguration. He'd picked up a copy of Alastair McIntosh's *Soil and Soul* that had been left in the house. A shakiness he'd not known he suffered left his hands. It was the soil he cared for, not the isotopes in the soil. It was the leaves he wanted to feel underfoot and in his hands, not the measurements of Sieverts or Becquerel found in the leaves. *That's* why he came; it wasn't to have an excuse not to talk. He didn't care about the size of the conductivity meter and not even, he's pleased to note, leaving academia. He didn't care about the missiles and the subs. He'd wanted to live near the trees and the beetles, the worms, the bees. It's hardly been any time at all, they've not had a chance to settle, there's been work to do on the cottage to make it habitable, the demands of Aggie's mother now that they're close by, and waiting for autumn and the midges to disappear. But now he has the chance. They have the chance. And all he has to do is do his work. Which also means not breaking the promise he's signed for.

'*You* wanted to work there,' Aggie says, quietly, finally.

'I don't work for the Navy,' he says, hating his whiny tone. 'The soil. I just want to work in sampling, again. Outside of the lab as well as inside it. I didn't come here to sign a piece of paper swearing me to secrecy.'

'So what's going on?' she asks. But he's said all he can.

Drago's told me so many stories of what his father told him about the Zone. Do you remember Trofin? He's dead now. He was a strong man. He had seventy-seven conditions and yet still he gave to the *hrupu*. And he secured his *sviaz* at Y, the highest rate saved for the *uchasnyky likvidatsii*. Why our family failed to get the same, Drago doesn't know. He does not say it meanly, he knows the difficulties we faced for father to gain only category II and E for us—for me and mama. Drago and his mama receive three times as much. But Drago is generous. He shares all he can after he's taken care of his family.

There is much Drago wants to tell you, even though he bids me not to write. You are nearly the same age. I know if he had the chance he would like to speak to you, brother to brother. His father shared more with him than our father did with us. You were not with us in Korosten' to hear what our father said in his last few months. His frenzied speeches, many I have never been able to make sense of, many I was scared of.

Drago's father lost the capacity to work, to live a normal life. Trofin was a *perspecktivnyi*, Drago says. Always digging for more from his invalidity, as if he were still mining copper and coal. But it wasn't just his ability to work that Drago's father lost. He could no longer *be* a father. What does that mean? Being a father is a special burden, says Drago. That there are things that only a father can pass on to a son.

Trofin used to hide his face in shame from his children, especially Drago, his eldest. I thought of you when he told me this, Anatolii Nikolaevich. A father is a sore loss for me, but for you, his only son... We never spoke about what this meant to you. Perhaps our father was sicker than Trofin? And who knows what doses he had? You can have three hundred rem but no *blat* and so you get no diagnosis, only VvD which we know means nothing. VvD is a curse, an obstacle when it should be a gift.

Our fathers were 'father-patients,' Drago says. They worried about what they could pass on to their children. The skills and manners of being men. Drago's grandfather had been a miner also, and his before, although before that they were soldiers. Drago's great-grandfather fought in the Ukrainian People's Republic against the Bolsheviks. Trofin blamed the catastrophe on Russian arrogance, and Drago does too. Not just the catastrophe of the radiation but the catastrophe of Ukraine, the catastrophe that has put our country into the dark ages. This is what Drago wants me to tell you, or rather would want you to hear from him. It's not their fault our fathers lost their capacity to father—*our* father too. But it was not lost. It was taken from him.

There is more Drago has to say, if you were able to listen. I think you would get on well with him. You would love him as a brother. He is kind to me, and loves me despite my sickness. But he is angry with you, more than with anyone I know. He knows how important it is for the sons of the men who suffered to hear this.

I hope you can write now and bless us with your acceptance, before it is too late.

Friday

He's awake an hour before he has to get up, and it seems as if in that hour their entire relationship plays before his eyes. For some reason the flood is the memory he dwells upon. It was 2007. The rain didn't stop. They watched the levels rise through sleeting, grey skies. Finally the Isis broke, and they rushed to help the couple in the flat below, moving the belongings up to their first-floor apartment to beat the creeping flood. The water filled their garden, drowned their herbs and the tomato plants and the blue plastic trampoline next door, emerging from the water like an eight-legged Kraken. The people from the flat below, James and Lyndsay, were overflowing in their gratitude. The four of them brought up boxes of clothes, books on music, three violas and a piano. Seriously! He could not get his head around finding himself in that moment—nature overrunning its channels, torrents of rain, climate changing, the moths and birds migrating northward—to be heaving an upright piano up one flight of stairs to help out flood-ridden neighbours. It made Anthony both angry at the world and proud of both he and Aggie to find themselves performing these acts of grace. He swelled with an awareness of their common generous nature. He was as good as her, then.

For three days they were flooded in. He and Aggie fed James and Lyndsay. There was a familiarity above the waterline that led them to share stories they'd all forgotten how to share. Or had never shared. In the intimacy of the siege water they learnt that James lost his brother in a motorbike accident. Lindsay's family farm had been ruined by foot and mouth; she'd watched from her bedroom and cried as the cows were carried in the claws of bulldozers and stacked in a pyre and burnt, burnt for days. Aggie shared the story of her upbringing, the Govan suburb and its tenements; how one uncle had died at thirty-four of alcohol poisoning or cirrhosis or just stupidity. They were not going anywhere until the water receded, so Anthony spoke about his past as well; his audience was Aggie but told by way of the two interlopers. He told them how he'd left his family that first time, was taken to Kyiv, and how his mama and sister went back to the Zone. How he lived with his uncle, how his uncle became his father. He explained what it was like to live on the other side of chaos as everything changed—the politics, even their nationalities—although all it really meant was more crime and less certainty. Ukraine's economy imploded after Independence, it shrank ten percent a year and there was hyperinflation. But he'd left for Britain before the worst of it, on the mercy convoys organised by the Irish churches, to Birmingham first and then to London, and then Oxford, and university.

The foursome sat on two sofas in the living room facing each other, with James and Lyndsay's boxes of belongings piled around them: the biographies of Mahler and Shostakovich, the violas and assorted smaller instruments, and the piano. No one got through their stories without crying. But more importantly in his memory was that, without saying it, he could see James and Lyndsay marveled at how this odd couple—a working-class girl from Glasgow and an orphan from the Ukraine—had come up to Oxford in the first place. And he remembers how virtuous he'd felt that he and Aggie had found each other, the odd ones out, and knew then, even if he only hoped now, that she had once, at least when they met, felt the same.

Oxford before Aggie had been a life spent within the silo of the physics department with fellow students at the bench. First a master's, then the doctorate. It was paid research, never felt anything less than a job. A desk in a room with the other PhDs with the best views in the department overlooking the University Parks. He and Michael would run at lunchtime, down the South Walk to the Cherwell, tip their winks to Parson's Pleasure and follow the edge of the Mesopotamia to Magdalen Bridge, if they wanted a long run, if there was a particular problem they needed time and air and movement to consider, and then back along Saint Cross. They shared a house with three others from the department, two of whom, Nina and Gurpreet, had desks in the same office. They shuttled between home and the lab and the conferences on their bikes, and felt engaged in important work. Neutrinos, Higgs, Dark Energy. They didn't work on them all, but discussions were in the air. The department had contracts with the Ministry of Defence and nuclear energy providers; the contributions they made had real-world impacts and were measured by awards and column inches. The department was taking a lead in climate physics. There was optical metrology. High energy frontier physics. Quantum and ultracold atoms. He could have specialised in any.

Their social lives outside the lab had been moored around pub quiz friendships at a regular Tuesday night at the Salmon and Compasses on the Iffley Road. He and Michael and Gurpreet, Nina and Xiao and occasionally others. Partners slipping in and out of the team, sometimes staying for months, years. The pub was a badly conceived cross between an old barn and a boutique hotel, with designer lamps hanging from bare sooty rafters. But it was their local and the quiz was enjoyable and winnable (seventeen times, each marked with a glowing sticky star on the fridge) although the prize money was laughable, forty quid maximum between five or eight of them. The highlight of the night was to hear the creativity of the student body crammed into the three- or five-word quiz names. What was his favourite? *Extreme Islam with Robson Green*? It seems too long ago, too puerile. He doesn't want to remember how young they were, or what other paths they could have taken.

Aggie joined the team in 2005, a few weeks after he and she met at a friend's party. He invited her to a comedy night. Then the pub. Then the quiz. She came to all three, and he was delighted. He thought he'd ruined it at first, with his talk of neutrinos and books and avoiding answers to things she asked him about his past. But she stayed. And she stayed as a member of their quiz team until they both left Oxford. When was that? Long after they'd begun to live together in the flat above the classical musicians. Long after the flood.

Aggie, Aggie, Aggie.

They chanted her name when she got a question right. Even then, in their late twenties, the joke was worn thin, and the reply, *Aye, Aye, Aye,* never stimulated many more round robins. Aggie wasn't the kind of woman who enjoyed her name shouted loudly (was there a woman who did?). She'd smile but downwards, never joining in. And then they weren't students anymore. They were postdoctorals and looking for jobs. The rituals of a pub quiz seemed outdated and fell away. Things got real as people departed with job offers, the first engagements, the weddings, the parental deaths. Michael went wherever he went, first Southampton on a temporary and then to Bristol. Nina left to work for EDF in France. Gurpreet was drawn back into family responsibilities and took a second postdoc at Leeds where he could shoulder some of the dynastic burden for his elderly father.

Aggie, Aggie, Aggie.

The things he remembers: Aggie correctly guessed the only Prime Minister to marry a divorcee was Margaret Thatcher. Aggie was the one who knew Microsoft was founded in Albuquerque. (They were all disgusted with themselves—scientists!—for not knowing that.) She was the one, because her father had been a fan, who knew the first British Grand Prix was run at Brooklands and not Silverstone. Michael had said he'd known too, but that was just a guess. Right at the start Michael had a crush on Aggie and wanted to '*me too*' her, to see if he could nip her away before she and Anthony had formed a bond. But out of jealousy or loneliness Michael met Rachel, who joined them at the quiz too.

Aggie, Aggie, Aggie. He says her name, softly.

That completed their stories: two couples who met briefly at the doorstep and shared a few words, now marooned in a two-bed upper, bearing their tragedies. When there wasn't much else to say, when the four of them had exhausted their memories, when it stopped raining, James went over to the piano and lifted the lid and sat on the stool they'd saved from the flood, and began to play a lament. Despite how saccharine it sounded, and despite the fact that he'd regularly cursed James and Lyndsay for the hours of musical practice (*It's a fucking shared building!*' he'd screamed more than once) he let himself be overwrought by the music. When James finished one piece he went on to another. He played for an hour, until in a gap between movements Aggie's stomach rumbled loudly, and they all laughed, and James slapped the lid down on the keys.

'I'm bloody hungry too,' he said.

'Let's cook,' said Aggie. She screwed up her face. 'It might be pasta again.'

The floodwaters receded. James and Lyndsay moved away for three months while the downstairs flat dried out. When they returned, the four of them attempted to build a friendship of couples. But it never worked. He hated Lyndsay like he hated the majority of the people at Oxford, now that he was being cast out. He thought he'd hidden it well; looking back, his contempt was obvious. But that puffy, breathy complaint in her voice, as if the burning of the cows was worst for *her*. He felt for James, though, and the loss of his brother, although somehow even this enraged him. He pitied James, and because of that did not want to see James's face. When he and Aggie left Oxford, James and Lyndsay dropped a card through the letter box wishing them *bon voyage*. On the day he and Aggie moved and were carrying out their boxes to a van, the downstairs couple were away in Hertfordshire, seeing James's parents.

He leaves a note on the kitchen table for Aggie, and a separate one for Michael. He's cutting it fine to arrange Michael's clearance. The air's gloomy as he approaches the long slip into the base.

There's the protest again. The same two people. Some tug on his conscience makes him slow to get a better look. They both turn and watch him. He pulls in, the engine fitful. He unwinds the window, a cold breeze filling the car. The woman pushes herself up from the camp chair and trots over. She bends down to look in through the window.

'Hello. You work at the base, then?'

'Well,' he looks beyond the woman. The man is standing up to come across. He's thin, made bulkier by layers. A bristly face, eyes a vibrant blue that peer into the car past Anthony at the mess on the passenger seat.

'Are you communications?' the man snaps at him. 'Security?'

'He's not any of those, Tom,' says the woman. 'Are you?'

'No, I'm not.' Now he's stopped he doesn't know what to say. 'I just—and—maybe, I thought, well you're out here a lot… I wondered if… Are you bored?'

'Oh fuck off,' says the man, turning away. 'He's mocking us, Mo.'

'No he's not,' she says, and smiles. 'Do you want to stop for tea?'

He shakes his head. 'I've got a busy day. I'm late. But thanks.'

'You'd better get on then,' she says.

A third person comes out of the largest tent. It's the younger woman he saw a few days before; he recognises the same aubergine hat. She comes over. Now he knows it was a mistake to stop.

'Hello,' she says, leaning into the open window, both hands tucked into the pockets of her ribbed winter jacket.

'Hi. I've got to get on,' he says.

'Do you know anything about the whales that washed up?'

'Sorry, I've really got to—' he says, pulling back from the window. He wants to wind it up, but can't find it in him to be that rude.

'If you know anything about the whale deaths…'

He turns away. 'Sorry.'

She lets out a humouring laugh, rummaging in a pocket. The older woman is staring at him, pinched lips and amused eyes. 'I'm trying to find out what happened,' the younger woman says, pushing a hand through the open window, offering him a card. Taking it doesn't mean he has to read it. He can scrunch it up and throw it in the footwell with the dog's chew toy. He takes her card and puts it in the drinks holder.

'Viccy,' she introduces herself. 'Victoria, if you're my mum.'

'And no, we don't,' the older woman says.

Anthony looks at her. 'You don't...?'

'Get bored. Do you?'

'Do I?'

'With the weapons. All that death and destruction. Or does that excite you?'

'I don't work with the weapons.'

'You know it happens a lot. People stopping and then not knowing what to say.'

'Oh. So I'm not the only idiot—I mean, not in stopping, I mean—'

She laughs and leans into the car. A whiff of talcum.

'I think you *are* mocking us a little. You don't believe in what we're doing here. Anyway, you'd better get off. Come for tea next time.'

He droops forward with relief. The old woman is waving goodbye. The man is gone. The younger woman is standing watching him. He winds up the window and accelerates, or what passes for acceleration in the old jalopy. He rubs his eyebrow with his gear-stick hand, has a confused thought about what just happened that makes him think of a *Monty Python* sketch.

He drives slowly along the road, high fences on either side, manicured greens that are lamp-lit every twenty metres, even in the daytime, so bright he can make out the individual chain links in the fence, the rivets along the hardened metal strips at chest height. *Blast height on a suicide belt?* He'd not thought of that before. He should be in a rush, but he's driving slowly. There are words he did not hear first in English, could not have, but understands that somewhere in the depths of his mind, without knowing, he's prepared their translation.

I am a mother of a child who is a sufferer. I am an evacuee from Zone One. My husband is a worker, Category Three.

He searches for the pebble. It's not there. He's left it in the pocket of his pyjamas, hanging over the chair in the bedroom.

At the gate he stops and gets out, talks to the guard, explains that there will be a visitor to the biomonitoring lab. The guard takes all the details.

'Not your breakdown recovery this time?' the guard smirks.

Anthony forces a laugh.

'I'll have to get clearance on this.' Anthony has a scan of the soldier's face, wonders how much he knows. He leaves the gate-room and parks and walks to the lab. He's glad David's not there. He opens his email.

David, I've got some equipment being delivered later for the marine testing procedures, the gate guard is going to call you to have it authorised. It's a bigger conductivity meter, had it sourced from Bristol. An old colleague has lent it to us. Just off to collect today's sample set. Anthony.

He grabs a sampling kit and leaves. An hour later, collecting new samples from the loch at the far northern edge of the base, his phone vibrates. New email. It's sorted. The thought that he's putting Michael in danger arrives clearly. The idea of what awaits them stops him breathing and he has to stand up and clear his throat.

He meets Michael at the gates. Michael waits patiently at the barrier as the guard checks his identity, hands over the visitor instructions, points towards the car park. There's a short conversation where Michael's face drops. He drives into the visitors' car park and gets out.

'Your man there says this is the closest we can get.'

'That's right.'

Inside the boot is the luggage-sized case. They carry the equipment, one at each end, and swap work stories on the way. He can't tell if this small talk is awkward or not, and if Michael really just wants to get away to meet Rachel and make a half day of it in Glasgow. At the lab he's prepared for questions, but no one's around. They pull the machine onto the bench. Michael unlocks the latches and opens the lid. The machine remains inside the hard shell case. It's the largest conductivity meter he's worked with. It will be a job to get it to where they can do the tests. He thinks of the two of them sitting on a raft, Tom Sawyer and Huck Finn, hanging the electrodes over the edge like homemade fishing rods alongside their dabbling feet. Swirling particles and gamma rays all around, ionising radiation, mackerel and sand eel gone awry.

'Can't believe we've got better kit than you have,' says Michael, looking around the lab. 'I mean, Navy and everything. The *nuclear deterrent*.'

Michael says it mockingly. But how else do you refer to the manifest materials for mutually assured destruction? M.A.D. was Python at its best. When Anthony first saw Monty Python he was confused, but every day for twenty years it has made more sense. Kubrick and Sellers got there first (there was barely an end of semester at Oxford that went by where he and Michael and others didn't celebrate with a *Doctor Strangelove* party) but Python satirised the strangeness best. Mutually Assured Destruction, or the Destruction of Mutual Assurance?

'Thanks for this,' he says, staring at the equipment.

'Was a good excuse to come and have a nosey.'

The door opens. Mariam cuts her stride when she sees them.

'Oh,' she says. 'We were expecting visitors?'

'Mariam, this is Michael.'

Michael steps forward and they shake hands. Mariam's is perfunctory.

'Right. Nice to see you. And you are...?'

'From Bristol. Physics department.'

'I didn't realise...' she trails off, looking at the meter.

'Here for your deadline,' says Michael breezily. 'Anthony and I did our PhDs together. Thought I could help.' He turns to the bench. 'Or rather, our kit.'

'Right,' says Mariam slowly. 'Anthony?'

Michael opts for a toilet break. When he's out of the lab, Mariam turns on Anthony, a hand tucked in her trouser pocket as if going for a gun on the hip.

'David *does* know?'

'David signed it off. Look, Mariam—'

'Does *he* know?'

Anthony shakes his head. 'Of course not. As far as Michael's concerned this is knowledge transfer. We've got a pressing deadline for updating our marine survey procedures and that we need the latest kit. Which is true. He was happy to come, he's signed the NDA. It scored him some teaching relief.'

'But what for? What good is that piece of kit?'

'Michael's colleagues with the expert on water testing. He knows more than us. If we want to be thorough—'

'Couldn't you have let me know?'

'It was all so—you've been up to your eyes in it.'

'And is bringing someone onto base a good idea?'

'There's no cordon,' he says, staring intently at the machine.

Michael returns and stops at the door. 'If you need a bit of time...'

'Mariam, do you want to come and join us?' Anthony slaps a hand on the shell of the meter. 'We're going to go and test this beast.'

'I've got a meeting,' she says, scoops up a notebook from the bench and leaves.

Anthony senses Michael's amused stare.

'She's feeling a bit undermined,' he explains.

'What, Anthony Fahey waltzing in and upsetting the applecart?'

They carry the equipment to the pontoon. They've obtained a small row boat, something used for sewage maintenance, from the smell of it, and decidedly un-Navy. They fumble the meter into the aft (he knows rowing boats don't have sterns and afts) and, almost having fun, they row the boat out into the loch. He sees the base from the water for the first time. Sees if he can spot the half-underground bunkers of the medical unit. Anthony rows them as close to the entrance of the marina as they can get without leaving the water perimeter. He suggests a place to get a measurement. Michael turns the machine on. The electrodes are much larger than on a handheld, with stiffened metal calipers that look like claws rather than cylinders. They extend out on four insulated wires, two of which Michael takes and dangles, one over each side of the boat, feeding them into the water. When they're resting he leans forward and switches on the flow.

'We're now in the centre of current,' says Michael. 'Don't touch the meter.'

'Instructions?'

Michael laughs.

'This is a setup, isn't it?'

Anthony freezes. 'Us?'

'I mean the base. Quite a setup.'

Anthony calms himself, sees it through Michael's eyes: an overgrown military boarding school, especially with boats lying about. They'd not been questioned getting in. That was one of the things he enjoyed about being on base: once you were in you were in, even if it looked like you were smuggling some very dangerous kit out of the base in a small rowing boat. They were both wearing whites. Although if they were terrorists they would have thought of that, wouldn't they?

'How did you end up working here again?'

Anthony makes a clicking sound with his tongue. 'That's a good question.'

'Is there a good answer?'

'Aggie, really.' He pauses. 'Closer to her mother.' He watches the electronic screen on the machine come alive, flickering. The light makes it difficult to read. 'But... I don't know. The city wasn't working out for us.'

'Too claustrophobic?'

He shrugs. 'I guess. We weren't getting on. Weren't sharing. So...'

'You theorised it?'

He can't think of a response. He looks at the machine.

'What's it saying?'

Michael leans forward and cups his hand around the screen to block the sun, which has, for once, burnt away the cloud cover. Michael leans back, implacable.

'And so you decided to get away?'

'I wanted something that got me outdoors. Soils, natural environments. Putting in new processes. Developing something.'

'For the military.'

'I don't work for the Navy.'

'You could have developed a research project,' says Michael, shifting on his end of the wooden board.

'Are we waiting for a reading?'

'You know, these questions interest me,' Michael says.

Anthony feels a prickle rise up his neck. 'I thought of moving out of nuclear into renewables. Would if there was a decent job.'

Michael is staring at the base. 'Nuclear? Well, it's better than coal. But... would you call it the *approach*? The *intention*—how the power is used? We're thinking of having kids.'

'You and Rachel?'

'It gets you thinking, doesn't it? Kids. What world you bring

them into. I guess you and Aggie have had the same conversation.
You couldn't not, really.'

He doesn't answer. Looks away.

'Don't tell me you've theorised that too?'

'Fuck off, Michael.'

'True. I've never really heard you talk about kids. Don't you
want them?'

He's not prepared for this. Not with what's going on around
them. He sees a girl from many years ago, hears his own voice…
Shall we get to know each other?

'What about Aggie? She want?'

'It's none of your business.'

'I'm just asking.'

'Of course we've…' he begins, but it's another lie, another
conversation he avoids. And he suddenly goes tight with the
thought: *that's why she's having an affair.* Because she does want
kids. Or at least to talk about them. And he won't. Can't.

'Working for the devil, so to speak, you have to debate it,
don't you? Bringing up kids around this type of facility.'

'You trained in nuclear too,' says Anthony, curt, and shifts on
the board. Michael finally takes the hint and stops questioning.

But I'd be worried, you know…

The girl's voice this time. In English. She was practising her
English with him.

…in case…

He closes his eyes. Lets the memory die. Michael begins
talking again.

'But then electricity,' says Michael, 'renewables. This
government shutting down the feed-in tariffs. It's crazy, don't
you think? Have you got solar panels? We got in just in time.
But then we're going to have to invest in nuclear too if we want
to beat climate change. That's obvious.' Michael pauses, and
looks down at the machine. 'These meters, they use an inductive
method so the sensors don't get wet. They're inductively coupled

coils. One drives the magnetic field'—and he holds and waggles the electrode on his left—'and then the other'—he waggles that one too—'forms the secondary coil of a transformer. Nothing really different from a handheld, but the increased size gives it more gradations to the sensitivity, a handful of extra dials, two more stages in setting the receptors.'

'I know all this.'

'I know you know,' says Michael sharply. 'And because I know you know, I know you don't need this machine. So now I'm here, and we've postponed our day out in the galleries, you ought at least to let me go through the motions.'

Anthony shakes his head as if he still needs to prove Michael wrong, but the ruse is wearing thin.

'Then the liquid,' Michael looks down at the water, 'forms a secondary winding of the transformer passing through a channel. From that,' he says, folding his arms and leaning over the meter, 'we get the compensation slope.'

Anthony's not planned for this. He'd imagined too long the knowledge he would garner, and the new processes he could tell David had been put in place. How he'd taken significant action to improve the base's capacity for measuring and responding to the situation. And Michael was coming up anyway. But that was as far as he'd got. What he might actually have to explain to Michael, he'd not theorised enough.

'I need to know about marine testing,' he says.

'My colleague James is the expert, not me.'

'You know more than us here.'

'Really. In the *fucking Navy*?'

'You'd be surprised how much they haven't planned for.'

'Well, that's encouraging.' He narrows his eyes. 'What's this for, buddy?'

Anthony looks to the hills beyond, the strip of blue sky. He feels a wind that is too light to rock the boat but has chilled his face.

'So what is it?' Anthony asks flatly, pointing to the machine. 'The reading.'

'Fucking hell,' is all Michael says, looking away into the water.

They spend an hour moving to different spots on the loch, taking readings. Anthony tells Michael most of what fits the truth. Deadlines. New procedures. The vote going through on Trident's renewal. The whales, the public misconception. They return to the pontoon and drag the meter back to the lab, and spend another hour looking at tables and making calculations and putting the scaffolding together for a comprehensive plan for water testing. Mariam, Elspeth and David are all in and out, and while Elspeth comes over to take a look, none of them interfere. Anthony absorbs all he can; Michael acts the professor, imparting knowledge, calm and superior. Even so, Anthony feels a new freedom. He knows, somehow, from Michael's posturing and guidance, that the academic life was not meant for him.

It's past lunchtime when they're finished.

'Rachel's going to slaughter me,' says Michael.

'I'm so sorry,' Anthony says, and he means it. 'You've still got time?'

'Sure. But I'm hungry.' Michael whispers, 'You need to talk to me, too.'

Anthony leads Michael to the cafeteria. They take trays and grab soup and sandwiches and sit opposite each other on a mostly empty long white bench in a half full hall, noisy enough so no one can hear their conversation. Michael eats most of his sandwich before Anthony's got his out of the pack.

'You know you've got a problem, don't you?' Michael lets out a long sigh, rubs his eyebrows and then picks up the spoon and dips it in the soup. 'Nice food,' he says after a mouthful. 'Wouldn't expect less from the Navy.'

'I always thought it'd be like school dinners.'

'I'm surprised they let you come here. With your history.'

'It's all known about,' he says, ripping the plastic off his wrap. 'The Commodore knows. It's not a secret.'

'I'm not saying it is,' says Michael. 'Don't be touchy with me, buddy. Not after what I've just done for you.' The cafeteria is a hum of chatter, plates and plastic and people who know nothing as much as he does. 'What's going to happen? What do those readings mean?'

Anthony takes a bite, looks away. Outside there's a view of the hills on one side, and on the other the loch, uneven glints of sun on its surface.

'There are contraventions...' is all he says. A little white lie about the levels: waste product again, like in the last Evening Star exercise. Already that's too much.

'Shit, Ant, buddy. You've not put us in danger, have you?'

'Of course not.'

Michael stares, not unlike how the old woman from the protest looked at him earlier. What if he *has* put them in danger? All of them? Him, Michael, Rachel. Aggie. The whole community. What if right now the base *should* be evacuated?

'You've got to do the right thing with these results. I don't know what that is for you. Now you're working for the Navy. What is it for you now? Whatever it is, you've got to do the right thing with them.' Michael gestures towards the loch with his chin. 'That's open water. That's the world. Where normal people live. What's in the water here will go out there. People, right? Kids swimming in the water, right?'

'They're not allowed. Not within the military range—'

'As if kids give a monkey's arse about that. They're *more* likely to, aren't they? Any authority tells them not to.' Michael puts both hands on the bench top. 'And we've just spent the morning pretty much tearing apart any concept of *military range*. If it's out there, then it's halfway to the Irish Sea. And then where? Then what? What's the Navy going to do about it?'

'I don't know,' he says quietly. His bowl of soup stares at

him. *Ducha, ducha.* His soul is out there, halfway to the Irish Sea. Floating like plankton, eaten by whales, rising and falling with the moon.

'What's your authority here? Can you say what's going to happen?'

'I'm not—' he begins. *Navy.* For what it matters.

'Well you'd better think how you can be,' says Michael, looking at his watch. 'Fucking slaughter me.'

Back at the lab, they pack up the meter and carry it out to the car park. He waves Michael off, to go and pick up Rachel and begin the long, argumentative drive to Glasgow to catch the last hour or so in the Mackintosh, or GoMA. The muscular Audi paws its way up the long out road, and then it's gone.

'Lift,' Mariam conducts.

He's back in the lab, helping Mariam carry the central bench across to the wall. They're making space in the middle of the room for a new bench with built-in tools. Superficial, he thinks. Icing on a burnt cake.

'There's no point excusing what you've done. You must know that.'

'Have you drawn the short straw?' he asks.

She goes to the cupboard to get a set of vials. He thinks, *Perhaps this will be the last time I enter the lab.*

'I'm not a stooge,' she says. 'But that was a very stupid thing to do.'

'You seem to have thought everything I've done here is stupid.'

She shakes her head, annoyed. 'You know that's not true.'

He's marooned in the middle of the lab where the bench used to be, an island to cling to. Strange how a small rearrangement can change so much.

'You know that's not true,' she repeats. 'You've made it difficult for me, but… Christ, Anthony, we may've made a good team.' He stutters at her use of the past tense. 'I still know a thing or two,' says Mariam. 'You could have learnt from me.'

'I know,' he says, quietly. 'You're a good scientist, Mariam.'

'Is it that you always fuck up, and this is just your pattern? We've read your CV, Anthony. You've never stayed long at any one place.'

'For different reasons.'

Someone walks past the lab door. He catches a glimpse of their face in the porthole window, and for a moment he's on a ward of a hospital... *vuzols*. Knots. He breathes quickly, takes in a lungful of the lab, the bleach, Mariam's antiperspirant.

Biostrata. Krizi.

He shuts his eyes and rubs his face with his hands.

'Anthony,' says Mariam. It is not his name. For a horrible moment he's lost his mooring. *What is my name?* The lab light shimmers. He's a boy surrounded by mistakes, who doesn't understand if they're his fault, or what he's done. With all his strength he pulls himself back to the conversation.

'David was aware. David signed it off.'

'Anthony.' His name like a stone. 'Don't be an idiot. The best thing you can do is go and see David. Speak to him.'

'But I've not—'

'Don't be a *fucking* idiot,' Mariam shouts. She breathes, pats down her whites. 'David signed off the *machine*, not the person. He didn't know you'd be spending half a day in a boat with someone from off base. You've made him look very inept. He's been digging this lab out of a security hole all afternoon.'

What a British thing, then, he thinks. For David not to say anything while Michael was around; to let the breach play out.

'Nothing?' Mariam continues. 'You didn't tell him *anything*?'

'He signed the NDA. As standard. You're being unreasonable.'

Mariam shakes her head. He wants to argue, but he knows what he did: the surprise email, the vague detail. He thinks other things: the chewed tennis ball. The face of a woman, not the crewmember from *Tartarus* in isolation, but a woman who used to come to their home. She would bring her young daughter, a thin, yellow-skinned girl. The woman's name was Hanna Kozlova. He doesn't remember the name of the daughter. Irina? Hanna is wearing a brown headscarf. Where's Irina? In the hospital. The next time he sees her, Hanna is standing in a corridor. Irina is in one of the wards. Hanna is arguing with a doctor. She is crying.

I'm an evacuee from the Zone, my grandmother was killed in the war, her sister was cannibalized in the famine after. Have we not suffered enough?

He hears her voice from far away. And then it's not her voice. 'Anthony, are you okay?'

Mariam sends him home. She's not his superior, but he takes the out, leaves early. He doesn't look to see if the young woman is still at the protest. He's not read her card. There's a proper crowd of them now, perhaps twenty, music and banners that say *Scottish CND, Fifty Today!*

He drives to the cottage. Aggie is home. She's in a good mood. Surprised, but happy to see him, and then concerned. He's relieved she's there, feels a weight lift from his chest. Mariam's words are ringing in his ears, muddled with other memories. *Is it your pattern? My grandmother died fighting in World War One. You must have told him something? Why did you cut off your hair? I pulled it out, it all fell out, in clumps. Are you lying? No! She's not, doctor. You, why hasn't your hair fallen out? I've not done anything wrong! Haven't we suffered enough?*

He has a cup of tea but is too restless to sink into the gift of a free afternoon. He asks Aggie to come for a walk. He changes into jeans, hiking boots, puts on a different coat. They drive north, past the turn for the Trossachs. Back past the base and the protest. Aggie looks out of the window delighted by the chanting and waving of flags.

'So where are we going?'

'I thought the beach.'

'Okay. Nice. Ant, you okay?'

He glances at her, then back to the road ahead.

In Garelochhead they stop and get a coffee and a tea from the local greasy spoon, and then they're driving again when he looks over and sees Aggie reading the business card the young woman gave him.

'Who's this?'

'I don't know. Someone looking for trouble.'

'Ant, really.'

'I found it on the windscreen, tucked under the windscreen wiper.'

'On the base?'

'Outside.'

'Why did you park outside?'

'In case the car broke down again,' he carries on lying. 'There's extra security at the moment because of...' But he can't think of any more lies. He lets it drift.

'Your deadline,' says Aggie for him.

He nods, relieved and ashamed. He drives to a shingly strip of beach, and they walk across shale that he knows might be carrying some dosage, although their rubber boots would protect them; it would be minimal, anyway, dispersed. His coffee's gone cold. He empties the remnants onto the shingle; it makes a stain the shape of New Zealand. He shakes out the cup and stuffs the lid into it for the ease of carrying it. There's no bin around. He will carry it back to the car and throw it in the rear footwell and they will drive on, and perhaps the chewed-up tennis ball will not be there, perhaps the woman's card will have disappeared too, perhaps they will drive on to somewhere else and begin the conversation pressing at his throat. Not only to share the secret he's keeping from her: of what has happened to the submarine and the crew who are lying under white sheets in the clinic; but what he's done about it. Perhaps Mariam was right. He's done some stupid things. He won't pass probation. They will move to

Glasgow and live in Aggie's mum's house and he'll find a new career. Or he'll wither away, workless, and Aggie will petition for a divorce, and the owner of the dog who chews tennis balls— *Greg*—will come to her wellbeing class and they will restrike their liaison, and Aggie will move to whatever island he's from, say Shetland, where he wrestles sheep and plucks their wool with his hands and plays the fiddle and loves his mother. And then Anthony will reach his mid-forties, half his life gone. Nothing left except to follow a new path. That's if it turns out well. And if it turns out badly? Five years in prison for breaking the Official Secrets Act, a battered anus and broken teeth, drug addictions. And—*ah*—isn't this what it's about? He'll be extradited. They'll send him back *there*.

'What are you thinking?' she asks. He jumps. He looks past her and across the shore to the pine hills of the Trossachs.

'Of a story.'

'Which one?'

'About us. Not boy-meets-girl —not that—not the happily ever after. There's the other one, when you get older. There's the other question. What happens *after* happily ever after.'

'Have we reached happily ever after?' she asks quietly.

His heart cramps. She's holding her tea with the lid on, determined to save its lukewarm dregs. He loops his arm through hers.

'Yes. But what's supposed to happen next? What if what needs to happen in your life is to, I don't know…gain some missing knowledge. You're on a path to wisdom but you keep missing the signs…'

'You, talking about paths to wisdom?'

'*You* are. On a path. Your classes. You've made the most of this.'

They crunch along the beach covered with broken mussel shells. Sharp edges of blue arcs, calcified life that could cut right through the boots to their toes.

'What do you mean, I've made the most of this? What's *this*?'

'You ditched your old life—your old job—began something new. That's a gentle beginning. A gentle fall from grace.'

'My father dying wasn't a ride on a bouncy castle, you know.'

He's straining to make sense. 'You're on a path to wisdom. Apart from marr—'

'Don't,' she interrupts.

'I'm being self-deprecating.'

'You're being an idiot.'

'I'm saying that...'

'Is our marriage part of this second story?'

'Of course. That's not—it doesn't mean you can't be married to someone...'

He gives up. He's skirting around what he *should* be saying. She's struggling to be tolerant. Either he tells her or he doesn't. Once again, she helps him out.

'You're saying that I've found the path I'm meant to be on?'

He nods. 'Yes.'

'And that you're not on yours? That you're still finding yours?'

'Fighting it,' he says, and knows as he says it that it's true, feels it in the footfalls along the beach and the way the air is light upon his face. 'Fighting it. When you've always fought your destiny, the fall is—'

Aggie laughs.

'You, destiny? Now I know something's up.'

He looks at her for a long time. Long enough for her to stare back, look away, and stare again. If marriage for Aggie was an adventure, an experiment open to learning from mistakes and to turning each mundane moment into a set piece; to live in amazement of the discovery of another person and of growing into that discovery without disillusionment; then for Anthony it was—or *had been*—an obligation. Every adult he'd known as a child was married, even the old men. His uncle, of course, never married. But that Anthony had understood, even as a boy, was a matter of temperament, of his uncle being the kind of man who wouldn't—couldn't—offer himself up to the necessary responsibility of sharing one's world, of explaining one's decisions, through actions if not in words, in private if not in front of the children. Of having children. Anthony didn't have that temperament. His uncle had not spent his life wading through the thickness of congealed emotions to reach his longings, as Anthony understood himself—self-pityingly—to have done. His uncle, who he'd grown up with, for a while, was free from the journey into that bog; whether by choice or not, Anthony didn't know, but he suspected not. His uncle was the cliché of an island, suspiciously watching the romantic tide lest it come in too far; spending a life plotting, like Canute, how to turn back the sea. Anthony wasn't like that. He wanted the tide to overcome him. Only when it did, he couldn't remember how to swim.

But he wanted it. He wanted the obligation. He wanted the bond that kept his mama and father tied until death, and beyond; he had the accentuated belief that marriage was a spiritual achievement he was obliged to attain, and succeed at.

That carried him through the romance, engagement, and first year of marriage. And then both his and Aggie's needs caught up with them. This was territory he didn't understand. He wasn't prepared for his own resistance to accepting the obvious: loving someone risked losing them. It was fear at the root of this retreat from what had been working between them. Not guilt, not shame; they were responsible for other things. Fear was the cause of why he'd closed up, that he couldn't bear to lose her. The perplexity of the conflict—between the obligation to make it work, and the fear of outliving the other person—to be left alive and in grief but also—

Who was he kidding?

Guilt. It was guilt. Of being the survivor. It was guilt, below the fear, and perhaps fear again below the guilt, or they were not layers at all but that mire he imagined when he thought of how to be better, how to love, his love a liquid he waded through, his grandpa's *bigos*—a hunter's stew—something wholly indigestible. His jealousy of Aggie having an affair was not the worst thing. The jealousy was a relief. What was worse was that he might outlive her, that outliving others would be his only success. But he couldn't dwell only in that soup. He had to hope that in succeeding in something as important as marriage, he would pull himself out of the sludge that was his fear, his guilt.

What he learnt from Aggie, from their intimacy and the times when he let her in, when they shared all that was reasonable and painful, was that it wasn't only *his* baggage now that he had to carry, but hers too. Like all relationships, good and bad. And she, his. Regardless of whether he *chose* to share or not. It wasn't possible across the membrane of real intimacy to maintain an internal Official Secrets Act of the unconscious for what they both carried, even if what was shared most was the afterimage of events. He wanted to share, didn't he? It was only something deeper and in more control of him that kept him from that.

'Maybe I've understood something,' he says finally. 'But if she dies—'

Aggie grabs his arm. 'What the fuck? Anthony... What's happened?'

He feels the grip of her arm and it doesn't release, because as the fear subsides it's replaced by a truthfulness that's gripped them both.

'Who dies?' Aggie asks, so quiet he hardly hears her.

He registers the strength of her fingers. The waves lapping, the gulls crying, and the marram grass rustling, the cars passing by on the road that runs alongside the beach ascending into tree cover, the road they drove down only a few hours ago, a road that will be different when they drive back. But no. That's too dramatic. Destiny! It's the same road. Nothing has changed.

Words come again. *Here, the worst is to be healthy.*

The pebble, it's not in his pocket.

110

Drops of water hitting a stone eventually cause the stone to crack.
But I've done nothing wrong.
This is me, he thinks. *This is where I am.*
Zolota seredynka.
The little golden centre of the disaster.

1986-87, Radynka, Radcha, Korosten'

They're in Kyiv for a week, before his uncle brings Anatolii and
Sveta back to Radynka so they can be evacuated with their mama.
Radynka is in Zone One; the liquidation is compulsory. Even the
women who refused to leave on the buses must go now. There
has been an announcement from a General over the tannoy in
the central square, and leaflets pushed through every door.
The General was not wearing one of the white masks, but even
the children saw the speech lasted less than a minute before he
rushed to his AKmaz. Go voluntarily within twenty-four hours
or be forcibly removed, and given inferior accommodation to
those who go willingly. So the women go home weeping and
begin packing. Take only essentials, the General warned them.
No furniture. Nothing from your gardens. No tools. No animals.
No metals. You will be searched on your way out.

Their father's away, driving. Not for the General but for
scientists, who have come to understand what happened. There
are rumours. It was an American plot, the CIA trying to undermine
the great Soviet vision. That it was caused by inexperienced
operators. That it could have been prevented. But no one knows.
It's all a conspiracy, says their uncle. No one can explain this
turning upside down of their world.

Anatolii is happy to see his mama. He's spent the week in
Kulyk's flat looking after Sveta. Kulyk had to work, because no
one in Kyiv thought what was happening was real, or serious, so
Kulyk's boss wouldn't give him time off. So Anatolii had to take
care of his sister. Feed her, stop her crying.

They pack clothes and pictures and his mama throws in the
kitchenware that was a wedding gift. She hopes in the rush they
won't get searched, but says this crying, *Where do we go? Where
are we going to live?* Kulyk says, 'Come to Kyiv. Live with me for
now.' His mama shakes her head. All they've been told is to go

to Korosten'. Someone tells them this is in Zone Four, which is safe. It has heightened radiological monitoring. She tells Kulyk to drive to Radcha instead. To go to their parents.

'But Radcha is in Zone Three,' says Kulyk. They're sitting in the car, waiting in the queue to exit the village. There's a roadblock. Soldiers are checking each vehicle. 'Zone Three is guaranteed voluntary resettlement. Mama and papa will leave too.'

He and Sveta are in the back, buried under black bags. Kulyk looks at them in the mirror. 'They should've stayed in Kyiv. Your children are taking up space.'

'Papa will never leave the farm. They won't go. Why should they go? Radcha is farther away. It's out of the smoke, the cloud never went that way.'

'Oksana, you don't know what you're saying. I'll take you to Korosten'.'

'Take us to Radcha!' she cries, and wails so loud and long that when they get to the checkpoint the young soldier who peers through their window, sharp brown eyes and a white mask over his mouth and nose, simply takes a look and puts out an open palm. Anatolii watches his uncle place a bundle of *roubles* into the soldier's hand. The soldier waves them on. Anatolii can see a snake of car lights heading southwest away from the Zone. Kulyk sighs heavily, turns northeast at the fork for Radcha.

It's two weeks since they arrived. Anatolii still has to look after Sveta while their mama scavenges for food in the near-empty market. He isn't allowed to leave the house. No one's certain if Radcha is more contaminated than Radynka, or less, or not at all. He can't go and play with other kids, there's no school, and so they hang around in the living room or the kitchen. *Babushka* tells them stories, their mama is too busy crying to take any notice, their grandpa is sick of them already and stays out of the house. Anatolii wants to run away. Sveta is always crying, always complaining of feeling sick. When she is sick, he has to help clear it up, wipe her face and undress her. It disgusts him. He doesn't know why she's being sick. He feels sick sometimes too, but if he throws up he does it in the toilet. Sveta doesn't understand, even when he drags her to the bathroom screaming, she still throws up all over the floor, over herself. The house stinks of cabbage and vinegar. It should be *babushka* who cleans up, but she has to work too. She goes out with grandpa to the farm, although returns earlier. *Babushka* shouts at him for how he looks after Sveta. 'Be gentle, Anatolii!' He doesn't want to be.

'We might as well go back,' his mama cries over dinner. He thinks of his father. They're trying to get a message to him: that they're in Radcha, that they haven't abandoned him. *He's abandoned us*, Anatolii thinks angrily, and is ashamed.

Finally one night, their father comes. Anatolii and Sveta are already in their makeshift bedroom on straw beds. Mama sleeps on her old cot. The house is so tiny he can hear what his father is saying through the walls. He's been driving the scientists. Sveta is breathing loudly in her sleep. Anatolii wants her to shut up so he can hear better. He throws straw at her. His father is explaining what the scientists have discovered. There's soil contamination. His father uses words no one understands, not even, he suspects, his father. Caesium, strontium, plutonium. There is one scientist, a young man called Chelovek, whose job it is to test the food: the milk, berries, mushrooms, fish, the potatoes. His team is coming soon, his father says. To Radcha. This *kolkhoz* will have to give up its food too. The scientists will take some to radiochemical laboratories; the rest they will bury.

'Bury potatoes?' his grandpa shouts. 'They want to bury potatoes!'

'How can they bury what's already buried?' his mama asks.

His father tells them to be quiet.

'They will bury earth within earth. Everything into big plastic bags, and then buried again.'

'There's no reason for it,' his grandpa is saying. 'This is

114

crazy. They're criminals, they're taking it all for their restricted access shops in Moscow. This explosion is just another excuse! This harvest is the best for years. And they say we can't eat the cucumbers! That we bury the potatoes!'

He hears his mama fussing. He throws more straw at Sveta, who wakes with a wail, and begins crying. He can't hear the conversation anymore. He reaches over and covers her mouth. She screams louder and he pushes down harder when the light goes on and his mama is looking at him in horror. She grabs his arm and pulls his hand away. She picks up Sveta, leaving a hollow in the straw mattress.

'What were you doing?' his mama shouts, holding Sveta on her shoulder.

His father is standing in the doorway. Anatolii sits up. He can see the bones in his father's face. A hungry dog, not even a wolf.

'What's your son doing?' his mama cries. 'What was he doing?"

'I was trying to make her stop,' pleads Anatolii. He doesn't know what's going to happen. He's terrified his father is going to punish him.

'Tell your son,' his mama says. 'Are you useless? You threw yourself at Chernobyl and now you are worthless! Won't you punish him?'

He can't believe his mama has said such things. His father grimaces, puts out a hand to lean on the doorframe. Then his father collapses.

They're taken away the next day. All the children in the village are loaded onto buses heading for the Black Sea. The wailing of women at the bus station is unbearable and he wishes for the bus to drive away to end the noise. Dozens of women in headscarves shaking their hands in the air. He and Sveta are bundled on with the other children, all crying. It smells of wet pants and engine oil. He's tied to his sister by a piece of string around their wrists.

His sister leans into him but he pushes her away as far as the string will stretch. She screams and tries to bury herself in his belly. Whose fault could it be? Why are they leaving? Where are they going?

It is September. They have returned from the Black Sea; the authorities have decided it is now safe for the children to be in cities. What has caused this change of policy, no one knows.

'You should've come here straight away. Now you will only get what is left.'

'Don't tell me, "I told you so," brother,' says his mama.

Their mama has spoken to the administrators in Kyiv dealing with the liquidation. At first she came back crying, saying it was 'too late, too late.' But then one day she came back with a red face but happier. She'd secured them a home in Korosten'. True to the General's word, the administrators have only small, unwanted places left. But they have no choice. His father has grown sicker and can't drive. His vision is blurred. He has blackouts.

They're in Kulyk's car, driving past the sign for Korosten'. His father is in the front passenger seat, he and Sveta on either side of their mama. They're rolling along slowly, looking for their new home. Anatolii doesn't like it. The streets are dirty, dusty. There's nobody on the roads. There are no trees. The Black Sea was beautiful, deep green, warm. He worried about his father but the people in charge reassured him everyone was safe, everyone was well. It was not true. Now he's back, and his father is sicker, his mother angry all the time. He and Sveta are afraid of both of them. 'Take your sister, look after her somewhere else,' their mama shouts at him. She waves them away like they're rabbits stealing her lettuce. Their belongings—or rather what his grandparents have given them—are in a trailer behind the car, clattering over the stony road. Anatolii cannot talk to his father, whose skin is yellow and scabby, his stomach bloated; his father only mumbles or shouts at them to be quiet, or shouts at things not there. His eyes are barely open, and when Anatolii gets close he can smell something rotten, like potatoes that have been half-eaten by beetles.

The address on the documents the administrators gave them is for a building on the outskirts. New homes made of concrete, small and dark. The windows are the size of prayer books. They sit in the car for a while before they get out and look around. The street is empty. No cars, no trees. He hates it. His mama is holding a tissue to her face. Their father is still in the car and needs Kulyk to help him out.

'Unlock the door, woman,' Kulyk tells his mama. She fiddles with the key in the lock and the door gives. A smell like dead rats. His father has a hand around his uncle's shoulder, walking slowly upstairs to the bedroom. His mama takes Sveta's hand and they go in. He is left on the street.

It's *Koliada*, the night of 7th January. His mama drags them around the town with a dozen other women who are also forcing their children through the freezing night. It's twenty degrees below and the snow is up to their thighs. They're dressed in boots and wrapped in their thickest coats. He's wearing his father's scarf and two pairs of gloves. He cannot feel his fingers and toes but he won't say anything. He carries the bucket for the collection, perhaps a hundred *roubles*, if they're lucky, for a whole night's singing. Usually they're on the inside, the ones who open the doors to hear the singing, who give away their money. This year they have no money. They need funds for the *hrupu*, someone says. What *hrupu*? Someone else asks, *What about food for us?* There are mutterings and murmurings. There are always mutterings and murmurings. He cannot remember any of the songs. His ears are too cold, perhaps, his mind empty like the bucket. He's overheard that the body reacts to radiation by blocking the senses. The men and women who stayed in the Zone have gone crazy that they cannot smell the apple blossom. Perhaps the radiation has blocked his ears too, so he cannot hear the words of the cheerful songs. He doesn't know. They're stopping at each door where there is a light on inside, thirty or so beggars waiting for their knock to be answered before singing, stamping their feet on the doorstep or garden path or passageway if they're in a block of flats. They all hoped being inside the walkways and corridors of these new flats would provide respite from the cold but the wind just runs faster through the stairwells. They wait. A man opens the door a crack, looks at them with one eye. *Get home, get home,* he says and wants to shut the door but cannot bring himself to be uncharitable. The wind blows down the Christmas cards on the mantel inside.

When they return home Kulyk is there. He's kept the fire burning. Anatolii strips off his layers and runs to the fire. His uncle puts out an arm.

'Slowly, slowly, you'll give yourself chilblains.'

Anatolii and Sveta fight to climb over Kulyk's outstretched arms. They want to throw themselves into the fire, a willing Hansel and Gretel. Sveta is giggling as Kulyk tickles her under her armpits, and Anatolii is laughing, fighting with his uncle's strength, until his uncle laughs and stands and grabs each one under an arm, pretends to shove their heads into the fire. Anatolii feels the fierce heat on the top of his head. Sveta is giggling loudly, Kulyk is laughing and then Sveta is screaming with excitement when the bangs come through the ceiling. They fall silent. Embarrassed, told off, even Kulyk. They stand silently in front of the spitting fire. Sveta collapses into a cross-legged position. Anatolii hopes he is not getting chilblains on his nose or his fingers, cannot be sure if it is from the heat of the fire or the fear of upsetting his father that his cheeks are burning.

Alex Lockwood

Saturday

There's stirring from the other room. Michael and Rachel are waking, after having stayed late in Glasgow for an appeasement dinner. Anthony rolls over, looks at Aggie. He thinks she's awake. He gets up, pries open the curtains. The sky looks as if it might be fine later. There's are bands of what could turn out to be blue. Behind him Aggie is getting up, wrapping herself in her bathrobe. Bathrobe or dressing gown? Suddenly he's not sure.

'If we get wet, we get wet,' he says turning to her, 'but it looks okay.'

'It's only rain if we do,' she says. 'It's Scotland.'

'No midges in the rain.'

She comes and stands with her arms around him, her chin resting on his shoulder. It feels good. With her there to settle him he understands how much he's been stirred up. The base, his errors. Michael's visit, even. The friendship is long rather than deep and it has unlatched memories of when his career was bound for somewhere else. And where is it heading now?

'Happy birthday. The midges will be gone.'

'I'll believe that when I don't get bit.'

They prepare breakfast, drink tea, make a packed lunch. Michael and Rachel come down after their showers. Michael shoves a candle in Anthony's porridge. They sing happy birthday and clink their teas and coffees. *So this is thirty-five,* he says to himself and blows out the candle.

He opens one of Michael and Rachel's two gifts, a copy of Dante's *Commedìa*.

'The classic age,' says Michael. 'It's the midlife now, buddy. It's the age that Dante begins his journey through the levels of hell. All downhill, as they say.'

'It's heaven,' Rachel says. 'Paradise. Not hell he's trying to get to.' Anthony remembers she's a classics graduate. *Ah.* She bought this as a gift for Michael on his thirty-fifth, and Michael's stolen the idea. But it's a good gift. Not one he'll ever read, but then it's only a playful contribution to the day's opening. He turns the book, reads the blurb: the protagonist lost in a dark wood, assailed by beasts. A lion, a leopard and a she-wolf. He puts the book down, eats his porridge.

Aggie fills up the biggest flask he's ever seen, nearly two feet long, bright green with a silver lid. He didn't know they owned it. Michael calls it a flagon and makes some comment about the Roman occupation. There are things that still surprise Anthony about marriage, and that he is not all-knowing of the properties of his wife is a good thing, usually. The flask looks a little beat up, a grail for the outdoors bound, full of the blood of life for those treading on the land: *here, drink this, it'll warm you up.* She packs it into the back of the car with their walking boots and rucksacks and freezer bag full of fruit and flapjacks and cheese and pickle sandwiches. He comments that it looks more like a missile than a canteen of English breakfast tea.

'Breakfast tea,' Aggie reminds him. 'The Scots occupied India too. It was called the *British* Empire.'

'Not something to boast about. Anyway, I thought you voted for independence?'

She ignores him, but playfully.

They leave the house in two cars as Michael and Rachel want to 'run a few errands later, before the party,' and neither he nor Aggie argue. They drive north, first heading to Garelochhead and past the base again. He doesn't look at the protest, swelled with the arrival of other protesters.

'Do they have jobs too? I mean, is it like a revolving protest? A tag team?'

'I don't know. We've never spoken about it at work.'

'You see them every day. Aren't you curious?'

'About what?'

'What keeps them going. I'd like to know.'

He imagines Aggie approaching them with the flagon. Then imagines if she did so holding it on her shoulder, pointing at them like a bazooka. He indicates right onto the A817. On the map there is a clear division between beige and green where they drive over the Auchengaich Burn and the Trossachs begin. But there is no such marked alteration in the landscape. It is heather and sphagnum moss behind and ahead of them for a mile. Then a stretch of pines line the road before disappearing again, and the land breaks through, hills to the right and a field of sheep to the left.

'So what is it, do you think?' Aggie asks. 'What keeps them going?'

He's doing a steady sixty, the road is empty, it is just them and the sheep.

'Okay, you grump,' says Aggie, and she turns away.

'Anger,' he offers. 'Habit? It's good to believe in something, I guess.'

'You think anger? Not compassion?'

'Sure,' he replies without commitment. 'But anger isn't all bad.'

She looks out of the window at the trees. He glances up at the mirror and sees Michael's Audi like something out of Dante's first circle, chasing them to hell.

'Through the winter as well?'

'They don't sleep there.'

'I thought you didn't talk about it?'

'I'm guessing. Maybe they don't sleep in the tents.'

'But they could, I suppose. If they wanted to.'

'On the side of the road? If a truck or a bus went off the curb...'

'I imagine it's the cold they're more bothered about.'

'Why don't you go and ask, then?' he says in a way that he immediately regrets. He's almost forgotten what he's said by the time she replies.

'I think you should, don't you?'

They're not far from the junction where he will turn left, away from the golf club and spa that has colonised this side of the forest, and up the side of the loch to Ben Vorlich. It will be his first Munro. It's an initiation, Aggie has told him many times. Perhaps that's why she's brought out the big flask. She has nearly a hundred Munros. He doubts if their marriage is going to make it to his second. He wants to drive straight on, not stop at the junction, through the golf club and the eighteenth fairway and straight into Loch Lomond to forever haunt the place, him and his wife who he makes eternally angry, and he can hear the stories, two people who loved each other once and got married and for no reason other than the fact he could not fucking open up to her, he drove them off a golf course to their deaths in an old jalopy that, when they dig it out years later, has a flagon of tea in the boot that is still steaming hot.

He indicates and turns left, and they drive on. If he responds to her anger now it will lead to an argument, and they've barely left home. He reaches over and puts a hand on her knee. She stiffens, then relaxes, turns the radio on. She scans the channels searching for something that isn't news, that isn't *The Archers*, that isn't something that will tell them how the world is this morning.

They park their cars half a mile from the foot of Ben Vorlich. The peak reaches into a cloudy sky, a craggy, green and black hill or rather a belt of hills that he guesses will be a tougher hike than it looks. Michael and Rachel are excited and daunted. They change into their walking boots and check they have everything. The bazooka of tea is staying in the car, reward for the return journey. There are a dozen cars but no other walkers in range. The sky is bright enough not to lead them to worry. This is what he needs. What they need. They haven't traipsed enough, swanned around enough; not, looking up at the Munro, that this is going to be like swanning around the city on a Sunday afternoon. He ties his laces, feels a breeze on his neck.

Once they're walking he feels good, and encourages Aggie to tell Michael and Rachel about her classes. About *Greg*, even. Rachel and Michael listen with that detached, middle-class concern he knows he was guilty of in the community centre. Seeing it on them makes him understand how it looked on him. They're not bad people, Michael and Rachel. But they are privileged—as he is. At least Aggie's dragging them both out of that world. Trying to.

There are red kites. A few, then a handful, then a dozen circling the peaks.

'There's a farmer near here who takes out his food waste and feeds them,' he says.

'What, the birds?' asks Michael.

'On a tractor,' Aggie adds. 'I don't know why he has a trailer full of meat.'

'Is he a chicken farmer?' Anthony thinks out loud. 'But yes, during the winter, the farmer throws out this whole load of slurry for them. There are pictures. It's something from a Hitchcock movie.'

'Why does he feed them?' Michael asks.

'We feed garden birds,' Anthony says. 'The farmer's doing the same. For us it's robins and blue tits. For him it's carrion birds.'

'With old chickens?'

'Better than pulping them.'

'Pulping?' asks Rachel, staring across at him as they tramp on.

'Old birds who don't lay enough eggs to be productive. Feeding them costs money, so they get rid of them. They pulp them into feed that they give to—'

'Oh, stop,' says Rachel. 'Stop, that's horrible.'

'It's what happens,' he shrugs.

'This way,' says Aggie, and they follow an incline and in a moment they're all breathing hard, hands on thighs for leverage up the path.

When it flattens out they walk on in silence. He's looking up at the birds. Wide fingered wings circling above some spotted prey, a small mammal that is too cunning and quick for human eyes but not for the kites. The ground is soft in places and it makes the uphill stretches an effort. The air has an autumn crispness that is reviving. They pass a fallen tree covered along its length with creamy, fan-shaped fungi which they stop and admire. The trunk glistens, and he studies the patterns as if they're oils and acrylics and he an art historian and this a gallery of grave beauty. The others have walked on ahead, and when they're out of earshot he hears the water that's running down the gulley. He recalls picking wild garlic in June along a stream. The garlic had flowers like white sparklers, but the leaves were turning, not as pungent as if they'd been picked a month earlier. It was their first weekend walk after moving into the cottage. The first time he had foraged for a long time. They made pesto with the leaves; put the rest into that evening's curry. It had given him hope that such days would be a fixture of their marriage, now they'd moved away from the city. But other demands encroached: fixing the cottage up, getting rid of the dankness, Aggie finding a job. His nine to five. Yet it lingered, the hope. They would spend more time outside, below the circling kites. He catches up with the others. They've been talking about him. They smile at each other and carry on in a silence that never quite loses its awkwardness.

Reaching the peak doesn't take as long as he was expecting. From the top they can look down to Garelochhead, and the base, but the day is too grey for a good view. Anyway, he looks east and north. There are five more walkers, another group of four and a single man, and they give each other the good grace of space to enjoy their summiting in the way they hoped for, free from the press of others. For a moment he takes Aggie's arm so that he's intimate with both her and the hill. He looks across the land, absorbs what he needs from its statuary ways.

They walk back mostly in silence. They're halfway down amongst the pines and ready for a rest when he catches a glimpse of something in a tree. Something red. He instructs the others to look.

'It's not one of those birds?' asks Rachel.

He points. One by one they see it, and even Rachel is taken with the squirrel. Sitting on a branch high up above them with its mucky crown of scarlet, balancing its long tail over the branch. Their sudden halt alerts the little critter and it freezes, wondering which way to escape, and then runs off. Not nearly as fast nor agile, he thinks, as the grey. The red has a courtlier shuffle.

They begin walking again, the path bending round to the right and down a slope.

'Always been good at spotting wildlife,' says Michael. 'Haven't you, buddy?'

'If you say so.'

'Yes you have, don't be coy,' Aggie says.

'It's where your career was heading at one point.'

'Was it?'

'The effect on animals. Those bugs. Didn't you help that artist identify her bugs?'

'I remember,' says Aggie. 'What was her name. She was European, right?'

'Camilla...' Michael guesses.

'Cornelia,' he says.

'That's right.' Michael turns to Rachel. 'Made paintings of mutated bugs from...'

'From?" Rachel asks.

Michael doesn't answer immediately. Then turns to Anthony. 'Was she, you know... Ukrainian?'

'*You know*, no,' Anthony says sharply, mocking his friend. *What the fuck?* He stops short of saying anything else. But he's left the others on eggshells. 'Swiss. She was...is Swiss.'

Michael looks down at the floor, tramps on.

'Bugs?' asks Rachel, keen to smooth over what's passed between them.

'The size of serving plates,' he says, and Rachel shudders. *Good*, he thinks, meanly. Michael shoots him a look. 'Sorry. I'm just joking. She was interested in the impact of radiation from the soil on the bugs. They all had missing legs. Oversized feelers, deformed body sections. That's all. They weren't massive or anything.'

'She painted them in watercolours, didn't she?' says Aggie.

He nods. 'Like botanic paintings. Out of an entomology textbook.'

True bugs, he recalls — that's what they were called. Malformed by their crouching and digging, purely for being alive and prey to human disaster.

'She's been collecting them for years. Still is. Since... She wanted to go back twenty years after, see if it was still the case. She asked me to go with her.'

'And you went?'

Rachel has her arms crossed over her chest, questioning him gingerly. She doesn't know how far to go into this past. She knows; Michael would have told her. But *he's* never told her. That makes a difference.

He shakes his head.

'The timing...' he begins, but he's fed up of lying. 'No. No, I didn't.'

'Wasn't only bugs,' says Michael, swerving the subject. 'Birds and mammals too. All deformed.'

'Oh that's horrible,' says Rachel.

It was. An ecology of distortion and collapse. He remembers the barn swallows with tumours and albinism; the bank voles with missing eyes. The spiders who could not spin webs. The dogs who became wolves again. He'd wanted to go back but that conference paper ruined things. By the time the artist assembled her team, he was being ushered out of Oxford. But then that was an excuse for other things he didn't want to admit.

'That was going to be your area wasn't it,' Michael says. 'The

Animals of—'

Its name still carries a residue, a curse. To say it is to do more than utter the word. They're like radioactive actors who won't mention the Scottish Play.

'But you didn't?' asks Rachel, breaking the spell. 'Carry on with animals?'

Aggie squeezes his hand to distract him. This is where he'd be angry. He *was* going to be the expert in the field. In the mutation of a swathe of living things out of sight of the world. He was going to discover the explicit ways that the radionuclides caused the germline mutations of sperm and egg. He was going to explore its interaction with the mutations in cellular DNA. Could he have applied for the postdoc funding elsewhere? Ridden out the controversies? *Not given that paper?*

'Look,' says Rachel. 'We're back.'

The trees part and they're standing in the car park. He knows he's going to have to drink tea and be cheerful. Aggie's hardly said anything. He wonders if she's disappointed in him. Not just now, but over their life together. If she's dreading the rest of his birthday as much as he is.

'Tea?' Aggie asks them, flagon in hand.

Michael and Rachel go off to run their errands while he and Aggie prepare the house for the party. Around twenty guests, mainly from the village. His colleagues from the lab are invited. Who he's most dreading seeing is David. Aggie busies herself with the food. He tries to create some space in the living room but then gives up, accepts that the chief feature of the room is its coziness. He clears away magazines and runs the hoover over the carpet, noticing the fractal pattern of the faux Persian rug, a diamond intercut with looping arabesques. Once he's done he flops down onto the sofa.

All he's been thinking about since their walk is that April more than a decade ago, and the Twentieth Anniversary Conference of the Chernobyl Disaster. He's standing at the front of the hall. Before him, two hundred attendees. The keynote still to deliver the final lecture after his brief ('keep it to ten minutes, Anthony') cameo. His palms are clammy. His hands are clamped on either side of the lectern. His heart expands to fill his chest. His ears pound. There was no one in the room to whom it meant more — that's why he'd been asked to speak. There were others from Russia and the Ukraine and Belarus, but older men. Men who had been men at the time, scientists who experienced the accident and political theatre firsthand. The radiologist from Belarus who'd seen the cloud rain down on his family home was the first to put a hand on Anthony's shoulder during drinks after the paper. But not even he had the story Anthony owned. And didn't he give it freely? His story validated everything these men worked for: a child survivor who'd come back to love nuclear power.

They'd invited him to give a brief presentation as way of introducing the keynote. For those few months leading up to the conference, he was invited to department meetings, brought in on applications. The conference promised to be a defining moment in his career. And it had, but not in the way he'd hoped.

He went beyond his remit. He'd delivered a paper that wowed the audience with his research on animals and the spread of radionuclides within exclusion zones, not knowing he was stealing the keynote's thunder. He saw Professor Challen squirm but thought it was the uncomfortable wooden seats in Lady Margaret Hall. Surely Challen should have checked with Anthony about the subject matter? Which made it worse, of course; his Professor made to look incompetent. He'd overreached himself. His academic career prowled like a wolf before being caught in a spring steel trap, lingering, yowling, to die.

It wasn't only the conference that marked him as politically naïve, according to the department later. Anthony's survivor status made him unpredictable. 'You've got to think about your place in the hierarchy,' Professor Challen reprimanded him. 'You've got a chip on your shoulder about this *thing*,' and Challen flapped a hand, pacing around his office. 'You're not the first young *protégé* to think he knows it all. You all get your comeuppance, and this is yours. Unfortunately yours was in front of two hundred people—and one very miffed one.'

'Fucking academics,' he'd said to Michael in the Salmon and Compasses after, commiserating over a pint of stout.

'We're academics,' Michael replied.

He shrivels at the memory. Professor Challen had liked him, up to that point. *This thing*, Challen had called it. His *childhood*. Waved away by a stuffy professor, who said he'd overstated its importance, his right to claim it. It was snobbery, fucking snobbery, and Anthony hated it, only knew how much the moment that snobbery turned on him and ejected him from its seat of privilege.

Oxford. A separate life. He luxuriates in the anguish and berates himself for the indulgence as Aggie comes into the lounge. He looks up at her.

'We're missing a few things. I don't think we've got enough spirits.'

After their conversation about the haunted cottage, this brings an arched eyebrow. But it's not more fairytale newlyweds he imagines, but a series of images that flash across his mind: the squirrel, the kites, then the whales. He follows her out of the lounge and into the kitchen. She gives him a list.

'A few other bits. I forgot olives.'

'That's because you hate them.'

'Hate is an overused word.'

'Is it? By who?'

She doesn't answer. She looks him in the eye.

'So who...the woman...' Aggie begins.

He's already picking up the shopping bags from the cupboard under the sink.

'Tonight. When my colleagues...you can't—'

'I'm not an idiot,' Aggie sighs. 'I won't mention anything.'

There's more than a note of wretchedness in her complaint and it turns his thoughts to brittle sticks. He goes out to the car and begins the drive to the shop, but knows that's not where he's going first.

The crowd from earlier has dispersed. The only two left are the usual pair. The man in the many-coloured layers stands up and waves a newspaper at him, pointing to the front page. Anthony squints. He can't quite see what's on the front cover, it's too far away, but it's a big picture, somewhere outdoors. A beach. He can't see it clearly, but knows it's about the whales.

He drives past the base's entrance and turns up a nearby lane that disappears behind a ramshackle shed and caravan on bricks. They belong to a smallholding, perhaps once a farm but now a scrap yard, all mud and crooked endeavours at breaking. When the car is hidden from view he pulls over and switches off the engine. There's no guarantee that, with the Hyundai in its decrepit state, the people who live on the scrapyard won't think he's dumped the car for them to dismantle. *Good luck to them if they can get it started without the key.* He gets out and slams the door. The air is rich with the smell of rust and cow shit. He puts his hood up and pushes his hands into his pockets, walks down the lane with his shoulders around his ears and crosses the road to the camp. The man is sitting down again, with the newspaper spread over his lap.

'Hello,' says the woman.

'Are you making tea?' he asks.

'Seems so. Tom, get another chair.'

Before the man—Tom—can say anything, she ushers him away. Tom stands and walks off with the newspaper, glaring at Anthony. The woman directs him to take the other man's seat. 'Go on,' she encourages. He sits down. He looks around at the tents.

'She's not here,' says the old woman. 'If that's who you're looking for?'

He shakes his head, but cannot, if the old woman's smile is anything to go by, hide the look on his face. He listens to Tom complaining and rummaging around inside the tent as the woman pulls out a third silver camping mug from a cardboard box under the table, followed by a teabag. Tom comes back with an old striped beach chair, which folds out like a gate. It snaps into position and Tom places it down on the other side of the table, looking at him.

'Not wanting to get spotted here?' Tom points, indicating Anthony's hood.

'Milk?' says the woman.

He shakes his head. 'Just black, thanks, and weak.'

'Wave the bag at the cup, right?'

He wrestles a hand out of his pocket, reaches over to shake the man's hand. 'Anthony,' he introduces himself.

The man stares without reciprocating.

'I'm Maureen,' says the woman. 'Or Mo, to most. And that's Tom.' She's pouring water in the cups, whips the bag out of his and puts it in a bin under the table. 'Tom isn't too trusting of people who come from the base.'

'Who would be,' says Tom, 'when there's shit like this happening?'

Tom holds up the newspaper. It's the local *Herald*. Anthony stares at the front page. Navy barriers around the whales. He's inside, hidden by those fences. There is no picture of the whales, just an inset photo of a pilot whale breaching, with a caption he can't read. The headline is incriminating enough: 'NAVY HIDES DEAD WHALES AT PORTKIL.' He's reading the first paragraph when Tom snatches the paper away and slaps it on the table.

'So what brings you to us this evening?' Tom asks. 'On a Saturday? Is that because none of your colleagues will see you? Had your cages rattled by the papers? You're not the most inconspicuous of spies, you know.'

He wonders how these people cannot sense what's been released by the accident. But perhaps they do. Perhaps that's why they're always here. He follows Tom's eyes as a noise reaches his ears. A car, turning into the base.

'Ah. Not officially here, then,' gloats Tom.

'Don't listen to him,' says Maureen. She says it kindly, but looks fierce. 'You're not the first to come from the base. Every now and then someone wanders over, has fun with us. But then you've probably thought of that?'

She offers him his cup. It burns his hands. The tea is the colour of cardboard.

'No, actually. I've not thought about it. If people come and join you from in there they're—'

'So you're *joining* us now,' says Tom, and laughs.

'Tom, stop it.'

'A comfy job in there with all the *lies*, or living with *the truth* out here?'

'Ignore him,' she says, 'plenty of people have come and stayed for a cup of tea at least. Do you want a biscuit?'

'You mean people who've worked at the base?' He takes one. 'Thanks.'

'Over time. Those who are on their way out.' She looks at him. He struggles not to look away. 'We've been here a while, you see.'

He nods, dips the biscuit and eats the soggy half. They rarely have biscuits at home. The shortbread—how clichéd—Aggie's mum makes them. Aggie will sometimes do a tray bake of flapjacks that Aggie's mum still turns her nose up at. *It's not what's done to oats*, her father always said, as if there was an ancient regulation in the land they'd transgressed by adding syrup and raisins and sugar.

'Can't think they care about us that much anymore,' Maureen carries on. 'But we stay on, don't we, Tom? Once you start something it has its own momentum.'

Tom picks up the paper.

'So come on. What about the whales? Aren't you even going to say sorry?'

He drinks more tea, stretching to see the paper.

'I'm not Navy, I'm civilian.' He speeds up. 'There's a distinction. It means I don't know about *a lot* of what happens. So those whales. What happened?'

'It doesn't say,' says Maureen. 'I suppose there are a few possibilities. But when you've been watching the Navy do what it does for as long as we have...'

'Like those sperm whales in Lincolnshire, last year,' Tom says, rolling the paper up into a baton and rapping it on his knee. 'All your military manoeuvres, the bombs. Deafening the poor buggers, sending them into shallow waters. You have some bloody death wish and you're not happy until you've wiped out all the other species who get in the way of your games.'

'Didn't someone paint a CND sign on the tail of one of those whales?' Anthony asks. He remembers the pictures of huge bodies on the wide, flat sands. True creatures, each a sad illustration, something out of *Moby Dick*.

'No one from CND would do that,' says Tom, waving the paper.

'No one *not* from CND would, would they?'

'They probably did,' says Maureen. 'Someone from CND. Which is wrong. Trying to make a statement about how your Navy sees whales as collateral. You understand the anger of people, do you, Anthony?' She sighs. 'Such beautiful creatures, whales. More intelligent than us. Their cerebral cortex is much bigger than ours.'

'It's a bloody whale,' says Tom.

'I mean proportionally. The paper doesn't say what happened, Tom?'

Another car passes. This time he doesn't shrink. He's thought of a cover story. The Hyundai broke down. He's imagining how he'll be lauded for reconnaissance, not wired to a polygraph. And as he's thinking it, he knows it doesn't matter anyway.

'You know, I've always thought of the base as an animal,' he says, not looking at either of them. 'People don't think of elements as alive. But everything is atoms. Everything moves at its core.'

Tom wants to speak, but Maureen stops him. Anthony takes a sip of his tea. She's made it perfectly. It comes out too strong from Aggie's pots. He doesn't mind, but this is how he likes it, and then laughs at himself. Tea. How British. He suddenly feels embarrassed for what he's said about the base. A living animal. But he's started now.

'If you think of the radioactive heart of the place... I'm not talking about the weapons so much as the subs. The submarines.'

'We know what subs are, thank—'

Maureen shushes Tom. Tom picks up his tea and drinks.

'We monitor the base. Or I do. That's my job. I'm one of the biomonitors. I was brought in to introduce some new procedures. For safety. The weapons, well, I guess the weapons are what you're protesting about, is that right?'

Tom lets off a loud, aggressive 'Ah!' and turns away.

'It's the readiness for war,' says Maureen, leaning forward, knees together. They could all be friends having lunch after a ramble. This could be an older couple that he and Aggie have adopted as new friends, elders of the mountain to lead them back to the path. 'The willingness for war, all of it. Not only the bombs.'

'Missiles,' he corrects her, and immediately regrets it.

'It's the hundred billion pounds,' says Tom, plonking his cup on the camping table. His tea erupts and spills on the grass. 'In this austerity, which is a load of bollocks by the way, it's a political choice, not a necessity, we're cutting people's tax credits and sending children to food banks and then spending a hundred billion pounds on a weapons system to kill millions of people in poor countries and it's a system we'll never use *because'* —

Tom takes a breath—'because *the world has changed*. No, that's fucking wrong. We *never* needed nuclear weapons. This whole fucking edifice of war, this whole *beast*... you want to think about it in those terms? Your base is an animal? It's a beast then, isn't it? You think a permanent at-sea deterrent is going to stop a fundamentalist from driving a car into people on the high street in Swindon?' Tom slouches, strangles a sigh. 'Or Burnley? If we didn't go around bombing everyone we wouldn't be a target.'

'If you're here all the time,' says Maureen, more softly, 'you have a lot of time to think about this. But tell us what you do. What is it you monitor?'

Anthony has both hands wrapped around the cup. It's not as if Tom's telling him anything he hasn't heard before—or thought himself. All the arguments he and Aggie went through before he took the job.

'I run the testing for the site. I mean the site. I didn't come for the missiles. I'm not actually Navy... The soil. The animals.' But it's too cryptic, and their attention hardens. Tom leans in.

'You're culpable. You're there to wrap the things in cotton wool and secrecy. There's always a few of you with troubled consciences. And you come out here, assuage whatever guilt it is you're feeling, and then fuck off back inside.'

Anthony looks to Maureen.

'Where there's smoke,' she says. She picks up the paper. 'They were here earlier. Scottish CND. Did you see them? Was a lot of fun. It's strange this happens now... the whales. They were coming anyway for the anniversary. Fifty years of CND this weekend.' She shakes her head. 'Fifty years, and we've not learnt much, have we?'

He wants to tell them that he's got nothing to do with the whales. That he's come back so he can help the whales, at least more whales in the future. The other animals.

'Hadn't you better go?' says Tom. 'Go and take some bloody samples?'

Back at the car it takes Anthony nearly five minutes to find the shopping list Aggie gave him. He's shouting in frustration when he finds it in the belly pocket of his hoodie, although he cannot remember putting it there. Also in there is the younger woman's card. He can't remember putting that there, either. He reads it, properly.

He puts it back in his hoodie, starts the car, knows that when he gets back Aggie will be wondering what's taken him so long.

Victoria if you're my mum.

He thought she was a journalist.

'Well, that was all a bit strange,' says Aggie.

It's midnight and the four of them are in the kitchen clearing up. Anthony's eyes are closed. They've been closed most of the night, if not actually then metaphorically. Closed as he was talking to people; as he blew out the candles on the cake Aggie had baked and hidden in the larder; closed as his friends and village acquaintances prompted him to make a wish, a different wish, one that wasn't tied up with the faces floating in front of his eyes.

His right hand is flat on the kitchen table. His fingertips feel their way across the freshly wiped wood. It's clammy, and he sees the tree covered in fungi. He breathes in saffron and preserved lemons, the lingering smell of the tagine they'd made for people to help themselves. Almond couscous. Too exotic for some of the villagers. He runs his tongue around the front of his teeth. He hears Aggie busy herself, Michael wiping dishes that Rachel has cleaned. The boiler bursts into life with every turn of the hot tap. Michael asks where the flutes go. Aggie says 'here' and opens the dresser door. He rubs the cool surface of the pebble in his pocket. A thousand perforations, the pebble more hole than stone. Atoms of protons and neutrons swirling, spinning.

Aggie leaves the kitchen. Rachel is nearly through with the glassware. Michael has put away all the flutes and is looking for where the tumblers go. Hans, Elspeth's husband, brought whisky—Ledaig, single malt straight from the distillery they'd visited on their tour around the islands. Anthony, Michael, Hans, Mariam's husband John, and two others from their village all had a tumbler of whisky. Some without ice. They'd questioned Hans on which was his preferred malt, how it compared to German liquor. Anthony withdrew from the small talk and Hans, with his Teutonic outsider status, became the focus of attention. All the while Anthony's eyes were closing. Mariam and John left after the first tumbler. John grumbling as he put on his windcheater that there was no rush to leave. But Mariam complained of a headache, kissed Aggie on both cheeks. Anthony shook John's hand and thanked him for coming, opened and closed the door, avoided Aggie's look and then didn't avoid it, then walked off, closed his eyes, bumped into the bannister.

Just then Elspeth pushed her head out through the lounge door. They got a burst of Miles Davis, and laughter coming from the room behind her.

'Oh,' said Elspeth, unsure of their silence in the hallway. 'Sorry. I—the loo.'

Aggie directed her up the stairs. Elspeth brushed past, her elbows pointing down as if she were forcing her way through a crowd. He and Aggie stood in silence as Elspeth ran lightly up the stairs and locked herself in the bathroom.

'How serious is it?' Aggie asked him.

'Not now.'

'Yes, *now*.'

He didn't reply. Upstairs, the toilet flushed.

'I mean your boss didn't come, your other boss leaves—'

'She's not my other boss.'

'You're mixing wine and whisky.'

'And water. Don't forget the water.'

The bathroom door opened. Elspeth passed through the middle of their argument and back into the lounge. Aggie put a hand on the balustrade.

'It's like you're going around your own party with your eyes closed,' she'd said. She looked like she might sing. He smiled and it irritated her. Aggie swung around and walked off. *Greg,* he thought. *Fuck you.*

'The tennis ball,' he said.

'What?'

'The tennis ball. The dog toy, in the car.'

'I don't know what you're playing at, but you want to think about how awkward you're making it for everyone else.'

Anthony opens his eyes, squints at the light. Aggie comes into the kitchen carrying one of the chairs. She scrapes the chair on the tile floor as she pushes it under the table. She moves some of the last dirty plates and bowls over to the sink, the final stragglers of the clear up. The *clean-up.*

'Funny your boss David didn't make it,' says Michael. 'Where do these go?'

Michael's holding a tumbler at arm's length, like a rock specimen. Anthony stands up and takes the glass.

'Here, let me. He's a bit stressed.'

He opens the cupboard door for the tumblers, joins in the production line.

'You've had a bit to drink, haven't you,' says Michael. 'You're tired. Mind you, midnight, it's way past your bedtime.'

'Anthony, why don't you go to bed,' says Aggie. 'You're half asleep.'

She's not doing it out of kindness. She doesn't want to see him. She doesn't want to come to bed while he's awake. He wonders if Michael and Rachel sense it. They resume the washing up. Michael hands him a clean tumbler.

'I don't think that's a bad idea, buddy. I've not had as many as you and it's going to be a job sleeping my load off.'

He's suddenly awfully tired.

'We can go for breakfast in Glasgow,' says Aggie, drying

her hands on a tea towel, still trying to make a success of the weekend. 'We're both driving in—'

'No!' begins Rachel, dropping a tumbler back into the basin. 'We have to...'

Michael gives Aggie a conciliatory smile.

'Well, that's awkward,' says Anthony. There's bile in his throat. He gives Michael and Rachel a stiff hug and crawls upstairs into bed. He can't be bothered to brush his teeth. He leaves the light on. He knows David did not come because David could not bear to face him. Could not bear to be humiliated, as he must have been, for the breach of security. Or rather, it is not Anthony's face that David cannot bear to see, but the faces they have both seen and that they would see in each other. Only he and David have seen the woman, know that she will die.

'So give me a fucking break,' he says, but no one's there. He's going to be sick.

He wakes up with a jump. The lights are off. Aggie's next to him. She's not saying anything; he thinks she's asleep. He listens for other sounds, twists onto his front. Puts his head under the pillow. Too much whisky. Too many faces. Too many words.

Krizi.

Crisis.

Numb arms, pins and needles. You can prick them and I can't feel them.

The words coming now, he knows, even when drunk, because they are the only things that can push away the face that he cannot bear to see.

May 1988–March 1989, Kyiv

He feels himself glowing red with shame, too old to be sitting on his father's knee. He wriggles, but he is held in place, his father's hands on either side of his ribs. He is told to sit still, and he tries to, he does. He feels the stare of the doctor's sad blue eyes from the other side of the desk in this stuffy surgery office. Behind the doctor are shelves, bundles of papers in brown files tied together with green and white striped string. One shelf is filled with thick black books. The rest are empty except for a coffee cup, a certificate in a frame, two jars with nothing in them. Anatolii's father puts him down on another seat with a bump. Then his father is rolling up a trouser leg. They all look. Just above his father's ankle is a ring of puckered skin. Anatolii has seen it before, this strange, dangling part of his father's leg that has formed itself into a hollow. The knot in Anatolii's chest pulls tighter.

'Come, come,' his father waves to his mama, who is sitting to one side. Anatolii's mama has lit a cigarette and is smoking. Anatolii's never seen her smoking before. She hands his father the cigarette, who pushes it through the ring of skin without touching the sides. The doctor is looking away, shaking his head.

'The result of direct contact,' his father says. His father is trembling with the effort to hold his leg at desk height so they can all see. His father used to hold Anatolii above his head with only one hand, so high he nearly touched the ceiling. They would both be laughing. '*You* told me it's a local skin burn.'

'I didn't tell you,' says the doctor, tapping a red pen on the desk.

'Direct contact with a radiation source. I was—'

'It must have been a colleague who saw you.'

'So I was hallucinating, and delirious,' says his father.

'You need to calm down.' The doctor is young. His voice is

sure, level. His father drops his leg and takes a long drag on the cigarette, exhales a great pall of smoke over the desk and into the doctor's face.

'Look at us.' His father coughs, chest shaking. 'Aren't we suffering?'

The doctor looks at them all, then brightens, as if he's thought of something.

'Do you want your children to go to the special school? They will need six conditions to qualify. I can arrange their tests if you prefer.'

'No one will hire me. Even with my good work history before the accident.'

'Before his service,' adds his mother.

'And what of your *lichnost*?' asks the doctor, now impatient. 'You're begging, you come to me begging. I do not dish out benefits, I'm not one of the administrators.'

Anatolii wonders, is this doctor a good person? Does he have children, and do his children sit on his bony knee and play Cossacks and Robbers? He wonders what kind of home the doctor has. It must be a big one, with seven rooms, and a garden. Perhaps they play Game the Bear. But even this doesn't make Anatolii want to be the child of the doctor. The doctor lives in the city, his children don't know the forest. They cannot play Rabbits in the Forest. But then that game is too young for Anatolii now. This makes him feel better, but he still wants to get out of the doctor's office.

His mother is crying. 'You can give us the tie.'

'To the accident?' The doctor shakes his head. 'Look, fill in these forms.' He pulls out a sheaf of papers from a drawer. 'Then come back and we'll put you through the tests.'

His father leans forward as if he's going to take the papers and then they can leave, but instead he picks them up and throws them across the desk. Some scatter onto the floor. The doctor leaves them where they fall and leans back in his chair. The doctor looks sad, undoes the top button of his shirt behind his tie. 'I've had the tests!' shouts his father. 'You've seen my results.' 'Vegetovascular dystonia?' asks the doctor. 'Was it VvD?'

'Caused by "environmental" factors in general,' his father sneers, and lifts up his leg again. 'How is this hole "in general"?'

'We should've bought chocolates,' his mama's saying, and then turns to the doctor. 'What do you want? Chocolates? Vodka? What can we get you?'

The doctor is shaking his head, as is his uncle Kulyk, who's sat quietly at the back of the room. Anatolii looks at him. His uncle shrugs.

'To be *poterpili* you must...'

He's heard this term before. Only *poterpili* get the tie to the benefits. Only when you get the tie do you get paid enough for being sick. But to get the tie you have to fill in the forms and see a doctor, and a doctor has to stamp the forms and sometimes, Anatolii is beginning to understand, that this is in return for chocolate and vodka. His father stands and without warning picks Anatolii up and holds him like a young baby, like Sveta's little cotton doll with the black eyes. He squirms, his father's hands are pinching his arms and it hurts.

'We are the living dead,' his father says, holding Anatolii as he wriggles. 'Two years now. Still nothing in two years other than the payment for the work, and that is all gone. The memory is gone. Oh my ancestors! How we live now, they're embarrassed for us... Yes, I'm *poterpili*. But what do survivors do? How do we live? I tell you this: we've lost everything—we go around like corpses.'

They return to Kulyk's apartment. Anatolii is given a few *kopecks* and told to go and buy ices, and take Sveta. There's a playground and he leaves Sveta there. There are other children about, they will watch her. She shouts at him and begins to cry but he walks off. His mother can see Sveta from the window, can't she? It will be okay. It's a short walk to the store. He has to cross a road. He's seven now. He knows how to cross a road. And he knows that his father didn't get what he wanted. Even so, the knot in his chest is less tight now they're not in the doctor's office. He feels calm and sad. He's let his father down, and his mama, but he doesn't know how; only that he was meant to show the doctor something, and he didn't. He would've suggested they play a game. Would that have been what they wanted from him, his mama and his father? He kicks the grass along the side of the road as he walks to the store. In the store he gets an ice for himself that is twice the size of the one he gets Sveta.

When he returns Sveta is not in the playground. He feels something he cannot name. He's eaten his ice, and hers is melting. He scours the play area. He jumps up into the climbing frame one-handed, sticks his head up the slides to see if she's hiding there. He asks the other children but they all just look at him. They don't know him, he doesn't speak with their accent. He runs back to the flat, unsure if he's more afraid of Sveta's ice melting before someone gets to eat it, or that mama will smack him for letting Sveta disappear. When he gets back there's an argument going on in the living room. Sveta is there already, sitting under the dining table with her doll. He's angry with her for leaving the playground. He stands in the doorway with the plum-coloured ice melting over his hands. It's like the rain, the sticky black rain that fell in the days after the accident and covered everything. He can't give it to her while she's on the other side of the room, so he begins eating the ice.

'You don't talk about *blat*. This is not how *blat* works,' shouts Kulyk. 'You embarrassed the doctor.'

'Well, what good did you do?' she shouts back. 'Why didn't you think of that before we went in? We should've taken the chocolates.'

'It wouldn't have made a difference. *Blat* needs a *Blatmeister*. You need to find someone who knows the doctor. But it's too late now.'

'Then why are you telling me?' Her face is streaked with black, and for a moment he's terrified because he's been thinking of the rain.

'Can you not think for yourself?' His uncle turns to look at his father lying on the sofa, an arm resting on his forehead, the other falling to the floor. 'Either of you?'

The skin around his father's eyes is red-black, like coals on fire.

Uncle Kulyk leaves early in the morning to pick up his father from Korosten'. Anatolii lives with Kulyk now. Kulyk drives a battered Niva that used to be owned by one of his taxi driver friends. The car is kept in a garage underneath the block they live in. The garage is a trove of brown-handled tools and mysterious jars with faded labels and dirty, musty smelling boxes. It's Anatolii's favourite place to run and play if he's alone in the flat, or if Kulyk is drunk and in a bad mood. This is where his uncle keeps his furniture-making equipment for when he can return to his craft, since the factory no longer needed his services. Kulyk talks a lot about setting up a small factory of his own. He rarely takes the car out—the petrol is too expensive, and the roads outside Kyiv are in ruins. But when Kulyk does he sometimes takes Anatolii, who pretends he's in the back of a KGB car. There are no handles on the doors ('Ah, *lapochka*, that's to stop the criminals letting themselves out'). They sometimes drive across Kyiv to visit Kulyk's buddies, and Anatolii sits in the back looking out of the window scanning for dissidents of the Chechen rebellion. He knows where Chechnya is on the map, they learn about it in school. The terrorists are attempting to break away from the Soviet to join the West and steal the Union's land. He lays low on the back seat, and transmits the details of the people he sees in the little walkie-talkie Kulyk has made for him out of an old transistor radio.

'You want to come collect your father?' his uncle asked the

night before.

It was a favourite thing, this adventure in the car. But his father might want to sit in the back with him, treat him like a baby. He could stay at Kulyk's and play in the garage instead? See if some of the other boys were around?

He decides not to go. Kulyk tells him to be in the house when they return, to have some tea ready and to warm the flat by turning the boiler on an hour before they arrive and getting the blankets out and leaving them on the sofa for his father. He agrees to all of this, but is already thinking of the garage, of what extra food there is in the pantry he can eat without Kulyk knowing. If he can find any coins lying around he can use them to buy himself some *Alenka* bars, or if the little grocer's doesn't have any, then *RotFront*. He's discovered sweets since living with his uncle. There was never anything in the shop in Radynka. Only fruit and salt and bread. He doesn't find any loose coins. Kulyk is careful with his money, even the *kopecks*.

He's in the garage opening boxes and looking through what he finds: old women's clothes, mainly. These are not all his uncle's boxes. It's a communal garage, just like on the *kolkhoz*, so he guesses he won't get in trouble, and anyway he's not taking anything, just looking. Then he finds some old newspapers. They're faded and brittle to touch. He flicks through. They're not that old, in fact, but turned brown by the stale underground air. He can read a little; some of the words he doesn't understand, but it's obvious they're about the explosion. The earliest he finds is 14th May then 16th May, 19th May. Copies of *Pravda* and *Komsomolskaya Pravda* and *Izvestia*, sometimes from the same day. In school they see the teachers only with *Pravda*, but his uncle reads *Izvestia* if he reads a paper at all. He pulls them out and lays them on the empty floor where the Niva usually sits under its tarp. He squats down with one knee up like a little mountain and he looks through the papers. There is a picture of their Secretary General, Gorbachev, Silly Spilly Head they call him when the teachers aren't around. There's a headline about *Western Lies* and a picture of a huge concrete building with lots of scaffolding, and pictures of the faces of firemen who are heroes. He thinks of the fire trucks and the hill and the smoke. The *vertolit* carrying their heavy bags. Sveta pulling on his arm. *'I want to go home now.'* He reads the article, as much as he can. It's about the power plant at Chernobyl. The death toll was nine—the firemen who are heroes—and a further two hundred ninety-nine were hospitalised with poisoning. Something called 'fallout' has been identified as far away as America. But the lies being told about the Soviet Union by Western countries were *merzennyy*. He doesn't know the world, but understands the situation was not as the Americans said it was.

He notices the time. He shoves the papers back into the boxes and runs out of the garage. In the flat, he switches on the boiler and scrabbles around, puts blankets on the sofa and a bucket on the floor next to it, and then boils the *samovar* and sits in the kitchen and waits. He's hungry but it's too late to raid the pantry. He sits looking out of the window at the flat white clouds, and waits.

His father coughs coming up the stairs. His father has yellow skin, and his hair is short and somehow darker. He's walking with a stick, and it's the best thing about his father now, this stick made from the aspen of the forest by one of the woodworkers of the Radcha *kolkhoz*. The Red Forest—the trees stripped of leaves and bark. He knows the aspen leaf is shaped like a dome, like the Kremlin.

His father gives him a weak smile and a stinking hug. He's come to Kyiv for an appointment. After a short lie down on the sofa, his father's up and they're all going to meet some other men. It's a *hrupu*. Kulyk drives them to the Pavlova Clinic of the Division of Neurological Diseases on the other side of the city. His father sits in the front while Anatolii slinks across the back seat, imagining the traitors from Chechnya outside, radioing in their locations to the KGB.

At the hospital they find the day room of Ward Four. This is where the men gather. Most are living here, his father says. There are more than a dozen, men of the same age as his father. It's difficult to tell. Anatolii thinks they must be part of the two hundred and ninety-nine that the papers talked about. Those who got sick but didn't die. The dayroom is chaotic; all chairs and sofas and tables thrown around with the arrangements of the ill and their visitors. The men are not allowed to smoke here, but on an occasion like this—a *hrupu* meeting—it's full of cigarette fumes and ash and his eyes begin watering. The resident men are in striped pyjamas and coloured housecoats, threadbare around the hems and elbows. He's the youngest son, although not the only one. The room is hot and feels greasy with spluttering and coughing. His father is a newcomer, an outsider, but not an unsolicited one. He's a sufferer but not yet official *poterpili*; the *hrupu* is going to help with that, his father told him on the drive over. These men know *blat*.

They're welcomed and introduced. A few ruffle Anatolii's hair, make comments about his likeness to his father. He stares at the lines on his father's face. Anatolii doesn't know what to say, and has the confusing thought that his father no longer knows what to say to him either.

There's a *Blatmeister*: Artem, a miner. The other men are silent as Artem speaks. He's not a big man, but his voice is strong, he speaks in a way that reminds Anatolii of the politicians he hears on the radio sometimes.

His father is invited to speak. Anatolii sinks into the sofa, down into its broken springs and damp, dirty cotton and sits as still as he can.

'I spent twelve weeks driving the bosses around non-stop,' says his father. 'I was in the Zone all that time. They said we'd be two weeks in, then out. But they kept us driving, they didn't pay us until we went back in, and who knows if they would have kept their promises if we'd refused? No one was telling us what was going on. How dangerous it was. We never had our doses. They would take them, and write them down, but they would never tell us. They would say: *okay, go. Two weeks now.* We would ask: what's my dose? But they said it was classified. Our own doses! But you didn't question the Party, did you? And this was the military now, by God. The first car I drove, they buried it. Buried it! They put me into a military car, this one with lead panels. The old women we passed on the road crossed themselves, asked us if there was a new war? The soldiers ignored the women. They were trained. We couldn't ignore them, though. I knew some of them. They were like my own family. One time we stopped and a woman asked if she needed to leave. Could she drink the milk? I couldn't drive anywhere, we were at a fork, we didn't know left or right, I was looking at the map, and this old woman kept begging, so the soldier by the door looks at her. "How old are you, *babushka*?" Seventy-eight. "Then drink the milk," says this soldier. "Drink all you like." She blessed him. Blessed him! He was only a boy but he knew he was going to get ill. They took from us and never gave us back a thing.'

When his father's finished the men applaud. Their clapping wafts the smoke around the room until it makes Anatolii cough. Someone opens a window and the fresh air blows into their faces, and the smoke lifts before a man in a red gown with a straggly beard and dark skin complains about the cold. Artem puts an arm around his father's shoulder. Anatolii watches from the sofa. He doesn't understand what he's feeling, or rather, feels too many things. There is *lichnost'*. He wants to be in his father's orb now. But there's still the way his father looks, as if this other man, Artem, is holding his father up after the exertions of speaking. His father looks...

How did his father look? The memories are like water; reflections on water. Was it Artem who put his arm around his father's shoulder? Did someone open a window? What was his uncle Kulyk doing? What colour was the sofa? What was *important*?

The men. The men were, to his father. To him, they're particles; attracted to one another; bouncing off one another. What was important was how the men took them under their protection. His father was accepted into the *hrupu*.

'We'll get you your tie,' Artem tells his father. 'Men, together we'll all have stronger ties to our rights. Fuck the doctors who tell us otherwise. It doesn't matter if we don't have our radiation passports. They only need to look us in the eye and hear stories like Nikolai's.'

Artem slaps his father on the back, whispers in his ear, and takes him round the men to hear their stories. Kulyk takes Anatolii to find a coffee machine, if there is one; which there isn't, at least not one they can find.

'Probably in the doctor's room,' Kulyk mutters. 'Shit, I'm thirsty.'

Back at Kulyk's flat, his father won't sit down. He walks around the *kvartyra* talking loudly, holding on to things. Anatolii sits at the table and gets up and sits down again as Kulyk asks him to chop the onion, or fetch something from the pantry. His father asks him if there's some of the old apple wine. He looks at Kulyk before answering. His father sees him looking.

'What, my own boy, watching what I drink?'

He doesn't say it unkindly—his father is in a good mood, perhaps the last good mood he will ever enjoy—but it makes Anatolii queasy. This is Kulyk's house, and Anatolii's not allowed to get things for himself or others.

'He's making sure I don't lose all my supply,' Kulyk replies.

'Come here, Anatolii Nikolaevich,' his father says. 'Bring the wine.'

Anatolii goes into the pantry and takes down the bottle, stopped halfway with a cork. His stomach turns. He returns and puts the bottle on the table.

'No, give, give,' his father tells him. 'What is this? Give the bottle to me.'

'Get glasses,' Kulyk says. Anatolii gives the bottle to his father and goes to the cupboard, gets out two small tumblers.

'Three,' his father says.

For a moment he's paralysed. He leans into the cupboard, looks through to the back, sees the dirty wall behind the cups and glasses, the Russian coffee pot, the small white bowls Kulyk uses if they eat peanuts or *paska* instead of a real dinner. He doesn't mind those nights. He'll go hungry, but it's better to sit at the table with Kulyk when he's in his relaxed mood eating nuts than to sit in silence eating watery *borscht* or stodgy *varenyky* heated up in the blackened pan. His uncle is happier when he's not really eating food, not really taking care of himself like his mama always nags him to. Although Anatolii thinks she doesn't really mean it. She'd rather have her brother sick than her husband. Even as young as he is, he understands this.

He pulls out three glasses. His father's uncorking the bottle. Kulyk is wiping plates at the sink while his father pours wine into the tumblers. Anatolii starts to feel sick. He watches as the wine fills up the glasses.

'Careful for the boy,' says Kulyk.

'He's *my* son,' his father says and bangs the bottle on the table, coughs. He's grinning at Anatolii, but it's a sick grin, the teeth are rotten.

'Come, come,' his father is saying, waving both of them to sit. 'Anatolii, we're not celebrating the fucking saints' day. Today our fortunes turn for the better. We'll be a family again. You'll come to live with your father again. We'll leave that shit town where they put us. Like prisoners! I'll have recognition for what I've suffered.'

'Don't drink it all at once,' Kulyk tells him. 'Nikolai, your son is eight.'

'I know how old my son is,' his father says. 'Don't I, *vovky*?'

The wolf. Tracks in the forest. Are the wolves ill, too? Are their teeth rotten with the same sickness that's in his father's blood? He feels sorrow for the animals. What did the wolves do to deserve their illness? And he's ashamed, because he thinks that, yes, his father *did* do something to deserve his suffering. He just doesn't know what.

'Come, we celebrate, we toast,' his father says.

'Your membership.' Kulyk raises his glass. 'To the *hrupu*.'

'Come, Anatolii, raise your glass, join us men.'

He picks up his glass, the wine is cold. It smells of sour apples.

'We toast,' says his father, and holds his glass out above the middle of the table. His uncle clinks glasses, and glances at Anatolii. He has to stand and lean forward for his glass to meet theirs. He feels proud and sick, excited and terrified, he doesn't want to drink the wine and wants to drink it all. And he thinks again of the wolf, and he thinks: *you aren't a wolf.*

He thinks: *you're dying.*

His father didn't want to join a group at first.

'They're all invalids,' his father had shouted at his mama once, in their new house in Korosten'. His father was sitting at the round table in the *kvartyra*, a small bowl of winter broth in front of him. Soup was all he could stomach. Even the barley had to be mashed. After his father had gone to bed their mama would let them eat potatoes and whatever meat they'd scavenged. Sometimes eggs. Everything had to be washed five times. (Mama stood in the middle of the *kvartyra* and held that blue bucket by the handle with both hands. Someone in the town told them to go as far from their house as they could and deposit the water in the same place each day, so only this place received the radioactive water, but then someone else said what did it matter, the water dumped into the ground would find its way into the soil everywhere, so in the end she just poured the water down the toilet. Then Sveta asked, 'Does the toilet need washing?' and their mama stopped this too.)

She wanted him to join a *hrupu*. But what could she say? Anatolii knew what she wanted to say: *You're an invalid too!* But she would never say that.

'The money we get isn't enough,' his mama said. 'You need to get more. Look at you. You deserve more! The *hrupu* knows how. Natasha's husband Kuzmenko—'

'Kuzmenko's a turd,' his father shouted. He had enough of the soup, threw his spoon in the bowl. The soup splashed on the table. Anatolii looked at Sveta, still eating her soup, focusing on each mouthful. 'A prospector. The man has no *lichnost'*.'

'And look at yours now. Is it paying our bills? Is it putting food in our mouths?'

Anatolii had never heard his mama speak like that. But she hated that house, that town, the water. It was so much farther from Radcha, from where she grew up. But Radcha was closer to the Zone. *People are going back,* this is what they heard. Back to Radynka. Back to Radcha. He heard his mama say this to his father when they were all in bed (the walls of the house in Korosten' were thin, he heard everything: his father's strangled breathing at night, his mama's sighs).

'I'm trying to sleep,' said his father. 'May your God bless me that I don't wake up. What will you do then? Go back? To those places?'

'This place is no better. It's all contaminated.'

'You go back then.'

His mama sighs.

Lichnost'. There's no direct translation. He's never found one. There's no such thing in non-socialist countries. It's a sense of duty in one's work for the collective, and Britain never had a collective, not since enclosure and the end of common land. It is all of these things and a meaning of personhood tied to the soviet. To collective labour, and honour. But it's more than this. It's what drove the men—not the soldiers, who were under orders, and who were excited for some action—it's what was kindled in men like his father, the miners and the drivers and the farmers. The men of the *kolkhoz*. Inspired by the explosion, the common catastrophe that struck them all that night. *Lichnost'*. Without this, what is a soviet man? What is any man?

I hate flowers and trees now. How sad is it to hate the things we grew up with? They say radiation is nature, only what men did with it is unnatural. Is this true?

I had other boyfriends before Drago. They were nice, but we were all sick. Only the sick can marry the sick. And none of us can have children. It's a sin. One boyfriend was a writer. He wrote poems about the disaster. He used to read them at nights in the *raion* but the organisers got bored with him. *Can't you write about something else? Can't you write about birds, flowers?* He was like me. Anyway, he did write about birds but they were all dead. I don't know what he does now, but I imagine he still writes. Why would he stop? His old best friend—his girlfriend, I knew, although he never admitted it—he found her dying. She'd hanged herself. She couldn't have children, the doctors had told her, but she didn't qualify for the tie. He would've married her, my poet boyfriend, but it wouldn't be enough for her. I understand that. She refused to eat in the hospital, so they sent her home. Her mama let her die. He never spoke about her but all his poems were about her. No one will write poetry about me, but then I'm too much of a coward to kill myself. I don't need to. And perhaps one day I'll look at a bunch of flowers and not hate them. Not think that they're going to kill me.

Where you are, is this how you look at the forest? It's only because your mother in London lets me know she's passed these notes on that I know you're reading them. At least receiving them. Why don't you reply? But then sometimes I feel I have no right to ask that. And I know, don't I? I already know what's happened to us.

I do feel guilty about hating the trees. Didn't Prince Myshkin say, 'How can you look at a tree and not be happy?' But then Dostoyevsky lived in a time when nature was not our enemy—or we nature's enemy. The tree has done nothing wrong, even now as it can kill us. We've killed thousands of them. Millions. Countless. Human life has been lost this way too—withered and thrown out. We are kindling for this fire.

I live every day with this sadness, and I'm too sick to fight it off. It's enough for me to go to night school and cook my husband's dinner without trying to improve my mood! And I don't want to. Why should I? Sometimes it's as if this very sadness is what keeps me alive. It's the life we could have had as a family if the accident had not happened. You and me, mama and father, still living in Radynka, making sense of the new Ukraine of course, we cannot stop all of history, or perhaps we have left for America. Mama is *bubba* to our children. You have married a good Ukrainian girl. Our children play together when we visit on Sundays. Our children run to the edge of the forest where we played—perhaps I wouldn't let them go farther, or I'd feel no fear at all, and send them to gather berries and sorrel. Mama begged for sorrel before she died. No one had any after the accident, it was said sorrel soaked up radiation better than any other plant. But imagine this future where our children gather the sorrel and bring it back and mama makes it into a paste that she spreads over the chicken and bakes for our lunch, where the flowers our children bring back from the forest don't glow in their hands. The forest is safe—or as safe as it ever was.

Do you remember what Chernobyl means in our language? Wormwood. But we never listened to the warnings— Ukrainians, the most symbolic people on Earth! We were... what? Scared of Russia? Too ignorant? I don't know, I was young. You, though, were you old enough? I don't think you were. How can they blame us children? It doesn't hardly matter now anyway, does it?

I talk to the old people about what happened. Many of them are in their sixties now, seventies or even eighties, so some of them, the younger ones, were our age now when it happened. Bringing up children, thinking about holidays from the collective. And now, what have they had? Thirty years of illness and uncertainty and the politicians breaking every promise.

They tell lots of jokes. Laugh and the world laughs with you, they say. There's a woman selling apples at the market. 'Lovely apples from Chernobyl,' she shouts. 'Shush,' the other traders tell her, 'don't say they're from Chernobyl, you won't sell any.' 'Rubbish,' she says, 'don't you believe it. They're selling well. People buy them for their mother-in-law or their boss.' Do you like it, brother? They tell me how confusing everything was for them—even as adults. It makes me feel better about how confused I felt. Can you believe our parents were our age when the accident happened? When our father was driving the generals around the Zone, he was the age you are now.

The old people have not come to hate nature as I have. The cuckoos they miss, and the magpies, the foxes who used to steal eggs from their yards if they could. They feel bad for what we have done to the animals, *that universe below us*, as Alina teaches us the poets say. We were innocent—everyone except the politicians, and the engineers—but weren't the animals most innocent? Roe deer run around the Zone now. Sometimes brave (or foolish) hunters go and shoot them and sell them, don't say where they have come from, but people know. Some buy the meat because it's cheap. The hunters go there for the thrill of being in that forgotten place. Wolves and bears, they live off the deer. There are horses too. The old people I speak to in the launderette or the grocers remember their dogs and cats they left behind. With tears in their eyes. They know their companions would have starved to death, or been eaten. It would have been horrible those first few months, always thinking if little puss had lived, or was mewling at the door for food. How it pains even me, who has come to hate the trees and flowers, to think of the suffering of those little cats. Some of the old people even bless the mercenaries who the generals paid to go in and kill all the dogs and cats. At least it saved them from starvation. Those men were paid in vodka. The tales they tell are unpretty, brother, the shooting of the puppies at point blank range, piling up all the dead dogs and cats onto a tipper, running out of bullets so that there were animals, for sure, they tell me, who were buried alive when they tipped all the bodies into the big pits. But what could they do? The animals haunt their dreams more than the loved ones they lost. Why is that, do you think? Because they were so innocent? What does it feel like to leave behind those innocent ones to their fate?

Sunday Morning

Aggie's got her stockinged feet up on the dashboard. In her lap she's undoing and reweaving the last strands of a wreath she's made from dried flowers. The petals are muted reds and browns, and in the middle there is a gathering of strands that looks Tartan. It's a craft she's learnt from the women in the village. The Thursday night classes she leads don't have a set subject; it is mindfulness focused on tasks, and the doing changes depending on what the women bring. They bring the culture of their hands. Aggie turns on the radio. He wants music, just in case there's something on the news and suddenly she's looking at him, *why haven't you told me?* But there's nothing on the bulletins. There's the fallout from a Friday late night second reading of a Housing Bill that got pushed through without scrutiny. The American elections. A farmer in Perthshire has committed suicide, and the ensuing discussion about the price of milk in which the supermarket's representative is tucked tightly into a corner by the pincers of the presenters. He can't stand Radio Four journalists—snobbish, arrogant twats— but it's now an even stronger revulsion, he's surprised to notice, since Aggie's poverty event, and the comparison of middle-class habits with the poor of Sheldon and Faslane. He presses scan. She casts her eye at him, scowling.

'It's an hour until *The Archers*. We'll catch it later.'

They both hear the vibrating of his phone. After seven rings, it stops.

'That finished?' he asks of the wreath.

She holds it up, turns it left and right.

'I've no idea. Maybe they're never finished. It doesn't matter. It'll fall apart in the wind.' She looks out of the car window. The clouds have come greyly over the mountains. There is some blue, but it is far along the horizon to the north. Not where they're going. 'I suppose they're meant to fall apart. And anyway,' she adds, 'he's dead, he's not going to worry. He bloody hated Tartan.'

'So you're winding him up, even now?'

'Like father, like daughter. Find BBC Glasgow, check the weather.'

BBC Glasgow doesn't let them down. It's practically uplifting. *Wichita Lineman* followed by *The Sun Always Shines on TV*. And although the weather report is miserable, it's accurate. They follow the A814 along the banks of the broadest point of the Clyde, as vast here as the Amazon, past the Coulport jetty where the nuclear weapons are loaded into the submarines, past Colgrain and Cardross before diverting inland at Dumbarton. The roads are not busy, and they make good time. He thinks Michael and Rachel must be halfway home. At breakfast, no one commented on the night before. The four of them moved around each other wordlessly, the kitchen ringing with the scrape of cutlery and whistling kettle. He tried to redeem himself with some grumpy humour, cursing his headache and Hans and the whole Scottish shebang for a genus of alcohol he's never been able to master. The banter eased the passing, and in less than an hour Michael and Rachel were heading south, and he and Aggie fell back into an expectant silence, packing up for their own road trip.

They hit morning traffic coming in on the M8, keen shoppers trundling their having 'lesses' into the Buchanan Galleries and Queen Street and the Mackintosh cafe in an attempt to have 'more,' despite them having most of what they needed already, if they looked. He and Aggie are not following that route. They stay on the M8 through the city as everyone else turns into Cowcaddens, and then past Sighthill Park. They turn north and drive up the eastern edge of the cemetery, past the Tesco's and the Lidl and the Costco and past the delightfully named Saint Rollox Brae, then left into the cemetery. Its stone walls and plane trees hide the graves. They roll into the car park at a respectful speed. The wind ('fifteen to twenty miles per hour, in gusts, it'll feel fresher than eleven') is upsetting the trees, breaking the stems of tall flowers and piling up fallen leaves against the stone boundaries of individual plots.

Aggie carries the home-made wreath while he grabs a plastic bag of potted flowers and a rucksack from the boot. The backpack's full of garden tools and a few trinkets for the grave. There's a flask of tea in the side pocket. The wind is blustery but not freezing. They pass the huge blocky black onyx tribute to what could only be Glasgow's Italian mafia, the Romeros, graves from 1888 to 2007, so far. All the way from Naples to run the ice cream and chippie empire of the greater Scottish city.

They walk hand in hand, reading the headstones. The dates are not chronological but they do follow a scattergraph, moving higher and later and closer to today. And then they're at her father's grave. John Irvine. Unassuming. Modest. Less than a year's moss gathered. Heart disease, diabetes. At the end an impacted colon and organ failure, a body agitated by its immobility, and a spirit embarrassed by the kindnesses of the junior nurses wiping away his piss and the little shit that came out. They had to lift him up off the pillows and wipe raspberry jelly off his chin. The last time Anthony and Aggie went to visit in the Western, Appleby Ward, bed sixteen, they both left understanding how shame could kill. Her father was sixty-three, a retired engineer, once a shipbuilder for Fairfield and then the Upper Clyde. Then a specialist repairman for heavy industry, regrinding the axle boxes for rolling stock on the railways, resetting the camshafts of ships, 'almonds on sticks' he used to call them, even had photos of the largest he'd worked on. A man proud of his hands and his stolidity. Agatha, he called her. Her father outlived the Glasgow Effect, at least, even if its symptoms caught him in the end. He drank and got away with it for most of his life. Gave up smoking a year before he died on doctor's orders. Meat every day for breakfast, lunch and dinner. Work was enough exercise, until work was concluded when the boss of the engineering factory died and the accounts revealed they were millions in debt. Then a fall, and the cracked hip. After that he could never shift the weight. He wasn't a huge man, but at that age it all counted. And Aggie has still not forgiven him for it, even though she is here today.

It's not the anniversary of his death, though. Nor her father's birthday. This was Anthony's idea to come today, his custom.

'So what do we do? Other than sweep up around him, like usual.'

'Careful, he might be listening,' he says.

Aggie shakes her head. 'We didn't bury him with his hearing aid.'

Anthony's got the small trowel and hand-fork out.

'Let's just tidy and then sit down. Have some tea.'

He passes a brush to Aggie. She tidies the grave, sweeping the jade stones off the frame of the plot and back into the bed. There is a flower border at the end of the plot, and he digs up the older plants to replace them with new. Heucheras, she tells him, North American plants, hardier than their delicate petals would suggest, and good for borders all year round. Names such as Key Lime Pie and Plum Pudding — another dig at her father, whose diabetes was in the end death's gauntlet that grasped hardest. The florist at Garelochhead, Geraldine's, was possibly the only flower shop in the world that regularly supplied spray presentations for a nuclear base. The Americans were over at least once a year for their 'shakedowns,' and the Commodore was a fan of floristry and arrangement. Yes, there in the middle of the coffee table when he was pulled in for that first meeting, was a muted bouquet.

He's on his knees. Hands dirty with the soil of the border. The scent of the heucheras in his nostrils, the flowers unworried by the wind. He knows how to extract a plant from its pot, even though he's not planted vegetables since he was a child. In Oxford there was a garden but no time and, anyway, he and Aggie were too young. Now, at the cottage? There's a small garden. A village allotment that he could inveigle his way into. Are they old enough to turn to the land? But he already has. That shock that ran up his arms. He understands it was the leak on *Tartarus*. The land registered it first. People here wouldn't believe it, but the locals in the Exclusion Zone, they would. The anglers couldn't find a worm within a yard of the surface. For twenty days the bees wouldn't come out of their hives. The dogs lost all sense of direction. There were no birds. The authorities didn't believe these peasant stories. Just like no one would be convinced he'd felt the flushing of *Tartarus* flash through his body. But this is how it happens. The uranium that drove the reactors was geological material. Uranium provides the radiation that powers not just the submarines but the circulations of the oceans in which those subs cruised. Nuclear energy at the core of planetary vectors. Gaia theory, quantum physics, spirit, call it what you wanted. The basis was the same: atoms, moving. The insects and animals registering the fluctuations. His body, too. Didn't that mean something?

He rests on his haunches surveying the job. The plants are aligned, the flowers tall and balanced. The plummy petals a good contrast with the bright cadmium gravel. Aggie squats on the stone lip of the plot, bumping next to him. She reaches for the rucksack and takes out the flask. She takes the lid off and presses the inner cap and pours. Steaming, brown and sweet.

'So what do you call it? This day?'

'The Day of the Graves.'

'No. Originally.'

He thinks of the word. He bids it to come and it does.

'*Hrobky.*'

'All those words in that small one?'

'It's a precise language. Sometimes.'

'And this is what you do? Tidy the graves, replant the flowers? Drink tea?'

'Usually something stronger. The adults anyway. I never...

And prayers. Singing. Stories, depending on who was there.'

'Other relatives would come?'

'It's the day for everyone, a national day. The graveyard would be packed.'

'Cemetery. I don't like graveyard.'

'They're graves.'

She huffs. 'So what stories would you tell?'

'About the person. Their family.'

'You start,' she says.

'I don't know enough about your dad.'

'Not mine.' She pauses. 'Yours.'

Him, start? He did suggest they come on *hrobky*. He thought it would help her mourn. He tries. But there's the treacle to wade through, the muffling in his head like someone's put down sandbags to stave off the flood. Isn't it too graceful a peace to break with words? They're beyond daily life for a change, where things have gotten tangled; where chewed-up tennis balls and *Greg's* knitted jumpers and the crewmembers in the clinic have besieged all hope for such a peace. She's waiting.

'Okay,' he says.

The stories told on *hrobky* are memorials to the person when they were alive. But the only story in his mind is of when his father is already dead. So he tells her that: his mama leading them from the house through the Korosten' streets. He doesn't know where they're going. It's cold. The wind is in their faces, it smarts against his skin. His gloves are thin and his hands are freezing as his mama pulls him along. He's pulling Sveta. He's tired—they all are. But his mama has the ghost of his father pulling her, and they carry on in a weary daisy chain, yanking and lurching along the street. His mama carries a wooden box containing his father's ashes, the size of a small loaf of bread. His mama is wearing her best black dress. They pass houses and then they're at the Lenin monument, beard as pointed as his finger. Lenin stands on faded red slabs of concrete above a fountain now filled with sand, as if children should play there, as if the Soviet Union is built upon this sand. Lenin leans over him. *Your father gave his life for our collective. He is a hero. Remember him as the wolf.* But Lenin doesn't say those words. Only the wind howls, the wind is *vovk.*

'Ant?' Aggie is offering him tea. He takes it. 'You've stopped.'

Their mama drags them on. Sveta complains but he doesn't listen. He buries his head deep into his hood. He closes his eyes, lets his mama drag him. His uncle had said, 'Not there, return him to his own family, to Ovruch.' But his father had disliked his family. They never went to Ovruch as they did to Radcha. So where then to scatter him? He'd hated Korosten', just as Anatolii hated it. Anatolii gasps for breath and the wind fills his stomach. Will Mama and Sveta come to Kyiv now? He screws up his eyes. The thought of them all in the same small flat makes him lightheaded.

They're on open land at the outskirts of town. They've reached their destination: a group of small mounds, the ancient settlements of Iskorosten. Made of clay, old homes of old people protected not by gates but by ghosts. The Drevlians were the race who once lived here. Farmers, makers of handicrafts, dwellers in the trees. The Drevlians fought with the Polyani, who were the city dwellers. The Polyani were the victorious ancestors, according to all the books, but the *kolkhoz* of the soviet was closer in spirit to the Drevlians (close to the Celts, too, he thinks, looking at Aggie). He knows he's descended from the Drevlians. When the Kievan Rus' conquered the Drevlians, Korosten' was burned to the ground. Its people left and made their homes in Ovruch. His father was from Ovruch. His father was a descendant, a tree dweller with a longing for the land. For tracking the wolves through firs. They should have taken him to the forest. But it doesn't matter. His father is not in that box. His father is somewhere else.

He listens to crows cawing and fighting with magpies in the trees around the graveyard. There are others come to tend their plots, dress flowers, stroll and read the names and dates of the dead. Not far off he can hear the supermarket traffic.

'Ant? Are you going to answer that?'

His phone is vibrating. He shakes his head.

'They buried everyone to begin with, in lead-lined coffins. No journalists were allowed at the funerals. The officials would send out dummy hearses to drive around the city and lead the journalists to the wrong graveyard. The families of the firemen all had KGB minders. They weren't allowed to talk about what they'd seen.'

'You mean how their husbands died?'

'Then the coffins were too expensive. And people gave up with the pretense. Gave up regulating. No one cared. The only thing in the end they cared about was the Plan, the crop yield—they didn't want to put the bodies into the ground and contaminate the soil. So they began to cremate. Anyone with ties to the accident was cremated. It became a tick box, how... to keep claiming the tie money.'

'And your father?'

'There's no grave,' he says. 'Just those mounds.'

'So on Grave Day?'

'The Day of the Graves,' he corrects her, and grimaces. 'We had a family plot in Radynka. They let you back in to the Zone one day of the year to mourn, tend the graves. We mounted the box, the ashes box, in a little...'

His mama stops. She lets go of his hand, and only then does he realise she's been squeezing it too hard. He lets go of Sveta. His sister drops both arms by her side and looks down, frozen as a statue. His mama walks up one of the mounds. The wind is a blade in his face, he can barely open his eyes. Sveta is almost blown off, so he grabs her. His mama struggles to open the box, to do it carefully, and he knows that this is to stop his father escaping all at once. But they'd come for the wind to take him far away from the cloud that killed him. What direction was the wind blowing? From the north. On a Soviet wind, blowing in the ice of Siberia. His mama takes her gloves off to open the latch on the box. She is a black goddess of the forest against a black sky in the wind and she fiddles with the latch, swearing. What must he say? Isn't it a day for stories? What is he, the man of the family, going to say? The lid snaps open and the ashes leap upwards and are blown away. The only words are his mama's, and they are not words at all but a howl. There's a ringing in his ears and it is the ringing of the wind but it is also Aggie at his shoulder.

'Ant, your phone. Your phone, it's got to be serious,' and she's leaning across to pull it out of his coat pocket. She looks at the screen and passes it to him and he looks at it and then stands up and walks a few feet away.

He's expecting it to be—but his mama is dead. He stares at the three dots pulsing left to right. For all the longing and the miracles it's not a ghost from the past. It remains David. He doesn't answer. He puts the phone in his pocket and sits down.

'Ant...'

'It's Sunday.'

'But that woman. It's got to be...'

He closes his eyes, runs both hands over his hair.

'You need to call back.' She grabs his arm. 'It's okay.'

He's furious that his story's been interrupted. But he phones David.

'Anthony. At last.'

'We're in Glasgow. At Aggie's father's grave.'

'Ah,' says David. 'It's Sunday I know but we've been called in. There's a situation.'

'Is it serious?'

'I'm not allowed to give out details on the phone, Anthony. But we really need everyone here as soon as possible. Can you make your way...'

Good is all David says before hanging up, and Anthony's knows he's not been forgiven for bringing Michael onto the base. He puts the phone away, and is struck by Aggie's easy movements standing up, gathering together their things. It's as if his wife does not know what to do with his news; or rather, he does not know anymore how his wife reacts. She lays the wreath she's made.

'I'll carry on to mum's and get the train back. You go.'

He's slinging the rucksack over his shoulders, scrutinizing her face.

'Maybe I'm not going back there,' he says.

'Why would you say that, Ant?'

He doesn't know. She takes his arm and they leave the grave. He feels her frustration through her grip. They have not stood and weathered the placing of the wreath, this thing she has made for her father.

'I'll tell mum you have to work. You do send your love, don't you?'

She's nudging a smile from his lips.

'We don't have to go yet. You've not said your—'

'I'll say something next year,' she says firmly. And he understands now the firmness of her grip steering them away; David's phone call has brought her relief. She is saved from having to tell a story about her father.

'Thank you for sharing, though,' she says as they pass by the Romeros, the names of the departed writ in gold leaf, the onyx spit-polished to a mirror. 'For telling me.'

1989, Kyiv and Moscow

Anatolii looks out at the road, the dirty net curtain drawn back. He's sitting on the edge of the foldout table that Kulyk drags into the middle of the room for special card nights, when there are eight men and they cannot fit in the kitchen. There's a car outside, stumpy and red. A man gets out wearing a big coat and heavy hat. He lights a cigarette, and stands leaning on the edge of the bonnet. There are others in the car, but they don't get out. His father comes into the room, and he slopes off the table.

'You're keeping watch?'

He nods. 'There's a car.'

'About time. It's a long drive. Do you know where we're going?'

Anatolii nods again.

'Do you know who is there?'

Kulyk comes in from the hall, carrying Anatolii's bag.

'Here,' says his uncle, thrusting the bag into his father's belly. His father looks down, irritated, and takes the bag.

'We're going on a trip,' his father says. 'And you're going to be my partner, little dagger. You're going to have my back with these other men.' His father shifts the curtain to one side and raps on the window. 'Hey! Hey!'

'Jesus Christ,' says Kulyk. 'Stop shouting. How are they meant to hear you? Anatolii, open the balcony door for your father.'

Anatolii runs over and opens the door.

'Tell them we'll be down in a minute,' says his father, 'go on, go on.'

He glances at his uncle who gives him a smile, but not the kind of smile like when Dynamo win a match. The wind makes him shiver and he wants to rush back inside and fall on the sofa, hide his face. He waves but they're four floors up, and the man isn't looking. Anatolii waves again, but the man isn't going to see that. Inside, his father and Kulyk are shouting at each other. He doesn't know how far Moscow is. His throat is dry. The man who's smoking by the car throws the cigarette down and looks up. He waves quickly, jerky and wild. The man sees him, and waves back, and gets in the car. Anatolii hurries back inside.

'He saw me,' says Anatolii, but his father is not there.

'Come here,' says Kulyk. His uncle grabs his arm. 'You'll be a few days. Respect your father. It's not going to be an easy trip, all those...the other men, don't listen to what they say, Anatolii. They talk bull—the things they say, they're not all in their right minds. You understand? The sickness, the things they've suffered since the accident. I don't know them, but you're going to Moscow to be one of the sick people. You understand? They all need to be as sick as they can, so they'll—you're not understanding this, are you?'

'They need to show the doctors in Moscow they're sick,' he says, proudly. It's like when he plays with the other boys who are bigger than him and he has to pretend to be—no, not pretend—'That's right. But don't lie. You respect your father, but you don't tell the doctors in Moscow, they might not be in white coats, okay... you don't lie. Do you understand? These men'— Kulyk points his chin at the balcony, and they both hear the toilet flush—'these men, maybe your father, they might want to get you to say more, that you're sick, that you suffer things. You don't do this. They think they know how to play the system for the benefits. They're crazy. Don't tell them I said this.' Kulyk lets go of his arm. His father is standing in the doorway, doing up his fly. Then his father points towards the sofa.

'Your bag, little dagger. Check you have everything. We can't turn around.'

Anatolii's bag is the tan holdall he took when they rushed from Radynka. He can't think if there's anything missing. What is he going to need? For how long will they be gone?

They drive from his uncle's to another block of flats, where a second car joins them. They don't get out, just flash their lights at the other car, which leads them from the city. The car smells of smoking and oil and always that smell now, of the medicines the men take, of the clothes that are wet with the creams the men rub on their burns and scars but never comes out in washing. They drive out of Kyiv, the men talking about the route, about how they've been sick, not too bad, sick again. They leave the motorway, and three lanes change to two and then to one. He sits by the window and watches the road signs that mark their leaving Kyiv. Moscow: 756 kilometres. He doesn't know how far that is. Soon the signs stop. The car jars over potholes and the men swear. Trucks come the other way down the middle of the road. He sits on the passenger side, behind his father. The driver is the man from the *hrupu*, Artem, who coughs all the time and spits out of the open window. He closes his eyes and tries to close his ears. The man sitting behind Artem complains that the wind is in his face. Anatolii doesn't know this other man's name yet, but he's in the *hrupu*. They shook hands when he got in—his father said, 'This is my son.' Between them is another boy, much older. Zhores is Artem's son. He can tell that Zhores is angry about being squeezed in the middle, but he couldn't do anything about it, his father said get in the car; and anyway, even though he'd prefer it if Zhores liked him, he would rather have the window. Their legs knock as the car jumps over holes and swerves around trucks. From his uncle's flat the car looked big, but inside they are big people too.

The men talk about their illnesses. They talk about Doctor Zoya and what is happening in the Zone. Is that Zone Four where his mama and sister and father live, or Zone One? He doesn't ask. A year ago a trip like this would have been his greatest wish—to travel with his father, without mama or Sveta. With other men was okay. And to Moscow! In his schoolbooks every picture is of St Peter's Square, every story begins and ends at the Kremlin. He looks out of the window, worrying that he's going to get carsick. He watches as they go through small towns and villages. They're on the E95. This is the farthest he's ever been from home.

'And then one born to a mother who was evacuated,' says Artem. 'Her infant has half a lung and no asshole.'

'It's criminal,' says the man sitting by the other window. 'And what do they do for her? For her child?'

'Nothing,' says his father.

'Another was born to a worker,' says Artem. Anatolii knows whenever they say 'worker' they mean at the power plant. 'There are six fingers on his left hand. He's missing a trachea.'

His father is shaking his head. 'And this, only three years later. What will happen in the future, when the children grow up and have their own?'

'His guts on the outside of his body,' Artem carries on. 'Can you imagine?'

Anatolii tries to imagine it. He doesn't understand what it means, or how it can happen. He does know, because of his sister, that babies come out of a mother's belly. But how? What makes it happen? And if they come out without their own belly, does that mean they don't survive? Are they even human? Can people have babies that don't survive because they aren't human?

'Six fingers,' says Zhores, and it startles him. Anatolii wouldn't dare join in the conversation. But then Zhores is older. He watches Zhores count out the fingers on his left hand. 'Four. Five.' Zhores adds the little finger from his other hand and shows it to Anatolii. 'See? Six. That's disgusting.'

Anatolii laughs.

'Like an alien,' he says, and regrets it. It makes him sound like a child. Zhores drops his hands and stares forward.

'It's not disgusting,' says Artem, 'it's not the woman's fault. You know whose fault it is? The idiots who couldn't operate a nuclear plant, the government that cuts corners on safety, who've left us with the mess. You pity that child with the six fingers.

You think what kind of life she's going to live. It won't be only her fingers that are deformed.' Artem shakes his head. 'You think she's ever going to marry?'

Anatolii can't see his father's face. He feels something is wrong, that his father wants to say something but doesn't know how to arrange the words.

The man by the window pulls a silver hipflask out of his jacket and begins to drink. His name is Dubinin; Artem shouts it as Dubinin jogs his knees into the back of Artem's seat. Dubinin hands the flask to the front. His father takes it and drinks, and swears, and hands it to Artem, who drinks and swears too, and hands it back.

They drive for most of the day, stopping to stretch their legs and smoke, although they also smoke while driving. One of the men in the other car feels sick for the whole journey. And because they're a *hrupu*, 'because this is why we are driving, right?' they do not complain, as other men would, about the one slowing them down. The other car has three men and one boy, who is older than he is. This other boy, Oleksandr, already knows Zhores and whenever they stop they're gone from his sight. They're not unfriendly to him but they don't take him with them. Their fathers shout: 'Don't break anything! Be back in fifteen minutes!' Anatolii stays by the car, his hands in his pockets, kicking the dust and stones.

They reach the small town of Zhizdra when it's dark. One of the men has a friend where they can park for the night and use the kitchen and bathroom. Zhizdra is a small town. They drive past rows of houses, stopping often as the car in front slows to look for the house. Artem and his father are both cursing. But then the other car pulls in, and they follow. They all get out with groans about how their legs are about to drop off. But they're not so far from Moscow now. It's only an early morning drive into the city.

It's a small house with four rooms. The man and woman

who live in the house have three young children. The house is decorated like theirs was in Radynka. The walls are white and covered in mementos. The mantelpiece is overflowing with pictures, large and small, in gold frames. The rooms are lit by faded ceiling lights. But the house is welcoming, it smells of how their house used to smell, of *bigos* with cabbage, the bristles of the hard brushes his mama used to sweep the house, before the chemicals they distributed for cleaning after the accident. The mama looks happy that her husband's friends have come. The woman says, 'We can help these *poterpili*.'

They're shepherded into the living room, where he sits on the floor with the children. The eldest boy of the house, Igor, is his age, and brings out picture books to share. Anatolii is grateful, happy to be out of the car. Zhores and Oleksandr sit at the back of the room, talking to each other in whispers and short laughs. The mama, whose name is Hanna, brings in extra chairs from the kitchen for the men, then runs in and out with tea, 'a few minutes!' she shouts. The men are happy, the fire is on, the man whose house it is, Ivan, is happy to see his friend, Trofin. Anatolii glances at his father, who's slumped in one of the sofas, looking tired and yellow.

'A long drive, a long drive,' says Ivan, with a hand on his friend's back. 'The food, it's ready soon. Hanna's a great cook. You'll see, it will send you right off to sleep.'

Ivan works in a factory outside the town. He's an administrator, a smallish man. He's wearing the clothes of someone who does not get dirty at work, a shirt and jumper and flannel trousers.

'I was lucky,' says Ivan. 'Was it two years ago? I wasn't going to take it.'

'You thought it wouldn't be as well paid as the plant,' says Trofin, a husky voice.

'Which is true, it wasn't, not to begin with,' says Ivan. 'But Hanna's family are in Moscow. And it seemed like a good company.'

'It is a good company,' says Hanna from the doorway. 'They're good to us.'

'They are, it's true,' says Ivan. 'For Christmas everyone in management got a hamper, and we let all the workers on the floor have a week off for the holidays, and they have special dispensations for activities in the town.'

'You got a hamper?' his father says, sitting up.

'And we brought in the butcher and the baker on the last day and they dispensed foods for Christmas to everyone.'

'You run a socialist factory,' says Artem. 'This is how a collective works.'

'It's not easy, of course,' says Ivan. 'Sometimes we have to let people go.'

'But you take your responsibilities seriously,' says Artem. 'To the workers.'

Anatolii looks at the other man from the other car, whose name he still does not know, but who sits quietly, always grimacing, as if he has a constant headache. The man looks back, winks, and then looks away.

'This is why we go to Moscow,' says Artem. 'When we see Doctor Zoya, this is what we must show him — their responsibilities to us.'

'You men.' Ivan shakes his head. 'What you've suffered...'

'It's our right,' says Artem, thumping his chest with a fist to stop his coughing. 'We will suffer whatever we have to, to gain our rights. Isn't that so, boys?' He leans across and puts a hand on Ivan's shoulder. 'We are in your house, Ivan Andreyivic, I am grateful. You understand what they've done to us, abandoning us. But they forget we have *lichnost'*. This is why we worked for them in the first place!'

'Speak for yourself, I went for the money,' says Dubinin, and some laugh.

'They knew we were hard workers,' Artem carries on. 'Even you, Dub*chek*.' They all laugh. 'You know what they did, Ivan?

While we were cleaning up their mess? They raised the limit for how many rem we could bear. From seven to twenty-five, which meant we could stay in the Zone for longer. It was always, "tell us our dose," but they didn't. They wrote it down, though. And those records are in Moscow.'

'They'd better be,' says his father. 'Or we'll give those bastards trouble.'

Artem gestures a pressing down movement with both palms.

'We talk like this amongst ourselves,' he says to Ivan. 'To the doctors, we are politicians.'

The men nod. 'The tie, the tie,' they say over each other.

Anatolii doesn't understand. What is this *rem*? It's something to do with the accident, with the time his father drove the car. But it's invisible. It's a small thing, *rem*, a part of a word, like *chek*, meaning little, maybe *rem* is the little part of sickness, the invisible part? It's bound up with this tie, which seems to be something they'll get in Moscow. It's what they're owed for their suffering.

'Food,' says Hanna, standing at the door. She startles them all except Zhores and Oleksandr, who are already up. 'Boys! Please, come and help yourselves and eat where you like,' and all the men, Anatolii too, rise with new energy, and he realises how hungry he is. He can smell the stew, thick with dumplings and warmth that's already filling his belly. He's famished, and he drops the picture book. The men are laughing and rushing at the door.

'My friends, you see! You see!' says Ivan.

After they've eaten they sleep. They can't all fit in the house, so only the drivers and Artem's son and Trofin sleep inside, while the rest are in the cars. But that's okay. There is only him and his father in their car, because Dubinin goes into the other car where there's more room. Ivan and Hanna have borrowed blankets from their neighbours. He and his father settle down in the car to sleep. They're far from the main road, it is quiet, the sky is black.

'Well, an adventure,' says his father, smiling. His father is stretched out on the passenger seat, which is reclined as far down as it will go. His father is deliriously tired and wants to sleep, but he's softer, too. The evening among a group of men in a nice house with a kind family has made him feel better.

'It's like sleeping in the forest,' Anatolii says.

His father reaches out a hand and grabs Anatolii's leg on the back seat. He's stretched all the way out with his feet tucked under the head of his father's seat. So his father grabs him, and squeezes him, and he laughs, it tickles. His father lets go.

'Ah, the forest. Remember, little Anatolii, our days in the forest?'

'Yes.' He smiles. He's happy to be with his father in the car, just the two of them.

They're up when it's still dark. They must reach Moscow in time for their appointment. They breakfast in the house. He sits and reads a picture book, eating bread and sausage and drinking warm milk. He and his father woke together. His father was groggy but not angry, and said the car stank of two men, which meant he and his father were the men, like in the forest. Hanna said the night before it was wrong for the boys to sleep in the car, but he'd disappeared from the room and gone to the car and then it was too late. His father understood, and agreed. *We men.*

They're on the road as the sun comes up behind thick clouds, and the black of the night never leaves them. Artem's silence doesn't last long. He talks of their strategy when they get to the hospital. He talks about Doctor Zoya. They stop once for everyone to piss. The men huddle together and the other two boys wander off. Anatolii is tired but enjoying himself. And soon they'll be in Moscow.

It's another two hours until they reach the city. The signs have reappeared, and he's been counting them down. The road is lined with blocks of flats, one after the other, many more cars, the traffic slower, people walking along with heavy bags and big coats. The road grows so wide there are covered bridges for people to walk across. The two sides of the motorway are divided by large grass islands with trees. They pass bigger buildings, a post office the size of their entire village. The roads are named in two languages, names he doesn't understand and has never heard of, foreign names as well as Russian. There are more people cycling here than he's ever seen, even in Kyiv. He is proud he's no longer just a *khlop*, a village boy, but even Kyiv has not prepared him for Moscow.

His father is sitting with a big map of Moscow open on his lap. They're looking for Hospital Number Six, the radiological hospital. His father and Dubinin argue about the next turn or straight ahead and whose eyesight is still working. Artem gives his commentary, as if he's their tour guide. It's not about the city, though, but about the history of the accident. Hospital Number Six is where the firemen and soldiers were brought in the days during the battle with the fire. By the time *they* started falling sick—Artem, his father, the other drivers, the miners, the metro-workers, the farm hands—Hospital Number Six was bursting at its seams, its staff overwhelmed, its doors closed to new cases.

'But we're owed our dues,' Artem says. 'Now their wards are full of people like us. Their staff have expanded. They've taken their responsibilities seriously, at last.'

'Or they'll toss us in the dustbin,' says Dubinin. 'Throw our claims out the door.'

The hospital is a five-story block of concrete and each window barred two thirds of the way across. It's hidden by lime trees that have lost their leaves. Between the trees and the building is a stretch of grass with benches and small, glass shelters to smoke under. There are many people there, some wearing normal clothes and some in bedclothes. In one shelter the smoke is so thick Anatolii cannot see their heads. He is pressed against the window and Zhores is pressing over his shoulder. Zhores speaks to him for the first time that morning, and they both laugh at the people standing around in the cold without proper clothes. The name of the hospital is made out along the edge of the roof in individual letters, each one outlined in black, with a light shining on it from below.

Artem turns off the engine and the other car parks alongside. They sit for a moment. No one knows what to do. Dubinin looks at his watch.

'Half past ten,' he says. 'We're an hour early.'

'Good,' says Artem, and places a hand on his father's shoulder. 'We've plenty of time to go over our plan.' He turns around. 'What do we do with the boys? Send them to find some decent coffee, the hospital coffee will be shit. And some breakfast.'

'We've had breakfast,' says Zhores. 'At the house.'

'I've been driving for hours,' says Artem, who doesn't seem bothered by Zhores's cheek. 'I need coffee. Decent fucking coffee. Here. . .' Artem digs into his trouser pocket and pulls out a dirty brown wallet. He takes out twenty *roubles*. 'And don't fucking lose all my money. Go and get…six coffees, and some bread and cheese if you find a store, and then whatever you boys want. Take Anatolii here, and maybe learn a little of how to behave.' Artem gives Anatolii a wink. 'Don't take forever.'

'And bring some cream for the coffees,' says Anatolii's father.

'But don't put it in. Wait, let me put it in myself,' adds Dubinin, who has his flask out, is holding it with both hands in his lap, jiggling it about.

Anatolii opens the door and falls out. There's a blustery wind. He stares up at the windows of the hospital. Black, curtains drawn. In one, a person, watching.

'Come on,' Zhores says. Oleksandr is out of the other car, and the two older boys walk off. He follows behind.

They find a cafe a block away from the hospital. He imagines the cafe as one of a million across the whole of Moscow. He feels a desire to go home. Not to live in Kyiv with Kulyk, but not back to Korosten' either. Back to Radynka, and the forest.

The cafe is warm but plain. There's a small television looming over them from a niche above the bar, blazing news. There are maybe half a dozen men, three at one table, and he winces from the smoke in his eyes and throat. Zhores and Oleksandr are at the counter talking to the waiter, a tall, fat man in a plain white shirt, an apron tied around his waist with the top half hanging down. Zhores buys them *all* coffee—all nine of them. The waiter sees the money so he starts brewing. The waiter is chatting to them, asking them where they're from, what they're doing in the capital.

'We've come to get our privileges,' says Zhores.

The waiter twists round while the coffee machine rattles and steams.

'Someone owes you money?'

Anatolii looks at Zhores, who doesn't seem scared.

'The State,' says Zhores, 'the State owes my father.'

The waiter's not looking at them now, but filling the plastic cups.

Two of the men sitting closest laugh, coarse and bitter.

'The State? The State is disappearing, boys. *Glasnost*. Whatever it owes you, you get it quick, you hear? You tell your country bumpkin fathers—'

'We're from Ukraine,' Anatolii says. The men and the other boys stare.

'Aha! We've got some independentists,' says one of the men wearing a square flat cap and a dark blue shirt buttoned to the top. He's holding a rolled-up newspaper. 'Like my comrade here said, country bumpkins. But don't take that badly, little comrades. We all work for the land.'

'My father's a miner,' says Zhores.

'And yours?' the man asks, pointing at Anatolii with his newspaper. 'Come on, little comrade from Ukraine. What is it the State owes your father for?'

'He's a driver,' he says. 'He worked on the *kolkhoz*. But then the accident happened and he got sick.'

The waiter leans over the counter, studying them.

'How are you going to carry these coffees? Where are you going?'

'The hospital,' says Oleksandr.

'Accident?' the man with the newspaper asks. His tone has changed. It's not mocking now. 'Your fathers are sick?'

'What accident?' the waiter asks.

None of them want to say more. Zhores is pushing the twenty *roubles* at the waiter, but the waiter ignores him. The man with the newspaper shifts his seat closer, scraping its metal legs along the floor.

'Little comrade, tell us,' he says.

He can feel their eyes on him. What would his father say? All the way here, hasn't Artem been telling them it's their right? That the world must not forget who they are and what they sacrificed?

'Chernobyl,' Anatolii says. 'We've come to get our tie to the privileges.'

The man at the table slaps the newspaper down and lets out a gasp.

'Take your coffees,' says the waiter. 'Go on.'

Zhores offers him the note, but he waves it away.

'We don't want your money.'

'Comrades,' says the man at the table. He and his friend stand. 'Take your coffees, you have a job to do.'

The waiter wraps the coffees in flimsy looking holders. He hands them across.

'Come on, come on,' says the waiter.

Zhores is still trying to give him the money. But the waiter shakes his head.

'I've told you, no money here. No money. No, no.'

Zhores puts the money back in his pocket.

'Quick now,' says the other man who hasn't spoken, 'quick,

quick.'

The men watch them go. They cross the road and when they're far away he looks back, just in time to see the waiter go inside.

'Why did you tell him that?' Zhores asks.

Anatolii isn't sure anymore. But he knows his father would be proud.

'Because we're here for our privileges,' he says. 'Why didn't *you* say it?'

Zhores kicks out at him. He jumps, and drops the coffees he's carrying. One spills over the ground, but the other two, wrapped in the holder, land on their bases and spill but don't break. He picks them up quickly.

'You don't mention it to strangers,' says Zhores, but he can see in Zhores's eyes that he wishes he'd been the one to say it.

His face is blazing when they get back to the cars, but not from shame. He hands over the two coffees to his father. One is half empty. His father looks at him angrily as he has to take the half-empty one for himself. Anatolii's happy he doesn't have a coffee. He doesn't like its bitterness. And Artem and Trofin end up shouting at Zhores and Oleksandr, who have drunk the coffee and are going wild. He gets into the back of the car and sits quietly, looking out.

Ask me what happened, he thinks. He wants his father to know that he was brave. He sits and thinks about the men in the cafe, their eyes, the man in the square cap, the questions of the waiter. The looks on their faces when he named it: *Chernobyl*.

It's time for their appointment. They're all going, including the boys. They enter the hospital and ask for directions and walk along wide, marbled corridors with huge wooden double doors, busy with nurses and doctors in clean, crisp uniforms. He feels a growing sense of impending shame of having to sit on his father's knee again. This time it would be in front of the other men, too, and Zhores. He can't imagine Artem putting Zhores on his knee. And even if Artem did, it would not eliminate the shame, only double it. Anatolii prays as he's never prayed before, to the spirits of the forest, to the wolf, to not let that happen.

The men argue over which way to go but finally find the office of Doctor Vasili Zoya. They knock but there's no one there. Artem looks at his watch. They're on time. A few minutes early. Artem looks up and down the corridor, wiping his face with his hand. The other men reassure him the doctor will come but that only makes him sweat more. Anatolii's father is sitting in one of the two chairs that are on either side of the door. Under the groomed moustache—the men spent as much time in front of the mirror of Hanna's dresser as he did eating breakfast—his father's lip is trembling.

A doctor in a clean coat, front-pleated trousers and shiny black shoes walks towards them, steps clattering on the marble. Artem jumps up to greet Doctor Zoya. His father opens his eyes and for a moment looks as if he's forgotten where he is.

'There's a lot of you, more than I was expecting,' says the doctor.

'We're a *hrupu*. In a way we've saved you time, all the same you see.'

'It's never the same across two people, let alone,' he stops to count, 'six. But come. You've come all this way. Have you had coffee?'

Artem nods, the other men say, *Yes, thank you*. The doctor pulls a set of keys out of his pocket and unlocks the door. Artem waves Trofin forward. It is Trofin who's been carrying the *blat*. Vodka, a carved wooden cigarette box full of money, the chocolate for the doctor's wife.

'Not the boys,' says the doctor.

The men look at the boys, but don't say anything.

'They'll stand,' says Artem.

'There's still no room, not for nine of you!'

The door opens into an office that even Anatolii can see will easily hold all of them. But the doctor won't let them in, and the men don't look back as they file in one by one, hats off in their hands. The doctor says, 'close the door,' and whoever's at the back does as he says. The door is latched quietly.

Zhores and Oleksandr are still crazed by the coffee. They've become mean and spiteful. They joke about him being a good boy. He's happy to see them jostle their way down the corridor. When it's quiet he rests his ear on the wall and can almost hear what they're saying.

He's startled upright when the door opposite opens and two people, a man and a woman, come out. The man is leaving while the woman, who must be a doctor too because of her white coat, is staying. The man is completely bald with a big belly covered in a striped shirt showing through his white coat.

'It's not possible to say?' She has big, yellow hair, and clear skin, even though she's older than his mama. Her voice is deep, like the headmistress at his school. He sits up straighter. 'Even now?'

The man shrugs. 'Perhaps. I don't really mind the overestimation.'

She shakes her head. 'It's a good estimate.' She notices him, then, and looks straight at him. She doesn't smile. 'Implement in wards six and eight. Then get me the results. We'll tell the Americans we can go ahead with transplants for those who've received over 500.'

'But Angela—' The man stops what he's about to say. She waits. 'It's only been tested on guinea pigs. The growth factors—'

'You don't like Americans.' The man attempts to deny it but she waves away his protestations. 'Doctor Gale is ready. We don't have many other options, do we?'

The man has a hand in his pocket, jingling some coins.

'Okay?' she says, and the man nods and walks off along the corridor.

The woman walks over to him. Anatolii's heart stops. He

jumps off the chair.

'Hello. Who are you?'

He thinks of his father. Doesn't want to let his father down.

'Anatolii,' he says. 'Nikolaevich.'

'You don't sound like you're from Moscow.'

He shakes his head.

'So where are you from?'

The image of the waiter from the cafe fills his head. Zhores kicking him. And the words of his uncle: *don't lie*. But now he's here, he knows it's different. This is where he's *meant* to say what happened.

'How about you,' she asks him, 'do you like Americans? Westerners?'

He knows America is the enemy, even though his uncle told him this was a lie that the Party made to keep people working on the farms. Americans had swimming pools and their kids had picture books called cartoons and they rode on skateboards. This woman liked Americans. Maybe he should too.

'Yes. They have cartoons,' he says.

She smiles. Her teeth are big and clean.

'Our future is in safe hands,' she says, straightening up.

He feels a wave of relief, and something else.

'We're from Radynka,' he says before the fear returns. She narrows her eyes, looks closely at him. 'We're here for the tie.'

She looks at him, and then at the door of her colleague, his name, Vasili Zoya, in gold letters across the wood panelling.

'Your father is in there, your mother?'

He nods. 'My father.'

'And your father, he wants to recover? He wants to work again?'

He nods vigorously.

'Then he doesn't need help from us,' she says. She walks away into her office and shuts the door. Anatolii feels emptied of everything; blood, thoughts, fears.

He hears raised voices from Doctor Zoya's room, including his father's. Then silence. Then Doctor Zoya. Silence again, or rather no talking but movement in the room. He unsticks his ear from the wall and sits upright looking forward. The door to Zoya's office opens and the men come out, Trofin first, then Dubinin, the other two, then his father and Artem. Then the doctor. They're shaking hands. He watches his father, who's animated, shaking hands with the other men.

'I'll write the letters, get them countersigned. Then you can have them. Wait, wait, be patient, it might take a month or two,' Zoya says standing at the door as the woman had moments earlier. A hand on the door, swinging it closed.

They walk back down the corridors and get lost finding the cars again, but it doesn't seem to matter. Even Zhores and Oleksandr don't get into trouble when they turn up half an hour later. The men drink from their hipflasks, and perhaps they're all drunk, even the drivers. They begin their journey to Kyiv, which they make in one night, stopping at a gas station for goulash with rice. The drive back is sociable for a while, then quiet. His father snores half the way. When they're dropped off at Kulyk's, Anatolii has to be shaken awake. His father's even more difficult to raise, as if he's a great black bear hibernating for winter. And this is the truth, Anatolii realises. His father was never a wolf, but a bear. This was a good thing to be. Strong, Soviet in heart and belly, a good protector, but mean too, sometimes, and not so cunning.

The cars honk their horns as they pull away, and he and his father wave back enthusiastically. They walk to Kulyk's flat, and his father puts an arm around his neck and pulls him close. He walks happily, still sleepy, as if he's part of his father's leg. They don't say anything. Inside, his father lets him go and ruffles his hair, pushes him gently from behind into his bedroom.

'You're tired, little *vovky*. Go in, go in. Sleep.'

He doesn't mention the conversation with the woman. He never does. It is fifteen years later, reading a textbook in the physics department library at Oxford, that he learns her name. Angelina Guskova, the lead physician who responded to the catastrophe. The collaboration with the American, Gale. How the Americans extended a silent hand of friendship outside the media's gaze. How it was accepted. Yet of the thirteen patients Gale's mission treated with experimental bone marrow transplants and blood transfusion with untried growth factors, eleven died. There is no guarantee that any would have survived. The texts he reads do not pass judgment whether the intervention was a disaster, or, for the two who survived, a success.

He does not know if Zoya's letter arrived. He doubts it. There was no legal document in his family that gave his father access to welfare benefits at the higher rate—the famed 'tie.' But for those few days, he was his father's son again. They had outwitted the bureaucracy. *We men.* It was there that for the first time he became aware of what it was he is tied to. What he has inherited.

Sunday Afternoon

He makes the journey back alone, and in that hour all the doubts of what he's done crowd his thoughts. Perhaps he really won't go back to the base, but drive to the cottage and crawl into bed, or pack his bags and disappear. Yet neither looking at the test results on David's computer nor stopping to talk to the protesters seem the cause for the latch in his chest to have opened. He wants to secure that latch again, but what if it's too late? What if Aggie doesn't come back from her mother's, if she's even gone to her mother's? He's unarmoured against the protest as he passes. He feels exposed to the extra guards on the gate who examine his ID. In the lab he's sure the others can hear the shame of his mama's howl into the wind, that their lab whites are covered in his father's ashen remains, that they're judging him for his inability to stop any of it; he's wearing the accident hung around his neck like a—no, a Cyrillic letter.

He shakes away those thoughts and with them his lingering headache; whatever crisis David is about to break upon him will be enough to deal with, without giving play to all that paranoia. David comes over.

'It was an error of judgment,' says Anthony, pre-empting the dressing-down.

He watches David's face grow red. There are heavy bags under his eyes. A sniffle. The last six days have been a stress that none of them have been through before. Except Anthony. David reels off no end of difficulties that Anthony has caused by bringing Michael onto the base, then runs a hand through his hair, bringing the reproof to a stop. The conditions of all the crew have worsened, David explains. The woman worst of all. They've brought in her family to lodge in a unit near the medical centre. And four additional crew from *Tartarus* have reported sick.

'So it's not contained?'

'No, it *is* contained,' says David with a pained expression. 'I don't want to increase the exposure—' but it's the wrong word and David baulks, rethinks, 'you and I have already seen them, they'—he indicates Mariam and Elspeth—'haven't.'

'What about the whales? That's going to get picked up nationally, isn't it?'

David closes his eyes, shakes his head. 'That's not for us to worry about.'

'And those boys?'

David looks at him.

'There are people here, Anthony,' David says quietly. 'People who are...'

The word you're looking for is dying.

But David doesn't say it. Another voice fills Anthony's ears.

I will never forget the mornings. We had to line them up in the square, and it was to become the routine of our life. One by one the children fell. They couldn't stand even for five minutes. They fell down and we took them away in pairs. It was a dreadful sight. I then began to realise that something awful had happened.

They scrub down, a coarse lathering on his arms and around his elbows, into the indent between thumb and index finger. He can smell carbolic, even though he's pretty sure what he's using is a new synthesis of chemicals and not soap at all. He closes his eyes and sees a hospital corridor, his father leading him by the hand. The clatter of shoes on a tiled floor. *Cerebral arteriosclerosis with arterial hypertension, osteochondrosis, gastritis, and hypochondriacal syndrome.*

'We'll go together this time,' says David.

They help each other with the tie-ups at the backs of the gowns, check that the crinkled edges of the hoods cover their hair. The pebble is in his pocket, but there is a shift in how he holds it: that when the words come now he doesn't want them to stop.

Some of the patients are conscious. He knows better than to

think this is a sign that they're recovering. What has changed is that some of the families are present. They enter the room of Midshipman Carter, and have to ask his mother, father and fiancée to leave while they take readings and blood samples. Each family is allowed twenty minutes exposure per four hours. Midshipman Carter's reading haven't fallen. David chats to the sailor while he draws blood. His name is John. Three years into service. An assistant to the chief marine engine officer. His skin is puffy, and it makes him look a stone heavier than the man in the photo on the bedside cabinet. The room smells of vomit. They say goodbye. He wonders if Midshipman Carter will serve again, or if the exposure will lead to long-term injury. If he will suffer from anorgasm, a loss of sexual interest. If it'll be the leukaemia that kills him.

The rest are in similar conditions, including the four new cases. Sickly, stoic. A few more panicky than others. Cadet Davidson. Sub-Lieutenant Baker. He reads their shock in having the dosimeter pointed at them, in registering how their bodies have become ionised. They're beginning to understand what it might mean for them.

Anthony and David come to the last room of the original eight. She's propped up in bed. Her skin is red, puffy, blotchy. Her eyes are open. Yellow and bloodshot. Her hair is gone. This time when he reads her medical records it divulges her name. Midshipman Louisa Darch. Engineering Officer.

'Hello,' says David. He's breezy; the task growing easier. They go around the same side of the bed, after finding that one each side made Sub-Lieutenant Baker freak out, as if they'd come to strap him down.

'Hello,' she croaks. Her vocal chords are swollen.

'I'm David, and this is my colleague Anthony. We're from the monitoring lab. We've come to take readings for you.' *For* you, not *from* you. They'd made that error too. 'Chart your progress.'

Anthony readies the vials for blood taking. David begins to

chatter about the conditions on the base and that her colleagues send good wishes. He reports on the wellbeing of the others while running the dosimeter over her body. There's no sound, like the old Geiger counters. It's an electric reading, and David keeps the screen pointing away from her—not that she'd know how to read one. But she's not looking at David. She's watching Anthony as he fits a needle to the syringe.

'Are you taking blood?'

'Just a little. To see how the measurements have changed.'

'Is it dirty? My blood.'

'No,' he says, and realises he's whispering. 'No,' he says louder. 'We're making sure the radiation is levelling off.'

He's unsure whether or not the lie is a good thing. David glances, then looks away. Midshipman Darch nods weakly. He takes hold of her right arm and puts the band around her bicep. Her arms were strong and smooth once, under the blisters. He holds her by the wrist as he fits the syringe to the cannula. It fills slowly. A missive written in the rate of that flow. When it's full he withdraws the needle. Her hand feels fleshy; resistance and tone gone.

The woman closes her eyes. Anthony turns to the cabinet at the side of the room where the perfume bottle stands, and fills four vials with her blood and places them in their holders and then wraps the syringe and drops it with the others in the medical disposal bag. David is chatting but it's clipped. What else is there to say?

'Goodbye, Midshipman Darch,' says David.

She attempts a smile. If it were him, he'd be screaming.

In the corridor they stop smartly as a crewmember's family leaves. He and David wait, knowing how terrifying they look in their blue suits. Once the family is gone, escorted by their military guide, who tilts a severe nod in their direction, they go back to the changing room.

'This is the choice you have,' David says abruptly, as he begins to disrobe.

Anthony looks up. 'My choice?'

'Once all this dies—' Another bad choice of words. 'Settles down. God knows what's going to happen. I mean politically. But they're not going to get rid of the subs. No matter what. Not even for this.'

'I get that,' he says.

'Bringing your friend onto the base...' David is stripping the protective suit off, as if the idea of what's been absorbed alarms him. He's fighting at the arms and pushing the blues over his feet. 'Is it your past? Your experience?'

'My experience?'

'Look... What the Commodore wanted to speak to... Did it cloud your decision-making? You came in with lots of ideas, Anthony, all good. But your manner...'

'My manner?'

There's nothing he can say except to repeat what David says. Because yes, it *is* his past. Something has clouded his decision-making, *and it was a fucking cloud*. He wants to thump David, beat him until there is nothing left, only gas and vapour.

David throws his overalls into the safety bin. Anthony's not even taken his off yet. David pulls at his chin as if to open his mouth mechanically, as if this might be the only way to get the words out.

'We have to work together, Anthony. Your six months' probation will be here soon. But bringing in...' David waits, but Anthony says nothing. 'We don't even have to trust you to begin with. You sign the Official Secrets Act. But over time, yes. We have to trust one another. You can't do this job without it. It's the nuclear deterrent, for God's sake. It's the real world.'

He wonders if David can see the lumpish outline of a pebble in his pocket. If he knows about the stops at the protest camp. If he knows about *"Safe Living Concept"* outlined for persons in *contaminated zones*. About the *istoriia*, the *baiky*, the *ekzotyka* of suffering, about the dusty city to which he was evacuated. *The whole town consists of sufferers.*

He pulls off his blue suit and pushes it through the sprung top of the safety bin, sits down and ties up his shoe laces and then stands to face David.

'You can trust me,' he says.

At five o'clock Elspeth offers him a cup of coffee, but he's not going to take it for some false camaraderie and then be up all night, angsty from the caffeine. Suddenly David and Mariam are there too. There's more work to be done before they leave. Another set of orders has just arrived.

'Can I call Aggie?' he asks. 'Let her know I won't be back soon.'

Elspeth barks with relief. 'Me too.'

David chides himself. 'Christie, yes.' He smiles. 'Good point.'

They go into the four corners of the lab. He dials Aggie's mobile.

'Ant?'

'We've got to work late,' he says, which is no explanation. Aggie's waiting. 'It's shipping out tomorrow, one of the subs, we've been drafted in to run tests that were missing from...' he says. It slips out easily. Why didn't they agree on what to say? 'Extra hands. Nothing exceptional,' he adds, in a light tone.

Aggie is quiet. She already knows about the woman, knows he's lying.

'We'd normally have much more time...'

'I'll stay at mum's.' It's curt. 'I can work in the Glasgow office tomorrow...'

He stops listening. But no, this is not about *Greg*. It's her dad. Today. The grave. He feels an unexpected sadness wash through his gut.

'I won't be long,' he says.

'I'd rather stay here if you're not going to pick me up.'

There's nothing else to say. He hangs up and returns to the bench to await the others. Of the four, David is the last to return.

An hour later he looks up and sees they've all left the lab; the three of them have attended another briefing, and he's not been invited. He turns to his work—*his* work, the only work that is improving the procedures that have stagnated for the last ten years. Of course the budget had been slashed; austerity reaches even here, so they'd cut corners. He writes up the results from the readings he and Michael took, finalizing the new procedures by which to ensure rigorous future marine testing, completes the rewriting of his section of the handbook, closes the laptop, cannot remember a single thing he's just written, breathes deeply with the thought that he's both proud and doesn't care.

He stares at the picture of Aggie on the bench from their honeymoon. They collapsed on the sunbeds of Ko Samui, drank the cocktails, wandered the streets of Chiang Mai in a daze, their minds numb with fatigue and the weight of propriety upon them, with vows made in front of witnesses to the contract they'd entered. They negotiated days of doing nothing on the honeymoon, and the newness of how he and Aggie related to each other took him by surprise. Perhaps he was just stone tired, but marriage floated down like feathers until it covered him. *A tonne of iron or a tonne of feathers?* It's the first thing he remembers of physics lessons. A trick question for boys eager to impress. He thinks of the helicopters that carried bags of sand over the hill. For the human bio-robots to shovel into the hole. A tonne is a tonne, although iron is not feathers, and feathers are not graphite. Feathers a slow, soft killing.

David pushes through the lab doors and looks at Anthony, but not with admonishment. He knows by the expression on David's face what's happened.

'Just now. Come on. We need to get postmortem readings immediately.'

For the second time he scrubs his hands and arms, pulls the blue suit on over his whites, hairnet, face mask and gloves on last. The clinic is quieter than before. He and David go in together. The chief medic is there talking with another doctor, a woman the same age as Anthony, with a grave face and suspicious eyes. The chief waves them in. It's quieter, Anthony realises, because the dead woman's monitoring machine has been switched off. The two medics finish their discussion; the woman clears Midshipman Louisa Darch's belongings into a blue thin canvas bag: tablets, a small brown cuddly toy dog, a headscarf, the perfume bottle.

'It's totally shocking,' says the chief medic to David, shaking his head. 'This changes things, doesn't it?'

'I really don't know,' says David.

The medic looks at Anthony. He's thinking of David's words. *This is the choice you have.* The woman zips up the blue bag.

'We've got a helicopter coming from the Western in Glasgow. It'll be half an hour or so. For the postmortem.' He looks at his watch. Anthony notices the medics are not wearing full protective clothing. 'Come on, Alice.'

The woman nods. She's holding the bag away from her body with both hands. Those belongings will not be returned to the family but will go straight to the incinerator, the blue bag too. The medics leave. He and David set about their business, taking the same samples as before. He takes a dosimeter reading, and then addresses the sample vials while David readies the syringe for drawing blood. It comes with a struggle—there is no heart, no pulse to drive the flow. Anthony's never taken samples from a dead person. He wonders if David has. As David fills each vial Anthony takes them, writes the name, time and date on each, and puts them in the case. He does this looking at the woman's face, which is still red, and feels heat rising from her body. It's the ionisation that's killed her. Her body may have stopped supporting her life but there is living matter there still, on the bed. He sees on the wheeled table that's been pushed away from the bed an open folder with her record. David takes a final blood sample, prepares to take tissue from her arm, a swab from inside her mouth. Every available toxicology source for their machines to interpret, for the pathologist to later request, for the inquest to later decide if they had done enough, for the government, perhaps Parliament, to choose whether or not the risk was worth it. Whether they should have more or less of this resource that is the at-sea deterrent, or if they should have more or less of the life of the young woman Midshipman Louisa Darch. But that decision is made. His hand trembles when David passes him the last swab to store in a large screw-cap container. He looks away, through the translucent window and the light softening as evening draws closer. It is Sunday. This morning he sat with Aggie on the edge of her father's grave, allowing memories to come that he'd not known he'd remembered. And now he's with this woman who is dead.

He secures all the samples in the case and closes the lid, snaps shut the two small silver latches. They leave the room, closing the door gently. They walk to the preparation room, and begin to disrobe. For the second time David's ready before him, throwing the blue suit in the secure waste bin, shoving his hands through the arms of his jacket and shucking his shoulders to get it on straight, putting on his whites. Antony is moving too slowly for David to let it pass.

'Are you okay, Anthony? You seemed...in there...'

He nods. 'It's not nice. You?'

'Well, I suppose. I've seen dead bodies before...'

'I might need a minute.'

David stares, then nods and leaves. Anthony watches the doors swing to and fro until they come to a halt. He's not taken his blues off. He raises the mask to cover his nose and mouth, and goes back into the corridor of the clinic. It's empty. Without waiting in case David comes back, he runs to her room.

She's died with a smile on her face. Flakes of her skin make a dandruff halo on the pillow. *Rozvalenyi.* The pace of ruin specific to each individual. He sits on the chair. He lowers his mask. For a moment he thinks she moves her head. But of course she doesn't. Her scalp is tender, enflamed. He puts his hand on hers. It's cold. There's none of the warmth he felt earlier.

The fear of being found seizes him, and he stands. He unzips his blue overalls and digs into his pocket. Not for the pebble. He takes out his phone and moves to the end of the bed and lines her up and takes a photo of Midshipman Louisa Darch. He's forgotten to turn the sound off and the noise of the fake electronic shutter makes him jump. Then he goes to the wheeled table and takes a photo of the top sheet of her medical records. The camera takes what feels like forever to focus. He turns the page, takes a photo of the next sheet. And the next. Then he puts them back in order, puts his phone back in his pocket, and zips up the blue overalls. He takes a final look.

Where am I?

Here. Here.

Soroksotok.

By the parcel of land.

Sviaz po smerti.

On the border with death.

25th– 26th December, 1991, Kyiv

In the morning, before he's allowed to open any presents, he goes downstairs and waits in line for the phone booth outside the supervisor's room. There's good cheer, a huddle of people, and someone is sharing around tree-shaped gingerbreads with icing decoration and which are the best thing he tastes all day. People shout in loud harsh tones and come away waggling their heads about how they can't hear a thing, the line is terrible. Then it's his turn. His mama and Sveta are waiting with other families in the house of a neighbour in Korosten', whose phone line is the most reliable. In the few months ('an abyss' his uncle calls it) since Ukrainian Independence there's been a flurry of activity in handing over power, which in reality has meant that no one's responsible for anything. Then the great storms in November knocked out much of the electricity. It's been repaired only in fits and starts. He reads the phone number off a scrap of paper and dials. When he gets through his mama is coughing. *'I'm so tired, my Anatolii, I'm so tired.'* He doesn't know what to say. He presses the receiver to his ear until it turns numb. His mama passes him to Sveta. They wish each other happy Christmas or at least he thinks that's what Sveta says. He has to shout to be heard, but Sveta cannot shout. Really, he only imagines she's saying the same as him. Then, silence. The people in the queue are telling him to say something or hang up, so he hangs up. He races upstairs and now Kulyk allows him to opens his presents.

What did he get? He can't remember. Give? He can't remember that either. Even so, calling them wasn't as bad as last year. Then he'd waited for more than an hour.

'Ah, less people making calls this year, Anatolii, none of the Russians want to call their families in public,' says Kulyk, shaking his head. Kulyk is sitting at the kitchen table, a large pile of potatoes sitting in a colander. There's a bottle of *horilka* on the table, half empty, and a small glass. Since Independence the 'ethnic cleaning' (a phrase picked up from Russian State Radio) continues in a casual way. No one is being thrown out officially, and no one is being attacked. Not in the cities, at least, where people have learnt to get along; but what about in the villages? And yet his uncle tells him, and he knows too, that people are leaving all the time. One day the Russian teachers at Anatolii's school disappeared, replaced by Ukrainian teachers, even if they didn't know the subjects. There were no more Russian history lessons. For a few weeks they had Mr Shokolov, but he was as unknowledgeable about Ukrainian history as they were. He tried to teach them folk songs but then he disappeared too; the rumour was that Mr Shokolov had a secret Russian family as well as a Ukrainian one.

'Rubbish,' Kulyk said when Anatolii brought the gossip home. 'This is getting out of hand. You can't sack people on rumours. That's as bad as Stalin.'

Anatolii nodded. Kulyk came and found him later in his room, where he was reading a book about stargazing he'd borrowed from the school library.

'Not as bad as Stalin,' said his uncle, leaning on the doorframe. 'Independence for Ukraine is a good thing, Anatolii, don't you think so?'

His uncle had been drinking the *horilka*. Anatolii hid his face behind the book. 'Not all good, but just you wait. We'll get you out yet.'

Anatolii didn't understand this thing about getting out. He didn't want to go anywhere, in case Miss Dorogatzev came back. He was in love, if he'd admit it, with Miss Dorogatzev. He'd liked the way she smelled of flowers and told them about the myths behind the stories they learnt in books. He didn't know what love was until someone told him what it felt like. This was how he felt about her. Then she disappeared.

He was also in love with stars. They'd begun to study astronomy in science class. That was one good thing about Independence. Mr Shalev had been replaced by Mr Kraznakov. 'Call me Kyryl,' he'd said in his first class. No one was brave enough. Mr Kraznakov taught them astrophysics. Anatolii was more interested in science now. Mr Kraznakov had worked at the State Centre for Space Research and Exploration in Moscow, and despite anything to do with Moscow and Russia being dangerous, Anatolii and the others were fascinated. Mr Kraznakov was young and enjoyed teaching them and came to class in a check shirt rather than Mr Shalev's jacket and tie. It was almost enough to make up for not seeing Miss Dorogatzev.

'You know, boys, not everything about Russia was bad,' Mr Kraznakov told them. 'Some things, yes, but we—' no one said *we* when talking about Russia anymore, but Mr Kraznakov didn't blink, 'were the first in space. Before the Americans. The hero, Gagarin. This is the real power of our science. To explore. This is what it means, yes? Question: Who would be a cosmonaut? A space explorer?'

'We should build weapons,' said a boy called Serhii, without putting up his hand. He was bigger than Anatolii, with straight brown hair that fell in a centre parting. The girls didn't like him. His father was in the police. 'We need weapons to defend our Motherland.'

'But what if every country put their money into building rockets to go to the moon instead? Into peaceful science?' Mr Kraznakov asked the class. Anatolii could tell Mr Kraznakov didn't like Serhii either. 'Would we need weapons?'

'If we're the only ones with weapons, we win,' said Serhii.

Mr Kraznakov sat on the edge of his desk and looked at Serhii for a moment, shaking his head. Then he stood and went to the board, and started writing down the names of different gases: oxygen, nitrogen, hydrogen.

'These are fundamental elements,' he explained. 'The stuff of life.'

Then Mr Kraznakov began writing names of words he'd never heard. No, that wasn't true. He'd heard them once, when his father spoke them after driving in the Zone. Uranium. Plutonium. Strontium.

'These,' said Mr Kraznakov, twisting to face the class, 'are elements too, parts of this planet and of space. The universe. But they're also dangerous. You' — and he pointed with the chalk at Serhii — 'believe these are better to make into weapons.' He shrugged. 'When Chernobyl exploded, these' — and he rapped the board with the chalk, underlining each of the words with a scribble — 'these were released and spread all over the country. Other countries too. Belarus, lots in Belarus. There was a plume of smoke and it spread all the way to Sweden. And here is where the Soviet Union did a bad thing. We tried to hide it. People in the West knew there'd been a disaster before our people did.'

The class was frozen, even Serhii. No one taught them this. No one mentioned the explosion. It was 'shoved under the carpet' his uncle said, although not as bitterly as he'd heard his father say it once, after their return from Moscow as they waited for the letter from Doctor Zoya. *I was there!* he wanted to tell Mr Kraznakov. He'd seen the plume of smoke. He wanted Mr Kraznakov to pat him on the back, ask him to share everything. 'You see, it was Swedish scientists who found particles of ruthenium in the air, showing that a meltdown of the reactor had occurred. Long before Premier Gorbachev went on the television and told everyone nothing had happened.'

No one understood what he was saying. It was six years until he knew what particles were, and remembered with fond surprise his teacher, Mr Kraznakov, that class and the other boys, even Serhii. He wished he'd called him Kyryl, just once.

'Come on,' says Kulyk, waving his glass at the potatoes, 'get these peeled.'

With nothing else to do they prepare dinner and eat on the stroke of twelve. Since he turned ten, Kulyk has allowed Anatolii a finger of beer with his dinner each Saturday. Now on Christmas Day he's allowed a small cup of wine with their dinner, which they eat at the kitchen table with the radio for company. They wash up and sit in the lounge, his uncle carrying the radio through. Anatolii feels lightheaded and reckless but also numb from the wine, and he falls into a chair.

Nothing else happens until the next day, when they hear the announcement that the Soviet Union is formally dissolved. Kulyk is lying on the sofa complaining about his headache.

'Nothing lasts. Nothing is infinite.'

'Uranium,' says Anatolii. He's reading his book on astronomy. His uncle rolls around to face him.

'What?'

'Uranium.' He's afraid he's irritated his uncle, who likes to lie down and think about these moments in history; that, or if he's got money, go to the bar and drink through them with his friends. But to Anatolii it seems they come along all the time. The world changes every day, since the accident at least. Something new happens that alters his life. It was Independence only a few months ago. Now it's the end of the Soviet Union. So what? What will it be next year? 'Uranium has an infinite half-life. Mr Kraznakov told us in astrophysics.'

Kulyk scrutinises him. Anatolii sinks into his chair, which is dirty and damp. He clutches his book, holds it in front of him.

'Okay then,' his uncle says, and lets out a long sigh. 'It's good you're becoming a smart boy. They'll let smart boys out of the country, to study in America.'

Soon his uncle is snoring. The radio is on, more news about the end of something that he hadn't realised he's lived under all his life. After a while he gets up and turns the radio off. He tiptoes to his room and falls onto the bed in a good mood. Reads his book on the stars. When he goes back to school in January, Mr Kraznakov isn't there. He's angry and doesn't know what to do. Then Anatolii starts the rumour that Serhii told his father the policeman to get rid of Mr Kraznakov. Everyone hates Serhii anyway, so they all believe him.

Monday

He leaves the car farther away this time, on a track off the roundabout before the base entrance in a parking space by a picnic outlook. It leads onto the hills so there's little chance of it being spotted. For a moment he hesitates. There's a view of the loch from the picnic rest. Despite its placidity he sees under its dark surface the scale of the crisis that's coming. He reaches into the back seat and pulls on a hooded jumper and walks down the track to the protest camp. He hears them inside the main tent. He calls out *hello* and puts his head though the entrance.

'Well, well. Back again,' says Tom.

'Come in then,' says Maureen. 'Don't let all the cold air in.'

Maureen mimes the pouring of tea. He smiles, nods. Tom shifts one of the camp chairs around for Anthony, and he sits. Maureen hands him a cup of tea.

'So what brings you back?' she asks.

He shakes his head. Drinks his tea. She's remembered: black, weak.

'Just to talk.'

'He's turning, Mo.'

'Leave him be. We're civilised here. We're capable of talking. No agendas.'

Tom's fixing a tarp, digging into eyeholes with a pocketknife and widening them to take a thicker twine. He's replacing old eyelets with sturdier ones, popping them into place over frayed edges of canvas. Anthony watches spellbound; such changes taken care of as if they were crucial to the success of the campaign. As if they were the only reason why it might succeed.

'You must have tough bones to stop the rain getting into you.'

'We're wild creatures now,' says Tom, not looking up. 'Grown fur.'

'We head off to the campsite down the road every day or two

for a shower,' says Maureen. 'We keep warm. Now what did you want to talk about?'

He stares into his tea.

'There used to be plenty of wildlife around here,' Tom says, and Anthony's shoulders drop in relief that he doesn't have to begin yet. 'I've watched it all in my time, their disappearance. The curlews and sandpipers, the hoverflies. Even the bloody hedgehogs, which let me tell you aren't as cute as people like to think. All gone. It damages us, them not being here. Our *wellbeing*. Fucking stupid word for it, something the charities say, ain't it?'

Tom's blue eyes have the hardness of a frozen lake as he waves the pocketknife in the air.

'What does it bloody mean? I'll tell you what it means. *Climate change*. Losing all these species. It's all connected, ain't it? Your military-fucking-industrial complex is the biggest sinner in greenhouse gas pollution. Got children, mate? If you have—'

'He's been like this all weekend,' says Maureen. 'I don't like it when the others come to join the protest. Oh, it's important, it feels good, but it leaves him like this.'

'You know what's really in decline?' asks Tom. 'The moths. I used to set a moth trap as a boy, just for the joy of looking at the things in the morning as they slept. I used to get every trap full every night. I knew the difference between a Hawk Moth and an Angle Shades. You seen one of them?'

Anthony shakes his head.

'You think I'm stupid?' Tom asks.

'Of course he doesn't,' Maureen says. 'Other people do, for good reason.'

'You can shut up,' says Tom, but says it lightly, an old couple bickering. He has a vision of himself and Aggie with silver hair, his back hurting, having tea on a campsite. He doesn't know if it scares or cheers him.

'I'm not stupid,' Tom says, leaning forward. 'You know what drives climate change? The same system that drives the desire for these weapons. Neo-lib-er-al-ism. The most dangerous -ism we've ever had. Ha!'

Tom throws himself back in his seat. Anthony's not sure what was funny. He looks at Maureen, her mouth tight with that question she's already asked.

'You want a dangerous -ism,' he says, 'you should've lived under Communism.'

'Okay?' says Tom, digging at the tarp and its knotted holes, confused. 'You want to know when it began? 1973. Torness, the other side of the country—Scotland,' in case Anthony misses the lesson. 'The old CEGB announced plans to build eight nuclear power stations at Torness. I was...? We'd set up Friends of the Earth in Edinburgh, my final year. Then I graduated and the Torness news broke. That's how it started. Not that I expect you pro-nuclear lot know our history.'

'It's not on the curricula.'

'Funny boy.'

'And Torness was built.'

Tom leans towards him.

'Yes, fucking gloat, like Dungeness, Hinckley Point. But you know we win sometimes. I was there at Druridge Bay, helped those women who built the Cairn. Delayed those bastards for over fifteen years. Then it was shelved. Ha! Although that Thatcherite Blair almost put it back on the agenda. They fought it off again. One of those trusts bought the land. It's a bird sanctuary now. Don't you think that's a better use? Rather than contaminating the landscape for half a billion years?'

Anthony deadpans the question, holds his tea with both hands. Warm drinks are meant to warm you to people, wasn't that the case?

'And then you came here?'

'There used to be quite a group of us.'

'Ask her about Greenham,' Tom says. 'Go on.'

He expects Mo to look away, but she doesn't. Her eyes are

defiant.

'You were one of the Greenham women?'

'Oh,' she says, not out of modesty but tiredness. She swirls her tea. 'We wanted a debate. That was all. We hoped a debate aired on the news would make everyone aware of the issue. Most people didn't know—'

'Didn't care,' Tom interrupts without looking up.

'Didn't know,' Maureen carries on, 'so *couldn't* care. You see, Anthony, this is the problem. People do care. No one doesn't care to be loved, to have those you love be safe. Wouldn't you say?'

He wishes Aggie was here. She'd be delighted.

'But we were ignored. We walked all the way from Wales to deliver a letter to the Commander. But he wouldn't take it. We'd guessed that might happen. So we stayed. We set up camp. A bit like this one, but bigger. There were more of us.'

'For nineteen years,' says Tom, holding the tarp up to his chest to look at his handiwork. Tom's smirking, then pointing at Maureen with his knife. 'Go on, ask her. What it was like. Whether she got *bored*.'

Anthony shakes his head. 'I never meant that.'

Maureen waves it away.

'We were singing, protesting. We didn't live ordinary lives. None of that "Go to work, take the children to school, have friends over, go out on a Saturday to shop." Our *lives* were a campaign.'

'Why did you stop?' he asks.

She laughs. It's deeper than he expects, happier. She grins. 'Who's stopped?'

'Fuck!' says Tom, shaking his fingers. 'Fucking plastic. He meant—'

'I know what he meant, you old dodder,' she says. 'And stop swearing.'

Anthony has to laugh at that. There's a pause while Tom gets a plaster for his hand. He and Maureen drink their tea. He listens to rain on the tent canvas, the wind, a car passing. He smells the place for the first time; old clothing, the rubber of airbeds and waterproofs and the mustiness of dried camping foods.

'Nineteen years, my dear,' she says, 'we were different women by the end of course. And the cruise missiles were gone, all flown back to the US.'

'Know your nuclear history?' asks Tom.

'I'm a radiologist. I don't work for the military.'

'Yes, you do.'

'We'd been there ten years,' Maureen carries on. 'Then the Americans left. But that place—Greenham—it was *common* land before it was a military base. We stayed because we had to secure the future of the land. It was the *land* we walked all the way from Wales for. Do you see? Not to protest *against* something. But *for* something.'

Her words make him shiver. He feels soil under his fingernails, hears the wet crinkle of leaf mulch he's carried in his arms from the corners of the base. Feels the glutinous, greasy black backs of the dead whales on the beach. Are these the things *he* is for?

'They took the last missiles back to America. Well, we were getting submarines, weren't we? And that's where you're implicated.'

Khlop. Just a boy.

'I miss the women,' says Maureen.

'"Con artists and communists in wigwams",' says Tom. 'Talking of communism...' Anthony's confused and, he's surprised to find, angry. But Maureen's laughing.

'Oh yes, that prat, the Conservative. What was his name? Davies? That's what he called us. He's an MP now. Ex-Army, too, surprise, surprise.'

'Although he does speak Welsh.'

She sighs. 'And he's married to a Hungarian. Does a lot for immigrant rights.' She looks at Anthony, sizing him up. 'You see, people aren't easy to pin down, are they? Even Tories.' She's standing at a foldout table making preparations for dinner.

'Oh, Thalia gave our Mister Davies a *right* talking-to at a rally in Carmarthen. He'd only gone and said that the memorial we wanted to leave behind at Greenham should be a statue of Thatcher.' Maureen stops halfway through opening a tin of sweet corn. 'All good women. Good friends. It was a way of life. Are you staying for dinner?'

'I've got to get back home. It's not fair on my wife.'

'Invite her,' says Tom. 'We could do with some company.'

'Tom, don't be rude.'

'I meant *more* company. So, then, man of mystery, are you going to tell us what you meant about living under Communism?'

He thought he was ready, but Tom's question takes him by surprise.

'Tom,' Maureen chides him.

Tom puts the tarp down. 'You want me to do something, Mo?'

'You get in the way. All these years, Anthony, and he still can't cook. He'd eat nothing but raw veg if it were down to him.'

Tom leans forward.

'So coming here. A radiologist on this base. Talking about Communism. What's that all about? Got something to say, or you mocking us again?'

'We're out of sausages,' Maureen interrupts.

They both turn to her.

'You have a car, don't you? Would you mind giving me a lift to the shops?'

Tom laughs.

'This is the test, isn't it? Seen in public with us?'

'Tom!' Maureen shouts. But breaking the Official Secrets Act would be nothing compared with the shame he'd feel if he refused. He pulls himself from the chair, bending to the low roof of the tent.

'I'll give you a lift.'

'Get me some tinned mackerel, will you,' Tom shouts after them as they leave the tent, much louder than he needs to.

Anthony winces. Cameras? Yes, he's on camera right now, he expects. He and Maureen walk up the track to the car. He gets in and sweeps the seat of rubbish and crumbs while scanning for anything incriminating.

'Don't worry about the mess,' she says, putting on the seat belt. 'It's a short drive into Garelochhead,' she says as they pull out, and then she's looking at the road, twisting round. 'But that's the other way?'

'It won't be open. The butchers. For your sausages.'

'Oh don't worry about that. The convenience store will be—'

'It's crap.'

'I'm not a fan of supermarkets. But then I guess you're not a fan of being seen with us, are you? Though I'd say the odds of you bumping into someone at the Tesco in—'

'There's a Spar at Helensburgh,' he says. 'More choice. Local suppliers too.'

Maureen interlinks her fingers so they rest over her stomach. They drive in silence apart from the slog of the engine through the gears. For a moment he's frightened someone will see them. Then the fear fades.

'Ever worked in a nuclear plant, Anthony?'

'No. It was mainly theoretical, I was at Oxford.'

'But you know them? Their names?'

He nods.

'They changed the names back in—but you'll know this. Changed the name of the plant down in Cumbria from Windscale to Sellafield. That was mainly because of the Yorkshire TV programme, "The Windscale Laundry." And the Black Report. You know the Black Report?'

He shakes his head.

'You don't know the Black Report? 1984. Or 1986. No, before Chernobyl.'

On the other side of the road a Land Rover passes by, pulling an animal trailer. He breathes out. Nothing has changed. It hasn't changed the world to hear its name.

'Not long after the Sizewell Inquiry, and those American pressure water—'

'Pressurised.'

'Okay, thanks for that.'

He winces, glows red.

'Sorry. That's a bad habit of mine.'

'It's alright. The Black Report found abnormally high levels of child leukaemia around the nuclear plants along the Severn Estuary. Four times the normal level.'

'I didn't know that.' Did he? Did he study that? Or did the professors keep them from such reports? They reach Helensburgh and he hits the thirty mile speed limit zone. The village opens into a wide main street but nearly everything's shut apart from the Spar, shining blurry green and red in the murky September evening. He pulls into a space in front of the store and turns off the engine.

'But of course, they couldn't prove a *cause*,' she says, sitting forward and unbuckling the belt. 'They really don't teach you this in your training?'

'We went through past events. They got me to...' Maureen doesn't ask what. 'I didn't pay attention to everything. We weren't doing site management. We were learning the physics.'

'Well. That sums up a lot. Just the physics, and not the management.'

'Other people were learning that.'

'They never taught you about the consequences, did they?' Her face hardens. 'About the leukaemia. The long-term sickness. Didn't you look?'

He stares out of the windscreen. Yes, he looked.

'You coming in?' she says, suddenly cheerful, nodding towards the Spar.

'We need some things,' he says, and he thinks they might.

She opens the door and then stops for a moment. She's looking down.

'Oh, you've got a dog. What type?'

He looks at the tennis ball. 'No,' he says, and gets out.

Aggie's not home. The cottage is full of damp tidings and her absence fills him with a quiet, wild desperation. He can't remember if she said she'd be late. He wanders around the cottage thinking of where she is, with whom. He stops by the mantelpiece in the lounge, looks at a picture from their honeymoon. They'd left opening all the presents until after they'd returned from Thailand. They were stacked in a large pile in the bay window of their flat, a gift to themselves to prolong the excitement. They settled down with a bottle of Languedoc left over from the wedding dinner and some of the cake that was still good to eat stored in little Tupperwares in the fridge. They sat on the floor with their backs against the sofa and worked their way through the pile. They unwrapped a set of plates from a pottery in Cumbria from their friend Hugh, who was obsessed with ceramics and travelled the country to all the *Polfests* (they really were called that). Bedding from Aggie's aunt Clare. Saucepans from his Irish cousins. The gifts were a statement that they'd made good on life's promise. Reward for the initiation not only into marriage but adulthood. To the secret of having understood who they were, enough to share that secret with another.

'What's this?' Aggie asked, handing him a package about the size of a good dictionary. He took it, expecting it to be heavy. It wasn't. It was wrapped in overelaborate wrapping paper. It brought back a memory of a woman standing in a crowd, wearing a dress of a similar design.

'Don't rip the paper,' said Aggie.

'Seriously?'

He put down his wine and undid the seal, peeling back the tape and unfolding the corners. It was a plain cardboard box. Taped across the top was an envelope.

The Chernobyl Privileges

'"To Anatolii",' read Aggie.

'Sorry. They fucking do that.'

She wriggled closer and rested her head on his shoulder.

'Why would you be sorry?'

He tore the tape and put the letter on top of the wrapping paper. Aggie gripped his elbow, as if all the pity he'd once felt for her—his sister, it was her handwriting—was returned to him by his wife. Aggie squeezed his arm and sat up.

'What's inside?'

'If it's not something to drink I'll be very surprised.'

He opened the flaps of the box and under a snowfall of white polystyrene clefs there emerged the shape of three eggs, two the size of duck's eggs and the third much larger. Below the eggs, set into a foam casing with jagged edges, as if Kulyk had carved the casement himself, was a miniature bottle of *horilka*, with two shot glasses.

'What are the eggs?'

'Here.' He offered Aggie the box. 'Take one, the big one.'

She lifted it out. Her hands jumped, as if it the egg was about to fly away.

'It's so light!'

'It's a real egg, although what animal...an ostrich probably.'

The egg was painted with a red background divided into a diamond by four white lines, and in each quadrant on both sides were geometric shapes that looked like tiny cathedrals, with a left and right steeple filled with yellow stripes, except for the bottom one, which had a line of yellow dots.

'Where would your uncle get hold of an ostrich egg?'

'It's an industry. There's demand for the bigger ones. Special occasions.'

'What are they?'

'*Pysanky*. Easter eggs. But they can be given other times. It's a big compliment. They're given to family members and respected others.'

'I'm a *respected other* now, am I?'

'There are two shot glasses.'

'So we're meant to toast the egg? What's that, in the bottle?'

'It's horrible.'

'We're still going to drink it, right? In honour of your uncle and sister?'

He lifted the smaller eggs out. One was black with a large red and pink flower with limp fronds. The other was geometric in reds and blues. They were emptied of the yolk and white but firm, the batik sealing the shell and giving it a strength undue to it, to travel thousands of miles and nestle among the other presents.

'And what do they mean? Are they symbolic?'

'It's all symbolic. You know the Eastern Europeans.'

'Not as well as I'd like.'

He didn't return her look. He took out the *horilka* and shot glasses.

'Those two, the small ones,' he pointed at the eggs, 'they're pretty traditional. That one you're holding, I don't know. It's not something I recognise.' He twisted the top of the *horilka* with a snap of the lid. It smelt of the plant world. 'The name *horilka* comes from *hority*.'

'And what does that mean?'

'Burning.'

He poured for them both. Aggie put the egg back in the box and took a shot glass.

'One, two, three.' They clinked glasses and drank. They coughed and cursed.

'Didn't we need to toast?' Aggie asked, wiping her mouth with the arm of her cardigan. 'Jesus. That *was* disgusting.'

'No toast. It's done. You're a member of the family, officially.'

'So that's all it took. What do they mean, the symbols?'

He told her why the ostrich egg was red: it represented life-giving blood, joy and love, and the hope of marriage. He picked it up and studied the pattern. He could not make out what it was, unless it was just the depiction of church spires. He told her of the importance of displaying the eggs in the house for the luck to be communed upon the receivers—to hide the eggs away was to refuse the blessing of love. The eggs would protect them from evil spirits and catastrophe, lightning and fires. That the *pysanky* with spiral motifs were the strongest protection, as demons and unholy creatures were trapped within the designs and could not find their way out of the mazes. He told her about the myths of the ancient Ukrainians who made their homes in the Carpathian Mountains, who believed the fate of the world rested on each *pysanka* and its making. As long as the custom continued, the world would exist. If the custom was abandoned, evil would take hold of the world in the shape of a serpent who was chained to a cliff. Without the eggs to keep the demons imprisoned, evil would unleash the serpent and it would overrun the world.

'So each year the serpent sends out his minions to see how many *pysanky* have been decorated.' He could feel the *horilka* on top of the wine making him lightheaded and queasy. 'And if the number is low the serpent's chains are loosened, and he's free to slink around. He causes all the world's ills, all the destruction and chaos.'

'But if the *pysanky*...?'

'If their number has gone up, the snake stays chained to the cliff face.'

'And good triumphs over evil for another year. Where will we put them?'

He stared at the eggs. He knew then what the design was, those white outlines on the largest egg. They were not cathedrals with two steeples. They were wolf's teeth.

'No one made any eggs in 1986,' he said.

He leaned across his wife and closed the box.

He leaves the cottage without taking off his coat. He gets back

214

Alex Lockwood

in the car, but has nowhere to go. He looks at the tennis ball. It's taken on a much greater meaning than it warrants, something he's magnified in his head until he is unable to see around it to whatever, whoever, is on the other side. The past week feels as if it has expanded out of control in the same way, too many crises for so few days. But crises, catastrophes, accidents and adulteries are not accounted for by linear time. They happen instantly, they tumble into a life. Is that where Aggie is now, with *Greg*? She probably is, he smiles grimly. In a training room with half a dozen others talking about poverty and narrative. Or at the pub after, having a Diet Coke before she runs to catch the train home, before she calls him with enthusiasm to ask him to pick her up at the station, that she is looking forward to seeing him. He checks his phone. No message. She's a good person. So is *Greg*. There's only one idiot in this story.

His desperation has gone, but it's replaced with a restlessness that makes it impossible to sit still. He could phone her to check. He goes into the cottage again and packs away the shopping from the Spar, thinks about cooking but isn't hungry. He turns on the heating and it cranks away under the skim of plaster and thick woodchip wallpaper. His skin prickles. It is, though, beginning to smell like their home; their brand of washing powder, their clothes drying in the airing cupboard. The knock of his shoes on the stone kitchen floor. The winnowing of dead women— Midshipman Louisa Darch—trapped in the walls.

He sits in the gloom, thinking of Aggie, thinking of stewed apples. The cottage creaks like an old tea-clipper and he thinks he hears someone coming down the stairs before he remembers that Aggie is not there with him. He goes into the lounge and sits at the computer and turns on the screen. Pauses in that strange, buffered silence while the screen glows dusky then light. He sees the diagnostic machines through which he runs the blood. The lists of radionuclides he checks for each sample. He sees her scalp, her perfume bottle. He is thinking about...and it comes in its own language. Her *dekompensatiia*, the decompensation the body enters when it cannot respond effectively. A loss of physiologically adaptive responses. Lethal doses. Death.

I sweat, I don't sleep. When I lie down, everything spins. The balcony attracts me. I want to jump. I'm on the fifth floor and the ground looks half a metre away. I walk and walk. Walk and walk and walk. I need movement.

Was that his father?

He digs his nails into his palms. The login screen flashes at him. He enters the password. Turns the screen brightness down. He plugs in his phone and downloads the pictures. He tries not to look at them while he moves them into a folder and buries them somewhere even he might forget they exist. He knows that's no real security. He unplugs the phone. He opens a browser and begins to Google names and email addresses. Opens Word. Begins to type. Just the facts. He finds the email of an editor at one of the newspapers. Creates a new Gmail account. Attaches the document. He can't believe what he's doing. Once it's done, he opens another Word document and stares at it. He doesn't know what this one is for. He begins to type.

Dear Sveta,

After all these years, after all the refusals to reply to her, he's going to *type* a letter? But that's just another excuse. She's right. He knows she's right. Unless he listens to her and accepts what is happening to her, he won't know what's going to happen to him. Because he's taken photos of a dead woman that he can be put in jail for; he's sent an email to a newspaper editor. And none of it seems wrong, or at least not wrong if what he is responding to, finally, is not the situation in front of him, the piece of paper he's signed, the chance of this career, but what happened before; to her, his sister. And to him. What happened to him.

But he's too agitated to sit and write. What does he say?

He goes out to the car again. In the space for pennies and phones beneath the dashboard is that woman's card. He picks it up and puts it in his pocket and brings it into the cottage and walks into the lounge where the landline sits on a small table next to the sofa. He is not acting mindlessly, he tells himself. He dials the number.

'Hello?' Her accent is how he remembers it.

'Hi,' he says, as if they're old friends. 'I'm the guy from the base.'

'Oh, hello,' she says. The energy shifts. He can hear her moving about. Perhaps she's standing up and moving away from someone. 'Thanks for ringing.'

He doesn't want to say too much over the phone. He knows it's ridiculous but there's the thought that if he gets off in less than a minute they can't trace it and won't know it was him. It isn't just the films that make him think that—it's how it was. The KGB on the line, listening in. She's in Dumbarton. They agree to meet at the big roadside Carvery on the A82 outside Alexandria.

He turns the key and hopes the old jalopy won't start, but it does.

The Carvery is low-lit, red carpeted and pine decorated, busy, he thinks, for a Monday evening. He walks in and sees her at the bar. He can see through the swinging doors into the kitchen, breathes in the overcooked vegetables and the stink of three different kinds of meat and mud on walking boots and the stagnation of Loch Lomond that has crept in with him through the door. He moves closer as this woman he's come to meet is asking the girl behind the bar if any of the desserts are vegan.

'What's that like, gluten-free?' the girl asks.

The woman sighs. 'No. It's no animal products.'

'Ah, I get you. You mean no dairy?'

'And no eggs. No animal products. At all.'

The girl puts a finger to her lips before pointing and silently mouthing at all the cakes in the revolving glass display to the side of the bar.

'No, I can't—I wouldn't think so, but I'll check.'

The girl runs off to the kitchen. The woman is facing him. Saying something.

'Pardon?'

She looks panicked for a moment. 'Sorry. I... It is you...?'

'You'll be lucky to find anything up here without butter in it,' he says.

The woman has blue eyes. Younger than he thought when she handed him her card. She's wrapped up in her Montane jacket and a big white and purple check scarf. The girl comes back from the kitchen shaking her head.

'No, sorry, not the cakes. But there's soup. I can do you a box of salad.'

'Not even the flapjack?'

The girl puts a hand on her hip. This is beginning to bore her.

'Okay, fine. Just a tea, thanks.' The woman looks up at him. She's shorter than Aggie. 'What can I get you?'

'I'll get my own, it's okay.'

'Might take forever.'

They're the only two waiting.

'Tea's fine.'

'So you work there?'

'Sorry to keep you waiting,' the girl behind the bar says to him.

'And another tea.'

'Aye, what kind?'

The woman looks at Anthony.

'Just normal.'

In the restaurant a man and woman in their fifties are sharing a piece of black forest gateau after their all-you-can-eat; three elderly women in different shades of knitted merino are sat at a round table by the window farthest from the door. All spies, he thinks, all obviously not. They wait for the teas. She gives him a nervous smile. The girl puts the teapots and cups on a tray, and the woman pays. He picks up the tray and chooses a table in the far corner on a raised mezzanine by the window. They sit opposite each other. He takes his teapot and lifts the lid and takes the teabag out, places it on a saucer.

'Okay,' she begins. 'You know about the whales?'

'I care, you know,' he blurts out. He's holding his cup, the steam wetting his face. 'About the whales. About the animals. That's what I did, for a while.'

She's looking at him, he thinks, wondering if he's a nutcase, come here to unload some guilt. *Is* that what he's come for? She's calculating how to convince him to do what she wants; and if he can't decide what it is *he* wants to do, she might just make him. But she doesn't know anything about Midshipman Darch.

'Well, that's good.' She pauses. 'What shall I call you?'

'Ant. You're an environmental investigator, right?'

'Wildlife crime, really. But cuts in the department, so I get to do both. This case, it's both. I worked in central government for a while.'

'London?'

'No, Holyrood. So, you care. That's good. They're incredible creatures, pilot whales. All whales. They're better adapted to their environments than we are, you know. Their social brains are more developed than ours. Do you know that many whales spend every minute of every day with every member of their family—'

There's a flash of what he once couldn't bear, when they all moved into the tiny house in Korosten', the bedroom his sick father never left again. If he doesn't talk, then that story will tumble out of him, so he tells her about the whales washing up on the beach. About the Navy cordon. About seeing the story in the paper. And then about his report. The readings on the whales' bodies. Samples cut from their teeth. She's fiercely attentive, not shocked.

'Why would they be radioactive?'

He feels hot, needs to move. He knocks the table as he heads to the toilet. It's too bright and he covers his face with his hands as he pisses. Curls fingers into fists and pushes the knuckles into the eye sockets. Digs deeper into his eyes until there are purple ovoid globules swimming in his inner vision. Someone comes in and he puts himself away, washes his hands and dries them, the blast of the noisy dryer a camouflage for his sharp breathing. He finishes drying his hands and takes a deep breath, puts a hand in his pocket. The pebble isn't there. But then it has no magic for this. Back at the table the woman hurriedly puts away her phone. Her eyes are scanning his face for whatever decision he's made. He sits down.

'There's never full disclosure with the military,' she says. 'They always control the flow of information. But we can hold them to account. With help. We're not in this to destroy anyone's jobs.'

'I understand.'

'So many whales have died…'

In another life he would be the one asking for the file. What would he do if he were her? What would she do if she were him?

'It's all going to come out, isn't it?'

He sits up sharply. 'What do you mean, *all*?'

She looks at him quizzically. 'It's already in the papers. It'll be in the nationals soon. Us having that report will get blown over. We'll sit on it until a reasonable time. All it means is we'll be able to react fully. We won't give you away.'

'You can't promise that.'

'Well, no. But you know why I'm asking. And you called me.' She pauses again. 'You said you care. There's a part of you that… Why were they radioactive?'

His mobile beeps. He takes it out of his pocket. It's Aggie from the station. He's half an hour away, at best. *Shit.* He stands up again.

'I need to go.'

She stands too. Her hands twitch, as if she wants to grab him. The three older women are laughing. There's a clatter of plates from the kitchen.

'I've got to go. My wife...'

He turns and leaves, not looking back. He texts Aggie as he strides to the car. Apologises, he's on his way. He drives as quickly as he can, recklessly, and when he arrives he can't remember the drive. *We took a different route out of Prypiat, through the centre of the Red Forest. It's called that because the radiation killed the bark and it all fell off. The wind was blowing to the west, towards Belarus, when the explosion occurred, and the most highly radioactive dust was deposited in an area of woodland some distance from the reactor.*

'Hi,' says Aggie, getting in. She leans across and kisses him.

This is the Plutonium Spike, though the radioactive material is mostly strontium and caesium. The real danger is drinking contaminated water and eating contaminated food: caesium is absorbed by the internal organs, and strontium by the bones. Both then continue to expose the body to radiation, poisoning it internally.

'Hi,' he responds. With Aggie next to him, it's as if the meeting with Viccy didn't happen. He turns forward and drives them home.

8th—11th November 1989, Kyiv

It takes them a while to find a parking space outside the bus station. Kulyk curses and throws insulting gestures at the other drivers as Anatolii sits in the passenger seat and sucks on a boiled sweet. Anatolii hasn't said much all morning. For once he's happy listening to the radio that's tuned to the football. The football is the only thing his uncle believes in. And this is despite Dynamo Kyiv always letting them down. 'At least you know the football is real,' Kulyk said to Anatolii once, unwrapping the red and white Dynamo scarf from his neck and throwing it into the cupboard in the hallway where they hang their coats, and where Anatolii had hidden once, when he first arrived in Kyiv and Kulyk hadn't come home after work. He was terrified of some fear he can't remember now; only that he was alone, and didn't know if he would see anyone he loved again. The football is interrupted by the news and the presenters talk about the Federal German Republic and a major announcement that's meant to be happening. Anatolii watches the city flow around him as they circle, looking for somewhere to park.

The bus station is as chaotic as a medieval village of the Kievan Rus' from one of the fairy stories in *babushka's* book. There's a scramble of old coaches chugging out choking smog and half the passengers smoking cigarettes while sitting on upended suitcases waiting to embark. There's a stink of petrol and people, women in headscarves wearing their travel perfumes and carrying a thousand babies. With only the one toilet block to change them no one dared risk the luxury—their buses could arrive and leave at any minute without them. 'Don't ever trust timetables,' his uncle tells him as they weave their way through the din, and it's a lesson he never forgets. Everywhere there are piles of baggage and clothing. The pavements that edge the station are thronged with stalls covered by drooping striped plastic canvas. The sellers

222

hawk dried fruits and trinkets and newspapers and cigarettes, the stalls only half full, like the shops that summer. It was a bad harvest and the Kyiv *raion* had wasted its budget, his uncle tells him. 'On God knows what, and I don't even believe in him, no doubt their own *dachas*, the bastards.'

Kulyk leads him by the hand through the crowds, looking for the bus from Korosten'. He's first to see his mama. She's being jostled by those trying to get on the bus she's just got off. She's holding Sveta's hand. They're waiting for their luggage as the driver throws bags around to find the right ones. His mama is in her long woollen winter coat and a plain brown headscarf. Sveta is curled into her legs. Then they're all together, hugging. When Anatolii sees his sister's face he gulps down a mouth of spit. Her skin is white. Sveta pulls her headscarf tighter, and he stops staring. He swallows again. 'Hey, let go, stop squeezing,' says his uncle. He stops crushing his uncle's hand.

They take the bags and Kulyk leads them across Moskovska Square to the car, which is jammed in between a taxi and a van. 'Fucking hell,' his uncle curses as he puts the bags in the boot. Anatolii's mama and sister climb in the back. He sits in front; so he is the man in his mother's eyes, he thinks.

Kulyk barely takes a breath as he drives. He swears at the Kyiv roads, the state of public transport, the corruption of government officials, and that they're lucky to arrive just before the storm. Anatolii's mama grunts every now and then, kisses her teeth at the potholes. 'Where are we, brother? Where are we? Is this the way?' Kulyk shakes his head. There's no anger in his uncle's actions, only the same discomfort that makes him stop from looking around at his sister. Sveta's buried herself in their mama's coat, hiding her face.

'She's feeling nauseous. Kulyk, stop the car.'

'She's fine, isn't she? We're not far.'

Their mama sighs. 'It's your car.'

At the flat his mama takes over the cooking. She peels potatoes and puts them in a pot with beans and sweet paprika. The cooking warms the room but it can't lift the sadness that's descended. Even Kulyk is subdued. His mama sends Kulyk out to buy some meat and there's a spat as she tries to give him money.

'We won't be beggars in my brother's house,' says his mama, trying to prise open Kulyk's fist. His uncle pushes her away.

'It's my house, you don't pay bills here.'

Kulyk turns away. His mama puts the money in the pocket of her cardigan. She looks at Anatolii, and there's a pain in her eyes he doesn't recognise. Sveta's sitting at the table. He can't bear to look at her. It's as if she has the eyes of her doll, big black coins. She smells, too, and he doesn't know of what.

The news is still about Germany. About the borders that Czechoslovakia has opened with the West and all the East Germans who've flooded the West German embassy. They're called aggressors, agitators. Traitors, the newsreader says. There are interviews with Party figures talking about the betrayal by the student movements in Budapest and Prague. Moscow and the Party has acted to end the radical movements swiftly. There's that word again: *glasnost*. His uncle is back with a skinny rump of beef that his mama adds to the stew. Kulyk sits and pours himself a glass of *horilka*. He comments over everything. 'Here, soon, too,' he says, 'the students at the universities won't sit by if the other *rentnyks* get away with murder.'

Kulyk turns the radio off when they eat but the silence is terrible. Kulyk abandons attempts to steer the conversation to the future. Each time he does, Anatolii's mama cries. They've come to Kyiv, Anatolii's been told, because Sveta needs to go to the hospital. Sveta picks at the food, pushing the vegetables around the plate. Anatolii's angry with her for not eating. If she ate she'd grow the same as him and make their mama happier. He stabs at his potatoes with his fork and eats so quickly it gives him a stomachache. He asks for more. He thinks this will make his mama happier, but all she does is look at him and put her napkin to her face. Kulyk takes Anatolii's plate and fills it with another ladle of the stew, which is tastier than anything his uncle makes. It's the first meal his mama has cooked for him in a long time. He barely remembers this used to be what they did every night; but instead of his uncle at the table it would be his father.

'Mama,' groans Sveta. Her face is a horrid mask. She grabs her stomach. Their mama pushes her chair back so it tumbles and she runs to catch Sveta. Sveta is sick on the floor. The vomit goes everywhere. He's never seen anyone be so sick. It's like a weapon, orange and yellow, a catapult of food. It stinks of the same smell on her skin.

'That's iodine,' his uncle tells him. Anatolii wipes the floor with a cloth as slowly as he can so he doesn't touch the sick. 'Sorbenty. She'll always smell of that. She's going to sleep in your bed tonight. We're in the living room.'

The room is cold and the camp bed is broken at one end. The springs have snapped and all night he's lying on a slope and about to roll off. In the morning he lies there achy and irritable until he hears his mama and Sveta getting dressed. He gets up and puts on his clothes without washing. His uncle is brewing coffee and a burnt smell fills the flat. They sit together at the kitchen table but only he and his uncle eat breakfast. Porridge with some jam to sweeten. There's something in him that knows he should speak to his sister but he cannot. It isn't like they're foraging and he's in charge of her and knows what to say. There are big bags under Sveta's black eyes, made worse by how white her skin is. Not white but yellow, like cream at the top of milk but cream that's stood for days and is spooned off into the pig trough. Their mama wraps a headscarf around Sveta's hair, and she looks frightening, both young and old, a tiny version of an old woman.

'You'll be better once they see you,' their mama says to Sveta.

She buttons up Sveta's overcoat. He's so afraid of how his sister looks and where she's going that he forgets he doesn't want to look at her. He thinks that where they used to gather berries and mushrooms there's now a sign in Cyrillic and Western alphabets warning people not to pick food there. He goes into the kitchen. A few minutes later the front door shuts. He goes into his bedroom and climbs into his bed but it smells of *Sorbenty*. And it's a school day, if he doesn't go he'll get into trouble.

That evening he's allowed to stay up to listen to the radio. What's happening in Germany excites his uncle. At nine o'clock they hear an East German called Schabowski say he's letting people visit West Germany. 'As far as I know effective immediately, without delay,' says Schabowski, his voice surprised, surrounded by journalists clamouring for more information.

'Jesus Christ,' says his uncle. 'You see, little paw, all things, all things end.' Kulyk pours himself a *horilka*. Anatolii is drinking warm milk with chocolate. 'This is Gorbachev. There'll be no Union left soon. What do you think, Anatolii, do you want to live in a democracy?'

He sips the milk, thinks of the woman in Moscow who asked him, '*Do you like America?*' He nods. 'Yes,' he says, and his uncle laughs, slaps the table.

'Then there's no hope,' says Kulyk, with a grim smile. His uncle tells Anatolii to go to bed but he doesn't, and anyway tomorrow he's not going to school; they're going to the hospital. It's at midnight they hear the announcement that the gates in the Berlin Wall are open.

'Who built the Berlin Wall?' He's almost asleep, his head on the kitchen table.

'We did. It's where civilisation ends and begins. Depending on which side you're on.' Kulyk laughs, leans back, yawns. 'Come on, boy, to bed.'

The next day Kulyk drives them to the Division of Nervous

Pathologies, moaning the whole way about the traffic. Anatolii is used to hospitals now. They find their way through the maze of corridors. After a particular turn, the colours of the walls change from dirty white to red and green. The walls have pictures on them, but stupid pictures, he thinks, drawn by children: of fields, and big yellow suns, and creatures with seven eyes. There are dozens of children running, walking or in beds. Some are attached to metal poles on wheels with bags of fluid hanging from them. There are lots of women in black skirts and thick cardigans. It smells of wet bedsheets and horrible medicine. The children are shouting and crying and playing. His uncle is pushing him on. 'Look, there they are,' says Kulyk, and Anatolii sees his mama sitting next to a bed. Sitting up in the bed is Sveta, whiter than the sheets. His mama's face is red. Sveta has a tube sticking out of her nose and it makes him want to be sick.

'Go get me some water, Anatolii,' says mama, and she hands him a flimsy plastic cup. 'There's a water fountain. Go on, go on.' She pushes him but he can't move. He stares at the u-shaped scar on his sister's neck. The stitches stick out like tiny shoelaces. His uncle grabs his hand and pulls him away.

'No,' says his uncle quietly. 'Don't stare. Not now, or in the future. Go, go.'

Everything moves in slow motion. He feels the cup in his hand, so flimsy, empty. He looks for a water fountain but can't find one. He stares at another girl. She's wearing a white gown. She's prettier than his sister; older. She has long blond hair but it's messy. She's sitting at a table meant only for children. She has the same u-shaped scar on her neck. He goes over. She looks up slowly.

'Do you have any knots?' Her voice is hoarse, as if she's been singing. He shakes his head. He's not angry with her like he is with Sveta.

'What do you mean, knots?'

'The doctors found a knot in my little sister as well,' says the

227

girl, and she points towards a bed farther down the ward. 'How many knots do you have?'

'I don't know. What are knots?'

'They're knots.' She shrugs. He wants to know her name. 'Ira.'

'Where's your mama?'

'With my sister. Are you going to see a doctor?'

'No.' He says it coldly. He wants to touch the scar on her neck but daren't.

'The doctors tell mama how many I have. If they go into my brain it will be too late. But if they spread into the lungs, they can still save me.'

He feels weak. He looks at the cup in his hand, then glances back at Sveta. He wonders how many knots she has, and if the doctors have taken them all away.

'Does the doctor untie them?' he asks.

'No, stupid,' Ira says, and turns away. It's like a stab in the chest, the most painful word anyone has said to him.

'The Berlin Wall fell down last night.' He knows it's stupid, more stupid than what he's already said, but maybe she'll be impressed. There's a green crayon on the table and she picks it up and drags a piece of paper closer and begins drawing.

'But everything is normal right now. I have to drink iodine and take daily doses of thyroxin. If I don't have that hormone I'll be faint, and I won't be lucky.'

He doesn't know what thyroxin is, or hormones. Ira stabs the paper with the crayon. He stumbles away looking for the fountain. He finds it and fills the cup and goes back to the bed and hands it to his mama.

'Thank you, Anatolii.' She pats his cheek. He sees something in her eyes that's the same as when Kulyk stops drinking, or the last time he saw his father. His mama leans over Sveta and puts a hand behind her head and tilts it towards the cup. Sveta opens her lips and their mama pours water from the cup, a little dribble at a time.

They bring Sveta home two evenings later. There's no room in the hospital. So many children having the same operation. He wonders why Ira stays there; perhaps she has more knots than anyone else. At home his uncle Kulyk carries Sveta into the flat and puts her to sleep in Anatolii's room. That night he sleeps on the camp bed again while Kulyk sleeps on the sofa and snores all night.

The next day Kulyk drives them to Korosten'. He wants to go too, but his uncle pulls him away. His whole body from head to toe is filled with anger. For a moment he panics and thinks that the anger is made of knots; that he's somehow caught them from the hospital.

The next morning he wakes up and the feeling is mostly gone. His bed smells of his sister. That evening over dinner his uncle drinks *horilka* and turns the radio on. More news from Germany, more protests in Prague, but all, says the newsreader, swiftly put down by the Party. The Soviet Union will stand for another thousand years, says one General. His uncle turns the radio off.

'You know what stands for a thousand years?' Kulyk asks over a plate of mashed potatoes and cured sausage and peas. Anatolii shakes his head. He doesn't like it when his uncle drinks all the time. 'Nothing,' says Kulyk. 'Nothing. Not ever.'

A tear falls from his uncle's eye into the mashed potato.

But I'm not writing to you because of the trees and flowers. Still I'm not saying what I should. So let me. I'm on the last of my nine lives. The hospital wants to do more tests—the blood takes so long to fill their tubes. I'm sluggish inside and out. What makes me saddest of all is that I'll soon have to give up my night classes with Alina. The great joy in my life for little more than a bare year (Alina says the phrase is 'barely a year' but she likes the way I've written it). It's so unfair. Who wished this upon me? Oh, there are so many people who didn't live as long as we have—the firemen who arrived on the scene, who dissolved in front of their wives' eyes. I know no one wished it upon us. You can waste a life searching for someone to blame for what happened. Of all lives, I was given this one, no other. And haven't I felt love? Haven't I been able to learn a little?

Many who lived through the disaster hate their memories. Can you blame them? We don't want to be a part of history. The Wall coming down, the end of the Union, Independence, the disaster. Now Russia invading Crimea, the killings at the freedom protests. History moves across us, back and forth. Will we always be a borderland? Isn't there a time when we won't have armies and winds blowing through us?

But there are some who've grown kinder, more loving, having lived through the same things. There are those who have conquered their tragedy. Alina asks if I mean this literally, and I do. There was a young boy born six months after the explosion with a count of 656 rems at birth. His mama told me that at first he seemed normal, that she was so overcome with relief she cried for a month, and she held the baby close all that time. But later they noticed things were wrong. He would stumble more than the other babies. His speech failed to develop. They took him for tests, but his heart and his lungs were fine. But he wasn't right. Then they scanned his brain. Brother, he has only half a brain.

The other half isn't there! His mother told me she cried for another month non-stop, but this time she wouldn't hold him. She was ashamed. They told her at the time she could have an abortion at the best hospital, no questions, but she was already dreaming of her little child. This boy is a man now, four years younger than me, and he's so kind. Perhaps the half he did not get is the hating half? He feels love for everything. He's always trying to help, although now it's obvious he lacks many things that you and I were born with. He loves nature, the sparrows and the pigeons and the storks, loves to put his feet in the river, he'll sit and watch ducks all day long. He wants us to enjoy life. Are we more complete than he is? He looks after the pigeons in our apartment block, the ones who have tumours where their feet should be. And the sparrows who sometimes are born without the wings to fly. Even now, these decades later. He loves moths and wasps. The storks, too, who also cannot fly and are born with eyes in the wrong places. These he cares for.

How can such generosity for what is broken come out of what he's suffered? But then he does not know he's suffered, does he? I watch him playing in the park opposite, I see his mother fussing around him. She holds the shame in *her* body. She knows what has been lost. How can such kindness be born of such a terrible day?

I sometimes sit with him and his mama and we feed peas to the ducks, and I pity him. And who is pitying me? I think you do, brother. You're ashamed of me, because you pity me. Why else would you never write back? But I deserve better, more than your pity. I deserve more... I don't know what. Alina says I deserve your comradeship. I cannot—no one can—demand love. Even if we deserve it. And I cannot ask for respect; I hate too much to be sure of that myself. But comradeship for what we were born into? I deserve that. Surely this is not too much to ask?

Do you remember the harvest of the Chernobyl year? We went, mama and I, from Korosten' on a bus that was sent for us and others to help. We worked with *babushka* and grandpa. Because of the evacuation and sickness there were not enough hands and the roots were spoiling. I was so sick, but mama couldn't leave me with our father. I could barely pull up a carrot without growing breathless, and anyway mama didn't want me touching the soil, so she kept me close as she worked. There were dead mice everywhere. The adults joked, of course, with no mice there would be no hares, and no hares meant no wolves, and if there were no wolves then there would soon be no people. And we children would live with no animals for company, not even the flies and wasps. This was how the adults joked our future was going to be. But we believed it. I never realised what they said wasn't real.

I don't know what happened to the vegetables. If we buried them in plastic bags, or if they were good to eat and made it to market, or were taken by Moscow for the Plan and redistributed elsewhere. And you, all this time were you playing football with other boys in Kyiv? Where the cloud never passed over, where the soil never stabbed at you under your fingernails.

Do you remember Easter before the explosion? It came early that year, it was still snowing. We painted eggs like they still do in the village. All the colours except black. You only paint black eggs if someone has died and you're mourning. Blue was for a long life—a long life! They say if you want to dream about someone you have lost, then paint an egg and roll it over their grave. I've painted red eggs for mama to come and hold me in my dreams. I painted white eggs too, when I met Drago, white eggs for the *busel-busko* to bring children. To bring me a baby I could hold to my chest. The storks my half-brained friend feeds at the river never fly, maybe one in three of the chicks die before they fledge. I don't know if this is normal. Or if it's normal for now. *Koolyko-koolyko*, they cry. It haunts me. Perhaps I'm rolling these white eggs over the graves of all the dead birds and they're coming back to me in my dreams. The *busel-busko* is meant to keep you safe from fires and also carry your babies to you from the mystery in which they're conceived, the old women say. But if the *busel-busko* cannot fly? If the stork has been caught in the fire it's meant to protect you from?

But thank God I could never have children. The women who had children after the accident had nightmares all through their pregnancies. They remember them like yesterday. I speak to the mother of my half-brained friend. She used to dream of giving birth to a huge queen bee with four faces. And the other women in the maternity ward at the same time, those who refused the abortions, they had dreams too, of giving birth to horses with no legs, or giving birth to a stork but with arms instead of wings, or giving birth to dogs, so many of the women dreamt of dogs, and one woman dreamt of giving birth to a worm wearing a crown with a thousand arms and each hand holding a weapon of torture. Can you imagine what these women went through to give birth... Some of them *did* give birth to their nightmares. So I bless myself, bless you, I thank my angels that it was easier for me as I will never have a child to hold to my breast.

In Russian, Chernobyl is called 'a black story.' A black egg for a black story. I paint eggs now every Easter for myself, and roll the black ones over my grave.

Tuesday

He wakes from a dream where he's in America, on the three-month scholarship organised prior to the disastrous conference paper. He worked on the properties of strontium in civil nuclear energy processing with a professor at the Ratnonfield research institute in Maine. The scholarship was a success, and at the end of that summer, back in Oxford with Aggie, life seemed almost as it was before. Some hope returned, unfolding from the material of privilege. Not just his place at Oxford, but the privilege of surviving. For a long time he chose to dwell in that present and the future it promised. To forget the past. But there's no choice now.

He gets out of bed and goes downstairs. His attention is on the computer, on the one thing he's done that can't be explained away. He logs in to his email. Nothing. So what now? Then he realises he's been checking the wrong Gmail. He closes down the window and opens another. If they're intercepting his browser history, then this makes no difference, but he's taken what precautions he can.

He logs in again. There's a message back from the editor. *Please, get in touch. We've seen the news. We need to hear more about your opinion on...*

It's not my fucking opinion. The rage that's been gathering in his chest since his visit to the sick crew returns. *No. Before,* he thinks; it was there when he went to the whales. *Before that?* He stands and fumbles around in the green-dark, clumsily pacing back and forth. The cottage is silent. His breathing is high up in his chest. He tries Aggie's technique of holding the left nostril, breathing out, then switching nostrils, breathing in through the left. He sits again, perches forward. He opens the document he sent and reads. A wave of tiredness engulfs him. Is it too late? But he gave nothing away of his identity. He wants to go to bed and forget about the base, the crew, the readings, the whales, the tennis ball. He logs out and clears the history. The IP blocker is on, but he doesn't want Aggie to see, nor does he want the temptation of going through her browsing. He knows she's not having an affair. It's made up in his head. Muddled and confused, like so much other stuff. The type of woman who would find him here at God knows what hour and squint with one eye into a computer-lit room and offer tea, the woman brave enough to marry him, who has battered away the obstacles of loving him (he feels the self-pity like the damp of the room, clammy across his skin), is not the type of woman who would have an affair; or, would keep it secret. He's glad of that, at least.

The sounds of the cottage settle around him, and he sits in a small ball of silence. He stands up and goes to the shelf in the kitchen and from behind the *pysanka* takes his sister's letter and brings it back to the computer. He opens it out to the last section he read. *A black egg for a black story.*

Vuzol. Knot.

'She wanted to be saved,' he'd told Aggie once, years ago. 'That little girl. Ira.'

'Maybe she was.'

He'd shaken his head. 'They didn't let her out. Too many knots already.'

'Your sister was. Saved.'

By then, in Oxford, he knew that radionuclides built up in forest floors, especially in the upper layer of soil, in moss and lichen, needles, twigs and branches. That caesium-137 transferred from soil to grass to cow to milk, and that ingestion resulted in increased internal dosages. That the families of the Zone were given the chance to use filters for the milk but they didn't because the filters removed the fat and then the milk couldn't be sold. His sister loved milk straight from the cows.

'The removal of the thyroid means they'll never mature properly. Their sexual functions. Those girls.'

He'd tried to say it calmly but it came out like a diagnosis. *Those girls*. Aggie had nothing to say to that.

He closes his eyes. Ira, his sister, they all counted. They marked the progression of their disease by the number of knots forming in their throats, their chests and necks. Ira did not live, he's sure of that. But what about her little sister? He wonders perhaps for the thousandth time what village they came from. He remembers his uncle's words, even after all these years, like a mantra.

Don't stare. Not now, or in the future.

He took it too literally. He's never looked back.

Dear Sveta, I—

Fuck. He turns off the computer, freezes for a moment as he thinks he hears movement outside. He peers through the window into darkness. Nothing. He goes upstairs and gets back into bed. Aggie rolls towards him. He's missing her like he's not done for a long time. Not her body—she's right there, he inhales the sleepy sourness of her breath—but what they could have built together these last few months—who is he kidding? *years*—if he'd been able to just keep sharing what was in his head. There's a void where that fostered love should be. He wriggles in and holds her. Pours his thoughts into that void and imagines it filled. Hopes that his life can still follow that bearing.

First thing in the lab he checks his email. There's a *communiqué* from the Commodore. It provides an update of what will happen next. The Navy are promising to act efficiently and in good faith to deal with developments. That includes a news bulletin going out. He thinks this must mean they'll reveal the death of Midshipman Darch. And when that happens he can delete the photos. No need to give the report on the whales to Viccy. No need to reply to the editor's email. He understands, reading the Commodore's words, how much he's risked—and why. But he won't stop at the protest again. He'll clean the car. No, he'll take it to that scrap metal merchant up the hill and he'll cycle to work. There'll be no chewed-up tennis ball. He and Aggie will talk. He'll tell her everything. He'll continue in nuclear power, he will do this work that he's good at, he will become the person that was his promise, once he'd left that old country. He'll rediscover his expertise in the lives of animals affected by radiation. He will remember, and although he will not control those memories, they will not control him. He will drop the knife in the snow in the forest. He will not go back to look for it. There are no tracks.

By midday the new procedures have been formalised. They begin immediately—or almost, once they've seen the news. Elspeth comes over with her laptop. She turns the volume up and they watch BBC Online as the bulletin spills out around the country. An incident at the UK's at-sea deterrent. The whales. The report to Parliament. His heart leaps at the thought of Aggie sitting at the kitchen table listening on the scratchy Roberts radio. But there's nothing about the leak. Nothing about two local boys. Nothing about Midshipman Darch. *Later,* he thinks. Perhaps this will come later, when the practical details of her death are dealt with.

At two o'clock he takes his equipment to the pontoon. He's met by two naval crew, young men in plastic insignia-marked waterproofs. This is the new protocol: all such civilian activities are now conducted with military accompaniment. He focuses on the list of tasks. The crew take him out on the water to sixteen mapped points in a small but nippy rib. The midshipmen enjoy the task, whipping the craft round the perimeter. Anthony holds tight to the safety bar. It's an enthralling ride and he shivers as he did eight days ago when he felt the beast rattle its chains; when Midshipman Louisa Darch was sent down to flush radioactive coolant into the loch. The wind rushes his face as they scoop through the water and he feels like an eagle flying above the Zone.

The meter readings are still beyond normal, but not as high as they were when he and Michael pushed out in the rowboat. And they're not in any danger. As long as no one goes swimming. The locals wouldn't swim on these rocky shores, not even the young boys of Garelochhead now the news has broken. He takes the samples back to the lab and processes them. He has a steady, almost preternatural focus on his work. At four he and David leave the lab and walk to the clinic. They don't talk. The receptionist studies her list of approved visitors and waves them in. They enter the changing room and scrub. Anthony breathes in the astringency. He puts on the blue suit, tightens the cord around his hairline, arranges his mask and gloves. They're both ready at the same time. There are guards now in the corridor, two at each end.

'Never seen so many eager pups,' says David quietly. 'You?'

He's glad David has broken the silence. David puts a hand on his arm.

'What I said yesterday… You understand how it looked?'

He nods. *How it was.*

'Too many things at once,' says David, but doesn't elaborate. 'I'll make it work.'

'Just follow protocol. Now, it's about them,' and David indicates through the window of the door they stand at. A woman is lying in the bed. He saw her before on their previous round. Sub-Lieutenant Kim Wilkins. The anti-inflammatories keep her from growing puffier but they can't stop her skin cracking. The door closes behind them with a sigh. For a terrible moment he thinks she's dead. Then the sheets rise and fall.

She's been in theatre. He didn't think they had an operating theatre here, or a capable surgeon. Perhaps she went overnight to Glasgow. None of this is in his purview. None of this is in his control. Instead, he stands and stares at the woman's neck and the u-shaped scar protected by a square of see-through gauze.

David is by the bedside unloading the sample case, taking

blood, holding out the syringe for Anthony. He fills the first vial, tries to write her name but his hand is shaky.

'Anthony?'

Your children must have six diseases to register as a student at our school, madam. I'm not your madam. I'm sorry, but those are the rules, we don't make them, we only implement them. But look at her! You must write to Moscow. Write?! I don't know how. You can see for yourself, can't you? Can't you see? I'm sorry, madam, there's nothing we can do for her.

'Anthony, are you okay?'

He pulls himself to the bed and it squeaks and moves under him.

'I'm fine.'

David glares.

'You don't look it. But okay, let's get on.'

There are fresh flowers. He knows their names, these poufy English blooms. Dahlias. Their scent fills the room. With the perfume comes the image of a family gathered around the bed. Giving consent for their daughter's operation.

The door opens. It's the chief medic and behind him a man and a woman in their fifties. Sub-Lieutenant Kim Wilkins's mother and father. Their faces are frozen in a limbo of not knowing. He expects them to look away, but they both stare at him and David seeking clues, if not answers, to what's happening. The chief medic smiles briefly. He and David are packed up and on their way out. Nothing is said. They stand a moment as the door closes behind them, and David walks off to the next room. Anthony looks along the corridor to where Midshipman Darch was yesterday.

Closer to Chernobyl is Narodychi, Zone Two. It's twenty kilometres west of the plant. There's another collective. A farm. You'll go there. But we want to go home! This is your new home, there's work to do. My children! Listen, the farm receives money from us for heavy metals to bind with the caesium in their cows to remove it from the cow's milk. They need good people who know the collective model. You'll go there. Inject the metal into the animal's abdomen, it binds with the radionuclides, removing them through natural excretion. The cows need to be herded. The grass cannot be cut. The cows cannot eat grass that is less than ten centimetres long. Keep the cows from the earth.

One of the guards is standing next to him.

'Sir, are you okay?'

'Fine,' he says again. 'Yes, sorry. Just thinking if I've forgotten anything.'

What? If you want to be like that, yes keep your children from the earth too. Get this bus. Here are the tickets. For you and your children. Go, they're expecting you.

In the lab he puts Sub-Lieutenant Wilkins's blood through its separation. He sees the panicked eyes of her parents in the tiny droplets. He thinks of what the news will do to them when it comes out that one of their daughter's shipmates is dead. It's better that the Navy control the release of information, he thinks. But at the back of his mind is what that woman Viccy told him: *the full story never comes out.*

He took her hand. He held it in his. The skin flaking off.

He leaves at six o'clock and glances at the protest as he passes. Mo and Tom are outside in their camping chairs, still as mannequins. Their lives will change when this is done. They see him, and Maureen waves. He waves back, but doesn't stop.

He thinks of Maureen. Mo. She had a husband and family in Carmarthen. She was active in her community. But driven by a fear of nuclear annihilation she walked for ten days with thirty-five other women to deliver a letter. He thinks of Tom. A life of opposition to the slowing down of the splitting of atoms. That's all—although if he said that to Tom's face he'd get stabbed like a canvas eyelet. It's the *purposes* to which those reactions are put to service that Tom detests. Trident. Torness. Sizewell. Faslane. Their home a menagerie of makeshift spaces and mended canvases on a knoll of grass by the intersection of road and military escarpment.

And himself? His life has been tethered as much as theirs to atomic energy. As tied to the mountain as the serpent that would devour the world if it were not for those people—*his* people—painting the *pysanky*. He's one of them; only their old traditions have become new ones in his hands. Perhaps it's when he stops sampling the soil, stops filling vials with water from the loch and blood from the crew that the serpent escapes. He's had days where he's understood everything about the movements of atoms and the release of neutrons, about the mantle of the earth and the force of its geological elements. But there have been the false starts too, the misunderstandings, his crashing stars, that paper, the sideways shifts... less than what it would have felt like to have excelled. To have made good on the promise of why he was sent away.

He looks at his hands as they hold the steering wheel. They are not the hands of someone working the land, worrying away at a canvas that needs fixing with stronger holdings before winter rains and northerly winds. Has he made his life, or been blown by those winds? Chased by the cloud? Where is his accumulation of the good of which he can consider himself the agent?

The State took my life away. They ripped me off, gone. What is there to be happy about? An honourable man cannot survive now. For what? For what? There was life. There was food. There was buha. I can't buy a wrench. Before I could buy fifty wrenches. The money was enough. But now my salary is less than the cost of one. What have we left?

Whose words, now his father is dead?

The cloud left its trace in my city too.

Whose voice is that? A girl. Sveta?

The trace in me is my scar. In others, there are other traces.

He sees a book full of fairy tales. Sveta sitting on the patterned rug on the floor. The stove is hot. Their bellies are full of potatoes and green beans and the little bit of pork they eat on Sundays.

Flowers. Dahlias. Dalia. It's a popular name where he comes from. He remembers the story as *babushka* told it. *Dalia*, the Goddess of Fate. The giver and taker of what is owed. The recorder of allotments of what one is properly due.

You see, my little ones, according to myth, just as a father divides his estate among the children, so the supreme god Dievas allots each newborn with a share of good and bad in life. You, little Anatolii, you have this share. And you, my Sveta, you have this too. And Dalia, Dievas's daughter, is with you for your whole life ensuring you keep your proper share. You see, Dievas is a god and he's too important to spend his time chasing little children like you. But Dalia is with you always. She'll decide if you have acted well and kindly with your lot. She appears to you as an animal. A lamb or a dog sometimes, but she loves most of all the rivers and lakes. She is a swan, like you Sveta. Or a duck, like you Anatolii. Oh shush, I am only teasing, little Anatolii. Oh yes, you are little! Okay, you want a bigger animal. Then she comes to you as a whale, Anatolii. She comes to you as a beast of the sea.

He's gone past the turn for the cottage, alarmed that he can't remember the last ten minutes of the drive. He wobbles awkwardly and then steadies the car. He carries on to Helensburgh and pulls in near the Spar. He gets his mobile out and puts it on his lap. He's missed three calls and two texts. A truck rumbles past pulling a bed loaded with huge pines. The car rocks and a jolt crosses his shoulders.

The mobile lights up. Another text. Viccy's been in these situations before, he thinks. She knows how to handle waverers. But he's not wavering. He's made up his mind. He needs to talk to Aggie.

But Aggie isn't home. By ten o'clock his stomach is complaining, but he can't eat without her. He goes upstairs, gets undressed. He lies in bed swapping between reading his sister's letter and Aggie's book, the one on poverty.

He discovers that his future-oriented mindset is a middle-class trait: that the middle classes concentrate on achievement and goals. The poor live in the present, never having time or energy to think about the future; their lot is immediate survival. The wealthy live in the past, concerned with tradition. With privilege.

He discovers that he has no idea who his sister is. He still thinks of her as a little girl. He sees her as he saw her last, at their mama's funeral. And before that. In the hospital. White-yellow, hidden among a choir of sick girls, all crying, all pleading.

He discovers that his future-oriented perspective means he's come to be poor in the skills of memory. *The one poverty you cannot dig yourself out of,* that woman Grace had told the hall full of people, *is relationships.* But there is another, more severe poverty, of what is lost when a person chooses to disregard the past for the fear that it will overwhelm him. Overwhelm that—

Khlop. Little boy.

He puts the book and letter down and summons up something for succour, a memory of the night he and Aggie shared together before he left that time for America. He went to Aggie's... not only for sex, but the new thing between them. Nothing so motivating, he'd thought, in love, than someone leaving. They had arduous lovemaking, they soaked the sheets of her bed. They'd found the positions in which they could look into each other's faces for longest. They'd talked during sex—something they hardly ever did now. A shame of familiarity had fallen across them. He could hardly look her in the eyes when they made love now for the pain of the exposure. But before he left for America and after he came back, for the good first year of their relationship, they urged each other on, told each other what they wanted, how to excite each other.

He remembers the arrival of the morning that followed. The sounds of the first bus passing her flat. On the roof, starlings and pigeons. Aggie put out suet balls and mealworms and rotting fruit so regularly the birds were semi-domesticated. He loved her for feeding them. Their robust, rambunctious singing was a chorus on the doorstep. He'd felt courage enough that morning to study her face. Her ears, so small, the outer canals almost painted on. The hard edges of her cheekbones that mirrored his and which, in the right light, gave her a Romany look. The two tiny puncture marks on her top lip, stars in constellation. *Remember these*, he'd said to himself. His old privileges were gone at that moment. He'd found new ones to replace them. He'd hold onto them.

It's past-midnight when he wakes to hear Aggie showering. He listens to the cottage pipes bang and rattle like the heating in that newly built apartment in Korosten'. Then the pipes are no longer rattling. The bathroom floor will be cold beneath her warm feet. *Bad for your ovaries*, Aggie's mum told her when she saw Aggie walking on the kitchen flagstones without slippers. Then Aggie is sitting on the bed with her back to him, her hair piled under the swish of a towel.

'I'm tired,' she says. She climbs into bed. He turns onto his side and looks at her. 'What are you doing?'

'Remembering your face.'

He cannot find those tiny indents. But he searches anyway. Of all the things she was expecting—jealousy, questioning, his excuses—this tender curiosity disarms her, and they go to sleep in each other's arms until she squeezes him and turns the other way. He passes into a blindness of sleep that he's not experienced for a long time.

1992-1993, Kyiv and Birmingham and London

Anatolii comes homes from school. He drops his bag on his bed and changes into a T-shirt, the one with Zavarov wheeling away after scoring a goal, hand in the air. He goes into the kitchen and pours himself a glass of milk and spoons in three heaps of chocolate. He can't drink milk without chocolate anymore. He buys it himself from the money he earns for doing chores. It's a good agreement; as long as the apartment looks tidy he gets five *hryvnia* a week. Anatolii is always waiting for his uncle to reduce the amount. Kulyk complains about money all the time. 'The economy is in ruins,' his uncle moans. No one at school admits their parents have lost their jobs but Anatolii can tell; someone grows thinner, another turns up less and then not at all. Sometimes the teachers don't turn up. The rumour is there's no money left to pay them. 'Kravchuk is an imbecile,' his uncle tells him often, 'he couldn't manage a toy store.' Anatolii takes his chocolate milk and sits in the living room and turns on the television. There's the news, and some children's programmes on another channel, but it's all rubbish and he turns it off. They're going to the bar tonight to watch the football. It isn't Dynamo playing, it's SKA but his uncle's happy to watch either team if it means a trip to the bar. He's old enough to go now; at least on football nights. Kulyk lets him drink from his beer, and the barman doesn't mind. He hears the front door open and then shut. He looks up and sees Kulyk's head round the door.

'You're here,' says Kulyk. 'Okay. I've got to make a phone call,' and then his uncle collapses on the stool in the hallway. They've all got phones now, although it hardly rings. He hears his uncle talking, then arguing on the phone. Suddenly his ears tune in; it's about him. Kulyk is speaking to his mama. He starts praying that Kulyk won't call him to go and speak. He's nothing to say. Then his uncle stops talking. Kulyk comes into the living room, shakes his head.

'Why do they stay, Anatolii?'

He hides behind his milk.

'Let me tell you. They stay because the authorities pay half their rent, because she has free public transport and free medical assistance if she stays. Outside? Here? Nothing. Or she thinks, nothing. She could come here, right?' Anatolii thinks there's no room. 'It's blackmail, Anatolii. If people like your mama left the Zone, the rest of the country would see her. But if they contain the sick people—'

His uncle stares at him. Does he have milk on his lip? He wipes his mouth.

'I'm sorry. These bastards said they would look after her. But only if you play the victim, isn't that true?' Does his uncle want an answer? He nods. 'And so what do they do? They make the sufferers work to get the payments. Their suffering becomes their work. This is what it is. But what can we do about it? I've told them—six years now. The sufferer's poison. You know what it is? It's an investment in suffering. When you've paid so much in, you don't give it up, right?' Kulyk stands. 'But not for you. We're going to get you out of here. I know you. You're a good boy. Once you're old enough you'll feel responsible. You'll want to go back and help.' His uncle shakes his head. 'If I do one thing right, it's this. Right, *lapochka*?'

The milk curdles in his stomach.

That night before the football begins there's a programme on television about Chernobyl. The journalist says a film like this could never have been made before Independence. There are interviews with soldiers who were sent up to shift graphite and debris from the roof of Unit Three to cover Unit Four, or to shovel it into containers for burial. They could only work for one minute at a time. 'Two shovels, then run for your life,' says one of the soldiers. A miner who was brought in to dig the tunnels for the liquid nitrogen says: 'We are alive. We didn't die. But we don't know how we survived.' He learns how men like his father were sent in to clean up the mess, or drive the cars, or operate the radios, or guard the fences. The documentary shows long lines of re-settlers at the doors to the clinics set up around the Zone. There's a woman, an academic from America, who's studied the disaster. 'The people suffered twice,' she says, 'not only from the accident and radiation, but from inattention.' The next interview is with a former Soviet politician calling the American a liar. Anatolii doesn't understand everything, but nor does he forget it.

The next day at school the boys pretend to be bio-robots because it's a cool name and they can act like machines. The bio-robots were men who took over when the real robots melted. Then one of the other boys calls him a 'glow-worm' and the class all turn on him. They say he's infected with radiation. They pile on top of him. Someone gives him a punch to the stomach, then they run away as two teachers break it up. When he explains what happened the teachers look at each other and tell him to go home early. The day after, everyone's forgotten about the documentary. No one wants to hear about tragedy. Nuclear power is part of Ukraine's future; he reads this in the *Izvestia* his uncle left on the kitchen table. But he doesn't forget. The programme said that between Independence and the fall of the Soviet Union there was a void in responsibility when medical care stopped. If Ukraine wanted nothing from Russia, then fine, Russia would give nothing to Ukraine. There was looting from the Zone and the soldiers who were guarding the perimeter took bribes. Expensive trucks and diggers that sat unused for years suddenly disappeared and were sold on the black market. The machinery was highly radioactive. Whoever bought it and handled it, or worse used it, would get sick within days. He thinks of men sitting in the cabs feeling sick and not knowing what was happening. His uncle worked in the black market after the furniture factory. Had his uncle been exposed?

A few weeks later, Anatolii's uncle tells him that he's going to be sent away. That he will learn English, and go to a good school. Kulyk tells him not to support Birmingham City; Aston Villa is a bigger team near where his friend Grigory lives. Grigory will look after him. Anatolii looks at the kitchen table, ashamed of wanting to cry. All he can hear is his uncle's breathing.

He doesn't understand that it would cost money, so he doesn't ask where the money came from. There's no excitement. England. It's nowhere to him. England was at war with Iraq, that's all he knows. England is cold and wet. England is full of capitalists who hate him. He hates his uncle that night, goes to bed without doing the dishes or any of his chores. On Friday his uncle leaves him his five *hryvnia* on his bed to pick up when he gets back from school. He throws them in the bin.

'When?'

His uncle can't tell him. 'I'm sorting things out, little Anatolii.'

'I'm not little,' he says. Is he little if he's going away on his own to live in another country? No. He is a man. Kulyk looks at him.

'Okay, Anatolii. I understand.'

Likuius.

Spoken by a child in the hospital. Which child? Which hospital? *I'm looking after myself now.*

Even so, when he's at the church waiting for the buses that make up the convoy, he's expecting his mama and sister to be there. Perhaps they'll beg him to stay, and he will, or they'll come with him. His father will be there too, although that would be a miracle. The ghost of his father.

But none of them are there. It's just his uncle, who's drunk and can't stand up straight without leaning on the wall of the church. He hates his uncle then. Suddenly he's glad to be leaving. There are hundreds of children just like him. Chernobyl children. There are women, women he recognises as Ukrainian, and others with red hair and pale skin, speaking a language he doesn't know. The writing down the side of the coach he's being ushered onto is in another language. All he's told is it's a convoy. A *mercy mission from God*. A crush of crying children thrusts him forward. He never thought for a moment there would be others leaving. Great Britain. What was so great about it? Yet here they are in their heavy coats with plastic laundry bags for luggage, hundreds of them, evacuating. The woman at the coach door checks her list against his passport—a passport he didn't know he owned until the night before—and looks at the lanyard around his neck that says where he's going, which recipient church at the other end of this cross-Europe journey. She says something about a man who is going to look after him. He's pushed through the bus door and up the small steps by the driver's seat, a hand on his back. He finds a window seat and looks for Kulyk but can't see properly. There are tears in his eyes and he wants to shout and get off the bus. Then he sees his uncle, who waves and turns away.

'He wants the best for you,' says Grigory. They're sitting in a small, square, dark living room in Grigory's house in Dudley, outside Birmingham. Grigory shows him on a map but the map is only a network of roads and he has no idea where he is in relation to where he was. The sofa is damp, Grigory smells of cigarettes and grease. They eat fried food without vegetables, smothered in a strange red sauce.

'Your uncle is a good man. It cost a lot of money to bring you here. Come on, Anatolii, cheer up. We'll play football. Your uncle said you played in goal.'

It's while sitting in Grigory's living room he realises he'll never play for Dynamo Kyiv. This makes him cry, although he's desperate not to. He wipes one eye and then the other with the cuff of his shirt. Grigory is his uncle's age. They worked together in the furniture factory. Grigory is a Ukrainian Jew.

'Easier to get a visa if you're Jewish,' he tells Anatolii, 'or an orphan, right?'

Grigory is not married, but he's met a British woman while working as a plumber. He'll be moving in with her in a few months. He can't take Anatolii.

'But that's okay, you don't want to live with me anyway, do you?'

Anatolii doesn't say anything. Grigory stares at him, then stands up, ruffles Anatolii's hair and leaves the room. Anatolii sits on the sofa. After a while he hears the front door open and shut. Anatolii doesn't move until it's dark. Then he goes to the kitchen and eats some thin white slices of bread and goes into his bedroom. He doesn't undress but crawls under the damp duvet and pulls it up over his head.

The house in Dudley is cold, and they eat cheap meat that comes packaged in white polystyrene stained with something that looks less real than blood. They have tins of stringy spaghetti and more of that thin white bread that's a little better if toasted. Grigory's getting meals cooked for him elsewhere. Anatolii doesn't go to school, either. He spends his days in the house watching TV learning English, or walking around the estate where Grigory lives. He's alert for noises and the shouts of other boys and the flat hoof of a football. Even when it's hot he wears his coat to hide his clothes, which are different to what he sees other boys wear.

Other Ukrainians come through the house for a night or a week at a time. Gruff men, Grigory's age or younger. None have anything nice to say, and they treat Anatolii with a roughness they think is humour. He goes to his room and reads his books. He's joined the library. He showed the women behind the counter his passport. They looked at it for a while and he panicked because he thought they were not going to give it back. Then they put it on a machine and a bar of white light ran across it; with a relief that almost made him wet himself, they handed it back to him. One of the women said a word and put a hand up to make him wait. Ten minutes later they handed him a card. The library staff are kind to him now—one woman in particular, older than his mama. She didn't trust him at first, but he returns every book before it's due and now she saves him the ones he wants. His English is getting better and she helps him. He spends his days in the children's area or, if they're free, in the big red seats that are like buckets. There are cups of tea from a small hatch into a kitchen, and although he doesn't have any money they give him squash for free, and a biscuit now and then. The biscuits are dry but also creamy. At first he wondered how they ate such dry food, but after a while he realises he cannot remember what biscuits were like back at home. Is this home now? Dudley? The library?

There are other children his age but mostly they come with parents. They look at him and they don't come near, as if they know he's from the Zone. He feels like a 'glow-worm.' But no one knows where he's from. Every now and then a girl will come over. Once he runs out of the English sentences he's learnt from the books, they drift away. His reading is good, but his conversation is embarrassing.

At night sometimes Grigory has short, loud arguments with Kulyk over the phone that end with calming hand gestures, as if Grigory is patting him on the head. Sometimes he gets to speak to his uncle but only for a few moments—the calls are expensive. 'Are you good? Fine? Grigory's a good man.' He wants to tell his uncle that the food is rubbish, he's always hungry, there's no school. But he knows his uncle doesn't want to hear those things. Grigory is standing halfway down the hall, leaning against the doorframe of the kitchen. He isn't going home. He knows that. Nothing he says will change it.

'Everything is fine,' he says.

Then one day Grigory tells him to pack his bag. He's moving.

The bus pulls in to Victoria coach station. He thinks of when his mama and Sveta came to Kyiv for the operation. This place is less chaotic, although he feels more lost. What if the woman isn't there to meet him? What will he do? He wants to cry again. Instead he imagines a great rip in the air the shape of a cat's eye, like in the world of the fantasy book he's taken from the library. The woman who was always kind gave it to him as a gift. 'The cover's damaged, we're getting a new copy.' He thanked her. 'You're a good boy,' she told him. She looked sad, but not only sad, and this other look in her eye made him angry. *Likuius.* He could look after himself. But he clings to the book. Through this rip in the air come warriors from a world made by seven gods. They are on horses. They're in the middle of a battle. They give him the choice: he can go with them and be a hero, but he will never be able to return to this world, or he can stay where he is. He goes. Every time. The driver is telling him to get off the bus.

He's met by Rose, as wide as she is tall, with red hair tied up on her head. She rubs his face and gives him a fish paste sandwich, which normally he would have thought disgusting but this time it makes him cry with gratitude. She puts an arm around him but doesn't take his bag. They walk together towards the London underground, a daunting and claustrophobic first experience he never forgets, even though he's travelled on the Kyiv metro. They ride north according to the map Rose shows him, to a place called Green Lanes.

Rose brings him to a place that looks like an old church. It's on a main street. The street is busy, noisy, full of greengrocers and shops selling fried food. There are hundreds of people, much busier than the housing estate in Dudley. There are people of all skin colours. The church has been turned into a centre for refugee children, Rose explains when he asks.

'Like you. You'll stay here for a little while,' Rose tells him. 'Until you meet your foster parents. They'll be coming soon. Linda can't wait to meet you.'

He only understands some of this, not all—his English is

not that good. So he doesn't know if Rose is lying or whether there really are people who are to be his new parents. Grigory explained what it meant. That a couple would act like his parents until he was eighteen, and then as an adult he could choose what to do.

'But you mustn't tell them about your mama,' Grigory told him. 'Okay?'

Grigory was holding him roughly by the arm.

'Answer me,' Grigory shouted. 'You're an orphan. Say it. Go on, say it!'

He wasn't sure what it meant, but said it anyway. 'Okay. I'm an orphan.'

Just before he got on the coach, Grigory apologised.

'Hey, no hard feelings? Your uncle, he made... you can't talk about your family in Ukraine. They'll send you back and Kulyk will get in deep shit, probably. Who knows? The whole country's fucked up. No hard feelings, hey?'

Grigory tousled his hair once more, and then turned and disappeared.

At the refugee centre he's surrounded by children who've run away from the Gulf War, from Iran and Iraq and Turkey. Most have dark skin that always looks dirty to him. There are children younger than him, who smile and laugh loudly, who play simply, and after a few hours things are easier. He makes friends. He runs around with Mehmet. That night they eat bowls of stew that tastes better than anything he's had in weeks at Grigory's place. His bed is in a big room with all the other boys. For the first time since he left his uncle's, he goes to bed happy, and sleeps.

He doesn't know why Linda takes him, at first. He trusts her, though. She's Irish. He doesn't know where Ireland is. He asks why she's taking him when there are younger children. Linda looks at him and there are tears streaming down her face. She introduces him to a man.

'Anthony, meet Peter, my husband.'

Anthony.

They don't have any children of their own. Linda says this sadly.

'I'm going to be your mother now, Anthony. Does that make you feel happy?'

There's something about you, she tells him, and a few weeks later he discovers what this 'something' is. Linda brings out the photos from the trip she made on the trucks that left Dublin in August 1988, the mercy missions to the Zone by the Irish Catholic Church. She came to the villages around Chernobyl. His village too, Radynka. His family had left the Zone long before then, but others had gone back.

Linda has scrapbooks of pictures and newspaper stories and tickets and doctors' notes and all sorts of other things she picked up on the journey, despite not being allowed to bring mementos back. He knows people in her pictures. Children he played with. Members of the *kolkhoz*. Some went back, despite the prohibitions and the radiation. If they went back, why didn't his family? The people look just the same as they did before the accident. At first Linda is delighted he's from this village; then she gets sad, and says they were all sick when they visited. Especially the children.

'We gave them all we had. Food, toys. We visited the hospitals. Oh, Anthony...'

Anthony is not crying, but he's gone white. She hugs him.

'I told you it was too early,' says Peter.

He's afraid of Peter, who's a big man and speaks slowly.

'He has a right to know. To see what happened to his people.'

He already knows. He was there. Or so he thinks. But it's in Linda's scrapbooks that he first sees pictures of children born with defects, the rows of cradles in the nurseries, the babies with no hair. The young girl with no left arm. The child everyone adores who's born with no bottom legs, whose feet come out of his knees and who moves around in a stunted lotus position so everyone calls him the Baby Buddha. Then Linda's favourite: a young boy born with no eyes but pools of skin where his eyes should be. The baby had 'a wonderful temperament, a proper cherub' and everyone fell in love with him.

'He died,' Linda says, wiping her eye with a pink tissue from a square cube of Kleenex she keeps on the coffee table next to her seat. She sits in the same chair every evening, as does Peter. They have their own chairs, as does he, until he leaves for university. 'He died before he was one year old. The little darling. The little angel. Heart difficulties. From birth, his mother exposed during pregnancy.'

His people. Even then, it's perfectly clear that for Linda he is that boy. They foster him, of all the refugees who come through the centre, because he's from Chernobyl. He thinks of Grigory, the tight grip on his shoulder, what he's promised. He never mentions his mama, or Sveta. And Linda never asks.

Wednesday

His phone is beeping. He stares at the coffee brewing on the hob in a worn silver Turkish pot. He looks through the kitchen window. When they first moved in, the woman from next door came round with an old brassy tin containing a Dundee cake, heavy as plutonium. They suffered a stilted conversation on the doorstep until Aggie pattered down the stairs and took over. He's expecting his neighbour to come over this morning with another cake, as if nothing has changed.

He picks up the red *pysanka* from the mantelpiece, from between a photo of Aggie's mum and dad and a candle. The egg was prominently placed, blessing their marriage. He weighs the emptiness, the yoke and white blown out, the batik holding the shell together, the four wolf's teeth that still look like cathedrals but now cathedrals of the forest where they foraged, that last time they foraged together. The smoke over the hill, the bags of mushrooms slung over their shoulders. He puts the egg back on the mantel. It rests there easily on a fraction of its surface.

What happened to the wolves in the forest?

Even wolves would have crawled sick into their nests and whimpered.

And the healthy would have left the sick to their fate.

But that is not true, he hears a voice. His uncle? His father?

In the lab Mariam explains with no embellishments: David is sick. Mild radiation exposure, minor symptoms, given a bed in the clinic. As the longer-serving member of the team she will assume David's responsibilities, and has been quick to do so. Even so, he knows she can't take them all on, and that he'll have a chance to prove himself. She smiles. He can't tell if it's full of *schadenfreude*. Then she leaves the lab. He completes the analysis of yesterday's samples, begins to organise today's.

David makes thirteen. A baker's dozen, he learnt once,

although he does not know the origin of that saying. One has died, leaving twelve. A normal dozen. A dirty dozen. *Is it dirty, my blood?* Elspeth comes over.

'What do you think... should we all...?'

'How do you feel?'

She shrugs. 'Fine. Not ill. Fine, yes. I wonder, though, if it was that first trip he and Mariam made to the sub... so Mariam...'

'We've probably all got some higher than usual readings, it's just that—'

'He's been more exposed—'

'More overworked.' He pauses. 'David will be fine.'

'This is all getting out of hand, don't you think?'

He sees a hospital room full of men, grey skinned and smoking, coughing, complaining. Elspeth crosses her arms, waiting for an answer. There's a chance he can get them to trust him, still. He imagines that future. Yet what he hears is the past.

Be quiet! Not in front of the children.

Who's listening? The soldiers? They don't care about us.

Just before eleven o'clock Mariam comes back. They've been summoned to the Commodore's office for a debrief before a midday news conference. They leave the lab side by side. There's a group of television camera trucks parked in the main car park. They enter the administrative building, march along the main corridor and through numerous double doors. They pass a room filled with chattering journalists. Most are sitting on dark wooden chairs in neat lines, others are crammed in tightly against the walls with their bulky cameras. At the front is a table on a dais, microphones covering a tablecloth emblazoned with Royal Navy insignia. There's a soldier checking IDs at the Commodore's office door. Anthony thinks of Midshipman Darch and of the photo he has of her buried in his computer at home, wiped from his mobile. Did he empty the phone's trash folder? It's in his pocket right now. He breathes deeply and as he does so feels the base breathing too, the land alive, the submarines submerged in the loch like crocodiles at a watering hole, the missiles a range of yellow pointed teeth.

He and Mariam are waved into the Commodore's office. There are two others: the commander of *Tartarus* and a woman in a black suit. He guesses she's PR. The Commodore is holding the new procedure book. Every gap and mistake rectified. Every possible thing they could do in the event of such a crisis, done. They've given the Commodore and the politicians the best chance of salvaging what they want from the mess. Which is not Midshipman Darch's life.

The Commodore praises Anthony's marine testing amendments. It's hyperbole. Even the PR woman's praise runs out quickly. The clock over the Commodore's shoulder ticks round. Perhaps there's no time for sitting down.

'So I need to be clear,' the Commodore says. He puts the manual on the desk, tapping the cover. 'I sit in front of the hacks and I tell them these new procedures have watertight guarantees that no further exposure has occurred and that none will occur in the future from this specific incident. That you've assessed and addressed all the... Look,' says the Commodore, 'I need a simple answer. These procedures are guarantees, yes? No more exposure from this specific incident.'

Anthony knows no new procedures could ever be *watertight*, and he pardons the terrible pun, the first time he's thought of laughing in a week. They're not the ones who have remedied the leak. The engineers are the only ones who could give that guarantee. Mariam say nothing. The Commodore raises his eyebrows.

'Yes. Absolutely,' Anthony says at last. Mariam turns sharply. 'The team... We've got a lot to thank Michael for. The Professor from Bristol. And David and Mariam—'

'Save the congratulations for later,' the Commodore cuts him off.

'Your sense of protocol has been lacking,' says the PR, glaring. Her words are a shock, then he realises he doesn't care. And she's wrong. He'd thought that nuclear engineering *was* about controlling the variables of atomic power. About its *protocols*. But that didn't work. The world was not so precise. It was a scene of calamity. His work, he can see clearly again, is conducted with a living being: a radioactive world. Digging into its skin, scraping off small grafts to test its health. Safe levels set at 500 Becquerel per kilogram of caesium and 100 Becquerel per kilogram of uranium before it's unwell. Surging levels of iodine and strontium in its bloodstream. This is what he's learnt of the tightly ordered world of nuclear force: that radiation cannot be mastered. There is no watertight guarantee.

'No one else will be exposed from what's already been released,' says Anthony, and he feels a set of blocks fall into place. 'You can have confidence in that.'

The Commodore sits behind his desk and picks up a china teacup.

'The time for confidence has long gone,' says the Commodore. 'Jesus Christ. Long gone.' And the Commodore lets out a sigh, as if he were a beetle and had just rolled a great ball of steaming dung up a hill only to watch it roll down the other side. 'Right now I'll settle for competent and effective. Okay, you can go.'

At one o'clock he and Elspeth watch the news. Mariam makes a point of leaving the lab, still angry with him. The press conference is the lead item. There's a fuller disclosure of how the leak happened: information that he hears for the first time of what form the accident took, what led to the flushing of the coolant into the loch, its impact on the environment and the whales. And then there's the book of the safety procedures, the majority of which he's written. There is his glory and his career, if he wants it.

He waits, and waits, but because it's not the first thing

mentioned, nor even is it asked by the journalists, he knows that the Commodore will not tell the press about Midshipman Louisa Darch. Nor David. Nor the rest of the crew. Not at this time. Until... when? The submarines have been renewed? In thirty years, when the papers under the Official Secrets Act are opened to the public?

He feels... He thinks of what he has given to that book of procedures. What they have taken, on the promise of what they would give back.

His phone beeps. Elspeth watches him. Slowly, he takes his phone out.

Jesus Christ, Anthony. I should disown you. You couldn't tell me everything, but you dragged me in there and that means you should have told me. The BBC's saying it was a proper leak. That wasn't a fucking thing to do to a friend, buddy.

He reads the next.

I get it, you would know we weren't exposed to high doses. Sorry about that text before, I freaked out seeing it on the news. Are you two okay? What happens now?

They finish watching the bulletin. He doesn't respond to Elspeth's freighted breathing, and she picks up her laptop and walks away. Anthony unlocks his phone and opens up the messages, closes Michael's text and clicks into the last from *Victoria if you're my mum.* He sends a text. Closes the phone and puts it back in his pocket.

He daren't look as he drives past the protest. Now Tom and Maureen will know why he stopped. Wasn't it as they said: to assuage his guilt, and then fuck off back to work? Isn't that what he's done?

At the cottage no one's there to arrest him. The cottage has not been ransacked. It's just as he and Aggie left it that morning. The hallway is dark but he doesn't turn on the light. He drops the keys on the dresser by the door. There's a pile of envelopes and papers on the dresser, a pair of gloves and a book on altruism by a French monk. Life has shunted him from day to day, and he's not stopped to see in which direction.

He enters the kitchen. They'll be able to stay here. There's no need to move, not now the news is out. Even so, his mind is agitated by the text he's sent, and her reply. He reaches into his pocket. Not the pebble. A USB key. He boils the kettle, then goes into the lounge and turns on the computer. He seeks a way through the many layers of folders to reach the images he took of Midshipman Darch and her medical records. Looks at not the images but the file names: *wolf, knife, bug, soil.* He goes into the kitchen to make a cup of tea straight into a cup. He reaches into his pocket for his phone to check the text—6:00 p.m. he'd said, Aggie out at her Wednesday class—but his phone's not there. He checks his coat hanging up in the hallway. Not there either. His pulse rises, sweat streaks onto his forehead and behind his ears. Where is his phone?

In the kitchen his cup of tea steams on the table. The seven teapots are lined up along the windowsill behind the sink, thyme and basil sprouting around the spouts and handles of Thursday's, the Wellington boot, when Aggie takes an early morning class. Sunday, the Mackintosh, and his winning appeal for coffee. The trivets are on the table, the cutlery is in the drawer, the salt and pepper shakers... all where he'd expect them to be. There's the woody aroma of the cottage and the stove, the way it smells different when it rains; rain is pelting the cottage. He listens. Where is his phone? Have they... Is this what it feels like to be the traitorous one?

He restarts his search. Under the Sunday papers, the pile creeping upwards, the bottom issues yellowing. As if somehow Aggie has mistaken his phone for a magazine and tidied it away, as if that were even possible since he had it half an hour ago. And Aggie isn't home. *Stop it.* He opens the cupboard under the stairs and turns on the light. Something scuttles away, one of the cottage's tiny mice no bigger than his thumb, one of whom he caught transfixed on the kitchen counter one morning amongst a lodestar of crumbs from a late-night snack. He and Aggie have left these mice alone. He's edged closer to the verity of this place and it has come alive for him: the mice are co-inhabitants, not eking a life out of the mess that he and Aggie make, but who have tramped lines along which their small feet scurry. Perhaps the mice, as in a Pixar fantasy, have picked up his phone and chewed through the hardwiring, destroyed the evidence—would they do this for him?

He rustles through the bags and coats, moves boxes. The dry, musty smell of exposed floorboards comes up to meet him. He flips open the flap of a shoulder bag but no, nothing's there. There's no reason he'd come in and put his phone there. He turns off the light and closes the door. *They have it.* If they have his phone there's no point doing anything. What, he's going to run? *They don't have it. You had it in the car. There's no reason to suspect anything. Check the car.*

He runs out to the car in the rain, jumps quickly in. Looks around in the wells, the back of the seat, the glove box, under the seat. The tennis ball is still there. Why the fuck hasn't he thrown it away? But his phone. Not here.

He calls his phone from the landline. Nothing. He turned it on silent after he sent the text. He switches on the light. It's too bright. He forgot how messy they are. But perhaps that's the space itself. Doesn't a space make a difference to how it's lived in?

This is good, he thinks, turning off the light, *this is good*, where would *the cottage* hide the phone? He understands the cottage is on his side. Their side. The cottage is not Bluebeard's *boudoir*. It is willing he and Aggie to succeed. He lifts up sofa cushions, shifts the board games they've piled around the hearth, more magazines, more books, nowhere a phone could hide, but he's looking with renewed hope. The cottage has been steadfastly on their side from the beginning. A difficult friend, but the dampness, the arrangement of the kitchen and how they sit at the table, even the windowsill exactly the right size for seven teapots, everything arranged to bring he and Aggie closer, to face one another at a soft conjunction, a trine not a square, as Linda might say. To come back to each other.

That's who the cottage reminds him of. Linda, who loved her tarot nights with the girls, who lived by Mystic Meg's pat predictions in *The Sun*, who knew much more than she ever let on about astrology, until that time he brought home the girlfriend from university, pre-Aggie, and did her tarot. Is this what the cottage feels like? At home with Linda, a spread of cards, the seven of cups, the Tower?

'So where have you hidden my phone?' he asks the cottage out loud.

The cottage doesn't answer.

In fact, it's not Linda at all. It's *babushka*. A fairy story, a cottage in a forest. It's fooled him, the cottage. It's not on their side at all. Not on *his* side, anyway. It's menacing. It's consuming. And what does it eat? *Khlop*. Little boys. Phones with pictures of dead women on them.

He sits at the kitchen table lost for where to look next, and he sees his bag where he left it: slid down on one of the kitchen chairs. He reaches over and drags it across. He takes the phone out and puts it on the table. Who would have thought security would be so lax to allow them to take their phones into the labs? As he's thinking this, a pair of headlights pierces the kitchen window, and he stands to see Viccy's red Fiesta pull up. He doesn't move until she rings the doorbell.

He offers Viccy a seat. He boils the kettle again, and takes from the windowsill the Wednesday teapot. He glances at the red *pysanka*, its painted-on maze imprisoning the serpent's minions. Its spired wolf's teeth. Behind it, his sister's letter.

He sits and they look at each other, both hugging cups of tea.

'I don't have any soya,' he apologises.

She shrugs.

'You saw the story on the news?' she asks him. 'I mean, from inside?'

'Yes. All the big boys were there. BBC, ITV, Reuters.'

'The big *boys*.' Anthony winces. 'And what they said. Is that the whole story?'

He hesitates, wonders if she notices.

'It's all out now.'

'Is it? Then why did you text me?'

He just needs to stop playacting. Make a decision, one way or the other. He scratches the middle knuckle of his left hand, then shoves it in his pocket.

'What did you think? About the news?' he asks.

'I think the Navy control what they want to release. There was no explanation of the cause of the leak. We don't know if it's worse than he's admitting. He said it was contained. Is that true?' A pause. 'And, of course, "radiation exposure" could mean anything. But your report would be specific about that?'

'Wait,' he says. He marches into the lounge and sits at the computer. He scrawls the mouse and the screen lights up. There, the images. He clicks on all four of them. Plugs in the USB. If he moves them onto the key, then everything changes. He looks at his hand as if it's not part of him, not under his control. It takes all his willpower to lift his hand from the mouse. He looks at the screen. The files stay where they are.

He hears the front door open and close. He grabs the USB key from the computer and runs into the hallway. Aggie's already in the kitchen. He hears them introducing themselves. His legs stop working, as if the hallway is filled with the thick black treacle he's had to wade through his whole life. It's only ten feet to the kitchen door, but it might as well be on the other side of the world. Slowly, one leg in front of the other, he moves forward. He has a foot in the kitchen but it's too late.

'I was just...' Viccy says, moving to get up.

'I invited her in,' he finishes off.

Aggie is smiling but confused. She puts her bag on the table and sits down, leans over and grabs the pot, pours herself a cup. She's not looking at either of them.

'You want more tea, Ant?'

It could be the last cup of tea he drinks as a free man, he thinks.

'Your class?'

'Cancelled. The heating in the centre had blown. A top up?' she offers Viccy.

'She's leaving soon.'

'Who's she, the cat's mother?' Aggie asks.

'It's fine.' Viccy's smiling gawkily. 'I know this is an imposition.'

'Of course it's not.'

They sit in awkward silence. He wants to be a little boy again, to run over to his father on the sofa and wake him and tell him not to go back into the Zone. But he's not that little boy anymore. He looks at Aggie. They lock eyes. She's on the edge of tears. If he goes over to her, will she throw him off? She'd hate it if he made a scene in front of a stranger. He puts his hands on the table and spreads his fingers.

'The nuclear—' he stops. 'The whales. She's investigating their deaths.'

He's waiting for Viccy to say she should leave. He wants to smell Aggie's hair, her sweat. She doesn't smell of iodine.

'Have you seen the news?' Viccy asks Aggie, calmly. Their domestic tragedy is not going to get in the way of what she needs.

'We'll talk again,' he interrupts Viccy. 'Perhaps you should go now.'

Viccy begins to speak, but he raises an open palm. It's forlorn and rude, as if she's no more than a bystander or worse, a dog he's trying to control. But he's lost the wisdom of how to handle this, if he ever had it. Aggie looks away, her body shaking. She's turned as bright as the crimson cover of her book on poverty.

'Sorry,' Viccy mumbles into the table as she drags her body out of the chair. He knows it's not over but only just beginning — that he's given her hope, and she'll come back. He walks to the kitchen doorway. He has the idea that in less than a minute a patrol will arrive and all three of them are thrown into cells somewhere in the underbelly of the base, and he will not see Aggie again for days, perhaps weeks, and he will die from the agony of not being able to explain to her why he has done what he has — not the whales, but Midshipman Darch, the photos... All he needs is to just take her and hold her and hold her until she is willing to listen.

Outside the night is already coal black. Viccy's standing on the lintel when she turns around. He puts a hand on the doorframe to steady himself. He sees his father and mama in the front seat of the car, his father driving. He and his sister in the back. What was it Viccy told him about the whales? *Every minute of every day with every member of your family.*

'I had a flight tonight,' says Viccy. 'Did I cancel it for nothing?'

He bristles at the suggestion he's imposed this upon her.

'To where?'

'The Faroe Islands. They slaughter them. The pilot whales.'

'Maybe that's more important. Maybe you should go.'

She shakes her head.

'The military kills more whales worldwide than a group of traditional hunters. Jesus, we all kill whales. You eat fish, you kill whales. You catch a ferry to Ireland, you kill whales. You buy plastic bags or bottled water, you kill whales. This report could save thousands of lives in the long run.'

He looks at her and a word shatters his focus: *Zakonomernyi.*

In accordance with natural law.

Words from the Moscow hospital, spoken by one of the men who they drove with when he and his father slept overnight in the car, when they had their best chance to secure the tie. *A doctor is vrach, but a witch is vrachika.* Was it Artem? Trofin? The men laughing, coughing, drinking.

He looks at Viccy and holds out the USB. She's momentarily shocked, then takes what's offered.

'Then I hope you save them,' he says, and shuts the door.

I want to know: were you happy on your wedding day? I was, brother. The twenty-four hours felt like a week, and I couldn't eat. Perhaps you did, we were always different. How did you spend the morning—with friends? And your wife, how pretty did she look? I am waiting to see the photographs, if you choose this moment to write to me. You'll be angry that your mother in London has been writing to me to tell me about your life. Only little notes. Please forgive her. She only wants the best for you. This is kind of her, to someone she has never met. You will forgive her?

So please tell me. I want to know what you felt when you became a married man. Do you remember the photograph that sat above our fireplace? Of mama and father and the priest in the hat with the horns, holding their hands on the book? Our father's face! He was looking upon you on your wedding day, I'm sure. Mama would have been happiest, though. I expect fathers everywhere think their sons make at least a little mistake in marrying, even when the woman is the most beautiful in the world.

I want to know what thoughts were in your mind. My single thought was: *will he turn up!* But no, this isn't the truth. It was this: *I am now boarding the train.* Strange, isn't it? I've almost never caught a train. Not like walking between the village and the factory, or catching the bus to Kyiv. Perhaps what I was entering into in marriage was similar, for me, of getting on a train. I stepped into a different world. I didn't know where it would take me. Only that I knew it would bring me there faster.

I didn't think you really invited us to your wedding—I guessed that came from Linda. But then I'm not well enough to travel. If I'd left here it would mean a train, a plane, and Jelena said I wasn't up to it, and I agreed. But what *am* I up to, now? If I couldn't go to my brother's wedding, what am I up to? Ah, this is so long ago now. You didn't want me there, your sickly forgotten sister. Perhaps this was your only thought throughout the day: *don't let her come.* Fine, my life is here, with my husband and our family. Mama's grave to tend. You boarded the train when you were young and it took you away. If I visited and saw your life in England and your friends, your pleasant weather and your health, it would make me feel too—

I don't—

So, it seems I'll never say to you what I feel.

I have written many letters that I've put straight into the wood burner. Why should I carry on when you never reply? After Mama died was the time I should have said things. But now? I won't even send this letter. Why bother? It's not my life that you need concern yourself with now.

All this is too miserable. I won't send it. I won't—

Thursday

He's swimming with a woman. They've jumped into the sea fully clothed as some extravagant gesture at the end of a party. The water is clear all around—but only he can see the huge eel-like creature that lunges toward them from the seafloor. He guides the woman away. The underwater world remains wonderful for her, and yet this prehistoric nightmare is chasing them. He swims with a hand on her back exposed by her backless gown. But before the monster attacks its head comes off and rolls in front of them. It's too late to stop her seeing it; he needs to get her to the water's surface to breathe. He pulls her clear, and they climb up and sit on the edge of a cliff looking down into the water. There is a great serpent chained at the bottom of the cliff, waiting for them to fall back down.

He goes downstairs. In the lounge Anthony turns on the television and stares at the early morning news. He hears Aggie get up, walk around. They haven't spoken since Viccy left. He'd gone up to bed and undressed even though it was only 7:00 p.m. The next thing he knew it was midnight, Aggie asleep next to him. He feels as if their marriage is a week old, a day, a minute, that he's never known her, this person he's shared his life with. Or more honestly, that she's never known him.

There's an item on the NHS. Next is an aerial view of the base. He turns the sound up. There's a to-camera piece from the journalist, the tents in the background, a gathering of about twenty activists. The journalist is explaining the story: *HMS Tartarus*, of the Astute class, was taken out of action a week ago. Twelve crew members affected and being looked after in the base clinic.

Twelve. Does that now include David? Or Midshipman Darch?

He mutes the TV. The programme flicks back to the studio, a pair of well-groomed presenters on a red crescent-shaped couch.

There's a picture of the Houses of Parliament and a superimposed image of the Greek god Poseidon holding a seaweed-strewn trident. The prongs of the spear are glowing like Christmas decorations. Professor Challen had mocked him for the mythic imagery he used as an epigraph in that paper. *But look at what they call their weapons.*

He punches the steering wheel when the Hyundai won't start, but on the fifteenth try it springs into life. Next week — if there is a next week — he'll upgrade. It might still work. The journalists will put through an FOI. What he's risked will be lost in the threads of an unravelling chaos. His faults might yet turn out to be gifts.

He reaches the base and is disoriented by what he's already seen on television. The engorged protest around the tents, Maureen and Tom within the melee, Tom no doubt still wielding his knife. There are four vans: ITV, BBC, Reuters, and an anonymous white Mercedes with the largest satellite dish of the lot.

'Bit of a scene this morning, sir,' says the guard at the gate. He sits in the car, waiting. There's extra security on, or seems so; the guard is running checks rather than handing him back his pass. The guard's grin changes and he glances at Anthony before leaning in the window.

'Commodore needs to see you, sir. There's an escort on the way.'

There's no loch view in the interrogation room — they must gnash their teeth at that. The two military police are both stocky, both have dark hair, although one of them is thinning on top. They sit him down in a chair while the shorter one, white shirt cuffs exposed beyond the jacket sleeves, sits on the side of the desk. The other perches on a low and wide filing cabinet, swinging a leg.

He tells them everything. The Hyundai broke down and the protesters helped him push the car off the road. It was impolite not to stop for tea. They'd said other people had stopped. The interrogator's face is implacable. Oh, and they showed him the paper. To not look would have been an admission of guilt. Of course he could have just gone online and seen the news… It was an error of judgment, sure. But not a purposeful one. He gives them more than they were expecting, or at least he thinks so, by their lack of questions. One of the MPs goes out and returns twenty minutes later. He indicates with his head they're leaving and then he's escorted, for the second time, to the Commodore's office.

It's just himself and the Commodore. He sits on the sofa. This time he notices the room's airiness. Light coming through the window paints a sun square on the carpet. It's quiet, lulling. He was expecting… to be arrested? At least that. He's confused by the Commodore's relaxed manner. He wants to throw up and sleep at the same time. It's the presumption that he's been followed to the Carvery to meet Viccy. That the cottage has been watched. That the ease he and Aggie were recovering is lost already because of his idiocy. Not just the stupidity of talking to an environmental investigator, not bringing Michael in, not even taking the photos, but of getting into nuclear energy in the first place, of thinking he could control its force. He returns the Commodore's smile as best he can.

'You understand it wasn't protocol, and you rather upset David, but bringing in that expert was pretty sharp thinking,' the Commodore says. Some of the earlier heaviness in the Commodore's voice is gone. Perhaps the severity of what's happened on the base means the Admiral of the Fleet has stepped in; maybe even the Prime Minister. And that means the Commodore isn't making the decisions, but also isn't carrying the burden.

Anthony leans back, hopes his face is apologetic.

'But since Midshipman Darch… that can't happen again. This story is going live with us in control. By the way, the politicians… as you can imagine. The vote for renewal was scheduled for a few weeks' time. No doubt it'll be postponed, kicked into the long grass. Football vernacular. Not my sport. Yours?'

He shakes his head. It's not only fear that is turning his stomach, he realises, but anger. *Football? Hasn't someone died?*

'Bloody politicians,' says the Commodore, smiling, but with relief. 'Forget I said that. But even the military has to accept we live in a twenty-four-hour news world. Social media. You'd think the Westminster lot got it. Are you on Twitter, Anthony?'

But perhaps this is how one ascends to higher office. What is one death in securing the nuclear deterrent? When there's a seat on the Security Council at stake?

'We've got no mobile signal in the cottage,' he replies.

'You and your wife? Agatha, isn't it?'

His stomach drops as the Commodore says her name, as it implicates her, and he knows the Commodore has done that on purpose. He feels the pebble press against his leg in his pocket; immediately words come. *We arrived in our new school. We were given special identity labels—red, green, yellow. If you got a red label nobody could touch you. If you had a green label, that was bad but not so terrible. A yellow label was okay.*

'Anthony, we've hardly got to know you. You've only been here...?'

'Nearly three months,' he says, dragging himself back into the room.

'I understand it takes time to get used to the military's way of doing things. Even for those of us who came up through the ranks. You're from the civil side. Which is why, you understand, when you stop and talk to the protesters, we need to keep you clear on what is tolerable, and what is not. For your own sake. As much as this kerfuffle.'

Perfectly controlled. Ordered, prohibited. He understands why he's here.

'This kerfuffle,' he repeats.

The Commodore puts down his coffee. 'So why did you stop?'

'The whales,' he says, before other words fall out. 'The paper. They were waving it at me. I thought... just thought I should see what was happening. I realise that...'

The Commodore looks at him, reading the lie on his face.

'And the second time?'

'It seemed... rude not to.'

The Commodore doesn't laugh, doesn't shake his head.

'There are two things we could do,' he says. 'Your work's of a very high standard, that's clear. David said so. So, we could do two things. We could suspend you now, for your breach of protocols, for the risk you've brought to the situation.' In the pause Anthony can hear his heart beating. He thinks of them sweeping the cottage. Checking his phone. Taking Aggie in for questioning. 'But that would seem quite unfair, after the work you've put into helping us clear up this situation. The other thing I could do, Anthony, is promote you. After your probation, of course. A reward. Recognition of your talent. I think you're a maverick, Anthony. Your past... Your work history, what you've turned around for me in a short period of time. And mavericks always have these rebellious elements to their character, which means one needs to keep them closer. Don't you think?'

The Commodore crosses his legs. The trouser rides up, revealing a navy blue sock with a red anchor sewn into the garter. Anthony catches a flash of the Commodore's fleshy yellow leg, his curls of brown hair. He looks up at the Commodore nursing his cup and saucer on the billowing folds of his jacket. He knows that when Commodore Thompson takes off his jacket and socks he's only Bill, or William, and he argues with his wife too, sometimes, would like to be better with his putter, is taking tablets for a hiatus hernia to keep down the reflux, doesn't understand why his daughter has pink streaks in her hair even now she's past twenty.

'Don't you think?'

He nods. The words in his head are not the words the

Commodore wants to hear.

'You understand with Midshipman Darch's expiration, how we must keep total control on protocols now?'

Expiration. He nods again. It's not nearly enough. He has to speak.

'What about David?'

The Commodore shakes his head. 'I cannot tell you how much I regret that. You've all been doing such brilliant jobs, without complaint. And the crew... There are the families. You know more than most about the effects, don't you?'

Khlop. Khlop.

'The two boys...' he says, avoiding the ditch into his past.

'We're monitoring them. My other doctors are.'

'I don't know how long they'd been on the whales for.'

'But you did the right thing. And reported it.'

'I had to.'

'That was absolutely right of you. Another chit on your account—the positive side. And we told the parents.' A pained smile. 'You can imagine their response.' Anthony doesn't say anything. 'It was one of them who told the press in the first place. Jesus Christ, if they'd only... Even though we didn't let them out of our sight. Perhaps they knew someone in the village. That's how it happens. Chinese Whispers, then it hits the front page.'

'Except—' he says, sharply, and stops.

'Yes, except it's not a whisper, is it?' The Commodore looks at Anthony until he's forced to turn away.

'What about Midshipman Darch?' he asks. 'When will we tell the press?'

The Commodore puts his cup down. Sighs.

'Some decisions aren't even mine to make,' he says. 'I wish it were.' Anthony doesn't believe him, but for the first time understands why the Commodore needs to believe his own lie. 'Everyone on base is my responsibility. Like a family. But, what's it to be Anthony? Are you going to follow protocols, or is this the last time we meet?'

Anthony swallows. Every decision has a half-life, he thinks. The decision—to marry, to begin to love—will decay, but the signature of the decision remains. He smiles at the Commodore but he's thinking of Aggie. How they used to talk made him happy. He thinks of their wedding, how they gusted with laughter coming up with names for the tables: the dullest distant family friends sat on Argon; his physics department friends on Ununtrium: extremely radioactive, an element that's created in a lab but isn't found in nature. The memory presses into him and hurts.

From within the moment he begins to understand the nature of crisis. *Krizi*. That it is survivable. That even catastrophes take place in a flow of time, and the decision, the secret, decays. That some may not survive, but the future survives. And afterwards the world is changed, but continues. Even the infinite decay of uranium-238, the more comprehensible yet near infinite half-life of uranium-235, even these pass, left in waste mines, buried underground, on ghost ships lulling outside Indonesian harbours, a permanent signature of the human race on the planet for all future records, but forgotten. And the decision whether or not to tell the press about Midshipman Darch, whether to marry Aggie, whether to talk to her, whether to…

He nods.

'Yes. Protocol.'

The Commodore stands, and he follows suit. They shake hands. He's shown out, and follows the corridor into the bright morning, where he's left by his escort and free to go in whichever direction he chooses. Free, to a degree; he's being watched.

He doesn't return to the lab. He looks at the loch, its grey waters silent, unyielding. He looks up, as a flock of pigeons scatters from the top of the cafeteria building. *Expiration*. To breathe out. A last breath taken, stolen. The ionising process that robbed Midshipman Darch—Louisa—of her breath.

Nuclear steals; some people call the process fission. But each transformation is a theft. A loss. Not a defeat—to terrorism, or to the anti-war protesters, the singers of songs, of *We Are Women, We Are Strong*. The loss is death's work. Human, animal, insect. *What are you reading? About loss.* He's carried loss in his body since the accident. Everything that was stolen. By destiny? No. By what then? What word? *Damn this fucking language.* Damn his uncle Kulyk for sending him to England. Damn his father and mother for meeting and marrying. Damn all their choices. Damn this present that's spinning and flinging itself ever farther from the core of what he knows. And damn its indifference: all that has been lost doesn't mean a thing to uranium, to the mantle of the earth. To the half-life of a degraded planet, its source sun, the expanse of core underneath. Everything he's lost means nothing to the thief who takes, takes, takes.

He puts a hand in his pocket and rubs the pebble. For the first time in a long time he hears the voice of his father.

It's only common men who hunt the wolf, Anatolii.

He arrives home prepared to talk, but the cottage is empty. He checks the calendar. Thursday, an evening class, but not late, and not far away, she's normally back by seven. He stares at the picture of Angkor Wat on the calendar, somewhere neither he nor Aggie have been, and wonders if they might go there together. Then he sees the note on the kitchen table, torn from a notebook and folded in two and stood up like a card. He hesitates. Sees his hand as he reaches for the note as someone else's, shaking and white.

Ant, I'm going to Glasgow for a couple of days to stay with mum. I can't believe what you've done, and I don't know what trouble it's going to get you in. It feels like you've disconnected from us. I don't know what's going on, but you need to get clear and then we can talk. Maybe you can undo it, get the thing back? Aggie x

He goes out to the car and sits in the driver's seat for a long time, until he knows for sure that her note was real and she's not coming home. The Hyundai starts on the first attempt. He drives on autopilot back to the base, past the protest, where there are still a group of twenty, electric lamps hanging from poles with their CND placards and a foldout table with a clutter of thermos flasks. He sees Maureen talking to a group of them. He can't see Tom. He drives through Garelochhead and past the buses that only a week before had him folding over the steering wheel as the memory of those buses in Radcha flooded his view. He drives all the way round the loch and into Portkil Bay where the whales washed up. He pulls in where there's a brown picnic sign and the rocks are less ragged. He's tired but forces himself to walk along the small strip of shore. There's no trace of the whales now. But that's not true. There will be a trace of their skin and mucus. The cause of death, the radiation in the water. It's cold and he wraps his coat around him. He listens to the wind as if he's not heard nature before. A moon behind grey cloud. The slow slap of the river on the shore, a whooshing up the beach, its fizzing sweep down into the water, bubbles dispersing and dissolving into the shingle.

It's only common men who hunt the wolf, Anatolii.

He is five years old. They are walking in the woods behind the house at Radynka. *The wolf is the European wolf, king of all dogs. It knows how to live in these forests, and to disappear when stupid men come through with their heavy feet. We see the wolf because we're more respectful.*

The shepherds hated the wolves for taking their sheep, and bred Karakachan dogs to fight them off. They lived in a fair trade—the weakest, oldest sheep would go, but the dogs would protect the lambs—and the wolf pack would be respected, like his father on the *kolkhoz*. Was he a good Soviet man? He gave his life following orders. Anthony knew for many in the *hrupu*, many men in Ukraine and Belarus, the accident saved them while it killed them. Before the explosion, their lives were anonymous lives of the collective. The accident warped some men into wolves. Hunted and feared, but tied to the land even more fiercely.

There were times that he went with his father to work. At sowing time and at harvesting. The work of the field was still by hand, mostly. The eggs were collected by the children. The herd was milked into buckets that they carried two in each hand but never spilling any. The milk straight from the cows was warm and thick and sweet and the smell made him think of the *vatrushka* his mama made, round pastries filled with cheese. It was Sveta who had the sweet tooth and would beg for their mama to add raisins, but if he had to admit it, he preferred them this way too.

Wolf. His father's love, in the forest. His father would talk about the wolves as they walked. *Vovky.* His focus was on keeping up, on listening. This was the tie between them. His father would talk about the others on the *kolkhoz*, the stupidity of Strokat, about the other men's poor decisions, and what benefits they were losing because of these decisions. But every now and then his father would stop and shake his head and tell him not to listen, not to repeat what he was saying, his words were not good Soviet words but the words of a tired man. *Too much work, Anatolii, as if we were having to live in the capitalist West!*, which is what they heard of America, that people lived in fine houses with televisions, sure, but government propaganda and advertising kept everyone brainwashed as wage slaves. *That's what's important about the kolkhoz,* his father said, *it's for the benefit of everyone and we work hard to provide for our community. For our land.*

He has the same love of the land. A yearning for a better life, to be responsible for balance in their small part of the world. He tries to reconcile what he might have once been with his responsibility for what's happening. He's not the academic. He's not the expert on wolves. Eleven crew members of a nuclear sub are suffering radiation sickness. One has died. David is in isolation. A nuclear incident is at the centre of his life again, less than twenty miles away.

He cannot parse the thought.

He hears movement and looks up. There's a couple walking towards him. He stands and looks around for somewhere to hide. He pulls the cuff of his jumper down over his hand and wipes his face. The couple get closer, and he feels exposed. What if he ran? Would it matter? He glances at them as they get closer. There's something familiar about the girl. They're too young to be military. Too young to be following him. She stares at him as they pass. When they're a few yards beyond him the girl tugs on the boy's arm and they turn, the boy reluctantly. Anthony stands with his hands in his pockets, a sticky sweat down his neck and back.

'It's you who came to see the whales, isn't it?' the girl says when they're six feet away. He knows her now. The girl from the cafe who gave him directions.

He's filled with relief, and the shame of panicking.

'That's right. Hello.'

'See I told you.' The boy shrugs. 'They were all dead, weren't they?'

'Yes. Before I got there.'

'Why aren't you letting anyone know about the boys? It was on the news.'

'Excuse me?'

'The two boys. You've taken them away, you lot have taken them.'

The girl looks at him angrily while the boy she's with is as still as rock. Anthony shakes his head. He could tell her he doesn't work for the Navy, that he's civilian. He shouldn't be the focus of her anger, of the locals' anger, of the fury of the parents—but he is. And none of those excuses matter. None of them are true.

'I know the sister of one. She's sick with worry. Says you're not telling them anything. Her parents are worried sick, and they've had to sign some paper saying they won't tell anything. Is that right? If they've got sick because of what you've—'

'Leave it, Mandy,' says the boy, grabbing the girl's arm. Mandy shrugs him off. 'Is it right?'

'No, it's not,' he says in a flat, lifeless way that disarms her. The Commodore lied to him about the boys: they're worse than he was told. The truth hits him in the stomach: *it will never all come out.* The anger that has been growing inside him is released. He fumbles in his pocket for the pebble while the girl glares.

'I'll find out where they are. I'll get some news for the families.' The girl looks surprised, then unconvinced.

'Come on,' the boy says again, walking away. 'Mandy.'

'Look, I will. I'll find out. I'll come to the cafe.'

She glares at Anthony, unsure of how she's won this argument. He returns her stare until she turns away and walks on with her boyfriend, strutting with a sense of power. He turns to the water and sees not the Clyde but the waters of the Caspian Sea. Remembers the letters his mama sent them, read to them by a woman in the camp at Odessa. *You're safer there. We won't forget you. We'll come for you.*

He picked up the pebble from that beach in Odessa. Was he five? Six? Scared. Alone, apart from Sveta, even more scared then he was.

He raises his arm, and throws the pebble as far out into the water as he's able.

1998, London and Kyiv and Korosten'

He's sixteen and nearing the end of his GSCEs—his physics project almost complete, the school prize almost won—when Linda and Peter sit him down. *Coronation Street* is turned off, so he knows it's serious. They hand him a letter. He looks at it, turns it over. On the back is his uncle's name and address in Kyiv. He opens the letter; is struck by the strangeness of an alphabet he's not seen for six years. He puts it down, doesn't want to read it. But Linda is telling him to. He would disobey her if Peter wasn't there. But Peter is there. He picks up the letter and begins to read.

Dear Anatolii,

We were never going to write. Then when you were eighteen, as a man, you could have told your new parents that Anatolii Nikolaevich is your name and that you have family still in Ukraine. Let me tell you, I understand that this letter is a terrible thing. I'm saddened too. I didn't want to disrupt your new life, after working so hard to give you a chance.

But your mama is at the Feofaniya. Do you remember visits with your father? It's where they moved treatment of the Chernobylites, but perhaps you had left for England. I was drinking too much, it's all a mess. Forgive me. Are you English, or British? What difference does it make to you, living there, is it similar to how it was here whether you said you were Ukrainian or Soviet? But your mother, Anatolii. She would write, but it pains her in too many ways. She needs you to come back. She understands you're studying. She understands it's important for you to be in England, to be British. But this is important also.

I went last week to help your sister take your mother to the Feofaniya. I would've kept your mother and sister there—the fresh air would do her better, but they go through the motions at the hospital. *Perspecktivnyi*, hey? One can't give up the prospecting once you're an invalid.

Your mama complains of emotional stress, of gastritis. The doctors don't believe it's to do with the accident. It came too late for her. It was all about your father and what he deserved. Ah, I'm not complaining. This is how it is. But now your mama's doctor, his name's Dmytro, he has a small office so he can't be that important, but he's the one we see. We bring chocolates and vodka but he's not old Soviet, instead he examines your mother on his bed, he places three fingers on her stomach and presses, and she oohs and aahs, she complains, your sister holds her hand, then he looks in her eyes with a light. All this is done with her coat on, Anatolii, she won't even take her coat off. What's the point, I ask you, to come all this way and submit yourself to the doctor and his pressing if you will not even take off your winter coat? But this is how it is. This doctor's not a bad man. He says it's age, her mood, her grief. I say it's all these things. She doesn't help herself. She wears her coat and complains that the State has withdrawn its support, less every year. It's true, but to say it, what good does this do? Your sister Sveta, she tries to calm your mama. This news, it doesn't help—

But your new parents will not want you to hear about the struggles of your old family. You were sent away to begin a new life. But your mama... I'm sorry, Anatolii, but there is not only the Chernobyl tie, there were ties before Chernobyl, too.

Your mama is very sick. You must come. She is asking for you. I told her you had an amazing scholarship to go to England, funded by our State, to become a worldly man. But she wants to see you once more, Anatolii. When you tell this to your new parents, they'll understand, I'm sure.

Beregi sebya,

Kulyk

Peter makes him translate the letter. Then Anthony is ushered into his room while Peter explains to Linda. He lies on his bed with his face on his pillow as he listens to Linda's wailing. Then, a few moments later, Peter opens his door, and tells him to come into the living room. He gets up, slowly, and walks through. Linda's in her seat. The television's turned off, and Linda is dabbing her eyes with a Kleenex.

'You should have told us,' is all she can say. 'My Anthony. My Anthony.'

He doesn't know what to do. She puts out her hands and calls him to her. He goes, and she wraps him in her arms. They're all crying. Later that night Peter gets off the phone from the Refugee Centre but doesn't tell Anthony what's been said.

A few days later Peter hands him a bundle, which includes money and tickets to fly to Kyiv. And a visa—he no longer has his Ukrainian passport, just his British one. He sinks into the stuffy, beige sofa. Via Amsterdam, tomorrow. Officially he has no mama in Ukraine. Linda is his mother, he must remember that. He mustn't tell anyone at airport security.

'He understands,' Peter says, putting a hand on his shoulder.

It's a summons from another life and he doesn't want to go. He was spending the weekend with friends revising for their exams, and as a reward they would watch the Arsenal game against Everton. He can't read Linda's face, it's too red and puffy. He can't imagine Linda *wants* him to go. Isn't she his mother? But Linda's credo has always been the same: family obligation outweighs one's wishes.

He's used to travelling on planes now. He and Linda always fly to Galway. They've been on holidays to the Algarve and Crete, too. And now he's sixteen he gets to travel as an adult. On the layover in Amsterdam he wanders around Schiphol Airport staring at people and imagining their lives. There are lots of Africans, lots from the Middle East. Everyone knows about Kuwait now since Saddam Hussein invaded. There's a family in long Arabic gowns waiting in the forecourt of a Burger King, six hyperactive kids drinking large cokes. He imagines they're a princely family from the desert ousted by Operation Desert Storm. Burger King! Perhaps this is as far as they've made it to the West. Linda's always telling them over dinner that the 'evil Major government' makes it almost impossible to help refugees 'like you,' she says, in case he's forgotten.

He flies from Heathrow with UIA, hears Ukrainian spoken for the first time in six years. His return ticket is not booked, it's on hold, the operator 'very understanding in the circumstances. It's all been arranged,' Linda told him. She'd sat next to him on the sofa for a long time with the television off. It's halfway through the flight that he understands that his mama is dying. It's looking down over the Alps and their snow crested ridges as the plane edges closer to Kyiv, to Boryspil Airport and his uncle, that the lie of who he is begins to creep up on him. That Linda's tears were not only over fears for his safety but the explosion of the greater lie: that they were a family. She was desperate for a Chernobyl baby and fostered him, which turned into something permanent. But he still has a mama. He watches the mountains pass underneath, solid, unbreakable. He thinks of what it might be like to be dropped down there, softly landing, to be stranded among the peaks and drifts, a hundred miles from a road or path, to have utter solitude amongst silent elements. *Geology*, he thinks. *Perhaps I will study geology.* The school's spoken to him about university. Where he might think of applying. His chemistry scores are better than his physics. But it's his sports teacher, Mr Flynn, of all people, who mentions Oxford.

He arrives after nine. He's not forgotten the cold and he looks for his uncle's old greatcoat among the waiting faces. Everything offends him: the beige walls, the lack of vending machines, the smallness of the doors out of the airport. It all seems so out-of-date.

Kulyk is older. His once sandy hair is colourless. He still has his large moustache but it's not so dark and is turning the same shade as his hair. His smile is wide, though, and he smiles for young Anatolii as they greet each other in a bear hug. 'Anthony,' he corrects Kulyk as they walk to the car. He sits quietly as they drive into town over the river, and remembers life in their three-roomed apartment: how he inhabited these streets and parks of Dniprovskyi District, how he and the other boys played football on the grass after school and each day of summer. His uncle carries his bag up the stairs and throws it into his old bedroom. Kulyk has a girlfriend, called Tania. She stays sometimes. It's a sort of apology, Anthony can tell, his uncle embarrassed that there are womanly touches to the apartment. It *is* cleaner. Cleaner than he ever made it for his five *hryvnia*. Anthony cannot believe his uncle has a girlfriend. It makes him smile and grimace at the same time.

His uncle shepherds him into the *kvartyra*. Anthony strokes the laminated tabletop with the coffee rings, stares at the bright green tiles on the floor reaching halfway up the walls, through the windows to the other blocks of flats. It isn't that dissimilar to London, or at least the parts he knows. Kulyk rattles around in the cupboard and then sits opposite with a bottle of *horilka* and two tumblers.

'So finally, we're old enough to drink together, man to man,' Kulyk says, smiling, even though Anthony remembers the times they went to the bar together and Kulyk allowed him a finger of beer with dinner. The language of his childhood flows into his mind. Kulyk pours proud measures and puts the bottle down. There's soreness round his uncle's eyes. The bottle is nearly empty. He wishes he'd brought vodka from England, but he's glad he hasn't, too. No one in England drinks vodka like they do in Ukraine. Beer, for sure, and gin, and wine, but not the same way. Not neat and burning. But he's a man now. He picks up his glass.

'*Nasdrovie!*' Kulyk shouts, and they clink glasses.

'*Nasdrovie.*' And then in English. 'To your health.'

'Ah, your English.'

The *horilka* burns his stomach.

'It's hard here,' says his uncle. Anthony starts to feel sick and happy. 'Your mama. She will cry to see you grown, Anatolii. But you have to know... Ah, it's easier in Kyiv. Here, we're almost Western. There's modernization. Everyone fights more, yes, but if you're good, you get a chance. Do you remember the *kolkhoz*, Anatolii?'

This time he doesn't correct his uncle. He nods.

'It's good you remember. And how is your school?'

'I'm going to university.'

'Ha!' Kulyk bangs the table. 'Another drink. Celebrate.' He pours—there's almost no vodka left. 'Here's to our self-made man.' Kulyk holds up his glass. And then in stuttering English, 'To your health!'

'*Nasdrovie*,' says Anthony.

They're both silent. He hears cars outside, the buzzing of the fridge's motor. He remembers the passing of history. The fall of the Wall. Ukrainian Independence. *Nothing lasts. Nothing.*

'You know who'd be proud of you, Anatolii Nikolaevich?' Kulyk picks up the empty bottle and stares at it. He tuts. 'That Tania,' he says, shaking his head but winking. 'You'll like her. She's a good looking woman.'

He wonders what kind of woman would put up with his uncle.

Tomorrow Kulyk will drive them both to see his mother and sister.

'Your mama won't come to the hospital anymore.' His uncle sighs and wipes his eyes, gets up and throws the bottle into the bin; it clatters and breaks upon the shards of previous bottles. Anthony asks to look at the old newspapers.

'It's for a physics project at school.' His uncle looks at him, confused. It will help him get to university, he says. 'In the garage. I found them once...'

His uncle leaves the flat and comes back with the saved papers. He doesn't ask if he can take them there and then, but he knows his uncle will give them up.

'Hold your breath,' says Kulyk as they drive past the sign for Korosten'.

It's still grey, still dusty. The roads are bare and broad and expose the houses to the wind. *I lived here once.* There's a flicker of memory but he turns away from it and looks out of the window at the surfeit of cloud, a thick depthless white.

Kulyk knocks and his sister answers. He holds his breath. She is—fourteen, fifteen?—but doesn't look older than when he left. She welcomes them both, she gives him a hug although she hugs him around the chest; he's a foot taller now. Do boys grow and girls do not? He doesn't look at her as they go into the house. The fire in the main room is burning, not freshly cut logs but pine, a cheap wood they buy from outside the Zone. Kulyk has made a new dining table and chairs from ash. They sit on a small sofa, the arms covered in lace antimacassars. His sister runs to the kitchen to make tea. The window faces north, it is April, there's barely any sun, the fire is embers and the lamp has a heavy red shade with tassels that lights only a small smear around the table. The *samovar* boils. He doesn't look at his uncle. He was expecting more people. Neighbours. Family. But who else is there? He shuts his eyes until he can see white and purple spots, until the idea of death has gone. His sister is there with a tray and two cups and a tall silver pot. His uncle chatters about the drive and the weather, but the words pass right through Sveta. She sighs, and an awful, tired look crosses her face. She drops into a chair behind the sofa where he and his uncle are sitting, as if she's uninvited to this family reunion.

'Do you want to come and see mama?'

He looks not at her but at Kulyk.

'Come on,' says his uncle.

They follow Sveta into the hallway and up the stairs onto the tiny landing, with its three doors leading to two bedrooms and a bathroom. The door to his mama's room is open. Sveta goes in and they follow. The room is unlit and the curtains closed. Sveta indicates they should sit down while she stands. There are bruises on his mama's face. She's been at the clinic, but wanted to come home, his sister is saying. She cried until she was allowed home. She's big now, and he has a memory of her shuffling along the road. Her breath is rasping, her eyes half open. She lifts a hand and moves it towards him.

'She wants to hold your hand,' says Sveta. He takes his mama's hand and holds it on the bed. It's cold and fleshy.

His mama speaks to him but her teeth are all gone and her words are slurred.

'Sorry?' says Kulyk, too loud for the dull room. 'No, no. You rest, Oksana. Rest, don't waste your words on silly apologies.'

His mama's name. His father used to call her *wife*.

She mumbles something childish. Her chin is resting on her chest, her breasts, he can't help but look at them spread out and falling under her arms. Her nightie of dark crimson. The room smelling of things it shouldn't. He thinks of his mama when she was angry, wailing as they scattered his father's ashes. Angered with the doctors and the hospitals, angry with their lack of *blat*, her inability to secure a better tie.

They sit like that for a while, for what could be ten minutes or a whole night.

'We should let mama rest,' says Sveta. He squeezes his mother's hand, and she squeezes back faintly. His other hand is in the pocket of his trousers, holding his old pebble. He'd found it in his bedroom last night, at Kulyk's. There on the bedside table, all these years.

In the living room they sit in silence. Above the fire is a picture of him and Sveta during a Victory Parade. There's a picture of his grandpa, his father's father, in uniform. A certificate framed in gold: his father's Hero's Certificate awarded six months after the end of the crisis. The 'end' was symbolic only, like so much to do with the Soviet Union. And a hero's status was worthless; only *poterpili* meant you would get the privileges you were owed.

Sveta offers them her room. But he can't imagine sleeping there. Kulyk drives them back to Kyiv and cooks a stew of sausage and potatoes and some cabbage from the allotments. Tania is staying away, Kulyk says, 'at this time.' The phone rings. Kulyk hands him the grater and instructs him to grate some ginger over the pot and give it a stir. He laughs at his uncle at this improvement in his cooking skills, and Kulyk blushes, then laughs. He grates the ginger with a flimsy grip, watching tiny strings of root fall into the stew, listening to the radio. Kulyk returns and stops at the door with his hands on his hips. Anthony glances, then looks away. Kulyk goes to the cupboard and pulls out the *horilka*.

'Come and sit down,' says his uncle.

He doesn't. He keeps grating until there's nothing left of the ginger except a stump in his hand, the rest dissolved into the simple chemistry of their dinner.

He lies in bed and remembers when Sveta came to Kyiv for the operation. Their mama had taught herself things about radiation that their father was no longer fit enough to know, that she hoped would help her care for Sveta.

'The radiation never ends,' she'd said, as Kulyk drove them away from the hospital. Sveta was asleep in her arms, a gauze over the scar on her neck. 'The plant, this land, do you know this, Anatolii? You know how long the caesium from the reactor stays in our soil?' He didn't know what to say, so said nothing and stared out of the window until they entered Korosten'. She'd discovered as much as she could about the explosion. All the women did, as the men fell away to sickness, or drunkenness, or impotency or anger, or committed suicide, or had given up and become hibernating beasts in their own homes, parts of the furniture to clear up around, or died. Everyone wanted compensation. After the men failed the women began their own *hrupu*. They joined invalid clubs and educated themselves on the nature of nuclear energy and the vocabulary of the atom so they could talk to the doctors and the administrators and petition for the money owed. But women had less *blat* and were easily dismissed. They were never valid witnesses. Only a handful worked the disaster, so his mama and all the mothers and sisters and wives began a toil that would neglect their own bodies. In the post-Soviet era there was a brief period, a moment of exchange when the Ukrainian government wanted democracy, so wanted votes, so purchased the stability of households with new facts and admissions, bought hope with benefits. But not enough to live on.

'You're nothing but a *cholovik-invalid*,' his mama cursed his father one time. Only once. A husband-invalid. He expected his father to strike his mama. His mama took a step back, gathered her skirt and apron between her legs. His father put a forearm over his eyes so he could no longer see the world. His mama stood waiting. In his memory Anatolii is spying through the doorway.

'What? Speak up?'

'Quiet woman!' his father croaked. 'When I die, get the tie. For Sveta.'

But not for Anatolii. Did his father know he wouldn't need it? He thought his father had meant that he was a man already. That he wasn't sick.

Sviaz po smerti.

The tie to Chernobyl, for the privileges, the benefits.

What it meant literally: in connection with death.

He has a memory of his mama at one of the hospitals, pleading: *I am a mother of a child who is a sufferer. I am an evacuee from Zone One. My husband was a Chernobyl driver, Category Three. Will you not help us, please?*

It comes to him from another world.

They drive to Korosten' before sunrise. It's English pop music on the radio. The news channels, once crammed with Party activists, are gone. The DJ plays *Take That*, which he hates, because all the girls at school love the band, especially Jason. He turns the radio off. Kulyk looks at him, but leaves it off.

They arrive at Korosten'. There are more people in the house. Some he recognises from Radynka and the streets where they used to live. Women and men from the invalid collectives sit around the body. The curtains have been thrown back, the windows opened. There's a priest, an old man with a white beard in a black cap, counselling people in low murmurs, holding their hands. There's an undertaker, a big man in a black suit, who talks to Kulyk. He supposes Kulyk has already begun making arrangements. Perhaps this is something he should be doing, isn't he the man of the household? He's glad Kulyk's there, even as all the neighbours, strangers to him, shake his hand. Some kiss him and hold his face as their grief overtakes them and threatens to overtake him. He wants to know where his sister is. He looks at his mama's body, dressed in her bed. He's not scared to see her, but the bruises on her face are worse, and perhaps, no, he doesn't want to look.

Sveta is in the kitchen boiling the *samovar*. He grabs her by the arms and drags her to the back door and pulls her out into the cold, stony yard, no bigger than the kitchen itself, smelling of their bins and cat piss and he doesn't know what—of this country, the Zone—Korosten' is barely out of range, it may be outside the official Zone of Exclusion but it's so close, so close to the accident and the forbidden places.

'What are you doing?' he shouts. 'Why is all you ever do is make everyone tea?'

'Let go of me.' She tries to shake him off but is too weak.

'You're not a maid. You need to stop.' But stop what? He doesn't know. 'Stop looking after everyone else. You need to look after yourself, not them.'

'But they want to drink. Mama would want me to welcome them.'

'It doesn't matter what Mama wants. She's dead.'

He lets go of her arms. He's worn her out. He's too angry to know what to do. He goes back into the house. He wanted to *help*. In the kitchen, he shoves her out of the way and finishes making tea. He puts two pots on trays with a dozen cups. Sveta hugs herself, watching him. He gestures to her to come and help. They each carry one tray up to their mama's bedroom, and don't talk again.

The funeral is a week later. He feels the school prize, his good grades, slipping away. He knows his friends have gone to the football without him, and are running around Finsbury Park pretending to be Dennis Bergkamp and Ian Wright. He wants to get out of Kulyk's flat. He's seventeen. Sixteen and a half. Old enough. He has friends in Kyiv, still? He uses his uncle's phone to call Demeshko. He tells his uncle he's going out to see some friends.

'Go, go,' says Kulyk, and shoves fifty *hryvnia* into his pocket. He's been a terror around the house and Tania, who came back for an afternoon, has left again.

'So our English boy, what are the girls like in England?' asks Vitalii, one of Demeshko's friends from college. They're going to a bar with a couple of older boys who'll get them in, no problem. Vitalii's got a crew cut and brown leather jacket and tight looking shoes that slap on the pavement as they walk along Shchorsa Street in the Perchersk. It's cold and there's a wind but no one is wearing great coats anymore. They dress like they're trying to be European.

'Pretty,' he tells them. He's thinking of Annette Flanagan. She's in his class but she also goes to the Irish Centre with her mam to volunteer. 'You want to come and *help*?' Linda replied when he asked if he could join her the next time she went. 'Well,

Peter, didn't I tell you he was a lovely lad?'

Annette Flanagan has copper-coloured eyebrows. He also thinks of the twins in the year above him with long blond hair. He's never talked to them, but he's fantasised about them, perhaps even more than he has about Annette Flanagan.

'So you've fucked them?' asks Vitalii. 'Or not?'

Demeshko laughs and puts an arm round Anthony's shoulder. 'They're jealous. Everyone wants to get out of this shithole.'

'How about you?'

'Sure, why do you think I answered the phone?'

'Come on, English boy, have you slipped them the finger?'

'They're not as lazy as Ukrainian girls,' he says, deflecting the question.

The boys laugh, and he's happy he's not thinking about his mama.

The club is dark, stinking and messy, but it's fun and he's feeling the effects of the vodka he poured into a plastic bottle and brought with him. He and Demeshko mess around; the older boys have abandoned them now they're in. They get talking to a group of girls. He narrows them down to one. She's pretty, but not the way the English and Irish girls are. She has the hard angles English girls are always pointing out about his face. The disco lights colour her purple, red, green. She has black hair which she sweeps away from her face as they dance. The music is stuff that wouldn't get on the radio in England anymore—New Order's 'Regret' gets played twice—but here it's exotic. As is he, he knows, and enjoys the envy of the other guys. The girl is in the same year as Demeshko. She's studying marketing. It's a new course.

'They got rid of all the Russian teachers,' she's telling him over the music, as if he doesn't know. She has pretty hazel eyes. 'They got rid of Miss Dragan, she taught piano. She was so cool. My piano is shit now. She came from Moscow, she performed at the *Olimpiyskiy*. No one saw her again. But you know, it's better.

Who wants to study Russian folklore? Everyone wants to work in the West. You're so lucky.'

He lists those things that make him English. His name. Linda and Peter. Their sofa and the living room, *Blind Date* and supporting Arsenal, his Gunners top with Ian Wright's name across the shoulders—a black man!

'So let's get to know each other,' he says. It's a line he heard one of the other boys use earlier. That girl laughed and walked off, but Anthony saw them talking later on in a corner so it must have worked. Besides, he doesn't have anything better to say.

'You're only here for a night.' She looks at him as if he should refute it.

'Say I'm not. Say I decide to stay?'

She laughs. 'Seriously? You'd stay here? I wouldn't.'

'You want to leave, really?'

'Of course I do.'

The DJ plays 'Into Your Arms' by the Lemonheads. It's a song he put on a tape for Annette Flanagan. She never mentioned it, and he never mentioned it either, but the word got out, and for a while everyone called him a lemon. He flushes, but not out of shame; his other life excites him. She's right. Why would he stay here?

'You could work in marketing in England. I live in London. Come visit.'

'You serious?'

'You can get a ticket?'

'Sure,' she says, but the way she says it he knows she can't. She turns as they dance, so he moves in behind her.

'We've got a spare room. You'll like London. It's amazing. It's huge. I can show you around. Everyone's got jobs in all the big buildings.'

She doesn't say anything, carries on dancing. She doesn't move away.

'So shall we get to know each other?' he tries again. She won't come to London. Or maybe she will. What does it matter? He's not asking her to marry him.

'But you're *Chernobylski,*' she says.

'I'm what?' He thinks he doesn't hear her right.

'You're *Chernobylski,*' she says again, into his ear. She's not saying it to curse him but it is a curse. She's not trying to be unkind but it tears him open. He can hear in her voice that it's just something, a thing to say. 'I'd be afraid to...' and she has the decency to look at him, 'you know...in case I got...'

The image of Baby Buddha flashes through his mind. His face is on fire. Red, purple, green. He will never come back again. Never.

They're waiting by the cars, saying goodbye to the people who were in the house and who drank their tea and said *look at them, such good children.* He thanks the priest. Then the priest leaves too.

'Forgive me,' his uncle cries, weeping on his shoulder.

Anthony doesn't cry. What is there to forgive his uncle *for*? It was his uncle who took him from the Zone. His uncle who found a way to send him to England. He'd hated it at the time, but now he understands. Tomorrow he's flying back.

Kulyk pulls himself off Anthony's shoulder and wipes his face.

'Where's your sister?'

The wind swirls around them, as it did during the service, muffling the priest's words. *A good woman... A diligent mother...* The sky is a thing unending and it dulls everything, the sparkling quartz in the headstone, the jade shingle set aside to cover the plot. Sveta is sitting cross-legged by their mama's grave. In her hands she's holding a small silver tin. He sits down next to her, feels wet ground seep through his trousers. Linda will be angry for the stain, but he'll get away with it. He thinks of the dinner she'll cook on his return. He cannot look at his sister while he thinks this.

'What's in the tin?' he asks. Her face is double the size, blown out. There are bags under her eyes so purple he did not know a face, nor grief, could turn such a colour. Still he doesn't ask what he should. Does not want to know.

'The tin?' he asks again.

She opens the lid. He's expecting some charm, a collection of hairs or threads or tiny little dolls. It is the desiccated body of a tiny bird. A sparrow. Its feathers and face preserved. He sees the deformities. The albinism in the body. The missing toes. Thinks about how old the body is, how tiny, how broken. His sister's hands are trembling, the tin too. He reaches out but she snatches it away. She sobs, great bubbles of air bursting out of her mouth, her nose. With a startling venom she throws the tin into the grave and it clatters on their mama's coffin. It is the worst sound he's ever heard, a rattle of the gates of hell, and for a moment he's terrified that it will wake his mama and she will rise from her grave and hug him, clasp him, pull him into the coffin. His sister is up and running. She bundles herself into Kulyk's legs. He gets up and shivers and follows. They drive her back to the house in silence, apart from Sveta's crying. Kulyk says the neighbours will take Sveta in. They'll sell the house, moaning that with what they have to pay back to the government they'll not even get enough to pay for Sveta's treatment until she's sixteen. And what will happen to her after that? No one has thought to tell him. And he, by the time he gets on the plane, has done his best not to ask.

Friday

It's nearly 10:00 a.m. when he gets to the lab. Elspeth comes over before he's even put on his whites. He's seeing her clearly for the first time since they went out to the dock.

'Where have you been?' she asks him.

'How's David?'

'Fine. Christie's with him. I hope you're not as much of a terrible communicator with your wife as David is, Anthony.'

'What do you mean?'

'So it's out.' She ignores him.

'What's out?'

'The cause. How it happened. It was on the news this morning.' She tilts her head. 'Have you not seen the news? Anthony'—she lowers her voice—'People think *you* leaked on the whales.'

He does up the buttons on his whites. Last button.

'People?'

He closes his eyes. Midshipman Darch is staring back at him. He puts his hands in his pockets. But there's no pebble now.

'For God's sake. All your... your incriminating—'

'My what?'

'Stopping at the protest, for one thing.'

'I've not done anything wrong. The Commodore knows that.'

Elspeth humphs, like a disconcerted child.

'What on earth, Anthony? Stopping to talk to those crusties.'

'They're not so different from us.'

'Really?'

'They knew about the whales. Anyway, it's all resolved.'

'Seriously, couldn't you just *buy* a paper?'

She walks away to her bench and sits on the stool. He follows her across, desperate now to share what he's been feeling these last few days.

'It was a mistake,' he says. He stands and waits for her to look up at him. 'But we've *all* dedicated our lives to this'—he waves his hands around—'what it can do. You come right round the circle and you join up again. We've all been working to keep this energy contained. Us in our way. The Navy in theirs. And those protesters too. We wouldn't have done such a good job without them out there forcing us to—'

'You're talking nonsense.'

'You must have thought it,' he says. He's sure of it. She must, once, have looked at night into the eye of the serpent and driven to work the next morning and thanked them, Tom and Maureen, for doing what she could not.

Chuzhe hore.

A foreign burden. The radiation in all their bodies.

He thinks of Aggie, Michael. David. His mama. Kulyk. And Sveta? What burden did she carry for him, when he was unable?

'You're talking nonsense,' Elspeth says again, demanding he reply.

'I didn't *have* to tell them anything. They know more than we do already.'

'What do you mean? Jesus Christ. Have they... What did they say to you?' There's a long pause. 'I mean... Anthony, oh Jesus, I really hope you've... You know you've really got Mariam's back up. Seriously, with what's going on here and you...'

She doesn't finish, and he doesn't reply. By one o'clock Elspeth has forgiven him, and comes over again with her laptop. It's been relegated to third story, after the shortfall in nurses since Britain voted to leave the EU and the decision to stop funding sex education.

'It was first this morning,' says Elspeth, piqued.

But the overcomplicated details of how the radiation got into the water is not a good TV story, and although there's an interview with an opposition MP on the safety of the Faslane base, because the vote on renewal of Trident hasn't yet been postponed, there's no furore. He knows, for all the assurances, they're not going to release the news about Midshipman Darch. For the sake of National Security. That the families of the crew will sign the Official Secrets Act. Perhaps even relocate. And if it leaks out, a Black Order will be issued. He's heard it all before. A long time ago. So instead he thinks of Aggie; of what he doesn't want to lose.

The next item begins. Elspeth closes the browser. She lingers, wanting to chew over the news and what they've been left with. He looks away. She takes her laptop and walks off. He has only one task, and it requires his focus. It also requires David.

'You're looking well,' he tells David as he readies the syringe.

David blows a weak raspberry.

'I wish they'd let me have a radio. Say I need to rest completely.'

'What would you listen to?'

'Is it still the main news? They told me that it'd gone out, at least.'

He nods.

'What about...' David begins.

Anthony takes David's hand and fits the syringe into the cannula and slowly draws the blood. He watches as the syringe fills.

'And you, Anthony?'

'Me? How am I feeling?'

David stares.

'Haven't felt ill at all.'

'Mariam?'

'She seems fine.'

'Elspeth?'

'Too.'

'And what we spoke about. Are you making it work? You're not, well...'

'You don't have to worry about me.'

David keeps staring, but he's tired. Anthony can feel David's lethargy in his hand as he holds it between finger and thumb. This is the same room, he thinks. The same bed where she died.

'They're not going to say anything, are they?' Anthony says. 'About her.'

'I don't know.'

'Don't they have to?'

'*They?*' David closes his eyes. 'They don't have to do anything. That's what the OSA is for. They're called secrets for a reason.' David catches his breath. 'Military personnel die all the time, Anthony. In war, in training. Do we know all the circumstances of those? Is this any different?'

'It's a nuclear incident.'

David sighs.

'To be honest, I'm more worried about my own health. I know that sounds selfish. Does it sound selfish? I'm more worried about Christie.'

The syringe is full. Anthony detaches, and turns to the vials. All the same tests for David as for Midshipman Darch. He puts the syringe in the waste box, secures the vials, closes the lid of the case and secures the latches. David has no external signs except the tiredness, the excessive bags under the eyes, the eyes redder than they would be usually.

'It's not selfish.'

David smiles at him. 'Thanks.'

'Those boys, were there follow-up tests? Samples?'

David looks at him, cautious but weary.

Anthony shrugs. 'I'm just concerned, that's all.'

'Yes, there were. I took charge, with Mariam.'

'They were quite bad, weren't they?'

David tried to pull himself up, then reaches out, grabs Anthony's hand.

'What did it feel like for you? I mean, when you were a child. Did you get sick from the exposure? It didn't say, in your file.'

He made it to the toilet and hid it from his family, usually.

He remembers the pictures Linda showed him in her album of the orphans. The children at the hospital where Sveta had her operation, all lined up with their scars, their tubes.

'I escaped the worst. Christie will be in later?'

'I understand now,' David says, half into the pillow. 'How this must be for you. Why you stopped at the protests. Brought your friend in without telling me. I think it was a mistake you coming to work here. For your own good, perhaps. You have a big burden to carry.'

Anthony shakes his head. The words are formed—*it wasn't a mistake. I'm making it work*—but they won't come out.

He leaves David's room and walks in what he hopes looks to the guards an authoritative way towards another of the rooms. Once inside, he counts to ten. No one follows him in. He breathes out. The woman in the bed opens her eyes. It's hard for her; the humour in her eyes has aged like the crust of old marshmallows.

'Hello again,' he says.

She looks confused.

'You're in the clinic on the base, don't worry. You're here. I'm here.'

Palata. Hospital room.

'Who are you?'

He walks over to the bed and sits down.

'I look after the testing of the radiation levels.' He pauses. 'My name is Anthony.'

'Is it bad?' she says finally.

He takes her hand and squeezes gently.

'There are twelve of you. Most of you are through the worst.'

'Most of us?'

'You've had an operation. They've taken out your thyroid. The cancerous bits. It's going to change your life.'

'The thyroid?' She wants to ask him what it is, what it does, but it's tiring her to talk. He waits, gives her time. She swallows, finds the energy. 'What does it do?'

'It produces hormones. You'll have to replace them. But that's normal.'

'Hormones,' she whispers. There's a silence in which he knows what will be her next question. 'Will I...' Her voice is wheezy and thin. 'Will it affect...'

'My sister,' he begins, and watches panic form in her eyes. He sees his sister, he's holding her hand and dragging her away from the cloud. 'She told me once about a dream she had. A magician came to our village with a travelling group. It wasn't quite a circus. She dreamt about it all the time after... After a thing happened to her like what's happened to you. The magician wore a black overcoat and carried a cane, and halfway through his tricks he would attack all the girls, poke at their eyes with the cane. There was nowhere she could... I'm sorry. It's not a very pleasant dream. I don't know why—it's like radiation. His cane. I think that's what I'm saying. What happened to her is what's happened to you... That's how I know that...'

He feels her hand tugging his.

'She was normal, my sister. Then she became small, like her doll.'

'Will that happen to me?'

He shakes his head. 'This has happened when you're already an adult. But you've had a really high dose. What that means for you... it means if you...'

He's urging her to understand. Sub-Lieutenant Wilkins turns her head away.

'I wanted a little girl.' He can barely hear her. 'And a boy. A boy and a girl.'

'My sister wanted children too.'

She turns towards him. He shakes his head, then looks away.

'I needed to be honest with you. I'm sorry.'

They're in someone's house in Radcha. A woman called Ivanivna is talking. There are other women and children. No men. Ivanivna is shouting at all of them. She's an old woman, or looked old to him, but when he saw her at his mama's funeral she looked just the same, and he understood that these women were never young. Ivanivna has rotten brown eyes, swimming in yellow; he can't look at her without wanting to be sick. Her mouth has been emptied of teeth, and when she talks it's like a yawing beast from a bad dream. She's wailing at him, spitting, swearing, while his mama is telling her to be quiet, but there's only weeping and wailing, there isn't a silent space in this shoddy, dusty, cramped house. Ivanivna is cursing the Zone of Exclusion. She's cursing the generals, cursing that there's nothing written down, only vague orders carried out by the soldiers in the white gowns, who carry guns on the outside of their overalls like strange, deranged, armed ghosts haunting the countryside. He knows all the soldiers will be dead. Those outfits were just cotton; they stopped nothing. And the women will be dead too.

We're liquidated. Our homes are off limits to humans! Who is this General Pikalov? Is this his home? Of course not! He'll go back to Moscow, back to his office on Red Square. To the dacha. They look after themselves.

Be quiet, the other women beg Ivanivna. *The soldiers are passing by.*

The soldiers are dying. They spit blood in the street. Look at them, already walking in their shrouds.

Not in front of the children.

Six miles away! Six miles away and we are in Zone Three. If it has happened, this great catastrophe, then why only six miles? Why here? This hole.

Quiet! This is where my parents are from.

If Radynka is off limits, why not Radcha?

I don't know, his mama mumbles. She wipes her face along the sleeve of her coat. None of the women or children take off their coats. They cannot get the heating to work. They huddle together in the kitchen. It smells of cabbage. It smells of the women and their hair. He and Sveta are hiding in the folds of his mama's skirt. Ivanivna leans down from her stool and looks straight at him.

Obman, she says, waving a finger at the room. *They're cleansing us. These soldiers, these politicians. You think they care about us, the country people? You think our deaths mean anything to them?*

For a moment he sees two faces: Sub-Lieutenant Wilkins and his sister. Their eyes are full of terror. Both have seen a wolf coming for them.

He returns to the lab and puts the testing kit on the bench and unpacks the vials of David's blood and sets the machines to process them. Mariam is still away, and while Elspeth is not looking he walks over to David's area of the lab and picks up his laptop and walks back to his testing station and puts his own laptop on his stool, out of sight. He opens David's laptop, but it's locked. His breathing is rapid now. If Elspeth comes over... If Mariam returns. *Shit.* Then he focuses. Types: *Christie.* Incorrect. He could just close it down now. Put it back, now. Changes the vowels for numbers: *Chr1st13.* And *shit,* it works. He scrabbles through the folders, thinks he's not going to find what he's looking for. Then does. Neither boy is as seriously ill as the crew, but they're under isolation, and military guard, at the Western in Glasgow. Neither is at risk of death, but at the levels they've received there may be long-term damage. He copies the results onto a USB, then closes the file. He walks back over to David's bench and puts the laptop back, and returns to his own and puts his laptop back on the bench and carries on with his tests.

Obman.

He rests his head in his hands for a moment. Then opens his eyes.

Obman.

Swindle.

Nothing has happened. It's all a swindle.

At the cottage he sits in the kitchen and thinks about phoning

Aggie. It grows dark and he goes up to bed. He shivers as the frozen sheets wrap around his body. He craves her touch. Touch first, then words. The light is off, the darkness its own cover. He wonders what it might be like to be blind, to be that boy born with folds of skin where eyes should be. He doesn't wish to be comforted by the idea, scared such fancies are heard by minions of the serpent. He doesn't wish to be the boy that Linda adopted him to replace.

He picks up his phone and calls her. After six rings, she answers. They're both silent. Is talking going to help now? But he needs her to know he did something right.

'Ant. Can we think about this, please? Can we talk about this?'

'We are. Now.'

'What are you doing, Ant?'

'Lying in bed.'

'That's not funny.'

He imagines she's there with him, undressing, putting on a T-shirt to sleep in. That she's come around to sit on his side of the bed.

'Have you lost—' she whispers down the phone. Her mum must have come into the room. Or *Greg*. Or she's stopped talking as she connects his acts with the outcomes they lead to. In her imagination she's packing boxes. Dealing with removal men. Dealing with the military police. Telling her mother. The truth sits on him with the weight of the loch and he doesn't have the energy to lift himself up.

'It's okay,' he croaks, clears his throat. 'I've—it's okay. It's already public.'

'I've seen the news. But what difference does that make? The...the...'

She falters. He has to hope her fear is not of him.

'There was a leak. It's what killed the whales. Don't—' He sounds official. He doesn't want this. 'It's not a threat. Honest. Not to us.'

'To anyone?'

'Some crew. Who were involved. Two boys. They were playing with the dead bodies of the whales. On the beach. The ones Viccy was interested in.'

'Viccy? It's *Viccy* now?'

'Please don't.'

'How do you know? How do you know it's not a threat to us?'

'I know. This isn't a reactor in meltdown. This isn't Fukushima.'

'Jesus, Ant. You said we could discuss it. Then you just gave it to her.'

'We're talking now. It was contained. You know I can't even tell you this.'

'Oh, but you can give some report to *Viccy*?'

He growls in frustration, a cowing, gruff sound out of the back of his throat. He'd read once—no, Aggie had read aloud to him from a book—that every marriage needed five good interactions for every one bad. What ratio were they at? But he knows she's right. Couldn't tell his wife, but emailed an editor at a newspaper. Couldn't share with her, but befriended two anti-nuclear protesters. Couldn't bear to have her see him undone, but handed over a report to a wildlife crime investigator.

'If I tell you things it implicates you,' he says.

'Protecting me? Don't give me that shit.'

'It's what they did under Communism.'

'But giving her the files on the whales... shit.'

'They won't know where it came from. It'll be okay.'

'Will it? This isn't about the whales, is it?'

He pauses, startled. 'Yes it is.'

He can hear her thumping something. Then she's breathing heavily, anxiously.

'Ant. It's not. Say it, can't you? What this is about. Say it.'

'Say what?'

'Do I have to say it for you?'

He recalls her face. Her cheekbones. There, above her lip, the tiny indents. He remembers what this is about, what she's asking him to do. *Say it.* Say it all: the radioactive pressure, the names of the whales in whale-call to their kin, the perfume bottle, the Dahlias, the dirty blood, the *Sarkofag* and scaffolding a solid fifteen metres of concrete around the ruined fourth unit, two hundred and sixteen tonnes of uranium and plutonium underneath. The knife his father gave him. His sister pulling on his arm to go home, the bag of nettles flung over his shoulder, the cloud at their backs. All pressing down on him, stopping him from speaking. *Say it.* He wades through the white molten memory towards that place before he can say its name. But he says it. Aggie lets out a long-suppressed wail.

Through tears she says, 'Again, Ant. Again.'

He says its name again.

It's somewhere way beyond midnight and he's sitting at the kitchen table. Two church candles throw overlapping discs of light onto the table where he's spread out a sheet of paper. He grips the pen and is already, before he's made a single mark, convinced that he'll not finish this reply before the military police come and arrest him for what he's done, and he'll know forever that this was always too late a time to begin writing to her. He's not even sure he can.

Say it, can't you? What this is about. Say it.

The cloud is above them, over the hill. She's tugging at his arm to go home.

He moans like a wounded animal as he leans forward and writes her name.

April and May 1986, Chernobyl

The accident wasn't in the plan!
The accident wasn't in the plan!
The unthinkable has happened.
It was too dark to inspect the site. They would begin observations the next morning. They circled in A-16s over the white plume that spired into clouds with a host of objects and debris, hot graphite consistents from out of the core of ruby incandescence. Huge spots of fire pulsing between violet and crimson, below them, the white, white tower around which they revolved all the time flying through the xenon-133 and krypton-85 without seeing. The cherry air above the ruined chamber of Reactor Number Four glimmering, fluorescent. The fires on the roof of Reactor Number Three smouldering, the tacky bitter taste of bitumen on their tongues, sucked into their lungs, as had the firemen who climbed the ladders to put out the fires and were now on their way to the Moscow Radiological Hospital Number Six. Reactors Number One and Two still operating! The emergency staff in the turbine hall of Reactor Number Three overseeing the cooling, ensuring the fuel elements were not engaged in residual fission.

Fissioning: not a word, not said, not a word in the plan.

'Shut down the other reactors,' someone ordered. Was it Shcherbina, Legasov? Not Pikalov. General Pikalov did not go up in the air with the others. Pikalov's men were the soldiers testing for surface radioactivity with the only dosimeters ready, as the only radiometer on the Chernobyl site able to record measures of roentgens high enough was *buried we don't know where. This is outrageous...* So Pikalov already knew, Pikalov didn't have to wait to be lifted up to the sky like the Eurasian eagle to peer down on the burning nest, its eggs aflame. Pikalov had taken a car out to the gates of the plant and peered through and seen up close the miasmatic fluorescence. Pikalov had returned to the commission in Pripyat and commandeered a heavily armoured vehicle specially prepared for radioactive reconnaissance and came back to the gates, and there turfed out his driver, sent him to headquarters, *get indoors, quick,* took the wheel himself and slammed the vehicle through the gates and drove right up to the burning reactor. It was Pikalov who established the graphite of the reactor was still burning, the first concrete evidence of the inglorious chaos and the significance of the hell on earth they were facing: the core was still melting. The core was alive and writhing. It was Pikalov who told Legasov, the academic, who then put himself at risk to discover if the nuclear chains of uranium-235 in the core were still reacting. By 7:00 a.m. the next morning, 27th April, he and Pikalov told those going up in the planes what they knew. They had no sleep. Shcherbina's phone call to the Kremlin was rattled and hoarse. Pikalov's call to the Ministry of Defence was short, curt, emphatic. Legasov had no one to call but his wife.

The accident wasn't in the plan!

The unthinkable has happened.

We've asked for troops.

This is where his father stepped into the battle. (Yes, the Battle of Chernobyl, the lust for Soviet heroism overwhelming the want for clarity, pragmatism, action.) The firemen first, then the Chernobyl workers who arrived for work at 8:00 a.m. on the 26th and were not sent away but put to work, then the policemen from Kyiv, a first thousand to create the roadblocks, and then fifteen thousand to keep the State from falling into chaos, before the patriotic coal miners from across the Union, the *kolkhoz* workers, and those like his father, the drivers. The men in their cars brought in to ferry the commission around the grounds, around the Zone of Immediate Exclusion for them to deliver their orders, operate their meters, make their phone calls from phones the size of spades connected by camouflaged curly wires to batteries the size of bales of hay, that took up the entire back space of a four-

310

seat vehicle.

Men like his father drove around men like Legasov, and men like Medvedev, whose book he read when he began to put the pieces together, and Legasov's reports to the International Atomic Energy Agency. Who was it his father drove around? Who exactly? He likes to think it was Legasov. Or Medvedev. That his father was close to the officials who directed the battle, who had a hand, good or bad, to play (he preferred to think good: Pikalov, Legasov, Medvedev. Bad: Shcherbina, Fimon, Bryukhanov, Il'in).

The unthinkable has happened.

We loaded ourselves into the cars and drove to the nuclear station. It did not even enter my head that we were driving towards an event of global magnitude.

Was it Legasov that his father collected from the airport? Poor Legasov, who committed suicide two years later, impaled by the acuteness of his radiation illness, unable to cope with a ruined stomach and legs that gave way and the weight of knowing that it was his reactors, his RBMKs, that failed to shut down.

The odds were that it was none of these men his father drove. It was probably rations, a car full of flour and *horilka* and apples. Or the inexperienced engineers, people like Kudryavtsev and Proskuriakov, the first two to die, the two probationary operators, neither older than twenty-five, who were sent to check on what was going wrong with the safety experiment, who came back after having seen the top of the protective plate come off the reactor. Even he, with all he knows of nuclear physics and fission reactors, can still only imagine something like the lid prised off of a tin of paint. The two young men came back with their death tans, their skin coloured to old bush leather; they were dead less than a few hours later, and still no one believed them. No one *reacted.* That was Akimov and Diatlov, the night shift manager and the plant manager. They couldn't believe what these two naïve young men were telling them. *The plate? Off? Ha! They'll never make operators.*

His father probably drove many different men—scientists, soldiers, politicians—in those first thirty-six hours. After that, he was perhaps switched to buses, like those in the square, multicoloured and rumbling, the drivers all smoking rollups. But the damage was done in those first hours. Before the extent of the radioactivity was known. When the core was spewing its ire, when the serpent was no longer chained.

And Professor Il'in, the chief medical officer for the Chernobyl precinct and for Pripyat—did his father drive him? He saw a photo of Il'in after the event. A tall man, a long nose, in a suit, not medical whites. This one man who held the authority to evacuate the whole region, but was sceptical of the seriousness of the accident. He was on the Shcherbina Commission, he was the one tempering the evidence of Pikalov, excusing the deaths of the firemen. Because most of the unit that had come from Pripyat were dead by the morning of the 27th April. They had been sent to put out the fires on the roof, where the bitumen had caught. The firemen didn't know what the graphite was, or if they did, why it was so dangerous. They died as much from what they inhaled as from the radiation. Hot spurs drawn into their lungs, rasping them open from inside. Even their deaths were not enough to warn Il'in to assent to an evacuation plan. But what evacuation plan? The Chernobyl plant didn't have one. A new one was formed the next morning, after Pikalov's findings were confirmed. Even then, the plan was distributed only by word of mouth so that Sunday morning life went on as normal in Pripyat and Radynka, in the villages north and south of the menace, the volcano. Women pushed prams along the road, families made ready to go to church, church bells rang, lovers lay in, the hands of the collective were steady on their coffee cups until at least 8:00 a.m.

Who did his father drive?

There's no record. There is nothing for the first ten days. The battle was all. Only later did the journal of Legasov and the notes of Medvedev emerge. The Soviet, the XXSU, the Politburo downplayed the severity. The Soviet nuclear energy programme was part of the Five Year Plan, which had only just been agreed. It was part of Plan 2000, how the Soviet Union was going to bring the countries of Eastern Europe into its political economy and energetic web. The future counted, not the men driving cars for soldiers and scientists through fired lands, not the names of the unaccountable who had 'volunteered' from the very beginning. There was no *glasnost* here.

His father would have volunteered anyway. Didn't his father marry the collective as much as his mama? Married to *lichnost'*. Every Russian and Ukrainian man wants to be a hero. That you were there would count more than what good you were. His father held it against Kulyk. Before the accident, too. Kulyk left the collective to work in a factory; his father moved the other way. There was honour in the grit of working with his hands (even though Kulyk did this with his furniture making; 'Ah, but that is for money,' his father had said). Honour in the *kolkhoz*.

So his father left his house that first time after receiving the call from the secretary of the collective, that all men were needed, and he took the Niva, a car shared by four families, and he took other men, and all of them could have driven, but his father was older, his eyesight better, or whatever the reason, and because he was driving he got picked as a driver. What happened to the others? What tasks were they set? Did they die sooner? Without protective suits or knowledge or guidance to the danger, without dosimeters or instructions to work for sixteen minutes every hour. They dug, dug, dug into the earth to cover over the disaster. He can remember them, men like his father, depleted in the village, dispersed across the Zones after the evacuation. Grey-skinned men, angry and vilified, *Chernobylski*. Men who wished they'd driven the other way, or stayed in bed, or been lazier than they were, not so full of the ale of *lichnost'*. They all died.

The accident wasn't in the plan!

The accident wasn't in the plan!

The unthinkable has happened.

Those bags of sand he saw hanging from the bottom of the *vertolit*: they were a mistake. They trapped the heat. They put out the graphite fire, but let the core burn on. The physicists arrived at noon on the 27th, perhaps his father was sent to pick them up at the train station or from their hotels in Pripyat—not hotels, of course, but Soviet accommodation for officials in the village. Or had his father been drafted in to fill the sandbags? At first it was the helicopter crew themselves who did this, because there were so few men around. The pretence that it was a minor incident meant the miners from the Donbass, the metro-workers from Kyiv and Moscow, only arrived when the Ryzhkov Commission was set up eight days after the explosion. By then the Zone of Exclusion for outsiders (but not for them) had been extended to sixty kilometres. The news reports, as brief as they were, said the farms were still working.

May Day. He remembers it. His father was home for a few hours, asleep on the sofa, coughing and vomiting into the blue bucket. He and his sister, all the children in the town, dressed in their best clothes, their white shirts and church hats, ready for the parade. The Mayor of Radynka, hand raised from the dais at the town hall, the town square that would be filled with buses a day later. His mama dragged him and Sveta from the house by the wrists, leaving their father. She was crying. She was short with them, and then smothering them with kisses and hugs as she passed them over to another woman who took them to the parade with her three children, while their mama went back home. There were mainly women and children as the floats glided by. The only men were the Mayor and his officers, and the male members of the brass bands, the old men who carried the flags for the miners' associations. When they returned home his father was gone.

Why does it matter who his father drove? What his father was asked to do? Perhaps he's holding on to this thread for no good reason. Or perhaps it does matter.

All he has is what happened to the soldiers, the firemen. Afterwards, they were the ones the newspapers wrote stories about, who were awarded the medals. Dozens to begin with, then hundreds. They received the *tie*. The *sviaz po merti*. Some men who did less got more. Some who died, got nothing.

What happened to the divers? The men who swam in the radioactive water in the bubbler pool underneath the reactor? Who were they? Whose fathers? When he imagines the long moments of their deed he can barely process what it must have been like to *swim under the fire*. To reach the release valves for the bubbler pool to drain the water. The water that was already radioactive, that would have killed them, for sure, immersed them in the wash of the serpent's venom. How dark it must have been. How quiet in the underwater world. How heavy. But the heat of the fire in the core was rising, and the threat of meltdown was imminent, the risk of a hot ball of radionuclides and sand and clay and lead all coalescing and sinking into that water and causing a steam explosion would have... it would have... they would all be dead. The entire *raion*, Kyiv, Belarus...man, woman, child, cow, hawk, wolf, for a hundred miles, a thousand miles all dead, then or in days. Because what actually happened was that only three or four percent of what could have been released, was. *Three or four percent*. Three or four percent killed *a hundred and fifty thousand people*. (Officially thirty-three to forty-four.) The men swimming in the bubbler pool couldn't have known. Did they volunteer blindly? Were they truly heroes? If the core had melted on them, they wouldn't have known a thing. Vaporised, blown to annihilation or God in a millisecond, as would have been every person at the plant, every person within the Zone and outside it for... Their deaths would have been the most peaceful. Swimming in the womb-waters of the serpent as it shook its chains and scattered them as far as Sweden (the outside world already knew; the Swedes had reported ruthenium in the wind, America's spy satellite had taken the pictures that appeared on the front pages of every Western newspaper by Monday morning; and still they went and stood on the square and waved their Soviet flags and smiled as the Mayor waved back).

His father could not swim.

Did his father drive a truck to collect the liquid nitrogen? The liquid nitrogen they injected into every nook and hole in Reactor Number Four to cool the metal and reduce the core, which released bluish gas that sat over the reactor like a shroud. Or was his father by then allocated as personal driver to one of the officers of the competing commissions? All the time he would've been exposed to the air, the releases of iodine-131, caesium-134 and strontium-90, the poison of the serpent's breath, and they too, Anatolii and Sveta and their mama, and the firs that lost their needles, the breath spreading over the sparrows and the zinnia, over the mushrooms that could no longer be eaten. He remembers being hungry all the time. (And then they ate, they drank. What else could they do? There was chaos and mealtimes and hungry children.) Maybe his father was driving Velikhov, the physicist who claimed victory on the 6th May, and telephoned Ryzhkov in Moscow who agreed for the Politburo to release a full statement, adhere to the tenets of *glasnost*, finally, after the blackout and refusals. This was to be celebrated on Victory Day, 9th May; but the parade was ruined when Legasov recorded a hot spot in the core, under the sand cap, above the lead and frozen concrete poured into the bubble pool. The victory was put on ice, and the core was flooded with boron which melted and reduced the temperature; and the celebrations were held when the immediate danger was really over, fifteen days later.

The question that has always gnawed at him: if his father had been in the house when Kulyk came to take them to Kyiv, would he have let them go? Would he have *made* them go? By this time his father knew what was going on; wasn't this after the first news report on 6th May? It was in the papers the next morning — not that his father ever bought a paper. The news went around the houses; the gap between what they knew and what the news reported was obvious. The official Politburo release: nothing about why the accident occurred. Nothing about his father coming home at 2:00 a.m. and being sick on the couch and then leaving again in the morning. Only men, old men in brown suits, some with hair and some without, sitting behind a table with the logos of the Committee on the Peaceful Use of Atomic Energy and the Ministry for Health and the Academy of Sciences and the Committee on Hydrometeorology and Environmental Control tautly hung behind them, while Soviet and Ukrainian journalists asked questions, while the journalists from the West (two West Germans, one Swede, one French, one Dane, one British) presented written questions submitted in advance and read out by an interpreter, asking the men at the press conference anodyne questions on the facts. *Have the fires been put out? Yes, the danger has passed. What are the long-term effects of the radioactive leak? They have been minimised, there is no need to worry. Who is responsible? Nuclear energy is a safe process, it is part of the Seventeenth Five Year Plan, you can rest in your beds, we are in control, we are always in control of everything.* Three months later every man on that panel had been sacked. Petrosy'ants, Vorob'ev, Sedunov, Yemel'yanov. Rebuked from the Politburo, dismissed from the Communist Party. Each one. And not the only ones.

The accident wasn't in the plan!

The accident wasn't in the plan!

We are in control, everything is under control.

But it wasn't. Not on 6th May. The next day the foreigners arrived, Hans Blix from the IAEA, who took a helicopter over the explosion site and made his own measurements with a dosimeter that could record higher levels. So the first accurate and trusted measurement reached the world. The West first, of course, and then Ukraine, but only months later in August when the important men all met in Vienna and the full extent—the full extent that the Politburo would agree to, anyway—was revealed. The cause: human error, and something of the poor nature of the RBMK-1000 reactor, its strange construction, its incongruous vulnerability to *ignorance and laziness*, which were, according to the politicians, the real reasons for the incident. It was an incident by then, the cause a failure of *lichnost'*, almost as if, you could hear the traditionalists argue, a man's integrity and bond to his labour was lost in inverse proportion to the growth of that other solely Soviet phenomenon, *glasnost*. As the Union thawed, the men melted.

Wasn't that the case? For some. Not for Gorbachev. But for some.

His father? No one could accuse his father of failing the test of *lichnost'*.

Did his father drive Blix from the IAEA? An impressive man, Blix, thirty years younger than the other officials and already Secretary-General, a man who would keep his job and go to Iraq and search for other weapons of mass destruction. A man who has seen it all and done it all, but a young man then; his father may have looked at him and considered him of no great importance. Another scientist sent from Europe, the world being let into the secret. Did his father, who knew no English at all, no German, no French, sit in the front of his small car and listen to the foreigners in the back discussing words of which he could not know the meaning? *Radionuclides. Half-life. Three hundred and fifty millirems an hour at a height of four hundred metres above the plant and at a distance of eight hundred metres.*

Then he and his sister left with Kulyk. His memories of then are patchy, scattered. That's what he used to tell himself. Once he began to focus, to talk, so much came back. He remembers nights where they slept on camp beds. The lights of the city bright through thin cream curtains. Nights where he and Sveta shared that room, before Kulyk told them all the children from the city were being sent to summer camps far away. They both had bowls of porridge they were not eating. Sveta was gripping her spoon in a stupid way, he remembers, she always gripped it like a baby with her whole fist, stirring the porridge around and around.

'Where are we going?' he asked.

His uncle shook his head and filled his cup from a coffee pot sitting on the stove.

'I have to take you to the local school, it's where they're deciding who goes where. Eat your breakfast and get dressed. Anatolii, help your little sister. Okay?'

He remembers Sveta crying. He wanted to cry too, but not for the same reasons. He remembers telling Sveta not to cry, and imagines that he will be with Sveta, only Sveta, for days, and she will not want to let go of his hand.

'Sveta, little Sveta,' Kulyk said. 'Stop crying. Eat your breakfast.'

But Sveta did not stop crying.

'I feel sick,' she said.

They were evacuated that afternoon. Their parents didn't even know where they had gone. It was weeks before they received a letter from their mama. It was shown to him by one of the women, one of the kind ones, a woman with grey hair and a round face, hard hands and a towel tucked into the belt around her waist. She read the letter to them. *We'll come and get you,* writes their mama. *Soon. But for now, you're safer there.* That's all he can remember. Then they're back in Kyiv and Kulyk's flat. The reasons for the evacuation had worn thin, or were forgotten under the weight of the chaos: the loss of crops, the banning of milk. The sicknesses that had started. So they went back to Kyiv, and their mama was waiting for them in the kitchen, and they both rushed to her as they heard her call for them, and she took both of them in her arms, he and little Sveta, and there was nothing he could do this time to stop himself crying, so he cried like he was a baby, and he was, he was only five, his mama, his mama, his mama, who is now dead, she is dead, he was never held by her again, what happened to their lives?

The accident wasn't in the plan!

The accident wasn't in the plan!

The accident wasn't in the plan!

It was Bryukhanov, the plant chief, put on trial in August the same year, with Fimon, the chief engineer, who said those words. *Actually said them.* Bryukhanov: *'The accident wasn't in the plan!'* Wasn't this why Gorbachev dissolved the Soviet Union in the end? That whatever wasn't in the plan could not happen, and that increasingly the Five Year Plans, the Twenty Year Visions, made less sense? That the USSR stopped functioning— if it ever functioned? No, it did. The collective, their lives were not unhappy lives, they were tied to the land, they knew the difference between edible and poisonous mushrooms, could read the tracks of wolves and recite the names of trees, what is this if not a world that works? But the USSR stopped being able to think outside of a plan. Who could legislate for such an accident? No one. Wasn't the catastrophe unthinkable? Of course.

The catastrophe was unthinkable!

The catastrophe was unthinkable!

And he's unthought the catastrophe every day of his life since then.

Shall I tell you about the day my life was revealed to me?

A person who makes films came into our evening class six weeks ago. That's all—six weeks ago. Can you believe I've lived this long without knowing the truth of my life? Alina wanted us to watch the film, because there are at least half of us in her class who were affected. This filmmaker has made a documentary for the anniversary. He's been back in and out of the Zone for years. But he's not been filming the people who went back. He's not been filming the ruins, which is what all the Western photographers like to show: the towns like Pripyat and villages like ours. He's been filming the animals. For years and years. He's made it in English, part of the reason Alina thought it would be good for our language class; but it's more than this. Let me tell you about the film.

This filmmaker has followed the deer, the wild boar, and the birds that have returned too, the sparrow and the sparrowhawk, the redstarts, the finches. There are elk that make you jump in your seat as they leap out of the buildings, their antlers the size of shopping carts, their breath steaming in the cold. There are bears too, but only from afar, as they move in the distance. He explained—he was here, he came and spoke with us—that it wasn't like a Western documentary where he could spend weeks hiding and waiting for the animals. In the Zone he'd grow sick even if he stayed for just a few days. So it was many small visits back, going through all the paperwork, but then sometimes just going back in at a place where there is no guard and the fence easily dug under. He's in his sixties now. He was a cameraman for a news channel when it happened. He's had cancer. He's suffered too. You can see it on his face... not fear of death, but the pain and a panicked look in people who felt... who feel... as if it wasn't theirs... I don't know. I don't know how to say it. He's tied to the place. I like him a lot—his name is Andrey. He's not tall, but rather round, and lively, despite this panic in his eyes. I don't know if the cancer has left his body.

He told us a story from the time of the accident. He was moved to do more than just point a camera for his bosses so he made a film then too. He interviewed people: workers, evacuees, everyone he could. But no one would show the film, not even with his contacts at the TV channels. He had to go abroad to show it in the end, and he showed it a few times, but by then no one was interested anymore. He came back after Independence. He toured the towns and villages, showing it in churches, in barns, wherever they'd let him. What a good man, no? The authorities tried to make him stop, but what could they do in all the chaos? He just moved on or he told them, 'Don't worry, it's a cartoon for children,' and it wasn't, of course, but he did show it to children. They used to shout at him for that. Parents and councillors would say we were too young and should be protected, but he argued with them, and he was right, he convinced them that the time for protecting children from the accident was gone, it was too late, the only protection we could have now was knowledge.

During a showing of his first film, a little boy asked him, 'Why couldn't you help the animals who were left behind?'

He didn't have an answer. *That* film was only about the humans who suffered. It was their story. But it changed his life, that question. That was the moment his life was revealed to *him*. He went back after that, year after year, to film the animals, to find an answer. It was too late to help the animals who'd been left behind, but he could record the lives of those who had made their homes in the Zone. He could widen his lens from humans to animals. Because how do you evacuate a sparrow, anyway? A beetle, a worm? You cannot. His film says this—both films, don't they? Isn't this the message of his first film too, a message by omission?— that there was a way to evacuate the pets with their owners, and the cattle with their farmers, but the wild animals? The only hope for them is that we do not act so stupidly in the first place to turn their homes into places that kill them. A home that becomes a trap. And a worse trap, because unlike me, brother, the animals cannot hate. They cannot hate their home, the trees and flowers. Hate is a human emotion. It is fear without recompense. It is fear that has become helpless.

'Why couldn't you help the animals who were left behind?'

The minute I heard this question, when this filmmaker recalled it being asked of him by that little boy, I knew it was the truth.

His film about the animals is called *Hostages*. A strange name for such a film, you think? Yes, to begin with. Say hostages, and you think of people on a plane, or in a building, and armed men. You think of Chechnya. How could the wild animals be taken hostage? Be held hostage? By who? But it is not 'by who.' It is 'by what.' It's true, isn't it? What holds these animals hostage is their misfortune and our stupidity. They're held hostage because this is their *home*. It always was, they don't have any choice. They can't leave. Can the worm leave its field? Can the bear leave behind its cubs in its den? Where would they go? We have trampled everywhere, not even the depths of the earth are safe for the animals to bury into. Not even the rivers can carry them away to somewhere safer.

So you might ask: what was revealed to me six weeks ago? Isn't it obvious? That I am a hostage too. Alina is crying. I am crying. My husband will beat me for saying it, he says I am a survivor, not a sufferer, but it's true, isn't it? I am the deer, I am the worm, who had no choice. I could not leave this field. I have been held hostage all these years, even after Mama died. Held by what happened. Held here by home. Like the animals. Like the filmmaker. Like everyone who was tied to this place. We've all suffered, and the suffering was not only human suffering, it is not limited to the human condition, but human or not, we hostages have all suffered the same fate.

But I have my own questions. Revealed to me by that film, by that little boy, and they are questions I understand, now that I've asked them myself every day since, and perhaps always. Why did I have no choice? Why did you get to leave and I had to stay?

And why has it always felt...why do I remember that you made it this way?

Saturday Morning

He's surrounded himself with Aggie's things: her Edinburgh marathon T-shirt, the book about poverty, one of her childhood teddy bears she keeps in a drawer under the bed. In the night it seemed like the right thing to do, although in the daylight—has he slept in?—it feels mawkish. He tries to focus on his phone to send Aggie a text, but his eyes are red and sore. His head, though, feels emptied. Into that lightness comes a memory of the two of them holidaying in another cottage, Aggie in her two-tone blue swimsuit jumping into the river at the bottom of the woods that were theirs to walk in, the river icy and quick, Aggie's face shocked with cold, hooting like a monkey, him laughing, trying to capture it on video but doubled up, crying too hard.

He tidies away her things. In the kitchen he uses Saturday's Kabocha cast iron pot they brought home from the V&A one afternoon, heavy as sin, which he puts direct on the hob. He nibbles on a banana, and then takes out his phone. He's recovered the images from the trash. He could just completely delete them, but there would be a residue. He doesn't doubt there's a black box of ways into the traces of its memory card. The images are probably already on the server farms of an industrial estate on the outskirts of Bucharest. Midshipman Darch. He knows she's dead, but to erase her images is to forego what might live on as *memento mori*. This is how people are disremembered: crossing their names out of address books, shredding their files, putting their letters in an old dovetail-jointed wooden box kept for such things, and closing the lid. So the easy option—to delete the pictures of her and say nothing—is no option, because it wouldn't explain what burden *he's* carried, nor would it help show the others what he needs them to know.

He goes into the living room and turns on the computer. He opens up a website. Types in dates. Selects. Pays. Types the confirmation code into the notes application on his phone. Prints, and the printer rumbles into life. The last sheet of paper falls from the tray. He catches it before it reaches the floor and looks at the printouts for longer than it takes to read. He knows it isn't just a matter of making sense of the gate times or seat numbers. There are a dozen things he could think to say to Aggie when he sees her, hopes he chooses the right one, but if all else fails he will just hand her these and hope she understands. It's like his ears have popped. He wants to tell Aggie all of it. He knows why, knows what he has done and what is left to do.

He opens the contacts on his phone, finds the number, and presses call.

'It's derelict now,' she says as they walk along one side of the walled garden of the old Balloch Castle. 'Abandoned a while ago. Some places are just not worth the upkeep.'

He studies the cool grey stone of the crenellated turrets. It's the light grey of a favourite mare in the Grand National, but then the castle was built as a country house, Mariam tells him, not as a keep. The walled garden is still in decent condition, though, kept by Tourism Scotland, ripe with lavender and jasmine and citrus trees in a glass orangery. They walk through a grove of acer tilting over a circle of white iron benches around a small fountain. Mariam gives her head a little shake, folds her arms so that she's grasping both elbows. There's a light wind. The sky is grey as usual, but although he's shivering he's not cold.

'David's going to be out soon. They're sending him home tomorrow. Maybe the day after. He'll be off for another week, though.'

'Not the best time to ask for time off then...'

'No.' A pause. 'You'll get the relief, if you need it. It's not going to look good on your record, though. Look. Is this about your marriage, Anthony?'

They pass the benches. There's no one around yet.

'Why do you say that?'

'Something Elspeth said. Look—'

'It was a mistake to work for the Navy,' he interrupts her. She opens her mouth to reply, but then closes it again. They carry on walking. 'David thinks it. He told me, and I agree. Six whales were killed. I helped them do that.'

He stops walking, closes his eyes. He feels Mariam take one step, then stop.

'This is about the whales?'

A pain floods his chest. Not inside, but on the surface of his body, between his ribs and the skin, as if this is how it would feel to be radiated, with the radiation working its way through his body, and out. No, never out.

'Not only the whales. But don't they count?'

Mariam glares. He'd not noticed before—she didn't wear them to the lab— silver rings on her fingers. She comes close enough to whisper.

'Do you know what you've done? You've flunked, is what you've done. The work might be good. But, what, you haven't been able to handle it? You're going to duck out now, when David is in the clinic? I told you... I said this, didn't I? Never stay in one place very long?'

He reaches into his pocket and takes out his phone. His hand is shaking.

'I need to show you something.'

He brings up the image on the screen. He can't look himself, and there's a sliver of time when he could just put it away, not conjure up this future. He holds the phone out for her. She screws up her eyes; has to, in the end, lean in to see.

'Oh, for Christ's sake.' She puts a hand over her mouth, turns and strides away. Half a dozen paces into the trees she stops and straightens up. He's sweating, but the trembling has stopped. He drops his arms. He hears birds, chaffinches maybe, or just sparrows, flitting between the shrubs and borders of the garden.

He can hear voices, other visitors to the country park, lovers of the serenity of the walled-in places under the castle's purview.

'I don't know why... I just took them. She'd died, for fuck's sake, and I knew they wouldn't release it to the public.'

'Oh Christ... have you?'

He wipes his forehead.

'No. I've not done anything. Except show you. It was a—' but *this* wasn't a mistake. It still isn't. Mariam stares at the phone in his hand, not wanting to look.

'So, this is the one who died?'

He nods. 'Midshipman Darch. I guess I didn't take it very well.'

Mariam rocks back.

'The photo?'

'Her death.'

'Christ, I'd say so.'

A couple clad in outdoor gear come upon them as if out of fog, smile and nod. They wait for them to pass. Mariam sits on one of the benches and after a while he joins her.

'Look, I'm deleting them,' and he scrolls through the four images.

'Anthony—what is this, some sort of masochism? Because'— and she is shaking—'I really do *not* understand you taking those pictures in the first place, but then doing nothing with them except to show me you're deleting them.' She pauses, her breathing fast. 'You wanted to be a whistleblower but, what, didn't have the balls? I—Christ, this is a bit much. You've imposed yourself. I'm going to have to report this.'

She's scared. He'd come prepared that she might not understand. But scared?

'I'm expecting you to. But I couldn't just delete her. I needed you—you and David—to know...that I didn't know how to deal with it. I'm sorry, it wasn't a question they asked at the interview, you know.' He sighs. 'Maybe I flunked. Maybe I wasn't prepared to see someone die, and be part of... I thought I *would* be that person. But then...' He shakes his head. She waits. 'They're not going to let it change anything,' he carries on, 'you know that.'

'I've no idea what's going to happen.'

'And you're okay with that?'

'Oh fuck off, Anthony. Christ, you brought me here for a guilt trip?'

'No. But I had to show you. I'm sorry I had to.'

She lets out a gasp. Then she pats down her hair, shakes her head as if giving her own thoughts short shrift.

'Is there anything else?' she asks him, curt.

'My marriage...' and for the first time in a long time he understands what he dares hope for. That his marriage is going to work. Away from the grip of a world he's been trying to control, and, he sees for the first time, protect, and how it has taken all his energy to do that. Despite what's happened, it still might work. 'If you want to see the messages. We've been mainly talking by text. It's been a tough few months.' He sits there for what seems a half-life of eternity with his arm outstretched, the phone offered up.

'I don't need to see details,' she snaps, waving off his offer. She looks away. 'I need to get back. We're expecting John's mother for lunch and she's not been well.'

They stand and leave the garden and walk back to their cars. He looks up at the castle the whole way. Up, and beyond that. They're parked next to each other. He offers his hand. Mariam looks at it for a moment, then returns the lightest of shakes.

'You've deleted them?'

He nods.

'And you've not copied them? You know I have to tell them...'

He nods again.

'And that I deleted them. You'll tell them that.'

'I can't wait until Monday, Anthony. I'll have to...'

'Unless you say we met—'

Her look brings him up short. She's not going to lie for him.
'Tell David first. Please? At least it's his responsibility.'
'You've not even given me that out, Anthony. I can't just go
and... Christ...'
'A few hours? Just to talk to Aggie.'
'Oh, hell.' A pause. 'I hope they don't find anything at your...'
'Only my work,' he says. 'Only what I was meant to do.'
'I hope so, Anthony. For all our sakes.'

He drives home and packs their bags. He runs around the cottage
checking everything's switched off. He stares for a moment at the
computer, then unplugs it from the screen and takes it to the car
and puts it in the boot. The lone screen is a giveaway, so he takes
that as well. He makes one last sweep of the cottage and carries
the bags to the car. He catches his breath, and goes back into the
cottage and comes out a few moments later with two letters, hers
and his, in their envelopes, and a small plain box, and then locks
the cottage door.

He drives past the base and the protest, reduced again to its
core, Tom and Mo, both sitting with their backs to the road in
their camp chairs looking at the base as if it were a cinema screen
at a drive-in; or worse, and the image is there, of the Arizona
Desert tests in the 1950s, the spectators in their directors' chairs
and thick black glasses waiting for the detonations. He shakes
away the thoughts and carries on up the side of the loch, turning
at Garelochhead and down the other side, pulling in at Portkil
Bay, next to the red Fiesta that's parked up by the shingle. Viccy
is staring out to sea. She turns as she hears him pull in. They greet
each other awkwardly.

'I thought you'd be off to the Faroes,' he says. 'Catch some
killers.'

She looks at him through narrowed eyes. He won't try humour
again.

'Next week,' she says. 'Thanks for calling. I'm guessing there's more.'

He motions for them to walk down the beach, and she follows.

'This is where,' he indicates, and they stop. 'Here was where the whales were washed up.' He remembers their sad, rounded bulbs of bodies, their bleak last moments and the sticky sheen. The woman challenging him, *you having your animal rights*? The sneers on the faces of the two boys whose lives he was trying to save, and probably did, by scaring them off as quickly as he could. Viccy stands with her hands in her pockets listening to the story, bored, or angry, he can't tell which, until he mentions the boys. At that her expression changes to a shocked enthusiasm, before shifting back to something less shamefully excited.

'They're not in your report.'

'They're not well. One of the boys is worse. The family are... It's going to come out, the family are already talking to the press.' He fishes around in his pockets. Phone, pebble, USB. 'But this is the detail. Sit on it, please.'

She takes the key, then looks around. 'This is a very open place.'

He shrugs. 'I need you to do something for me.'

She doesn't agree. She's too experienced to be overly thankful for what he's done.

'A small thing. Please?'

But she doesn't say no, so he leads her from the beach up the road. At the cafe he opens the door and she follows him in. The girl is there, behind the counter, with her back turned to them, emptying a five-pound packet of brown sugar into a large glass jar. There is a scatter of people in the cafe, holidaymakers and the retired, who give them only the briefest of glances.

'With you in a minute,' says the girl. They're at the counter before she turns around. 'Okay, sorry. What do you —'

Her eyes widen, her pride and power gone with the surprise. Then her face hardens and she twists a tea towel around her hands, wiping off the sugar.

'This woman,' he says, and he moves aside so the girl can see Viccy. 'She's going to let you know about the boys. Then you can tell the family. Okay?'

Rather than swell with pride, there's a worried look on the girl's face as she acknowledges her task. He turns to Viccy.

'Okay?'

Viccy looks at him briefly, then turns to the girl and smiles.

Outside they walk briskly back to their cars.

'You're really pushing your luck with this. You've broken the OSA and you're standing in a cafe telling half the people there.'

He turns to watch the Greenock ferry depart, its diesel engine chugging and pulling the bow into the water. There's a steep scream of gears and then a noisy lug.

'You're going to sit on the report, right?'

'The boys, what—'

'They're getting treatment. They're not going to die. But you can investigate it properly, but later, right? Like I said, it's coming out in the press anyway.'

They reach their cars and before they separate she puts a hand on his arm.

'Look. Thank you. You didn't have to do this.'

He shrugs at that, wants to say—but doesn't. They stand together for a moment, then she drops her hand. He watches her drive off. She waves briefly, as if they're old friends and will see each other again soon. He starts the car, takes note that it has started first time every time today. He laughs, then bends down into the footwell and grabs the tennis ball and gets out and strides down the beach and hurls it into the water. It floats on the surface, slowly moving out into the channel, and then disappears from his view in the wake of the ferry.

Viccy is right—he's taking too many risks. But he's not stupid—not completely—so he parks farther up the road towards Garelochhead this time, and walks down to the protest. He looks at his watch. He pulls the phone from his pocket and sees Aggie has replied to his text. *No, I'm not!* An emoji smile.

He replies: *I'm coming to Glasgow. Two hours. Meet me at your dad's grave?*

Tom is sitting in the camp chair, staring at the base. Anthony's on top of Tom before he turns. Tom looks woken from a deep reverie and stands with great effort, as if the years of living outside have suddenly caught up with him. The bristles along Tom's jawline are rougher, the skin through the bristles redder.

'It's you.'

Anthony nods. He turns as he hears Maureen come out from the tent.

'Lunch—oh. You again.' It takes her a moment to smile. 'What news have you got for us today then? It's been rather a week. Are you joining us for lunch?'

'Jesus, Mo, can't we have some peace for a change,' says Tom, leaning forward with his hands on his back. 'We don't want his type here.'

'Oh, go back to sleep, you old dodder.' She turns to Anthony. 'Well?'

'Thanks, okay.'

'It'll get you into trouble, coming here. They don't care about us, but they probably do about—'

'Too late,' says Anthony. He laughs. 'I told them my car broke down. You helped me jump-start it. It's—'

'Japanese is it?' asks Tom. 'They're normally reliable.'

'Korean.'

'That isn't really the important thing, here, Tom,' Maureen snaps. 'Well, okay. Come on in, it's nearly ready.'

Tom stares at the small box Anthony's carrying, but doesn't ask what it is. Anthony's glad for that, for now, and follows Maureen into the tent. It's close from the steam of cooking pasta and vegetables, the smell of tomatoes and oregano, canvas and dirt. She offers him a seat while she stands in the cooking area.

Tom comes in carrying his chair, throws it down and falls into it.

'So to what do we owe this pleasure?' Tom drawls, leaning back.

'I didn't finish what I started last time.'

'And what was that? Pulling the wool over Mo's eyes? She's a lot more gullible than I am.'

'Oh, I am, am I?'

'Communism,' he says. 'We didn't finish our conversation about Communism.'

Tom stops, his eyes narrow. Maureen has her back to him so he can't see the look on her face. She doesn't stop her preparations for lunch, though.

'And what about it?'

He looks above him, as if he can see through the canvas to the rain.

'Do you remember 1986?' he asks, and hesitates. 'I mean, Chernobyl? When the explosion happened?'

'What is this, a fucking history quiz?' shouts Tom.

Maureen shushes him. 'Tom, please. Let me think. You could too, before you speak.' There's a pause where the only sound is the boiling pasta. 'Yes, of course,' she says to Anthony. 'We were five years into the Peace Camp. Everything was about nuclear. The decade was the one...well, it didn't stop everything. But it was the battle's heart. You might not...how old were you?'

'Five. Did it change things, here? When you heard about it?'

She thinks for a while.

'They probably didn't teach you this at university, but there were scandals in Britain the whole year. There'd been leaks at Windscale in January, February and March. Then Chernobyl. Then Dounreay and Dungeness had scares. Without Chernobyl we might not have heard of those. Every paper and tele programme was covering nuclear accidents. So then everyone's thinking, well, how bloody safe are these things anyway? Tom's crowd up in Druridge Bay, you know they'd started doing backyard monitoring, before and after readings, in case they ever built a nuclear station up there. They were well organised as a campaign. Got the unions to donate money so they could buy a proper radiation counter, one that couldn't be discredited. So when Chernobyl happened they were able to take readings when the raincloud passed over. The gamma radiation jumped by forty, fifty percent. That was big news. This wasn't the government telling us everything was safe. This wasn't scientists. This was people like us—' she stops and looks at him, '*us*. Citizens. Our figures for the radiation passing over were credible. The government had to listen.' She pauses. 'You know what I like about all the Eastern Europeans I've met, Anthony? Their directness. It's such a different culture from ours. We have seventeen thousand words for death but nothing that allows us to grieve. We think we're a lyrical people—well, the Celts are, I'd say, but much of that culture is lost—but the English, the Angles always package everything up in dull wrapping. We had a lot of contact with the Ukrainians and Belarusians, after the accident. Campaigners.' She looks at Tom. 'Gullible. *Really*.'

He smiles, looks at Tom, who is glaring at him.

'So what have you got to say about it, then? Got some spiel about the Communist way of life that you want to attack us with? You think we're Commies?'

'Did you know about the Mayak plant in Chelyabinsk?'

Tom looks through him.

'I think so,' says Maureen. 'But I'm not sure. Why do you ask?'

'It was wrecked by two nuclear disasters, one covered up for a decade. Years before Chernobyl. They evacuated a whole region, told nobody.' He looks up, feels time slipping over him. 'It was never something we knew as children.'

His words cut through the steam rising from the saucepan, and there's a stillness in both Tom and Maureen that, though he was expecting it, he's not prepared for.

'No one knew,' he carries on. 'And if you did know, you

didn't tell. Not in 1957. The Party would send you to Siberia for a whisper. You'd disappear. You were relocated, and said nothing, and nobody asked you why you'd been moved. Mayak wasn't even a plant failure. They were dumping waste from nuclear bomb production into a small lake.'

He's out of breath. Things he's known. Things he's buried.

'How many people?' Maureen asks.

He laughs but it barely fills the tent. He shakes his head.

'Dead? Nobody of course. There were no records. *There was no incident.*'

'But you wanted to know? You looked?'

He nods. 'I wanted to know.'

There's a pause before Maureen asks, 'So why you?'

He's said it—last night to Aggie, and as good as with Mariam this morning, but he doesn't know if he can again. Even though he hopes once he does, this will be the last time. Or perhaps, once more.

'So what's in the bloody package?' Tom asks, breaking the silence.

He looks at the box he's been holding on his knees.

'I've brought you a gift.'

Maureen turns towards him, pointing with her paring knife. 'What is it?'

'Something bloody radioactive, I bet,' says Tom. 'We don't need your baubles here, thank you.'

Maureen shakes her head. 'A gift? That's kind of you.'

'No, Mo,' says Tom, learning forward. 'No it's bloody not. Kind would be fucking off and stopping what—' He turns to face Anthony. 'Why the bloody hell have you brought us anything? Anything more than the crap you've already brought us? We've all seen the news. We know exactly what's been going on. How fucking dangerous it is here. And here you are, bringing toys like it's our birthday. Fuck off.'

The box is light on his knees.

'Tom, you take it, I've got my hands full,' says Mo, calm and sure. Tom looks at Anthony as if he would rather poke his own eyes out.

'No, I won't,' says Tom.

'Tom. Go on.'

Maureen stands above him, and although she's not threatening him with the paring knife there's a hierarchy between them that was there all along, but has only now been brought to the surface. Tom shakes his head, then snatches for the box and sits with it in his hands.

'Well, open it!'

'Bloody alright, Mo.'

Tom peels back the flaps and narrows his eyes before putting his hand into the box and lifting out the large, red egg with the white wolf's teeth.

'So what is that?' Maureen asks.

'*Pysanka*,' he says, his gut full of a feeling he's not...since the forest, running. Watching his father vomit into the bucket. He explains the story of the egg and the folklore of his people, the symbolism of the colour, the way the egg came to him, and what blessings it confers. What it's done for him.

'We can't take that,' says Maureen. She drains the pasta with a *splosh* into a metal colander that's discoloured to a silvery carbon sheen.

'It's something to keep you safe,' he says. 'I think it works.'

Tom lets out an ugly laugh.

'Keep us safe? From what? Communism? You?'

'I'm from Chernobyl,' he says. And there it is.

Tom barely bats an eyelid. 'Bullshit.'

He shakes his head. 'I wish.'

'What, so it's lent you some mystique then? Some justification for this shit?'

'Used to believe that.' He laughs, despite the spite. 'Thought I was special. It gave me a right. That I knew more than my colleagues. That my work was authentic.'

'Can't undermine the testimony of the sufferer, can you,' says Tom. 'Can't tell a black woman she's not oppressed.'

'Don't open those doors,' says Maureen. 'Let him speak, for God's sake.'

A part of him is trembling.

'There wasn't anything special about me just because I'd...'

'Survived?' snaps Tom.

'Understood. Understood.'

'Ha!' shouts Tom, but bereft of humour. Maureen waves at him to be quiet.

'I grew up in a town called Radynka. It was in the Zone.' A bus goes past outside. 'I was five. I used to play in the forest—' he stops. 'We used to go there and collect mushrooms. We lived off the land. We were part of a...a... *kolkhoz*. It was Soviet. But you'd know that. You were at Greenham. I came over here on one of the convoys. I still don't know how. My family sent me away when the wall fell, the Berlin Wall. We could move around then, when the bloc collapsed. My sister, my mother were living in the Zone. They were ill. It was difficult, and my mother, she didn't want to leave. Thousands went back, you know? Despite the radiation. The government...it was complicated to get benefits. The tie.'

Only for that. All their sufferings for that. His eyes fill up.

'You've got quite a past for someone working in nuclear power,' says Tom.

He nods. Tom leans across, so close he can smell Tom's breath.

'So you knew,' Tom says. 'Fucking completely. You knew what it could do to people, and you fucking end up working for them. You turned *killer*.'

Tom looks like he wants to plunge a knife into Anthony. Those blue eyes in the sharp, fatless face, all those days battered by wind and rain, a life focused on one thing: hating people like him.

'If you understood anything you would not be working for

the fucking—'

'Thank you,' Maureen interrupts. She's offering Anthony her hand, and he takes it. She places the palm of her other over the back of his to stop him trembling.

'I wanted to learn how to control it. To see if it could be—'

'And what have you found?' Tom interrupts. 'Can it be?'

'You were sent away, is that it?' asks Maureen. 'On the convoys? Fostered.'

He nods. He's five years old again, in the back of his uncle's car.

'Well, lucky you got out, wasn't it,' says Tom. 'Lucky you got away.'

There's a silence in which no one moves.

'They kept everything from you?' asks Maureen.

'Took,' he says. 'Took.' He breathes deeply. Cars go past outside. They shake the tent just a little, like a mother rocking them to sleep in a cot. Then Tom is leaning across, one hand on the arm of Anthony's chair.

'And can it? You said you wanted to control nuclear power. Can it be controlled?'

He looks at Tom, then at Maureen, imagines the world outside, but imagines it differently. He looks at the *pysanka*, showing out of the rip in the box that Tom has put on the ground. He hears a voice, far away, but the words are still clear to him.

We didn't want to know the truth. We deceived ourselves. Somewhere deep down, isn't that the case? But now we don't want to admit that to ourselves either. We blame Gorbachev. We blame the Party. We were blameless. We were victims.

He stands up.

'Not by me,' he says, finally. 'Not by my hands.'

1987, Korosten'

'The whole town is nothing but sufferers,' says his uncle. *Poterpili*. The official word, the word that would bestow upon them access to the higher benefits. Korosten' is full of sick men and women. The children at the school are not separated by age but by dosage. Some of the men have dosimetric passports they're told to keep safe. His mama and sister get sick too, but they don't have books. Only those who worked in Zone One. When he's sick he runs to the bathroom, pretends to be washing. Flushes the toilet. For him it's only every now and then. He doesn't know why, or only knows as much as Mama tells him. 'You're like your father,' she says. 'A hero. You're strong, little Anatolii. Stronger than I am, stronger than your sister.'

When his uncle hears her talk like this he *tsks*, shakes his head.

'Come and live with me,' says Kulyk.

His mama won't. They need to stay in the town. Here they get basic benefits automatically; it's something at least. If they live in Kyiv they'll have to fight. Harder. It's here that they have the best chance of securing the tie.

'Nikolai won't leave. Can't leave.'

'And what's he doing?' His uncle points up at the ceiling.

'Resting.'

His uncle sighs and throws himself on the sofa. Looks around.

'You don't have enough chairs. I'll make you some chairs.'

'We have enough.'

'I'll make you some chairs. A table.'

'We don't need anything.'

Kulyk looks at Anatolii. 'Let me take the children for the winter.'

His mama ignores Kulyk. But it's said. Anatolii hates this place. He doesn't understand the feeling that comes up through his feet like water, except that if he doesn't do something with it, it will burst through him. He goes into the other room where Sveta is playing with some coloured blocks of wood. He sits down next to her. He's seen what's been happening. The wisps of hair on her pillow, in the bathwater. Even if his uncle takes both of them, wouldn't that be better than staying here? But if his uncle takes just him, then he won't have to look after Sveta. Their mama will be able to look after Sveta more easily. He's not so sick—he doesn't need to stay for the tie they're always talking about. He sits next to Sveta. She annoys him. That's all she does now, look sick and cry. He pulls her hair. She screams, a long bellow. He doesn't let go. He pulls harder. Her head is tilting towards him and she's screeching. He only has to make her keep screaming. He's pulling hard on her hair when it comes off in his hands like straw after threshing. He looks at it with revulsion for what it is, a living snake stuck to his palms. Sveta screams louder. She's pulling it out herself now, falling away in tiny fists. She's kneeling in the middle of a half-moon of hair. Her screams are short, sharp, lung emptying. Their mama and Kulyk run into the room. They both stare at him, his hands full of his sister's hair.

'Take her to the hospital,' says Kulyk sharply.

His mama holds Sveta tightly, wraps her in a blanket.

'I'll look after you,' says his mama, kissing Sveta on her scalp.

Kulyk shakes his head.

'For God's sake woman, let me take them away from here.'

'I'll look after you,' his mama repeats, many kisses on Sveta's head.

Kulyk makes a strangled noise, and throws his hands up in the air. Then Kulyk looks at Anatolii, the hair he's still grasping. His uncle understands, at last.

'Let me take the boy at least.'

His mama looks at him. Anatolii stares back, frozen. Then his mama nods.

Yes. Take him.

He's loping through the forest, following a trail of wolf tracks. He reaches the edge of the trees where he sits on his haunches and watches the smoke rise from the far side of the hill. He leaps up and bounds over the fence and runs across the fields. He looks down. It's not his feet sinking into the sod but his furred paws. On the other side he scampers up the hill and when he reaches the top he sniffs. The air has a shining but it also has a burning. It's a smell he knows has come from the earth. Buried deep inside the rocks. He scratches at the stone with his claws as he runs. Sharpens his eyes and breath. Below, there's fire. It would burn his coat but he's too quick, he moves before his fur is singed. He's a lone creature now, a king of the forest; not even the bear knows the tracks and traces he makes through the dark.

He opens his eyes. He's lying on the rear seat. He stares up sleepily at the back of his uncle's head. It's dark outside and they pass many houses with their lights on. He rests his head on his holdall. Schoolbooks, clothes, his little knife. He turns to see his sister's knees curled up by his nose and to smell her skin. But this time she's not there. Instead there are the legs and paws of a wolf. The deep musty smell of the animal's pelt in his nostrils.

Alex Lockwood

Saturday Afternoon

Only once on the drive to Glasgow does he think he's being followed, when a black Vauxhall with two men inside sits behind him for a few miles along the M8, but then keeps on while he turns into the city. Police cars fly past with their tocsins blaring but they pass as quickly as they come. His phone rings once, and it's No Caller ID. Someone from the base, maybe Mariam. How long did she give him? An hour, maybe two. They've already searched his bench, taken his laptop. Then the cottage. They won't find anything. If he phones, he can delay their search, but what would be the point? He's nearly at the grave—the cemetery. At Saint Rollox Brae he slows and turns left at the entrance.

He gets Aggie's number up. He texts rather than calls. *I'm here x.* Then he sits in the car until he feels the stares of other visitors. Who comes to a graveyard at such a time to sit in the car except grave robbers, or those ashamed of their grief? He locks up and walks past the Romeros, towards Aggie's father's grave, tumbling the mobile around and around in his hand. Thinks of what Mariam called him. *Whistleblower.* He went halfway. But perhaps that was far enough.

His phone beeps. *I'm on my way. x*

For the first time in a long time he knows they'll talk. He panics, wondering if she's really forgiven him, or if she really has had an affair. His world hinges on whether or not they'll talk. He busies himself at the grave as best he can with no tools. He tidies up the stones and flattens down the jade. The heucheras are still in good shape, not wilted or broken by wind. He kneels and pulls out some weeds and lets his fingers dig into the soil. There's a tingling at the base of his neck, and he understands it's been there this whole time, since the accident happened; not since the incident on *Tartarus*, but since *that* accident. He puts both hands out in front to stop him falling forward. He closes

343

his eyes and sees the cloud, blue and billowing, above the hill. He sees his mama running towards him and Sveta. '*Poklasty yikh vnyz! Poklasty yikh vnyz!*' Sveta holding his hand, struggling to keep up. He sees her hair in his hands and the look in his mama's eyes as she kisses Sveta's scabbed and peeling crown.

He wrenches his hands out of the earth, brushes them off on his trousers, then sits down and waits. It's a while before Aggie arrives. She walks towards him, holding up her palms in a lighthearted private greeting, how they used to salute each other when they bumped into one another without expecting it, *look, how did this happen?* It tells him what mood she's in, which is good, or perhaps what mood she wants him to be in, which is just as good. He could do with some instruction on this day.

'No flask?' he says as she sits down next to him.

'Worried I'd poison you?'

'You could have done that a long time ago if you wanted to.'

'Trust me, I've wanted to...'

They sit in silence for a moment not looking at each other.

'How's work been?' he asks.

'What, small talk? After all this time trying to get you to ease up, and you choose to start with the small talk *now*?'

'I was just asking.'

'Ant...'

And he feels her slipping away. It takes all his effort not to put his arms around her to stop her from leaving. He would have no right to, even though putting his arms around her might be exactly what she wants.

'What about Greg then?'

'What *about* Greg?'

'I don't know... I—'

'You thought I was having an affair? Jesus, Ant. Where have you been the last couple of weeks? What planet? Have you even looked in the mirror? Every time I've tried to talk to you you've been stuck in your own head. I knew... You working on the weekend. Your boss David not coming to your birthday. The news. My mother's been at me all bloody week.' She pauses; she's been shouting. She looks around, but they're the only people left. 'She asks what you've been telling me. I had to fight not to laugh. *You, telling me.*' She breathes out heavily. 'Like you've been on a different planet.' Sighs. 'You think you've been hiding it? Jesus. Well at least I know now. Bloody hell... What about the leak? The community?'

'The village?'

'Yes, *the village*. Are they in danger?'

'No. None.'

'You sure?'

'There's nothing I can do now.'

'So, that's it?'

'You haven't answered the question.'

'What question?'

'About Greg.'

'Greg?'

'Whose is the chew toy? The dog's tennis ball in the car?'

'There's a dog's toy in the car? How would I know? You take the car every day. Maybe you'd given someone from the village a lift.'

His head rocks back. Had he? Was it from months ago? When they first moved in he used to stop at the bus stand, against his will but to keep Aggie happy, to give people a lift. There's half an image of someone waving, him stopping. Had there been a dog? He didn't have to work hard to convince himself that Aggie's telling the truth.

'God knows you'd give me reason to. All this time you've been acting like a shit because of a dog's toy in the car?'

'No...' he pleads. He puts a hand on her knee. She shakes him off and it's like a knife through his skin.

'You don't even try to deal with the problem in front of you. You're so busy holding on as tight as you can to the past that you can't even... can't talk... You just hold on to it all, don't you? Jesus. I thought you'd let go, the other night on the phone. I thought you'd let it go.'

He knows it's true. That the reason he cannot get past things — like Greg's chew toy; like not talking, and the letters, why he'd never replied — was that he simply wouldn't let go of what was hurting him long enough to look at it, to face it. The past as pain; no. The past as history. Just history. What he held in his hands was not even the thing that hurt most. And now he has to let it go, and hold on to the present.

Out of his jacket pocket he pulls the letter he's written and hands it to Aggie. She looks at it. It's already sealed, it's just the envelope. But he's written her name on the front. *Sveta*. Aggie looks at him.

'You're replying?'

He nods.

'There's no address.'

He takes it back and puts it inside his jacket. 'I know.' After a while, he says, 'You need to talk now.'

'*Me?*' It's almost a scream.

'About your father. It's your turn to talk about your father.'

She looks at him, and in the dark he can just about make out the lines at the corners of her eyes and the anger she's holding onto.

'I told you mine, remember,' he says, and he puts both hands on her knees this time, and takes her hands and puts them under his, and this simple gesture releases her, and she sobs into his chest, and whatever was slipping away has come back. He no longer needs to protect her from seeing what he sees, because what he sees is no longer shame. What he sees, finally, is what he has done. And although he is responsible for much, he is not responsible for it all. Not the cloud. Not for his father. Not his mother. Not the accident.

When Aggie is finished he stands and pulls her up. He looks

at her and their wedding floods his memory; he cannot remember the courage it took to marry but she made it easy for him, and he knows that if he looks he will find his way to that courage again. There's more than a toe in the door now. He weaves his arm through hers and wraps the other around her back as they walk past the Romeros, her head sinking into his shoulder, this head of hair he smells for the first time in a long time, of hibiscus shampoo, of Aggie. Agatha.

In the car he leans over to the back seat and grabs his rucksack and pulls out the printed tickets. She's dabbing at her mascara. That she wore mascara to meet him prods him in the gut. Once she's finished he hands them to her. It takes her some time to grasp what they are.

'Two?'

'Respected other, remember?'

She grunts, her nose full of snot. She wipes her face on her sleeve. 'Oh shit. These are for tonight, Ant.'

'That okay?'

'Ant... Your job?'

'Cross that bridge...?'

'Jesus...' she sniffs. 'I don't know if I can just drop everything...'

'It's okay if you don't want to come.'

She's sniffling, wiping her face, thrown by this last act of his.

'No address,' she says. 'On the letter. Jesus... What will I tell mum?'

'That I'm going home? That I need you to come with me?'

She stares out of the windscreen.

'Since her letter arrived,' she says, putting it together. 'Last week. Isn't it? All this... Everything... Don't I need a visa?'

He shakes his head. 'Waiver.' He holds her gaze. 'I'll tell your mum. We need to leave the car there.' He breathes deeply, sighs. 'I need to do one thing before we go. Is there a tip on the way? You know, for dumping stuff.' He laughs. 'Sorry.'

'Jesus...' she looks out of the window. It won't all be easy, he knows. But it will be honest. She turns back to him. 'Half of Glasgow is a tip.'

'Shhh, he might be listening.'

She shakes her head.

'I told you. We kept the hearing aid. We'll just drive through Govan, for God's sake. Put whatever it is on the side of the road and it'll be gone in two minutes.'

He starts the Hyundai and drives. They don't talk, and neither of them reaches for the radio. There is a peace that is not merely, this time, a truce.

As he drives a story comes to him: not from *babushka*, not from his sister's letter either, but, and he smiles to think of it, from Linda. She told him one time as they were driving through the country lanes of Galway about Saint Ailbe, a sixth-century Irish bishop, born the son of a slave girl. The mother's owner sent the baby away to the wilderness to be eaten by the animals. A wolf took pity on him and cared for him. When he was grown, a hunter found him and took him back to the village. When years later he was Bishop of Emily, a grey wolf pursued by hunters ran into his house and laid her head on his lap. 'I will protect thee, old mother,' said the bishop, drawing his cloak around the wolf and hiding her from the chasing hunters. 'When I was little and feeble, thou didst nourish and cherish and protect me, and now that thou art old and grey and weak, shall I not render thee the same love and care? None shall injure thee. Come every day with thy little ones to my table, and thou and thine shall share my crusts.'

Alex Lockwood

6th May 2009

That this House is deeply disturbed at the revelations of at least eight liquid radioactive leaks into the sea loch over the past ten years from radioactive waste storage facilities at HM Naval Base Clyde at Faslane, near Glasgow, the home port for British nuclear-powered and nuclear-armed submarines, made public on 27th April 2009, following an investigation carried out by Channel Four News and investigative reporter Rob Edwards; notes with alarm that these latest leaks bring the total number of leaks acknowledged at Faslane over the last three decades to more than 40; welcomes the release of around 400 pages of internal e-mails, letters and reports by the environmental regulator, the Scottish Environmental Protection Agency (SEPA); further notes with concern that one of SEPA's internal reports indicates that many of the ageing facilities used to process, store and dispose of radioactive waste at Faslane are 'not fit for purpose'; further notes that the Ministry of Defence has admitted its facilities fail to meet modern safety standards requiring that the 'best practicable means' are used to minimise and control waste; further notes SEPA is pressing for the legal power to inspect and control Faslane's nuclear operations; therefore calls upon the Ministry of Defence to urgently tighten safety standards at Faslane, and to evaluate the future environmental hazards to those living around the River Clyde, from Faslane; and calls upon the Government to consider urgently the benefits to the economy and the environment of abolishing Britain's current nuclear weapons, including the planned £76 billion Trident replacement.

— House of Commons Early Day Motion 1442

About the Author

Alex Lockwood is from London but now lives in the North of England. He writes fiction, non-fiction and journalism, and is a Winston Churchill Fellow and a Fellow of the Royal Society for the Encouragement of the Arts (RSA).

From the Author: If you would like to connect with other books that I have coming in the near future, please visit my website for news on upcoming works, recent posts and to sign up for my newsletter: http://www.alexlockwood.co.uk

Roundfire

FICTION

Put simply, we publish great stories. Whether it's literary or popular, a gentle tale or a pulsating thriller, the connecting theme in all Roundfire fiction titles is that once you pick them up you won't want to put them down.
If you have enjoyed this book, why not tell other readers by posting a review on your preferred book site.

Recent bestsellers from Roundfire are:

The Bookseller's Sonnets
Andi Rosenthal
The Bookseller's Sonnets intertwines three love stories with a tale of
religious identity and mystery spanning five hundred years and
three countries.
Paperback: 978-1-84694-342-3 ebook: 978-184694-626-4

Birds of the Nile
An Egyptian Adventure
N.E. David
Ex-diplomat Michael Blake wanted a quiet birding trip up the Nile
– he wasn't expecting a revolution.
Paperback: 978-1-78279-158-4 ebook: 978-1-78279-157-7

Blood Profit$
The Lithium Conspiracy
J. Victor Tomaszek, James N. Patrick, Sr.
The blood of the many for the profits of the few… *Blood Profit$* will
take you into the cigar-smoke-filled room where American policy
and laws are really made.
Paperback: 978-1-78279-483-7 ebook: 978-1-78279-277-2

The Burden
A Family Saga
N.E. David
Frank will do anything to keep his mother and father apart. But
he's carrying baggage – and it might just weigh him down …
Paperback: 978-1-78279-936-8 ebook: 978-1-78279-937-5

The Cause
Roderick Vincent
The second American Revolution will be a fire lit from an internal spark.
Paperback: 978-1-78279-763-0 ebook: 978-1-78279-762-3

Don't Drink and Fly
The Story of Bernice O'Hanlon: Part One
Cathie Devitt
Bernice is a witch living in Glasgow. She loses her way in her life and wanders off the beaten track looking for the garden of enlightenment.
Paperback: 978-1-78279-016-7 ebook: 978-1-78279-015-0

Gag
Melissa Unger
One rainy afternoon in a Brooklyn diner, Peter Howland punctures an egg with his fork. Repulsed, Peter pushes the plate away and never eats again.
Paperback: 978-1-78279-564-3 ebook: 978-1-78279-563-6

The Master Yeshua
The Undiscovered Gospel of Joseph
Joyce Luck
Jesus is not who you think he is. The year is 75 CE. Joseph ben Jude is frail and ailing, but he has a prophecy to fulfil ...
Paperback: 978-1-78279-974-0 ebook: 978-1-78279-975-7

On the Far Side, There's a Boy
Paula Coston
Martine Haslett, a thirty-something 1980s woman, plays hard on the fringes of the London drag club scene until one night which prompts her to sign up to a charity. She writes to a young Sri Lankan boy, with consequences far and long.
Paperback: 978-1-78279-574-2 ebook: 978-1-78279-573-5

Tuareg

Alberto Vazquez-Figueroa

With over 5 million copies sold worldwide, Tuareg is a classic adventure story from best-selling author Alberto Vazquez-Figueroa, about honour, revenge and a clash of cultures.
Paperback: 978-1-84694-192-4

Readers of ebooks can buy or view any of these bestsellers by clicking on the live link in the title. Most titles are published in paperback and as an ebook. Paperbacks are available in traditional bookshops. Both print and ebook formats are available online.

Find more titles and sign up to our readers' newsletter at
http://www.johnhuntpublishing.com/fiction

Follow us on Facebook at https://www.facebook.com/JHPfiction
and Twitter at https://twitter.com/JHPFiction